Arthur P. Vivian

Wanderings in the Western Land

Arthur P. Vivian

Wanderings in the Western Land

ISBN/EAN: 9783337196257

Printed in Europe, USA, Canada, Australia, Japan

Cover: Foto ©Andreas Hilbeck / pixelio.de

More available books at **www.hansebooks.com**

WANDERINGS IN THE WESTERN LAND.

LONDON :
GILBERT AND RIVINGTON, PRINTERS,
ST. JOHN'S SQUARE.

THE MOUNTAIN LION, OR AMERICAN PUMA.

WANDERINGS IN THE WESTERN LAND.

By A. PENDARVES VIVIAN, M.P., F.G.S.

"Go ye, and look upon that land,
  That far vast land that few behold,
  And none, beholding, understand ;
  That old, old land, which men call new,
  That land as old as time is old.

"Go, journey with the seasons through
  Its wastes, and learn how limitless,
  How shoreless lie the distances,
  Before you come to question this,
  Or dare to dream what grandeur is."
                              JOAQUIN MILLER.

WITH ILLUSTRATIONS FROM ORIGINAL SKETCHES BY MR. ALBERT BIERSTADT AND THE AUTHOR.

London :

SAMPSON LOW, MARSTON, SEARLE, & RIVINGTON,

CROWN BUILDINGS, 188, FLEET STREET.

1879.

INTRODUCTION.

In the following pages I have endeavoured to record the recollections of a few months' wanderings in North America, spent chiefly in "hunting" in the Rocky Mountains. My principal objects in making the trip were to obtain a thorough change of scene, and to see something of a country of which we have all heard so much.

I make no claim to having done or seen more than any one else could have done, having the same time and means at their disposal, and possessed of the same keenness for sport as myself. I believe, however, that I was "in luck on the hunt;" at least, I am told so by some well able to judge.

I would endeavour at once to disarm adverse criticism, by acknowledging numerous faults, perceptible even to myself, and by pleading very broken leisure for writing. My main object has been to describe in a plain, unvarnished manner the leading incidents of a short but very enjoyable run to regions many parts of which are within easy reach of all.

I must record my sense of the general courtesy which I experienced throughout, with scarcely an exception; even the rough western men, the hardy sons of the Indian frontier, accustomed from boyhood to fighting for existence, were hospitable and generous to a degree hard to find in more civilized life.

I have availed myself of the admirable reports of the Surveys of the United States Government, not only to confirm my own observations, but to supply information when I have been unable from any cause to speak from personal experience.

In conclusion, one word of thanks to my old friend and brother sportsman, Lord Aberdare, who most promptly and kindly consented to wade through my manuscript, and gave me the benefit of his most valuable advice. For many of the woodcuts I am indebted to my friend Mr. Bierstadt, that true delineator of nature's beauties in the Western Land, who most courteously placed his original oil sketches at my disposal.

A. PENDARVES VIVIAN.

7, BELGRAVE SQUARE, LONDON,
    July, 1879.

CONTENTS.

CHAPTER IV.

CHAPTER V.

CHAPTER VI.

CHAPTER VII.

CHAPTER VIII.

CHAPTER IX.

CHAPTER XII.

CHAPTER XIII.

CHAPTER XIV.

CHAPTER XVIII.

CHAPTER XIX.

CHAPTER XX.

LIST OF ILLUSTRATIONS.

FULL-PAGE ENGRAVINGS.

SMALLER ENGRAVINGS.

—

MAPS.

.

WANDERINGS IN THE WESTERN LAND.

"GOOD-BYE." THE OLD HEAD OF KINSALE.

From a Sketch by A. P. V.

CHAPTER I.

" PER MARE—PER TERRAM."

Voyage out—St. John's, Newfoundland—Inhabitants—Country—
Sporting—Trade—Mining—Passage to Halifax—Cape Race—
French Islands—Sable Island—Halifax: Approach, Situation,
Environs, Fortifications, Defenders.

AFTER a prosperous and uneventful voyage of six
days two-and-a-half hours from Liverpool, we ran
through the narrow entrance into the harbour of

B

St. John's, Newfoundland, on the dull and gloomy
evening of the 14th August, 1877. The voyage
had been, on the whole, very prosperous. Our ship,
the "Caspian," of the Allan Line, had met with
some knocking about at the very commencement,
in encountering, between Liverpool and Queenstown,
what is meteorologically noted as a "moderate
gale," but after this, for the remainder of the
voyage, had had no reason to complain; in fact, so
well had the elements behaved, that, although a slow
boat, she had been able to average about 290 knots
per twenty-four hours. We, her passengers, had
undergone the wearisome routine of daily life on
board ship with as many comforts and as few dis-
agreeables as were possible. We had ate and slept
with regularity, walked or tried to walk the deck
daily, watched the heaving of the log, speculated on
seeing icebergs, and discussed our future plans *ad
nauseam*. But now all was over, for here we were,
going to set our sea legs once more on mother earth;
some of us, it is true, only for a few hours, but
others had reached their final haven, and I cannot
help confessing that I envied them much. Such a
quaint little harbour as this is, which we have
squeezed into through the narrowest of entrances,
formed by a rent in the granite cliffs; how it
was ever discovered must always be a matter for
wonder. It must be difficult navigation to accomplish, but when once in, there appeared to be perfect
shelter from every quarter. About two years ago
the entrance got blocked by an iceberg, which had
to be blown up with powder before a free passage
could be re-established. The whole place has a
West Highland look about it; but the odour is pecu-

liar, thanks to the cod and seal fisheries, which are
the staple trades of the place.

ENTRANCE TO ST. JOHN'S, NEWFOUNDLAND.
From a Sketch by J. P. V.

The little town, consisting chiefly of wooden houses,
is built on the side of the hill facing the harbour; the
Roman Catholic cathedral and Government House
being perhaps the two most conspicuous edifices.
The present Governor is Sir John Glover, V.C., of
Ashantee reputation, a most hospitable and popular
ruler. The Government House possesses no archi-
tectural beauty nor anything of interest, beyond a
fine collection of cariboo antlers from the interior
of the island, amongst which is a great curiosity,
namely, two pairs of antlers locked so firmly together that they cannot be separated, the poor
beasts having evidently got entangled in fighting
and so perished by starvation.

Newfoundland, with a population of over 200,000,
is still a separate colony of Great Britain, having

refused to join the newly-formed Dominion of Canada, fear of an increased taxation being, I believe, the principal reason against amalgamation. It possesses no military of any sort; a police force of seventy-eight foot and six mounted constables is sufficient to maintain order. A few years ago, on the occasion of an Irish riot, the six mounted constables did excellent service in dispersing the rioters by repeated charges on the ice of the frozen harbour, since which it has been an annual motion of the irreconcilables in the House of Representatives to reduce the vote by the amount required for their maintenance, but hitherto without success. The inhabitants, as a rule, are said to be most loyal to the British crown, and in this respect resemble the rest of the British North Americans.

The general appearance of the country at a little distance from St. John's is very like some parts of the Highlands of Scotland. There is the same sort of moorlands, with here and there bare patches of rock cropping up through the wild herbage. Lower down and nearer the town cultivated plots abound, in the midst of which, and surrounded with clumps of spruce and birch, nestle snug-looking homesteads and cottages. The interior of the island is said to be barren and unproductive and but very thinly inhabited, most of the aborigines having migrated northward towards the sea-coast.

I was told that, with proper guides, good cariboo hunting can be obtained, but that it is a difficult country to pass through. Much of the travelling must be done in canoes, which have, together with the stores, to be "portaged" by Indians between the different waters. Wolves abound in parts, and in consequence of the severe cold in these northern latitudes, their fur greatly surpasses in quality that of the same animal on the American continent.

The black bear is also to be found, but is far more common in Labrador, and on Anticosti, where they are reported to be very numerous. There are no moose on the island, but attempts are now being made to introduce them.

At the proper seasons of the year the gunner may find himself at home here. The so-called partridge—which in habits and appearance resembles much more the grey hen than any European partridge—is very plentiful. When disturbed off the ground, this bird generally takes to a tree, from the branches of which it can be shot down by the merest tyro. But, besides this doubtful sport, the lover of the shot-gun can get most excellent goose and duck-shooting on the inland waters, which harbour many varieties of the *natatores*.

For those who care about fishing, I am told that salmon abound in some of the rivers, but that there is at present great difficulty in getting to many of the most favoured spots, on account of their distances from any inhabited localities or roads. But this is all hearsay, as I had no opportunity of testing the accuracy of my information by any personal experience.

In Newfoundland I naturally expected to see in great perfection the far-famed Newfoundland dog, but in that I was doomed to disappointment. It is said that the pure breed is as rare here as it is in England. Quantities of black animals there are, no doubt, running about the streets of St. John's; but "all is not coal that's black." My local infor-

mant—an Irishman—who seemed to be a con-
noisseur in dogs, said one of the characteristics of
the true breed is a web between the toes. They are
now very valuable, and are becoming more so. I
understand as much as 30l. has been given for a
thoroughbred dog.

An import of Newfoundland of no mean merit is
port wine. This trade has been carried on direct
with Portugal for many years, the wine being sent in
exchange for the dried cod-fish, which is in much
request in that Roman Catholic country. It is
curious that the severity of this climate seems to suit
the wine, and that it rather gains than loses in
quality by being frozen. Good port can be purchased at the time I write for about 14l. per quarter
cask in bond here, a price which, considering the
quality, can scarcely be said to be exorbitant.

Our ship got out the Newfoundland portion of
her cargo during the night. The rattling of the
steam cranes did not conduce to refreshing sleep,
notwithstanding that the operations were carried on
with as little noise as circumstances would allow.
The following forenoon we were again under way,
steaming steadily southward towards Cape Race.
That part of the coast near St. John's is very fine.
Bluff headlands of granite and Killas slate stand out
grandly into the sea, reminding me much of the
wave-worn front of old Cornwall. As in the latter
country, there are here also great mineral deposits,
and mines of considerable reputation are being
busily worked at Betts Cove, on the north-eastern
coast of the island, where a rich yellow copper ore
is being shipped, most of it across the ocean to
Swansea in South Wales. I should have been glad

to have visited these mines, but the communication
with St. John's is very irregular and uncertain, and

CUCKOLD'S HEAD.   THE COAST OF NEWFOUNDLAND.
From a Sketch by A. P. V.

the expedition would have taken far more time than
I could well have spared.

After leaving St. John's we had a smooth time of
it, and were able thoroughly to enjoy this portion of
the voyage. We passed a good many fishing and
coasting craft, generally of the regular American
fore-and-aft rig, with sails as white as a yacht's.
In the afternoon we were abreast of the far-famed
but unimposing Cape Race, eighty-six nautical miles
from St. John's. In old days the Liverpool and
New York mail steamers were wont to make this
headland, and, in order to save the loss of time in
going into St. John's, used to throw the mails
overboard in a water-tight tin case, a gun being
fired from the ship to attract the notice of those on
shore. A reward of ten shillings was paid to the

hardy fishermen by the shore authorities for each
case delivered to them; and, wonderful to relate,
very few were ever lost. Nowadays railroads
and telegraph cables have changed all this, and the
New York liners pass far away to the southward,
giving this often fog-hidden headland a very wide
berth. The coast itself is low, having gradually
lessened in height as we came southwards. The
cliffs are covered with a short stubby undergrowth,
apparently a sort of dwarf pine, and no trees of any
size seem to grow near the coast.

From Cape Race the coast bends away to the
west and north, towards Cape St. Mary and the
Gulf of St. Lawrence. On this south-west coast
are many French settlers, with certain peculiar rights
as to fishing, &c., which are likely to require before
very long the attention of the two Governments.
Not very far from here are the very small islands of
Miquelon and St. Pierre, the last footholds in these
parts left to France by the Quebec and other treaties.

The following afternoon we were about fifty miles
north of that curious spot on the ocean, "Sable
Island," a low flat bank of sand (hence the name)
heaved up from the bed of the ocean. It is situated
off the coast of Nova Scotia, and is about 220 miles
east-south-east of Halifax. Its westernmost end is
in N. lat. 43° 56′; W. long. 60° 71′; and its eastern
end N. lat. 43° 59′; W. long. 59° 42′. It is about
50 miles in length, from end to end, with bars of
sand running out for 16 miles on the north-western,
and 28 miles on the other end; both bars are from
1 mile to 1½ miles in width. On these bars a most
fearful sea breaks in bad weather. As a dreadful
proof of the dangers of this bank, two hundred lives
are said to have been lost here in one year. No

shrub or tree grows on the island, only bent **grass**, with some cranberry and whortleberry bushes.   **One** of the sand-hills on it is 100 feet in height.   This curious storm-swept island was first colonized by forty French convicts, who were landed on it in 1598 by the Marquis de la Roche, **and** who would have been starved had it not been for some sheep which happened to be thrown ashore from a vessel. **In** old days, before it was **well** lighted, many a terrible wreck used to occur **on** this inhospitable shore, and starvation generally awaited the poor unfortunate seamen who escaped the fearful surf. The authorities endeavoured to lessen such horrors by turning **out** a few cattle on the island.   They thrived, and **did** well on the scanty herbage; but such is the greed for filthy lucre that scoundrels used to land from vessels for **the** purpose of killing and carrying away this provision for the shipwrecked, and in this way the stock has disappeared.

The present inhabitants **of** the island are the lighthouse-keepers and their families, and, curious to relate, some wild horses.   These latter are supposed to be the descendants of some Spanish horses cast ashore very many years ago.   They subsist on the scanty sand-grass, and obtain water by pawing **up** the sand with their fore feet.   Occasionally parties land and capture some for the purposes of sale.   A more uninviting abode than this island can scarcely be conceived, and one can well imagine the intense horror with which it used to be regarded by the ancient mariner.   Now, although well lighted, the universal instructions to all captains are to give **it** a very wide berth.

A night's steaming brought us into the harbour of Halifax, the approach to which is very pleasing.

The western entrance, up which we sailed, and which is the only one for large vessels, is well protected by forts on both shores, and on the McNab and George Islands. The former of these divides the western from the eastern entrance. The forts mount very heavy guns of the most modern pattern, and are manned by English artillerymen, but the complement is said to be far short of what would be required to work the guns. This matter should have the attention of our Government; for it is of national importance that this, our only naval station, and now the only garrison of English troops in North America, should be in such a condition that in time of war it should be able to afford shelter and security to our imperial and mercantile marine. If it is worth holding at all, it is worth holding well, and everything should be done to make it a secure haven for ourselves and an object of terror to an aggressor—a haven to which, in time of war, our merchantmen could run for safety, where our war vessels could refit in security, and whence they could issue at any time to harass the enemies' shipping, blockade their ports, or descend on their vulnerable positions.

The so-called McNab Island, derives its name from an old fisherman, who, having been seized outside the harbour by the French, in one of the expeditions of by-gone days, and forced to pilot their squadron into Halifax, took the opportunity of the darkness of night to steer them into what is now termed the north-west arm of the harbour. Here the water is very shallow, and the vessels soon grounded. History does not say how the old salt himself escaped, or, indeed, whether he escaped at all; but the result of his piloting to the French was

the destruction of their squadron, and to himself, or
his family, the gift from the British Government of
that important island which now bears his name.

THE NORTH-WEST ARM, HALIFAX, N.S.
From a Sketch by A. P. V.

Halifax is a picturesque town, situated on the
side of a hill overlooking the harbour, on the summit
of which is the well-known citadel. It is old for
America, having been founded about the year 1750.

Amongst other novelties to be encountered on
first landing in America, are the peculiarities of the
hotel life. The system is, as it were, *en pension,* so
many dollars per day (generally from $3.50 to $5.50
= 14*s.* to 22*s.*) for rooms and food. The meals
take place at fixed times, between stated hours;
they are served at separate little tables, the waiters
being usually coloured men. The functions of the
various officials do not quite coincide with what they
are with us. As for instance, I found out on my
very first morning that brushing clothes does not
constitute part of the duties of the individual

answering to our "boots." I had rung my bell several times with no effect, when at last a very small boy appeared. I told him, perhaps rather shortly, to take my clothes down to be brushed; he and the clothes quickly disappeared, but there was no reappearance of either. I again had recourse to the bell, and at last the boy again presented himself, but without the clothes. On my demanding an explanation of their whereabouts, he said no one would brush them "as the weather was too hot." I apologized for having asked for such a service in such trying weather, and was only too glad to get them back and be released from my bedroom in an unbrushed condition. I found out that one is expected to have them brushed, or rather whisked over *in situ*, by the individual who takes the hats, at the entrance to the *salle à manger*.

The weather was somewhat hot, but not intolerably so—in fact, very enjoyable. The heat does not, however, last long at this time of year—the latter end of August—and is soon succeeded by the fresh " Fall " weather.

In the environs there are many very beautiful and varied drives and walks. Some of the most popular are along the Bedford Basin ; through the Park to the North West Arm; from Dartmouth on the other side of the harbour, round by some lovely freshwater lakes, &c., &c. Melville Island is worth a visit ; it is situated down the harbour, not far from the North West Arm, and is now used as a Military Prison. When we were there, about fifty prisoners were employed in breaking stones for the roads. The stones were doubtless necessary, but could be obtained from inferior labour, and it seemed as if such a mass of men would have been better employed in erecting the forts which, I am told, have been decided upon, but which are still in the future. When these works are finished and armed, then comes the all-important question of manning them efficiently. The Dominion artillerymen are, I believe, good, but are far too few in number, and, moreover, at present, have not been drilled to work our new and improved ordnance. As for our own Royal Artillery, but few probably could be spared in time of war from our more important European positions. I am told, however, that the native fisherman is the finest raw material possible. During that portion of the year when he could not carry on his natural calling, he would no doubt be willing, for a very small remuneration, to put himself through a course of training. Being strong and very hardy, intelligent and keen-sighted, he would soon render himself an effective gunner, and in the hour of need could be relied on as a sturdy defender, not only of those forts which now exist, but of those which are to be erected hereafter.

OUT OF MY WINDOW AT HALIFAX, N.S.
From a Sketch by J. P. V.

CHAPTER II.

"This is the forest primeval. The murmuring pines and the hem
    locks,
  Bearded with moss, and in garments green, indistinct in the
    twilight,
  Stand like Druids of eld, with voices sad and prophetic,
  Stand like harpers hoar, with beards that rest on their bosom."

Longfellow's "Evangeline."

Start for the Hunt—Outfitting and Outfit—Railroad Cars and
    Conductors—The Intercolonial System—Canadian Forests—
    Waste by Fires—Causes—Legislation—Spring Hill—Coal
    Mine—New Line—Cumberland County—Settlers—Varieties
    of Timber—Maple and Sugar Making.

I HAD spent nearly a week very pleasantly in Halifax,
when one day I got a telegram from my brother-in-
law, Lord Dunraven, to say he had landed at New
York, and that if there were bears in the province,
he would come up for a "hunt." This led to an
Indian, who had been with him on a former occasion,
being telegraphed for, to give his opinion on our
bear prospects; and his opinion was so favourable
that an answer was sent to D. to come up "right
away," and that I would meet him with the Indian
hunter and my Scotch stalker, at a station called
Spring Hill, on the Intercolonial Railway, and bring
with me tents, camp-utensils, and sufficient stores
for a fortnight's hunt.

As I had never done any real "camping-out," I was perfectly ignorant as to what sort of stores were required, as well as the quantity of each necessary. All this was, however, made very easy to me through the kindness of Col. Clerke—a very old campaigner—and the general knowledge of Scott, grocer and outfitter. Colonel Clerke, at D.'s request, had kindly procured for me an excellent tent from Hemmenway, New York, which turned out so good, that after several months' experience, I had no fault to find with it. It remained perfectly water-tight to the end of my campaign (except where holes had been torn), and stood the rough usage it was subjected to in a most exemplary manner. It was not furnished with poles, which for use in Canada was no disadvantage, but for hunting on the plains of the Rocky Mountains certainly ought to be forthcoming, and these should be so arranged as to pack with the tent. If winter weather is to be encountered, a small stove should also be provided, when a hole for passing the stove-pipe through, must be made in the canvas. Stoves of all sorts are quite a *spécialité* of America, and the small tent and cooking-stove is no exception to their general excellence.

But to return to my preparations for my first camp out. All the necessaries being provided for me, nothing devolved upon my own responsibility but the luxuries; these consisted of a few reindeers' tongues, cans of potted soup, a little preserved milk (which, by the way, nearly always leaked out and bedaubed other things), and a few tins of preserved or "canned" salmon. The third day found me ready and keen to make a start.

My " out-fit " (as a party is termed in America)
on starting from Halifax consisted of myself and
Sandie Macdonald, a true Highlander and a good
stalker, of Glengarry birth ; " Ned," a short-haired
colley dog, hailing from Glen Nevis, and reported to
be a first-class deer tracker ; and an Irish water-
spaniel called " Sailor," who had already seen great
sport with me on the Nile, and in Albania and
Greece, and who accompanied me now in case of my
having any duck or prairie-fowl shooting.   This was
a somewhat large party to move about by train, in
addition to the stores and other *impedimenta*, but as
I had been kindly given a general letter of introduction by a Canadian railway swell, or, as he
would be termed here, a railway " boss," my travelling was made very easy.   I may here say that,
throughout my travels, I met with the greatest
civility from all officials, the only exception being
from certain jacks-in-office, in the shape of the
baggage-men on the Union Pacific Railroad, who
on more than one occasion annoyed me much about
my guns.   It appeared that these gentry are allowed
to extract, as a perquisite and part payment of
their services, so much for each gun from any
passenger having such an article amongst his
baggage.   As may be supposed, this leads to much
questioning on the part of these worthies, as to first,
whether you have any, and secondly, how many guns
you have in your baggage.   I have not met with
such a practice in any of my other wanderings, and
I would submit that such a way of partly paying
their *employés* is scarcely worthy of a great railway
company.

To return to my present journey, however.   Every-

thing was made as smooth and agreeable as possible,
and without any vexatious haggling or bother of any
sort or kind, I found myself seated in one of the
long cars of the Intercolonial Railway, bound for
the happy hunting-grounds of the Parsborough
country. It is unnecessary to dwell upon the peculiarities of American railway travelling, as they have
been so often and so well described, and are well-
known to many from personal experience.

The great difference in the appearance and arrangement of the cars or carriages from our own, strikes
an Englishman at once. These are usually about
sixty feet long, with a passage down the centre,
having a succession of two seats together, on each
side. They are carried on four pairs of small bogie-
wheels, two pairs at each end. The locomotive is
remarkable to our eyes from the well-known bell-
mouthed smoke funnel, and the useful " cow-
catcher," like a great ploughshare, protruding in front
of the wheels. The ease of travelling varies much on
different lines. On this it was smooth and steady, but
the pace of even the fastest passenger trains is not
great, seldom exceeding twenty-eight miles an hour.

The conductor is the great personage on an
American railway. His authority is paramount,
and his terse order, " All on board," must be
obeyed " right away," or the lagging passenger will
assuredly find himself left behind. To be sure,
unless the train has actually got well away, he can
generally get on to the last car, and pass through
the central passage into his own car; but should he
be too late for this on his way across the continent,
the punishment of being left behind is not a slight
one, for there he will be planted for twenty-four

c

hours, until the corresponding train of the following day arrives. By the conductors being allowed to collect money from passengers having no tickets, railway companies naturally stand a good chance of being considerably defrauded, and many amusing stories are told of such occurrences. On one occasion a conductor who had been long in the employ of a company, was discovered retaining money to a very large extent. He was had up before the Board of Directors, reproached for such behaviour, and asked whether he had anything to say why he should not be instantly dismissed. His reply was forcible,—" Well, I guess, you are making quite a mistake in shunting me. You see I have made my fortune, but the gentleman who follows after will have to make his."

One of my hunters in the Rocky Mountains had had a friend a conductor. The first day he was on, he collected about $50; he thought of this sum he would hand in about $30, keeping the remainder for his own uses! " Hallo, what's this?" said the inspector. " Why the money I took yesterday," was the reply. " Well you did have a big day of it anyhow. The gent before you never took more than $20 in a day"!! So much for their ticket system, which I do not think we need copy, however far ahead they undoubtedly are in many other particulars connected with the comfort of railway travelling.

This Intercolonial Railway is a new line, having been only opened a few years. It unites Halifax with Quebec, joining the Grand Trunk system at Riviere du Loup. The distance from Halifax to Riviere du Loup is 561 miles, which is run in 20 hours.

At Moncton, 187 miles from Halifax, a branch line goes off 89 miles to St. John's, New Brunswick. On leaving Halifax the line (or, as it is called here, the "track") runs for a long distance through a flat well-timbered country, passing many a likely-looking lake, on the margins of which one could imagine the gigantic moose disporting himself, but not a sight of game of any sort gladdened my eyes throughout the whole journey; there appeared, in fact, a general want of wild animal life.

Here and there might be seen patches of hundreds of acres of burnt timber, testifying to the fearful ravages made by fire in these grand Canadian forests. These fires sometimes originate from sparks from locomotives, more frequently perhaps from carelessness on the part of the settlers themselves, or other parties, camping out in the woods. It is really too sad to contemplate the wreck made by such conflagrations, and it is high time for the Government to adopt some practical measure for enforcing as much care as possible on those with whom these disasters originate.

The United States have already very stringent laws for this purpose, which are put in force whenever proof of carelessness can be obtained.

The Canadian forests are indeed grand heirlooms, but heirlooms which are getting less and less year by year, even at the present rate of legitimate consumption. A time must soon come when Canadian timber will be far more difficult to get than at present, and far more costly. Why then should this comparative scarcity be hastened on by needless carelessness or reckless mischief? Sometimes the embers of a fire, not extinguished before the camp is left, kindles up

into a flame again ; at other times the careless lighting of a pipe or the wanton mischief of a boy may
start a fire, which results in the destruction of
hundreds, aye, thousands of acres of magnificent
forest timber. It is truly distressing to see these
blackened stumps and poles, stretching away for
miles, where, only a few months before, forest giants
luxuriated in their primeval grandeur. Let us hope
that ere long effective measures will be in force which
will check this sinful waste.

But to return ; at Spring Hill station we
branched off from the main line of the Intercolonial
Railway, and having to wait here some time, I was
able to learn a little about this, one of the most
important coal producing districts of the Dominion.
The Spring Hill colliery has been opened about
three years, and is one of the largest undertakings
in this locality. It is in communication with the
main line by a branch of about four and a half miles
from the Spring Hill station. The "out-put" at
the present time is about 300 tons per day. The
measures are steep,—that is, lie at a sharp angle,—
about $35°$ I was told ; the coal is won by a slant
driven down over 100 fathoms in one of the veins.
Three veins are being worked ; the largest has a
thickness of about nine feet of coal, the quality is
said to be strong bituminous. I see the analysis is
given as $60·95 °/_o$ carbon, $25·38 °/_o$ volatile matter,
the remainder ash, with a little sulphur. It is used
exclusively by the locomotives on the Intercolonial
Railway Company, and seems to answer well. There
are about 300 men employed in connexion with the
colliery, for whom cottages have been built by the
company.

About a quarter of an hour's rail from Spring Hill station landed us at the colliery, where we changed from a mineral into a baggage-waggon, which, with a few "lumber" or timber trucks, formed the train for the remainder of our railway journey. A run, or rather a crawl, of three hours to perform fourteen miles, brought us through a well-timbered, thinly-inhabited country, to a cross-road called Halfway River. Here ourselves and baggage were deposited on the side of the track, this being the nearest spot on the railway to the country of our future hunting operations. Leaving the *impedimenta* in charge of Sandie Macdonald, I set off on foot for a settler's homestead about a mile away, and arranged with the owner to convey us to another settler's, called Harrison, from whose house we hoped the next day to make our start into the woods. A very comfortable home was Harrison's. A plain, well-built plank-house, lined inside with birch bark to keep out the cold and draughts, and covered with creepers; the interior was plainly but substantially furnished, and contained more comforts than might have been expected so far away from any town or stores. Outside, it possessed an important addition to good living in the shape of a capital garden and orchard. Wild hops grew luxuriantly, as is generally the case in this country, but I never saw them cultivated as a crop by the Canadian farmer. I could never ascertain why this was, for all I asked seemed to agree in the suitability of the climate and the ready market which could be made for them.

Our host was a good specimen of a well-to-do Canadian settler. He had emigrated from the "old

country" as a poor labourer some fifty years ago,
and had settled at once where we now found him.
He has acquired a considerable estate, and has
reared a large family, the youngest of whom is
already in her teens. A large portion of his land
is covered with timber, on which he sets a great
value, foreseeing, that, owing to the vast quantity
which is felled yearly, and the immense destruction
by fire, the value of timber (or "lumber," as it is
here termed) must increase enormously.

The timber hereabouts is principally "black
spruce," which grows so fast that when thirty years
old, Harrison told me, he could cut "deals" out of
it twelve inches wide by three inches thick. Besides
the spruce, of which there are three varieties, there
are three kinds of birch and two of maple.

In addition to the wholesale modes of destroying
timber of which I have spoken, there is individual
or retail waste constantly going on. If a settler
finds a fine tree encroaching on his clearing or
road, instead of felling it and making use of the
timber, he will often, as they say here, "nick" it,
that is, cut a deep notch in the tree about four
feet from the ground all the way round. Circula-
tion is stopped, and the tree dies and falls. Then
again in hunting, if an Indian wants to mark his
way, he will pass along breaking the leading shoots
off the young firs as he goes. If it suits his fancy,
he will make his camp-fire at such close proximity
to, it may be, the finest tree of the forest that the
roots are consumed and the tree itself destroyed.
This was the case at our first camp, and when I suggested the removal of the fire a little further from
the splendid spruce, a contemptuous smile lighted up

the face of our hardened old Indian, accompanied by
some light remarks about there being plenty more.
By the end of our week's sojourn the roots and side
of the stem nearest the fire were completely charred,
and the gigantic old fellow had but to die.

From the variety of maple called here the rock
maple (*acer saccharinus*), a fine white sugar is
made. The process—which takes place in the
month of April—consists in cutting a V in the bark,
in the point of which a plug of wood is inserted
which serves as a tap for the juice to flow over.
This is collected into vessels, and concentrated by
boiling until crystals are obtained, in much the
same way, I believe, as the ordinary cane-sugar is
manufactured. It is stated that a very good tree
will yield in a season, without injury to itself, thirty-
two gallons of sap or juice, which would make about
8 lbs. of sugar; but I believe such a yield to be far
above the average, which would be, probably, nearer
twenty gallons of sap per tree. In appearance, the
maple sugar is very like ordinary white sugar. Both
in the States and in Canada it is in much favour, as
well as the syrup made from the same source.

The consumption of syrup in North America
must be enormous. No meal is considered complete, even in the backwoods, without this " fixing,"
and to such an extent is this a necessary that
it is a regular item in the fitting-out stores of the
hunter, miner, and lumberman. This would seem
to confirm the theory that to a great extent saccha-
rine matter supplies the place of alcohol in the
human system, as but little spirits are, as a rule,
consumed by this class of " outfits."

Amongst the other principal forest trees of

Canada are the pines, of which there are said to be four chief varieties, viz. the Weymouth, or white pine (*pinus Strobus*); the yellow pine (*pinus mitis*); the red or pitch pine (*pinus resinosa*); and the grey pine (*pinus Banksiana*), of no commercial value. Then there are four principal sorts of spruce, viz. the hemlock (*pinus* or *abies Canadensis*); the white (*pinus alba*), and the black (*pinus nigra*), and the balsam spruce (*pinus balsamea*). There is only one variety of larch, namely the black larch (*larix Americanus*). The birch is a magnificent production of these forests, growing to such a size as we have no idea of in the old country. There are three varieties, the black, the yellow, and the white (*betula alba*). The bark of this latter is one of the most useful, if not the most curious, productions of the great Canadian forests. It is truly marvellous to hear of the many and varied uses to which it is applied. It is a true friend alike to all—to the Indian, the hunter and the settler. Of it, the Indian makes his camp utensils; with it, he covers his canoe, and forms the outside of his wigwam, for which his Western brethren use the skins of the buffalo and the deer. In it he has a torch always ready to hand; and however wet the weather, it will "start" his fire, an invaluable blessing in such a climate as that of Canada. On one occasion I call to mind, we had to make camp in the dark; the difficulties of this proceeding were considerable, from having to grope about for everything, when of a sudden one of our Indians encountered an old birch tree, the bark of which he forthwith fired; a grand blaze ensued which greatly facilitated our endeavours, and we soon got fixed for the night.

The Indian squaw is said to be able to boil water in vessels made of birch bark, by dropping heated stones into the water. Very great ingenuity is displayed by the natives in making utensils of this bark; the corners are turned up and secured with the supple roots of shrubs, which seem to be always at hand, and as pliable as whipcord. The less ingenious settler has found out that he can make his plank house warmer and more comfortable by lining the inside with sheets of birch bark, and this plan is now very generally adopted in the better class of houses. When the country is left in which the birch flourishes, the want of the ready friend is keenly felt in more ways than one, but more especially about the camp-fire, where it can only be supplied by much additional labour in finding and cutting up the very small dead sprigs of the neighbouring pine trees.

CHAPTER III.

After Bear— My Indian Hunter—Woodcraft—Ferocity of the
Bear—Our First Camp—Camp-making—Food—Sleep—Stillness—Unsuccessful Hunting—The Moose—Close Time—Legislation—Cause of Scarcity—Modes of Hunting—Snowshoe
Running—A Successful " Creep "—" Calling " and Mosquitoes.

THE next morning we were off at an early hour for
the country in which we intended to make our hunt
for bear. A waggon was chartered to convey our
baggage, Sandie being told off as baggage-guard.
We left a message for D——, to inform him of our
movements and the whereabouts of our future camp;
while the Indian, John Williams, and myself went
ahead on foot, to hunt some of the most likely places
on our way to the camping *rendezvous*.

John was a famous companion, besides being a
most killing hunter. He was of the Micmac tribe,
to which all the Indians in Nova Scotia, and a great
many of those now located in New Brunswick,
belong. They are a quiet, peaceful, inoffensive
race ; hard working and money earning. They are

said to be able to do as hard a day's work and earn
as much money at the lumber trade as a white man.
But John was not one of this sort; he was evidently
meant for hunting, and not for hard manual labour.
He delighted in the chase, and was an undeniable
hunter; but his *specialité* was his woodcraft. Many
as good a stalker (or, as it is termed here,
"creeper") could be found in the Highlands of
Scotland; but in his dense native forests it would
be difficult to find John's equal. Not a thing escaped
his notice. When the ground was too hard to show
a track, the fallen *débris* of the pine and hard wood
were carefully scrutinized; twigs of the neighbouring shrubs, which a beast might have rubbed in
passing, were consulted; should a morsel have been
nipped off a sapling, it was sure to attract John's
hawk eye; and woe betide any beast which he once
got on the trail of; not the finest-nosed sleath-
hound could follow with a greater certainty of a
view than my companion of to-day. In appearance
he was peculiar, though not striking in any way;
he stood about five feet six inches, was wiry in
make, sallow in complexion, with long, lanky, black
hair; in gait he was rather shuffling, but capable
nevertheless of great endurance and considerable
speed. His costume was not strictly in accordance
with one's Scotch-conceived ideas; it consisted of
a dirty tweed shooting-coat, a pair of blackish
overalls, and a white straw hat; a pair of mocassins
of his own make took the place of shoes. With
what a marvellous quiet stealth did those mocassins
glide through the timber, not breaking the smallest
twig; whilst I, trying to follow most carefully in my
London-made shooting-boots, broke so many dead

and rotten twigs, and made so much noise, that I felt truly ashamed of myself, before I encountered John's half-astonished, half-reproachful looks at my misbehaviour. When game was near, and tracks became what is called "burning hot," the joyful twinkle in John's dull eyes was worth seeing, it seemed to say, "Hurrah! I am all right, it is only for you to do *your* part now."

To-day it did not much signify how much noise I made, nor how skilful John was, for not a fresh track of bear did we come across; there were plenty of old ones, and other signs, too, such as stones and pieces of timber turned over in search of ants; but nothing denoted any recent visit on Bruin's part to the "barrens" we searched so diligently. These so-called "barrens" are open spaces in the timber, off which the trees have been destroyed by fire or axe; a short undergrowth quickly comes up, consisting chiefly of "blueberries," as they are here termed; which are very sweet and attractive to the bear, and on them and beech-nuts at this time of the year he largely subsists. But if I had no actual sport, I had at any rate a good lesson; for old John initiated me in all the different signs of the bear. The track is not unlike a child's foot in a mocassin, from the fact that the animal places the last joint of his leg on the ground at the same time as his paw.

Having never come across a black bear, I cannot say anything from personal observation on their behaviour when brought to close quarters; but all I heard satisfied me that, unless cornered and unable to get away, from wounds or any other cause; or unless in the case of a she-bear defending her young, they will always "skip" (run off) as fast as

they can. I believe nearly all wild animals will do
the same; the rhinoceros, African panther, East
Indian tiger, and grizzly bear being perhaps occasional exceptions to this general rule.

As this was our first camp, we were anxious to
reach pretty early the spot previously arranged on
by John and the teamster. The *locale* selected was
a ridge in the forest, on one side of which was a
valley through which crawled a small sluggish
stream. In this little brook were plenty of small and
indifferent trout, of which we were always able to
procure sufficient for our wants with but little
difficulty. On the other side of the ridge, at a
higher level, was a small spring as clear as crystal,
trickling down a gentle slope, very small in quantity,
but of excellent quality, and it was from this we
got our drinking supplies. Of the other great
camp necessary, firewood, there was indeed an
abundance; we were established in the midst of a
clump of gigantic spruce, against one of which our
camp fire had been lighted; and all around, as far
as the eye could reach in every direction, were to
be seen dense masses of fir, spruce, and other forest
trees; the underwood and younger saplings were
excellent materials for the camp fire.

The process of making camp was new to me,
and as it may be so to some of my readers, and
may interest them, I will briefly describe the *modus
operandi.* The general *locale* being selected, the
next thing is to pick out the exact spot most suited
for the camp fire. This is chosen with regard to
the number and position of the tents to be pitched
around, and proximity to wood and water. Having
selected the spot, a fire is at once " started." In

this, as in many other things, to make a commencement is the chief difficulty, and often requires a great exercise of patience. A small quantity of dry birch bark or, where this is not procurable, of the driest twigs is first collected, a handful of which is gathered up, and the ofttimes precious match is then struck and carefully applied; when well ignited, the bunch is gently laid on the ground, and a little more of the same material is added very gradually to it. By continually adding larger and larger pieces of dry branches, the fire is fostered and encouraged into a certain substance of blazing materials, on which may be gently laid, crossways, two or three logs of dry spruce, or fir (in the Rocky Mountains, cottonwood or pitch pine). Now all is safe, at any rate for a considerable time, and the individual to whom is deputed the culinary department, can look after his pots and pans, and viands, and the others set to work chopping wood for the night, cutting tent poles, clearing spaces of dead wood and rubbish for the tents, clipping off the small branches of the spruce for forming the beds (of which more anon), or the many other little things which have to be looked to for future comfort. It was indeed a fortunate thing for me that I was regularly instructed in the art of making a fire early in my camping-out life; otherwise, when afterwards "lost" in the Rocky Mountains, it would have gone hard with me.

But to go on with our camp-making: as level and dry a spot as was obtainable near the camp fire having been cleared of all rubbish, such as dead boughs, roots, young growth, &c., the tents—of which we had three on the present occasion—are pitched and securely fastened to the pegs, tree-roots, or brushwood.

The tents are placed so that the doors face the fire, and as near to it on the probable lee-side as safety from the sparks will allow. Often in cold weather the hunter is tempted to pitch his tent too near the fire, when he is lucky if he escape only with holes burnt in the canvas, through which water may in future drop on his prostrate body, as a punishment for his indiscretion; sometimes, however, the total destruction of the canvas home is the sad result of trying to secure warmth at the expense of safety.

The tents being pitched and secured, the "floor" is covered when procurable with the small branches of the spruce, laid a couple of inches thick, with the prickly side downwards. Nothing can exceed the comfort and luxurious lying of a fresh-made bed of this description. It is soft and springy, and it has about it a delicious, comforting aroma, satisfying and soothing in the extreme. The evening meal is being seen to all this time, and by the time our beds are made, the food is pronounced ready. Laying hold of our tin plate and a knife and fork, we proceed to operations, and find that this half-hour of supper is by no means the least pleasant of the twenty-four. On the present occasion, we were obliged to be content with bacon and canned viands: but we had most excellent bread, baked in a frying-pan on the red-hot wood ashes. We were generally able afterwards to vary this too civilized fare with some game, most commonly the so-called "partridges," of which there are two varieties, locally called "the common" and "the birch partridge." When in the haunts of venison, the meals are real events. If meat is plentiful, only the choicest parts

are taken for camp use, and when these morsels are
fried in lard or elk's fat, and supplemented with the
most delicious new bread, made of the finest
Colorado flour (of the "snow-flake" brand), and
eaten in that wonderfully pure and invigorating
atmosphere, we have a meal not to be equalled for
enjoyment by the best dinner of the civilized world.

I cannot say that I slept as well on this my first
night in camp as I probably should have done in
my own bed after a stiff day's walking. All was so
strange and new. The novelty, not to say discomfort, at first, of sleeping in an unaccustomed garb;
the chilliness which comes over one towards morning, when camping out in hot weather; the sense of
loneliness and the absence of all sounds of life,
except the shrill, uncanny cry of the owl—all
tend at first to light sleeping and constant waking.
Then the intense stillness of a Canadian forest,
even in the daytime, naturally much intensified
at night, must be felt to be understood. No one
can fully estimate the value of song-birds till after
they have experienced their want. Here not a chirp
is ever heard—nothing but the melancholy "tap,
tap, tap," and the peculiarly wild note of the wood-
pecker. How one longs for the rich, full notes of
our own familiar birds! and how welcome would be
the chirp of even the much-despised London house-
sparrow! The howling of the many-tongued coyote
would be an actual relief to the death-like stillness
of the night, but even this is denied to the Canadian
forest, where an unbroken quiet reigns around,
made more lonesome only by the wailing of the air
in the branches of the pines.

The break of day came at last, but all remained

oppressively still until our outfit began to move about; then chattering and chopping commenced in earnest, and everybody was busy and at work at something. The first thing to be done in the morning after "fixing up" the fire is to boil the water necessary for ablutions; then the bread has to be baked, and the meat fried for the early meal. Often, if well banked up on turning in, the fire will be all aglow in the morning, and only require the addition of some fresh fuel, and a skilful kick or two, to make it break forth into an active flame. How comforting is its warmth to one's bones, when waiting eagerly for food after a bitter night, during which it has been somewhat difficult to keep warm enough for sleep! In what form one feels by the time breakfast is ready! and what a quantity is consumed before the meal is over! There is no doubt about it, that camping out gives an appetite and a relish which are never forthcoming in the domesticated routine of home life, and however many meals are consumed, that miserable production of civilized life, indigestion, is a complaint unknown in the backwoods.

After doing justice to our provender, John Williams and I started off for a morning's hunt. The result was nothing but a good walk and plenty of talk, chiefly on hunting and the mysteries of woodcraft. Although we saw no fresh signs of bear, there were plenty of indications that we were in the country of that largest of the deer tribe the moose (*Alces Americanus*, or *Malchis*), but this was the close season, the Legislature of Nova Scotia having deemed it prudent to prohibit the killing of moose for three years, which period expires on the coming 1st of October.

A few words about the advisability and working

of this law. I begin by saying that I most fully concur in any legislation which would tend to the better preservation of this grand animal, but I doubt very much whether prohibiting their being killed altogether for three years, and then allowing them to be slaughtered at pleasure during the winter months, commencing with the 1st of October, is calculated to attain this object. Every one who has had anything to do with the deer tribe in general, knows that the male about this time of year begins to get out of season, and I believe that the moose is no exception to this general rule. From what I am told, the bull moose is in prime condition from about the 20th of August to the 1st of October, and is at that time well able to take care of himself in his native fastnesses; but after the snow has fallen he is out of condition and weak, and falls an easy prey to the hunter shod with snow-shoes. The heavy brute himself breaks through the crust formed on the surface of the snow, whilst the broad snow-shoes bear the hunter over the fickle skin of ice. The cows heavy with calf fall easy victims, and are killed chiefly for the sake of their hides; hitherto both sexes seem to have been slaughtered indiscriminately. Is it any wonder, then, that this grand deer is becoming rapidly extinct? What would become of our Scotch red deer if stags and hinds were to be killed all through the winter? The only wonder to me is that there are so many left as there still are.

Another of the endeavours of the local Legislature to protect the moose (and caribou) is a regulation that no one in any one year shall kill more than two moose and three caribou. But who is to enforce this law? How is it possible to obtain proof of an offence against it, considering the extent of the thinly inhabited and thickly timbered regions which have to be dealt with? I believe that if the Legislature were to enact that no bull moose should be killed except during the months of August and September, and that no cow moose should be killed at all for a certain number of years, and then that they should have the same close time as the bull moose, making the penalty for killing or possessing double what it is at present—viz., one hundred instead of fifty dollars—that there would soon be plenty of moose again. Against this it will be urged that the winter is the great time for moose hunting, and that it is such "sport" on snow-shoes. I have never tried it, so am unable to form an opinion; but I can hardly believe in the enjoyment of this sport, which consists in running down a fine animal, wasted and miserably out of condition, floundering through the crust of snow, which is strong enough, however, to support you on your snow-shoes.

Then again it will be said, that it would be hard on many poor Indians, and some settlers, who now subsist largely on moose meat through the winter. Well, under any circumstances, these individuals will soon have to find something else to subsist on, as under the present system there will soon be no moose at all; besides which, it would be quite open to them to cure for their winter's wants any meat killed in the autumn, as is often done now.

These enactments should of course be made equally applicable to Indians and whites, and a good portion of the fine should be allowed to the informer on whose evidence the conviction is obtained.

Various causes are assigned by the inhabitants for the increasing scarcity of the moose. It is said that, on the occasion of our troops going out to Canada at the time of the " Trent " affair, a most lamentable slaughter took place by both Indian and white hunters to provide mocassins for the soldiers, which the Government thought to be necessary. The bears are often accused of assisting in the destruction of the moose by killing the young calves ; but I could not find out that this was the case, at any rate, to any considerable extent.

I believe that the slaughter which has taken place in the deep snows of winter is the main cause of the present scarcity, and that this will, unless checked by effectual legislation, eventually cause the total extinction. I do not mean for one moment to assert that the three years' rest which has now been given in this province, has not been of very great service; on the contrary, I believe from what I am told that the moose has increased enormously during this period; but I am very doubtful whether the coming winter will not leave as great a scarcity as has ever before existed, and for the following reason : every hunter and would-be sportsman knows that they are more than usually plentiful now, and that the Legislature may at any moment re-enact a fresh close time; consequently, all are anxious to be at them, and the poor beasts will get a very hard time of it from all sides.

And now to close this dissertation on the protection of the moose, and to say a few words about the animal itself, and the two other modes of " hunting " it, besides that on snow-shoes in winter. Judging by the only specimen I ever killed, and from what I heard and saw, the American moose is

identical with the elk of Northern Europe. The bull
is of great size, weighing frequently, when "gralloched," from 600 to 700 lbs., or even 800 lbs., say
from 40 to 60 stone. He sheds the velvet off his
horns about the beginning of September; and
commences "running" about the middle of that
month, remaining with the cows about five or six
weeks. He generally has only one or two cows
with him, but does not remain with the same for
long. At this time of year he usually frequents the
thick undergrowth of the Canadian forests abutting
on damp, wet ground, and seems perfectly at home
in the water. Both the bull and the cow have
something comical and antediluvian in their appearance; but, notwithstanding their great size,
their movements are surprisingly rapid, and the
the pace at which they can get through the thickest
growth is most astonishing. Their senses of sight,
smell, and hearing are all very acute, but more
especially their hearing; and it is a matter of the
greatest difficulty to get near them, unless a smart
wind is blowing to make a stir amongst the
branches of the timber.

The other ways of "hunting" the moose, besides
that to which I have already alluded, are "creeping,"
or what we should call "stalking"—and "calling."
The "creeping" is pursued chiefly in the "fall," or
autumn, and consists in walking most carefully,
and against the wind, the likely places of the forest,
watching narrowly the signs you may come across,
such as the foot-tracks, browsing of the shrubs, &c.,
&c., and looking out sharply for a snap shot. A
good Indian can tell to a nicety and with certainty
the exact age of each track, the probable size of the
beast, how long such a small twig has been browsed,

&c., &c. When it is deemed that the beast is in close proximity, the utmost caution is necessary; the cracking of a piece of dried stick might "jump" (start) him at any moment, and he would be away without your getting even a sight of him. You may be lucky enough, as was my case, to sight him standing broadside on for a moment, just long enough to get your rifle off, and to know, notwithstanding

THE DEAD MOOSE.
From a Sketch by Albert Bierstadt.

his rapid disappearance into the densest of thickets, that you were well on him. Ah! then comes the thrilling joy, the inexpressible feeling of delight, which repays the sportsman for many a bad night and real rough work, when on taking up the track you come first on his blood, and then a little further on his gigantic body, lying prone and helpless! I need not dilate on the rhapsodies which your hunter and yourself pour out over the fine beast; nor on

the interest of the after processes of "gralloching," or
" dressing," and the way in which the prized morsels,
such as the " muffel " (or nose), and tongue, &c., are
commented upon and packed for that evening's enjoyment over the blazing camp-fire. But keen as all this
enjoyment is at the time, and enjoyable even now to
recall, it is soon over, and a long and severe trudge
back to camp, partly in the dark through fallen
timber, soon takes off somewhat of its freshness.

The third mode of hunting the moose is " calling."
This is followed from about the middle of September
to the end of the first week in October, the most
favourable time of the twenty-four hours being very
early in the morning and very late in the evening, when
the moon is at her full. I believe that no white man
can call well, and that an Indian must always be
employed. His instrument is a piece of birch bark,
twisted up into the shape of a speaking-trumpet. The
call, or cry, is in imitation of that of a cow moose, but
it is skilfully varied with the note, or perhaps " roar,"
of the bull. The noise made is not unlike what I have
occasionally heard from red deer stags, but not the
regular roar of the latter. To " call " well is a
matter requiring great practice and skill; and even
the Indians themselves vary much in their pro-
ficiency. The *modus operandi* is to take up a position with your " caller " towards evening, or very
early in the morning, in some clearing or " barren "
in the forest, taking care that the wind shall be
coming from that portion of the forest where you
think it is most likely that a moose will be. Being
tolerably well hidden by brushwood, the caller emits
one of the prolonged grunts or calls; if no answer
of any sort is made from the neighbouring forest
after an interval of ten or fifteen minutes, the pro-

cess is repeated, and so on until the calling time is past. If any answer comes, the greatest skill has to be displayed by the caller in order to allure the moose within range of the rifle. Should he come out into the open, and get drawn on within one hundred yards, the calling must not be attempted, or he would at once detect the imposition. Sometimes he will stop two hundred or three hundred yards off, and refuse to come any nearer, being what a Highlander would call "suspeecious;" then there is nothing for it but to try a steady shot at that distance.

This mode of hunting is often very effective, and some sportsmen speak with enthusiasm of the excitement of it. I have had but little experience of it, and that little brought me no success, so I am but ill able to speak of its enjoyment; but I must confess that what little I saw did not commend itself to me as a sport. All, except the actual shooting, must depend on your caller. It may be that my judgment of this sport is influenced by the vivid recollection of having become, one warm evening late in the "fall," a living victim to perfect swarms of mosquitoes and black flies. It may sound "soft" to care about such trifles when in pursuit of such noble game, but let any one who has not the skin of a pachyderm try for one hour what it is to lie still on a quiet warm autumn evening in a swamp of a Canadian forest, unprotected by gloves or veil, before he gives an opinion, and then I think he will agree with me in acknowledging that he had grown somewhat desirous of a move, and did not care for a repetition of the entertainment. That evening, I remember, even the Indian took it seriously to heart, and proposed an earlier return to

camp than perhaps the prospects of sport (for we
had had a reply from a bull moose) fully justified.
Glad was I that night to roll my head up under my
blanket, the branches of a fine old tree my only protection overhead, and the ground my mattress, but
at any rate I was now safe from the savage attack
of those venomous pests, whose marks I bore for
many a week afterwards.

But I have gone ahead some weeks, and must
return to our present camp and doings. Dunraven
and Dr. Morgan joined me the day after I arrived;
but several unsuccessful days' hunting for bear,
forced us to the conclusion that it was no use trying
any longer in this district, and that we had better be
off into the neighbouring province of New Brunswick, where there are bear, and where, moreover, it
is lawful to kill moose and caribou at this or any
other time of year.

A MICMAC WIGWAM.

From a Sketch by A. P. V.

CHAPTER IV.

A key of fire ran all along the shore,
　　And lighten'd all the river with a blaze ;
The waken'd tides began again to roar,
　　And wondering fish in shining water gaze.

To every nobler portion of the town
　　The curling billows roll their restless tide ;
In parties now they straggle up and down
　　As armies, unopposed, for prey divide.

Those who have homes, when home they do repair,
　　To a last lodging call their wandering friends,
Their short uneasy sleeps are broke with care,
　　To look how near their own destruction tends.

Those who have none sit round where once it was,
　　And with full eyes each wonted room require ;
Haunting the yet warm ashes of the place,
　　As murder'd men walk where they did expire.
　　　　　　　　　　　　　"Annus Mirabilis," Dryden.

Saint John's, N. B.—The late fire—Extent—Suffering—Destruction of property—The night following—Relief incidents—Energy of inhabitants—The St. John's River—Reminiscences of the past—Fredericton—Cathedral—Houses of Representatives—Members—Business—The Lumber Trade and Lumber Men.

It was the first week in September when we left off hunting in Nova Scotia. The weather was still as warm as summer, and I at least, felt loath to leave the old camp, but having decided, as we thought, for the best, we hurried back to civilization as speedily as we could. Two days' travelling, partly driving, partly by rail, brought us to the once fine city of Saint John's, New Brunswick, which to distinguish in conversation, from the city of the same name in Newfoundland, has the accent thrown on the "Saint," whilst in the other it is made short. The next morning the rest of my party went on to Fredericton, to make arrangements for a contemplated canoeing expedition down the great Miramichi river, whilst I remained behind to have a look round at this "burnt-up" city. The "Waverley," the "house," or hotel, we were stopping at, was the only important hostelry which escaped destruction from the terrible fire.

I shall not attempt to give more than a very brief account of the fearful calamity to this once prosperous and go-ahead city. Nor can I describe the curiously depressing effect on one's feelings on visiting the hundreds of acres of blackened earth and *débris* of all sorts, where existed but a few months ago streets and houses alive with thriving industry. The fire commenced about half-past two in the afternoon of the 20th of June of this year (1877), and by eight o'clock in the same evening it was nearly over. In that short time there was not only a considerable loss of life, but such a vast amount of human suffering consequent on the disastrous destruction of house and other property as to be truly heart-rending to hear of. It is believed that between twenty and thirty persons were killed on the spot, and many more seriously injured by falling materials. Nearly two hundred acres of buildings were

destroyed, and nine and a half miles of streets! the
value of this property and effects is computed at
about five and a half million pounds ! 13,000 people
are stated to have been made homeless ! !

Let the reader try to conceive what an amount of
misery these data mean ! As a sample, one poor
woman, who before the calamity was rated on nearly
3000*l.* worth of property, was now literally without
a cent, and dependent solely on charity ! She, like
many others, was uninsured, and the general sufferings were aggravated by the inability of some
of the insurance companies to meet their liabilities
at once.

The work of destruction was so fearfully and
almost supernaturally irresistible that, to use the
words of my informant (himself an eye-witness),
" It was as if the air itself was on fire ; as if there
was something unnatural in the atmosphere." Not
only were all the wooden houses and structures
swept away as if they were straw, but I saw myself
great masses of stone and brick buildings in crumbled dust and ruins. In some cases the blackened
brick chimney-stacks stood alone amongst the
ghastly *débris* to mark the site of some of the finest
structures the city could boast of. It was curious
to observe how much better bricks stood the fearful
heat than stone. It would appear as if the stone
(principally granite and sandstone) had got previously so heated that when played upon by the
water it flew and crumbled to pieces. A fine flight
of dressed granite steps had become calcined sand,
and some of the most substantial stone structures
appeared to have fallen the easiest victims to the
sheets of flame. In fact, fanned by a strong north-

west wind, the fire from the very commencement seemed to have defied the efforts of the gallant fire brigade, and to have swept all before it.

The insurances are said to have covered about one and a half million pounds sterling of the total loss of five and a half millions. The Dominion Government Property which was destroyed was stated to be worth 100,000*l.*, and was uninsured. The building of the Bank of British North America escaped in a most wonderful way, having apparently had fire on all sides of it, and was the only "money house" in a condition to resume business the next day.

The night of the fire is said to have been a most fearful one. Misery, destitution, helplessness, blank despair, reigned on all sides, and yet there were found even amidst all these horrors, miscreants hardened enough to take advantage of the dreadful visitation, and to plunder the helpless sufferers. On the other hand, to the credit of human nature be it stated, that no sooner was the fire known abroad than supplies began to pour in from all quarters. More especially did the towns of the United States distinguish themselves in this good Samaritan work. Everybody and every public company seem to have exerted themselves to the utmost to alleviate the terrible amount of suffering and misery which ensued, and which would have been intolerable but for the timely assistance so promptly rendered. Relief Committees were organized; quick trains were placed at the disposal of the authorities by the Intercolonial Railway Company for the instant conveyance of the much needed supplies, and perfect order was restored and guaranteed by the arrival of a detachment of regular troops from

Halifax.   Then assistance in money began to pour in, and here again the philanthropy of the inhabitants of the United States was remarkable. Chicago, which had herself suffered so fearfully, and so recently from a like disaster sent 4000*l.*, Philadelphia 1200*l.*, and I am told the amount from Boston was not less than 11,000*l.*   The Dominion Government contributed 1000*l.*, and the town of Halifax 2000*l.*   Besides these there came smaller amounts from the old country, from Glasgow, Liverpool, and Manchester.

At the present time—the month of August—many small wooden shanties have sprung up here and there on the blackened ruins, in which business is being temporarily carried on, and many fine structures of brick and stone are being rapidly erected; but one cannot help shuddering to see that wood is still used very largely in the construction of the new buildings. Surely this—" the Great Fire "—with the three or four large ones which have occurred in previous years, must have taught them a lesson. And so it has to a certain extent, for the Insurance Companies refuse now to insure wood, but it is said that the mass of the people are so poor that they cannot afford brick or stone, and that therefore they are forced to rebuild their wooden habitations. Mercifully a plentiful supply of water is always at hand, and the water's edge seems to have been the only defined line of arrest to the sweeping flame in the present instance.

Many must have been the incidents of excitement and agony of mind during that short but awful reign of fire. The landlord of my hotel himself must have had rather a *mauvais quart d'heure.* He was absent on his farm a few miles from the city when the fire broke out; the second in command got all the horses out of the stables, which were threatened by the fire, and drove as hard as he could to the land-lord, and told him that "St. John's was in flames." Our host's feelings were not to be envied during the fourteen miles' drive back to the city. He did not know but that his all—namely, his house and stock in trade, which were entirely uninsured—might not be a blackened mass of ruins by the time he got back. Three times did the flames attack and actually ignite his well-built brick house, and three times did the gallant gang of workmen repulse the enemy. In front and in rear the fire raged, but this building stood comparatively uninjured. At last the battle was won, and my host has been able to drive a thriving trade ever since in his well-tried edifice, and is one of the very few gainers by this awful calamity.

It will of course be some time before this city can quite recover, but such is the indomitable perse-verance, the latent vitality, of these young towns on this side of the Atlantic, that its restoration will be far more rapid than we could believe possible in the old country. I am told that the population of about 40,000 is not believed to have decreased since the fire, but that it has accommodated itself to the cir-cumstances by packing closer, only awaiting the erection of buildings to expand itself again, probably with redoubled energy.

I was glad to leave this now melancholy city. Its situation is not only beautiful by nature, but is also well adapted for a large commercial centre. The splendid river St. John, here more than eighty yards across, is the great channel of

commerce from the interior. Down it are brought
masses of both Canadian and United States timber
or "lumber." Wharves, constructed of piles, line
both the St. John's and the Carleton bank, and the
harbour exhibits a forest of masts, which testify in a
marked manner to the importance of this port. The
suburb of Carleton on the right bank of the great
river (formerly called the "Richelieu") is connected
with St. John's proper by a fine suspension bridge
200 yards long, which cost 16,000l. to erect. Being
about one hundred feet above the water, a grand
view is obtained from it. At the entrance of the
harbour is Partridge Island, forming a magnificent natural breakwater to the heavy ocean swells.
The tide rises and falls as much as thirty feet,
which is a great preventive to the accumulation
of ice.

The city of St. John's claims to be the fourth
largest port of commerce in the British Empire,
coming only after London, Liverpool, and Glasgow.
The two great sources of commercial prosperity
seem to be shipbuilding and the timber or lumber
trade. The most busy time of the latter is from
April to July inclusive, but at all seasons plenty of
evidence is to be seen of its importance in the
voyage up the river from St. John's to Fredericton.
Large rafts of logs are formed early in the season in
different places, and then as soon as the depth of
water will allow, they are towed by small steamers to
the numerous saw mills. Often the surface of the
river (in some places more than a mile across) is
literally covered with sailing boats of from twenty
to thirty tons, carrying deals in their holds, and such
a deck cargo as would excite the indignation of Mr.

Plimsoll. Nevertheless they seem to make capital weather with their handy fore and aft sails, and are admirably adapted for the trade.

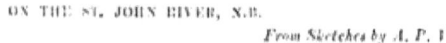

ON THE ST. JOHN RIVER, N.B.

From Sketches by A. P. V.

LUMBER BOATS AND RAFT.

For some little distance after leaving St. John's when bound up the river to Fredericton, the banks continue high and picturesque. Here and there precipitous limestone rocks start sheer out of the water, covered with a luxuriant growth of firs and underwood. Gradually as we ascend the banks become flatter, and the scenery same and uninteresting. Many settlements are to be seen on both sides, some of them having quite an ancient appearance. St. John's was founded by the French at the commencement of the seventeenth century, and the banks of the river were no doubt very rapidly settled from this centre. In old times, before the days of steamers, the British troops quartered at Fredericton used to be conveyed up the river from St. John's in large rowing "flats" called "durhams," with about twenty oars in each. The distance (eighty miles) used to be accomplished in two or three days, the soldiers camping on the banks *en route*. My informant was seventy-eight years of age, and old enough to remember those days which he recalled with evident pleasure. The water of the river is blackish, as if it contained much peat, but such was the effect of a bright sun and a clear sky after a heavy thunder shower, that at one time during our short voyage it looked quite blue. The soil in the vicinity of the river is very rich alluvial, with scarcely any stones. So fine and loamy is it, that, as my informant expressed it, "you could not find a rock big enough to heave at a robin." Why a robin (which by-the-bye is no robin, but a blackbird) should be "heaved at" did not transpire, but it clearly illustrated the fineness of the soil. On an ordinary season it is said to grow two tons of hay per acre.

Fredericton is reached from St. John's by the steamer in about eight hours, and by rail in somewhat less. It is a very taking, clean-looking little town of about six thousand inhabitants. Notwithstanding its very inferior size to St. John's, it is the seat of the Government of the Province of New Brunswick, and possesses a Cathedral, a Government House, and Houses of Parliament. These last are of no exterior beauty, but of them and their contents more anon. The cathedral is a very pretty

Gothic building of the native sandstone, erected about twenty-five years ago. The seats and wood-work of the interior are of "butternut" wood, a sort of walnut of much repute in this country. The present bishop (Dr. Medley) has held the appoint-ment for thirty-two years, and is much respected. The stained glass of the windows was the only drawback to the general pleasing effect of the interior; it was of that light, dazzling, unsubstantial character, of which so much is to be seen in France.

Parliament was now in session, but it was a special session to deal with the difficulties arising from the conflagration at St. John's; the regular session being usually from the 1st of February to the middle of April. The hours at which the Houses sit are far more sensible, in a sanitary point of view at any rate, than are ours in the old country; for they meet at ten a.m. and sit till one p.m., when they adjourn for the day, unless business is very pressing, when they have a short sitting after tea at six p.m. Both the Upper and Lower Houses hold their sittings in one building of insignificant appearance; the Upper House occupy-ing the room exactly above the Lower. The Upper House, I am told, consists of some fourteen or six-teen members selected by the Government; they have generally been members of the Lower House who have been of service to the Government. The Lower House consists of forty members elected by the constituencies. I heard the Upper House go through a Bill in Committee, and can only say that in expedition they emulated successfully their English compeers.

The Province of New Brunswick sends nineteen

members to the Dominion Parliament at Ottawa. It is a cause of complaint here that the maritime interests of New Brunswick, Nova Scotia, and Prince Edward's Island, are swamped in the Dominion Parliament by the overwhelming number of members from the agricultural provinces of Central and Western Canada.

The members of the Provincial Parliament appeared contented, hard-working, shrewd, and most loyal, and well calculated to deal with the local interests of a young and developing country.

We spent some few days in Fredericton laying in fresh stores, purchasing canoes, and engaging Indians preparatory to a canoeing expedition. But before leaving this great lumber river, I must say a few words on that trade of which so much is to be seen around on all the big rivers of this country.

Most of the trees made use of for lumber are of the fir tribe, for although there are many others, such as birch, maple, &c., which come into the market, yet the logs, deals, and battens cut from the *coniferæ* form the chief staple of the trade. My informant was a very intelligent merchant of Cornish descent. His principal business was supplying the lumber camps with flour and the other necessary stores for their winter campaigns. For the information of the uninitiated, I must explain some of the local and technical terms. By "lumber" is meant timber; a "lumber man" is one who cuts or "chops" the lumber during the winter, and later on takes his part in the various subsequent processes on the streams and main river; a "lumber camp" is the log hut or huts in which the lumber men live or "locate" themselves during the winter operations.

About the month of October experienced men are sent out into the forests exploring, or to use their own term "cruising;" their object being, in the first place, to find suitable lumber for chopping; and, secondly, that it shall be in such a locality as to make it remunerative to get it to a market. Having selected a suitable site—generally a district abounding with large spruce, and in near proximity to a good stream of water—they return to civilization, and enter into negotiations with those to whom the timber belongs. The Government, or a Railway Company are usually the proprietors, the latter receiving it as a grant for making a line through that part of the country. An arrangement having been entered into, about November a suitable place for a camp is selected, and to this spot a rough road is made through the forest. Then a log hut is built to accommodate as many men as are going to "operate" during the winter—sometimes as many as eighty men are located in one place—and to this encampment stores of flour, tea, coffee, tobacco, molasses, salt pork, &c., are forthwith hauled. In old times there was an open fire in the middle of each hut, but nowadays a stove is used instead. Every chink and crevice is caulked as tight as possible, so that when the door is closed with all the occupants inside, and wet clothes are being dried around the parching hot stove, the atmosphere had better be imagined than described. By the beginning of December all is ready for the lumber men, who at once take up their abodes in the encampments, most of them not revisiting civilization till late in the following spring.

The spruce they fell is generally chopped, so as

to measure not less than ten inches diameter at the small end, and to lengths of from twenty to forty feet. These logs are hauled over the surface of the hard snow to the "browse," which is the bank overhanging the stream down which the timber is to be "driven" or floated when the ice breaks up in the spring. Piles of logs are here formed by driving in very strong retaining posts and heaping up the lumber against these in such a manner that when the uprights are cut away the whole pile shall be free. When released it crashes madly down the hillside into the stream below. These operations of felling, hauling, and stacking go on all the winter months.

When the spring comes and the ice breaks up, the lumber camps are abandoned and the "browses" are let go. The lumber is then "driven" or floated down the smaller streams into the main rivers, such as the St. John, Miramichi, &c. Here it is stopped and gathered into what are called "boombs;" these are bays of the river shut off from the rest by large "boombs" or logs of timber chained together, and made fast to the shore at one end and to a mooring at the other with the opening up stream. From these depôts, rafts, or, as they are called here, "joints" are formed, which are towed down by steamers to the various saw mills on the banks of the river. These rafts contain usually about 5000 cubic feet of timber; a steamer may have as much as a million cubic feet in tow at one time.

In the saw mills the logs are cut up into "deals," that is, planks three inches thick, and seven, nine, and eleven inches in width; if less than seven inches they are called "battens." The thin ends cut off

from the tops of the trees are split up into " laths "
for building purposes.

I fear the foregoing description is dry, but it
is difficult to make it otherwise. The operations
themselves, however, are not without excitement,
and even danger. Two of them are really very
ticklish, involving risk to life and limb. The
first of these is, cutting away the uprights which
retain the browse, when it sometimes happens that
the browse comes away before the unfortunate
lumber-man can escape on one side, and then he
must inevitably be smashed amongst the masses of
rolling logs, tearing wildly down the hill into the
stream below. Sometimes it happens that the
operation is so evidently hazardous that the lumber-
man is let down from above by a rope and pulley.

The other dangerous operation is when what is
called a " jam " occurs in driving or floating the
lumber down the smaller streams. This happens
when logs get caught in an obstruction and gradually
form a barrier, which stops the further progress of the
floating lumber in rear. Then comes into play the
services of a not only very active man, but one well
skilled and experienced in the work which has to be
done. He finds out first of all the offending logs
which cause the " jam," and then sets to work with
his axe to cut them away. Of a sudden the mass is
freed. To fling his axe away, and skip for dear life
to the shore, jumping like a cat from log to log as
they spin and whirl down the stream, is the work of
a few seconds; but even surprisingly nimble as he
is, he sometimes finds that he cannot reach the shore
before the mass is on him, and he is driven to take
the last chance of plunging into the water and

diving underneath the surging mass, allowing it to pass over him. Should he get hit by a log his fate is sealed.

Yet with all these risks and dangers, and the discomfort of being shut off from his friends and civilization for a great portion of the year, the life of the lumber-man is most popular. In fact, it is a common complaint that it is difficult to get any young man to take to anything else, and that agriculture suffers in consequence. The lumber-man's wages are not excessive for America, varying from $14 to $18 (2*l.* 16*s.* to 3*l.* 12*s.*) per month, everything except clothes and tools being found. The life itself must be a very healthy one, for it would be difficult to find their equals in strength, activity, and endurance. I should say they would average about five feet eight inches in height, and would weigh between eleven and twelve stone right through. What a fine, raw material for soldiers we have here! Accustomed as they have been all their lives to roughing it, the labours of a campaign would come to them not only quite naturally, but as an actual enjoyment. Should it be the misfortune of the British empire ever to be involved in a vital war, I feel sure that a Canadian contingent would prove a most important addition, and that it would leave its mark on the nation's history.

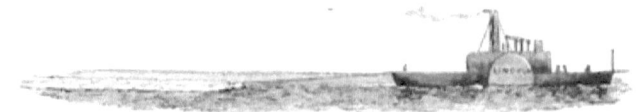

STEAMER TOWING RAFT OF LUMBER.

"ON THE MIRAMICHI."

From a Sketch by A. P. V.

CHAPTER V.

"And the forest life was in it,
All its mystery and its magic;
All the lightness of the birch tree,
All the toughness of the cedar,
All the larch's supple sinews;
And it floated in the river,
Like a yellow leaf in autumn,
Like a yellow water lily."

Longfellow's "*Hiawatha,*" vii.

Start for our canoeing trip—Indian Birchbark Canoes—Disaster—
Across to the head waters of the Miramichi—Glashville—Hard-
ships of its early settlers—Gray's Mill—McEwing's—Afloat—
Beaver—Bear Incident—Camp-making in the dark—Slow

By the 1st of September we had refitted and were
ready for our canoeing trip down the Miramichi, one
of those grand rivers flowing into the Gulf of
St. Lawrence, or more accurately into the Bay of
Miramichi, which abuts on that magnificent gulph.
Our " outfit " consisted of Lord Dunraven, Dr. Morgan, and myself, Sandie Macdonald (my Highlander),
and four Indians. Two of these, our old friend
John Williams and Hood, we had brought with us
from Nova Scotia, and were of the Micmac tribe;
the other two were Milicetes, a father and son, of the
name of Gabe.

To carry ourselves and our *impedimenta* we had
hired, bought, and borrowed, three birch canoes, of
Indian construction. As I was not well, D. started
ahead of us with the canoes and Indians, leaving me
and Dr. M., who was kind enough to stop with me,
to follow on as soon as I was sufficiently recovered
from the very severe chill I was suffering from. A
couple of days found me ready, but in the meantime
a disaster had occurred to our transport service, for
the team of horses which D. had hired to convey the
canoes from the nearest railway station, Kent, to
the head waters of the Miramichi, had been scared at

the whistle of the train, and bolted with one of our canoes on board. The result was the irreparable annihilation of the frail bark, which meant the loss of the fourth part of our means of transport. A telegram arrived before leaving Fredericton, acquainting us with the misfortune, and telling us to replace the smashed canoe. This we did, as well as we could in so short a time, but, as often happens, the canoe which was destroyed was our best, and that we now bought was as bad as could be, consistently with floating at all. The after consequences to our expedition were great loss of time and temper in pitching and plastering to keep this last ship afloat.

The drive of sixteen miles from Kent station to Gray's Mill, on the head waters of the south-west branch of the Miramichi, is at first through a country well covered with birch and other hard-wood trees; then we got into denser forests, chiefly composed of coniferæ, as well as maple and birch, the latter attaining a size inconceivable to those accustomed only to the English growth. Our progress was slow and tiresome; the roads were very bad, and we had to be careful not to strain our canoe or smash it against the overhanging branches. But all around was new to me, and there is always a charm in looking out for novelties in Nature's works. There was little to be seen of animal life. We disturbed one covey of " partridges," which caused us to descend from our conveyance and demean ourselves by shooting a few off the tree " for camp use." I mention that they were for food, as affording extenuating circumstances in the eyes of my fellow sportsmen for the dastard deed. In the vegetation, however,

there was much strange and new, and I often
wished on this and other occasions that I knew a
little of botany.

About midway we passed through a new small
settlement called "Glashville," consisting of a few
log houses and an inn with the high-sounding title of
"Glashville House." The inhabitants are hardy
Scotchmen, who had been induced to clear and
settle here by a grant of one hundred acres free per
man, they on their part undertaking to make a road
free of cost to the settlement. The first winter after
their arrival from the old country was terribly hard
for them, poor people! They were all quite new at
a settler's life in this very severe climate, and seem
to have suffered fearfully. However, with the
indomitable perseverance of Scotchmen, they stuck
to their work, and have established a fairly prosperous settlement.

Nine more weary miles brought us to Gray's mill.
Here we had hoped to find D—— and our advanced
guard, but here they were not; and all we could
ascertain from the Irish inhabitants was that they
believed they had gone on to a settler's called
McEwings, eight miles farther down the river.
Taking on the same team of horses, we made the
best progress we could, but the pace was slower
even than before, and it was getting on towards
dusk before we made McEwings's. We found
here two of our Indians and our canoe; they
had pitched our tent, but as we were very
anxious to overtake D——, we determined not to
stop the night here, but to take to our canoes and
get as far as the remaining daylight would allow.
It was a lovely autumn evening; Dr. M—— and

I, with the Indian, Hood, were in one canoe; Sandie and the dogs, and the other Indian, young Gabe, were in the other. I did not aspire to being a canoeist, so contented myself by lying at the bottom of the frail barque on a bed of soft young spruce shoots, whilst Hood and Dr. M—— did the propelling part. Unfortunately the water was rather "small," and consequently the shallows frequent, so that a great deal of scraping, and shoving, and lifting had to be encountered, with a fair chance of getting capsized, where the current was strong. So nearly did this happen that on several occasions we took in water over the gunwhale. Where, however, it was tolerably deep the motion was most delicious and soothing. Nothing disturbed the almost unnatural stillness of the blissful evening but the lapping of the water against the canoes and the slushing of the paddle or the pole; a deep quiet pervaded everything. The tops of the trees were tipped with the warm madder of the rich and gorgeous Canadian sunset. Thick, almost impenetrable, forests ran right down to the very water's edge, dense enough to harbour any amount of any kind of big game. But the only "signs" we saw, were those of the beaver, which were frequently to be detected on the soft mud of the shelving banks. Judging by the amount of tracks, these little animals must have been very plentiful, but we could not stop for such small game. Had we known, however, as much as we did afterwards, I should have been very much tempted to have delayed our movements; for it afterwards transpired that, near where we had embarked, a black bear had been encountered the previous afternoon by the oldest of our Indians.

He had been loafing about, as Indians are apt to do, just to " take observations" of the locality, when he came suddenly on a young but full-grown black bear. Being unarmed, and the bear in very close proximity, Hood speedily made up his mind that the best thing to do was to try the effect of the *vox humana*, and commenced forthwith to yell and halloo vociferously. This had the desired effect; the bear was scared, and bolted; and Hood lost no time in making back tracks for camp. It appeared that he had had quite enough of bear-hunting for the present, so took care not to mention what had happened— at least, to any white man—until we had placed a goodly distance between us and the scene of his adventure.

We had canoed about five or six miles when the light began to wane; and as making camp in the dark is a thing to be avoided if possible, we went ashore at the first suitable place. It was, however, very late before we had completed our camp arrangements; the selection and chopping of the fire-wood having to be carried out by the blazing light of a fine old birch tree, which one of our Indians had fired for that purpose alone.

The next morning by half-past seven we had struck camp and were again under way; our rate of progress was very slow, owing to the continued shallowness of the water. We kept a sharp look-out on both sides for any signs of our party, and were in the afternoon rewarded by a sign-board, curious in device, of D.'s design and manufacture. After close study—some difficulty arising from a portion of it having fallen to the ground—we made out that he wished us to

follow him up a small stream which ran into the
main river here from the Miràmichi Lake. The
Indians judged from the signs that our party had
been here the previous day, so we determined,
although it was getting late in the afternoon, and
none of the outfit had been in these parts before, to
push on up the brook as far as we could, before the
night overtook us. At first the water was very
shallow, and consequently our progress was anything
but rapid; but after about a mile it became deeper
and more sluggish, and we were able to get along
famously.

This night was one of the most uncomfortable I
experienced whilst hunting in Canada. We were
making good progress up the small stream, when a
most fearful thunderstorm broke quite suddenly upon
us. To get ashore and make camp as rapidly as possible, was all that could be done. Fortunately we
struck on the very spot where our advanced party
had passed the previous night, so we had no clearing
to do. Almost everything, however, got soaked in
no time. One dripping tent was soon pitched on
the soppy, spongy ground, and under it we piled all
those things we wished most to save from the downpour. During the process of camp-making, the
storm was at its height, and the peals of thunder
and flashes of the most dazzling forked lightning
were appalling. Once I saw something like a
bomb burst apparently not far from us, the rain
coming down the whole time in perfect sheets.
Although the intense fury of the storm did not
last very long, the rain continued to fall heavily
during the greater part of the night. Most fortunately my tent, although wetted through during the

operation of pitching, proved really waterproof ; and
not a drop came inside during the whole of the subsequent downpour.

What a lovely morning succeeded that terrible
night of storm !   One could hardly imagine it possible
that the serene, peaceful scene now before us was
so lately the battle-field of so fierce a struggle of the
elements.   The quiet but swollen stream flowed
sluggishly before us, disturbed now only by the
jumping of fish or the splash of the musquash or
musk-rat ; and all was so still and calm, not even a
sigh of air moving to stir the bright green spruce
branches on which glistened the rain-drops in
the blaze of the rising sun.   All nature seemed
exhausted and reposing after the conflict of the
previous night.

But we had no time to linger and admire; we
must away again as quickly as possible in pursuit
of our companions, whom we thought could not
be far ahead of us.   A short distance more of
dead water between mud banks, on which were
plenty of signs of musk-rats, beaver, and otter, and
then we got again into some steep rapids.   Here
we had to turn out and walk through the dense
timber on the banks, the water being so shallow as
to necessitate the canoes being emptied of all human
freight.   The canoes were then shoved along from
the stern, or dragged by the bows, by the Indians.
Soon after entering these rapids we were surprised
to come suddenly on a canoe, which we were
delighted to see was being propelled by old Gabe,
one of D.'s Indians.   He had heard some shots we
had fired last night before the storm, and had come
down to render any assistance we might require.

He told us that we were not far from the Miramichi
Lake, on which D—— was encamped. But before
reaching camp Dr. M—— and I came in for another
ducking, the result of our being together in the
same canoe, and one of us attempting to fly-fish.
Over went the crank piece of bark, and the first I
knew of it was the difference of temperature to my
body between lying on my side basking in the sun
and the cold water of the river. The contrast was
somewhat startling, but dry clothes and all the
requisites for a good fire were close at hand, and I
soon got fairly comfortable again. I came, however,
to the conclusion that these canoes are not to be
trifled with, and are certainly not adapted for
fishing, being almost as tender and crank as a
Thames outrigger. When it is considered how and
of what they are made, this peculiarity is not to be
wondered at. A skeleton of light tough wood,
generally cedar, in appearance something like the
backbone of a small whale, over which are nailed
and tied layers of birch bark, the outside to the
water; the ends of the canoe are squeezed in, closed,
and turned up so as to be quite sharp, and form
a cut water. Most ingenious and light are these
crafts, but neither safe for beginners, nor calculated
for any rough usage. The white settlers do not
patronize bark canoes, but construct for themselves what are called "Dug-outs," that is, stems of
large trees, shaped on the outside like a canoe, and
scooped out in the centre; these are far more lasting
and are not nearly so crank, but are far heavier and
more clumsy than the bark canoes. Both sorts
are either "poled" or punted; the pole is used
when the depth of water will allow of it, and the

F

paddle when it becomes too deep for the pole.   A
good bark canoe, capable of carrying say three
persons and some baggage, is worth from fifteen
to twenty dollars (3*l*. or 4*l*.); the weight is about
sixty or seventy pounds.

To return to the Miramichi Lake, into which we
entered very soon after the little incident just
narrated.   We found that D. had selected a most
charming spot for a camp at the south end of this

OUR CAMP ON LAKE MIRAMICHI.

From a Sketch by A. P. V.

really very beautiful little piece of water.   A clear
streamlet discharged itself into the lake within a
very short distance, and magnificent spruce, maple,
and birch covered the ground in all directions.   The
lake itself was about four miles long by three broad,
surrounded by tolerably high hills except on the
eastern side, where the ground was flat and very
swampy.   Our encampment was close to the lake

shore, upon which we soon found old tracks both of cariboo and moose, exciting to behold. Not far off was a very small trail leading through the forest to another little lake, called " Napadurgan," of which more hereafter. As we should in all probability remain in this delightful spot some few days, our outfit had taken much trouble to make it as habitable and comfortable as possible. The two tents for our own use were pitched near some fine large trees with their backs to the lake, and sheltered from the cold air and fog which drifted down the lake mornings and evenings by some underwood. A space had been carefully cleared in front of the doors of our tents for the main camp fire, on the opposite side of which was a marvellously constructed " lean-to," the handiwork of the Indians, and made of fir poles covered with sheets of the ever-useful birch bark. Here on every spare moment they would squat on their haunches and chatter away in their own native lingo, in great enjoyment of the many good stories of which they had a large stock, judging by the almost incessant chuckling and laughter which proceeded from the little shelter. The floor of the lean-to had been carefully levelled, and was strewn, inches thick, with the deliciously-soft and turpentine-smelling shoots of the spruce branches. The men's tent and the cooking fire were a few yards off. Gabe the younger was our cook, and a very good one he proved.

The first evening after we arrived D. and I went out with our old friend John Williams, to " call" moose. The spot selected was a small " barren" two miles from camp, and not very far from the edge of the lake. It was oppressively and strikingly still; not a sound was to be heard except the occasional, wild, melancholy cry of what is called here the "Loon" bird (the great northern diver), a constant frequenter of the Canadian lakes. The beating of one's heart sounded like the thumping of an engine when waiting with intense eagerness for any answer from the surrounding forest to the Indian's call.

There is a curious feeling of enjoyment in this intense stillness in the midst of these boundless and magnificent forests. A feeling of quiet repose comes over one, producing a soothing, calming effect on mind and thoughts, which is hard even to understand in the haunts of civilization. The season was not sufficiently advanced for calling, nor had we seen any fresh signs of moose in this locality, so we were not sanguine when we went out, but I was glad to try it, although I cannot say that it impressed me much as a sport, and after about an hour's "calling" we re-embarked in our canoe and made for camp.

The next morning I was all ready for a day's "creeping," or "still hunting," or, as we should call it in the highlands, "stalking," after moose, cariboo, or bear. D. most good-naturedly lent me old John Williams, and very early he and I and Sandie started away for a barren, which D. and John had seen the day before near the Napadurgan Lake. We ought not to have been very hopeful, for there were no very fresh signs in the vicinity, but somehow I thought something would come of the day, and Sandie seemed to share my hopes. A trudge of five or six miles along the trail through the forest brought us to the little lake, which was surrounded with much swampy and partially-wooded ground, just the favourite haunt for moose and caribou.

Our movements now became very slow and careful. The cautious old Indian who led the way examined with "skinned" eyes every fresh piece of ground which came in view, and I followed close on his heels with my favourite little "express" ready to open fire on the slightest provocation. All of a sudden the Indian drops on his knees, followed *instanter* by Sandie and myself; then he whispers eagerly that he thinks that he has seen a stag caribou lying down some little way off, but he was not certain, for it was so far off, and he had been so anxious to get out of sight again, that he had dropped down before he had made quite sure. All doubt is soon put an end to by my old stalking-glass, which revealed to us a most exciting little family party, consisting of a very fine caribou stag, his wife and child, all peacefully lying down and ruminating. The ground was well-adapted for stalking, being covered with patches and clumps of short stubby cedar; but there was no wind, and it was so very sloppy that there was great danger of the slushing of our footsteps being heard by the acute-eared beasts. Leaving Sandie behind to watch the deer with the glass, John and I started off on the stalk. I must confess to feeling more than ordinarily excited. It was the first caribou I had seen; the stag was an unusually fine one, and large caribou are getting scarce; moreover, as my stay in Canada was to be but short, probably I might not get another chance, at any rate not at so fine a specimen. Fortune favoured us, and my nerves did not desert me; some friendly cedar bushes allowed us to get within about ninety yards of the stag, and by kneeling as high as

I could, I was able to see about half the depth of his body. Taking him low behind the shoulder, I pulled. Off he went at a gallop, but I soon saw that he was badly wounded, and I felt happy; and well I might, for within about 150 yards he fell dead. A sudden impulse made me snap at the hind with my second barrel as she galloped away, but fortunately—as I thought afterwards—I missed her.

Sandie was soon on the spot, and gralloched the stag *à l'Écossaise;* during which process most lavish was the admiration poured by all of us upon the grand beast. His head was very fine, possessing both length and span of horn, and no less than twenty-five little points. Being in excellent condition, his haunches were covered with inches of fat, and the hair of the skin was sleek, glossy, and thick. We had no means of ascertaining his weight, but Sandie, who had had great experience of red deer and cattle, estimated it to be about 450 pounds —over thirty-two stone—"clean." Sandie packed the head back to camp on his shoulders, a distance of six or seven miles, through thick and fallen timber, and over some infamously swampy ground, a feat which raised him much in old John's eyes, who, I fancy, rather looked down upon the *modus operandi* of the previous gralloching. On reaching camp many were the congratulations on my luck, and most excellent were the tit-bits we had brought home with us for supper.

The next day four of our men started off early, and having skinned and cut up the deer, brought him back in four parts. They calculated that they carried over 100 pounds each, besides the skin and head, which bore out Sandie's estimate. The meat

was excellent, and having set apart for use as much
as we could consume fresh, the Indians smoked and
dried the remainder. Even from a commissariat
point of view this was a great piece of good fortune;
it kept us well supplied with meat for the rest of our
voyage, and even smoked caribou is very superior to
salt pork and bacon, which would otherwise have
been our portion.

MY CARIBOU.

And now to say a few words about this fine and
sporting representative of the deer tribe. The
caribou, or cariboo (*tarandus rangifer*), is the
reindeer of America, in the same way as the moose
is the American elk, though in the latter case the
American and European representatives are much
more nearly identical than are the cariboo and the

reindeer. Authorities seem to recognize two varieties of caribou in North America, namely, the "barren land caribou" and the "mountain caribou." The former is found in Newfoundland and Labrador, and is generally larger and coarser than the mountain caribou, which inhabits Nova Scotia, New Brunswick, and other parts of Canada, and some parts of the United States. The specimen I was lucky enough to get was as fine a mountain caribou as Professor Ward, of Rochester, New York State (a gentleman of vast experience), had ever set up. These deer go in herds like red deer, but the difference of size between the stag and the hind is much more marked. The colour of the skin is a greyish brown, the stag having a broad white stripe extending from the shoulder to the neck; the feet are large and broad. With the fore feet they clear away the snow when in search of food, for I am told that it is a popular fallacy to suppose that this process is performed with their brow antlers, and it is evident that if this were so, the hinds would fare but badly, for although they generally have small spike horns, they never have the brow antler. The stag sheds the velvet about the middle of August, and commences to go with the hinds about the end of that month, or the beginning of September.

In point of size, the caribou comes about third of the American deer kind, the Moose (*alces malchis*) and Wapiti (*cervus canadensis*) being both larger. It is a matter greatly to be regretted that this fine animal, like many others, is becoming yearly more and more scarce. It would seem pretty certain that eventually it will be extinct, unless means are taken, and that speedily, for its protection.

After this piece of luck, I was laid up with a bad cold for some days, and could not get out of camp much, but D—— hunted most perseveringly. Beyond seeing the hind and calf belonging to the stag I had killed, and hearing a bear near his camp-fire when sleeping out one night, he never came across any sort of big game. We therefore decided on "pulling out" from this beautiful locality and continuing our voyage down the river.

My canoe was navigated by the old Indian, Gabe *père*, a most excellent canoeist, skilful but at the same time very careful and slow; moreover he got no assistance from me, whereas D—— was himself almost as good as any Indian, and Dr. M—— and Sandie worked hard, poling or paddling, as the case might be; the consequence were that our usual order of progression was as follows: First canoe, well ahead and leading easily, D—— and John Williams (Indian); second canoe, Dr. M—— and Hood (Indian); third canoe, Sandie and young Gabe (Indian), with the two dogs (who generally spent half the time in the water or running on the banks), and in the fourth and last, old Gabe and myself. The *impedimenta* were divided between all the canoes; the cooking utensils being with the cook, young Gabe, whose canoe (our last purchase), as I said before, leaked like a sieve, but without detriment to the pots and pans, or apparently to the canine and human occupants. The river was so "small" that much dragging over shallows had to be done; and the bottoms of the canoes got chafed, and all more or less leaky. At nights they were pulled up on the banks, and turned bottom upwards so as to dry well; then in the morning we were able to see any fresh-made holes or rents, and these were patched over with bits of rags and hot resin. Sometimes, if the water came in too fast and entailed too much baling, this operation had to be repeated, in the middle of the day

The weather was lovely, and fortunately continued so the whole of the voyage. Our daily routine was somewhat as follows: Having every morning, after breakfast, to strike our tents, repair and pack canoes, &c. &c., it was generally nine o'clock before we got fairly under way; then we kept going till about midday, when we stopped about an hour for lunch, after which we paddled on till we brought up finally for the night, about five o'clock. From fifteen to twenty miles a day was about our average rate of progress in the first part of our voyage, until the water deepened.

The upper part of the river was full of trout, of which we were generally able to get a good dish for supper when we made camp early enough for an hour's fishing before dark. The almost total absence of animal life is a great drawback to the enjoyment of these splendid Canadian rivers. Beyond a few of the large kingfishers, an osprey or two, and a few red-breasted mergansers, we saw no sign of life for days together. The hopes of sighting a bear on the banks kept us always on the lookout, but none was forthcoming, and except a pair of young lynxes killed by D——, our canoeing trip on the main river was devoid of all fourfooted game.

The banks got higher as we proceeded down the river, and the scenery reminded me of the neighbourhood of Cliveden on the Thames, above Maidenhead. Where they had not been cut for lumber,

the banks were clothed down to the water's edge
with the dense sombre greens of the firs, spruce,
and cedars, but here and there refreshing patches
of bright maple and birch relieved the eye. At this
time of the year—the middle of September—the
maple are brilliant to a degree scarcely to be
believed by any one who has not visited North
America in the fall. On the same branch, aye,
even on the same leaf, of delicate light green, may
be seen every shade of red, from a rose madder to
a bright crimson lake.

A few days of this slow but enjoyable and luxurious mode of travelling brought us to Burnt Hill,
one of the chief "fishing stations" of this well-
known salmon river. We were too late in the
season to expect any real sport; in fact we were
within a few days of the close season, but we
thought we might kill a few fish, and with this
object determined to give the best pools a good
trial. We set to work with a will, fishing hard
in the early morn, and again as soon as the
sun was sufficiently low in evening, for during
the day, when the bright rays of the still fierce
sun fell on the pools, it was perfectly hopeless
to attempt it, more especially with the water as
low as it was now. The pools themselves were
both promising and numerous, and the whole of
them can be fished from one bank or the other.
The width of the river here is about that of the
Thames at Marlow, but it is not so deep, and is
more rapid and stony. We flogged away most
resolutely, but, whether owing to the lateness of
the season or smallness of the water, with scarcely
any result; one fish of about 5 lbs., of a very dis-

creditable colour, was the sole result of nearly two
days' labours.   There were, therefore, no attractions to keep us here (with the exception of the
most delicious "blue-berries," which grew in pro-
fusion), so we soon re-embarked, and resumed our
downward voyage.   One pest we were spared, which
is always, unfortunately, the concomitant of good
fishing in Canada, and that was mosquitoes and
blackflies; we had had a fair taste of them further
up the river, but from all accounts slight in comparison with what they are when the fishing season
is at its height, say in the months of June and
July.   I must say for myself personally, my new
acquaintance, the blackfly, is a perfect gentleman
compared to his *confrère*, that persistent, indefatigable, poisonous little miscreant, the well-known
mosquito; but I feel assured from personal experience that in northern climes the latter is far more
poisonous and hurtful than in the sunny south.
Tweed material will not keep him out; his proboscis
will drive through anything short of leather, and
even then he will take mean advantage of the
seams, and make use of the same holes through
which the threads have passed.

The "blackfly" in appearance is remarkably like
the common house fly; but wherever he pitches on
the flesh, he drives a small hole, from which a small
drop of blood quickly oozes.   This operation is
sharp while it lasts, but no irritation or inflammation
follows.

Many preventives against these veritable and
sometimes actually dangerous pests are recom-
mended, some sounding almost as bad as the evil
itself, such as being smeared with paraffine or coal

oil, or a mixture of tar and castor-oil, or pork fat; but I found a liquid called the "Angler's Defence," which I had bought in Halifax, of very great service, without being offensive to oneself and others. No spirit or beer should be indulged in on these expeditions, the blood becoming much more inflammatory under these circumstances. I found a mixture of equal parts of glycerine and chloroform of very great value in allaying the inflammation arising from the bites, and well worthy of forming part of one's small amount of baggage.

Some short way down from Burnt Hill, we passed a party of four men and three women "on pleasure bent" from a neighbouring settlement, in two "dugouts," on an expedition after blueberries of some days' duration, for they had not yet reached their destination. Their daylight was spent in travelling, and the nights in camping out on the banks as best they could.

From here on, in order to save weight, the dogs and myself walked along the banks wherever the water appeared likely to be too shallow. This is possible and even easy below Burnt Hill; but above, in most places, the banks are covered with dense impenetrable forest to the very water's edge, which render it impracticable.

A few days after leaving Burnt Hill, we arrived at the first settler's abode, situated about fifteen miles above the first little village, called Boiestown. Here we came across a very hospitable farmer, by name Wilson, who furnished us with such stores as we required, and gave us much information as to our route, the fishing of the river, &c. &c. No spearing, or "burning" is allowed anywhere on the river, and the law is expected to be enforced by certain persons appointed by the Government, who receive for their services a very small remuneration. It is doubtful, however, whether these water-bailiffs are always immaculate themselves, and whether some of them do not indulge in a little spearing on their own account. The best part of the rod season is about the commencement of July, and it continues good throughout the month. The portion of the river suited for the rod may be said practically to cease at Boiestown, below which there are no good salmon pools, and quantities of nets.

We now got into much deeper water, which favoured our progress, and we were able to float and paddle about twenty-eight miles in the day. This part of the country is quite settled. A stage coach runs three times a week from Fredericton to Newcastle, passing through Boiestown and Docktown, and "tapping" all this district. The through journey occupies about twenty hours.

A short way further down signs of the fearful fire, which swept over this region more than half a century ago, are still grimly visible. Large areas on both sides of the river were at that time completely burnt up, and are even now only sparsely covered with undergrowth, through which protrude white, weird-looking stumps, silent but striking monuments to the power of the dreaded element. This terrible fire, known far and wide out here as "The Great Fire of Miramichi," occurred in the month of October, 1825. Upwards of 100 miles in length of country was burning at the same time, so that the district was fitly described as a "sheet of flame!" The fire extended over 6,000 square miles, more than 500 human beings fell victims, burnt, suffocated, or lost, and over 253,000*l.* worth of property was destroyed!! A relief fund was raised, in order, as far as practicable, to alleviate the most urgent cases of distress and suffering, and it eventually reached the sum of 40,000*l.* The towns of Newcastle and Chatham were almost entirely destroyed, and many of their inhabitants lost their lives in the raging and irresistible flames. The Indians and even many whites to this day regard this terrible fire as a judgment on the inhabitants of this part of the country, who are said to have been at that time unusually depraved and wicked.

In some places which were swept over by the fire, a young growth of firs has come up, and is now nearly large enough for lumber; in others, only hard wood has grown, and in others again no good growth at all seems to have followed.

Near Indian Town, a village on the left bank, we had the pleasurable excitement of shooting a rapid called the " White Rapid." The river is here of considerable volume, and as it is much narrowed, and a sudden difference in level takes place, a grand rush of water is the result. Points of rocks pop their heads up here and there through the surging waters, adding much to the feeling of excitement and pleasure, for I had very full confidence in my old Indian, which was not misplaced. Preparatory to the shooting I took the precaution of lying down flat in the canoe, whilst old Gabe, as cool as a cucumber, stood erect in the stern, ready with his paddle to steer the frail craft. Away we dashed most deliciously, acquiring more and more speed,

shaving rocks which seemed an instant before bent
on putting a sudden end to our further progress,
but which a slight dash of Gabe's paddle had just
sent us far enough off to avoid. Saved from this
Scylla on one side, the same movement seemed
destined to wreck us on a hungry Charybdis on the
other, only again to be averted by the Indian's
timely stroke. No flurry about old Gabe—he was
of very different stuff to the screaming Arabs of the
cataract of the Nile,—not a word escaped his lips
until we had landed, or rather floated into the deep,
still waters of the pool below, when I felt only sorry
that we had not a series of rapids before us.

Not far below we found further progress barred
by a boom of timber, stretching across the river
and enclosing a mass of lumber. To negotiate
this obstacle we had to engage the services of a
friendly lumberman, who guided us to a very narrow
channel, where the canoes were partly shoved, partly
lifted into the open water beyond. Soon after this
we brought up for the night, in a small inn kept by
a man called Jardine, who was the master of this,
the Renous Post-office. A little above the Renous
stream flows into the main river. The tidal water
reaches up as far as this, and the white trout
fishing is said to be excellent, the fish being numerous, and regular whales in size, running up to
$6\frac{1}{2}$ lbs. in weight.

From the Renous Post-office we were able to get
down in one day to Newcastle, having been assisted
over the last six miles by a large " skowl," or flat-
bottomed barge, manned by four Micmac Indians,
who most good-naturedly took us on board and
towed our canoes. This " skowl " had been engaged

in carrying the bark of the hemlock-spruce to a
factory on the river, where it is heated, and a product is extracted from it, which is used largely
instead of oak-bark in the tanyards of England. I
am told that fearful waste of timber occurs in
this business; the finest trees being often felled
solely for the bark, and the timber itself not even
fetched out of the forest, but allowed to rot as it
fell. We made out roughly from hearsay that for
this one factory alone the bark of over 100,000 large
trees was required yearly—a large portion of the
wood of which is wasted. Some of the timber is,
however, sawn up into boards; but it would seem
as if there was more demand for the bark than for
the planks; or else that the power of hauling from
the forests is limited.

About nine miles above Newcastle we passed a
large lumber station, called " Parker's," where quantities of timber are " boomed " (that is, collected
between " booms " previous to its being divided
off into rafts or " joints "). This place swarmed
with active-looking lumbermen, who amused themselves with a wholesale abuse of our inoffensive
Indians, who seemed accustomed to it, and took it
very coolly. The skill displayed by these lumbermen
in their vocation is really wonderful; they are said
to be able to shoot a rapid standing on a single log,
with no other aid but a pole to steer it with. One
of their favourite amusements is for two of them to
take up a position one on each end of a floating log,
and then to spin it round with their feet, trying
which shall turn the other off into the water. This
is often done for a bet, the survivor receiving the
wager. It is said that sometimes the log is made

G

to spin so fast that you cannot see it revolve. To all appearances they are as much at home on these mean and shifty *pieds à l'eau* as we should be on a Thames barge. They wear high leather boots, and how they are not always taking involuntary headers must be a problem to every one who has only occasionally tried the slippery, treacherous footing of a floating log, which apparently has but one object, and that is, to pitch one into the river with all possible despatch.

About five miles further down, the river is spanned by a fine though slender iron bridge, on which runs the Intercolonial Railway. A little beyond this and the North-West branch of this grand Miramichi river unites with that on which we have been voyaging, namely, the Great South-West branch. The name " Miramichi " is said to be of Indian origin, probably derived from some old Indian tribe which has been driven back before civilization, and has now ceased to exist. The present Indians call it in their own language "The Little Resticouche."

Newcastle reached, and our enjoyable canoe voyage was over. We had here to separate; D—— and Dr. Morgan turning their faces again towards the hunting-grounds of Nova Scotia, whilst I was obliged to desert them, and—after a few days more hunting in New Brunswick in the neighbourhood of Aulac—to betake myself to Quebec, *en route* to the Rocky Mountains.

CHAPTER VI.

"Amidst the clamour of exulting joys,
  Which triumph forces from the patriot heart,
  Grief dares to mingle her soul-piercing voice,
  And quells the raptures which from pleasure start.

"O Wolfe, to thee a streaming flood of woe
  Sighing we pay, and think e'en conquest dear;
  Quebec in vain shall teach our breast to glow,
  Whilst thy sad fate extorts the heart-wrung tear.

"Alive, the foe thy dreadful vigour fled,
  And saw thee fall with joy-pronouncing eyes;
  Yet they shall know thou conquerest, though dead!
  Since from thy tomb a thousand heroes rise."

                    Goldsmith's stanzas on the " Taking of Quebec."

On the rail—Quebec—Situation—History—Wolfe's Victory—
  Citadel—Garrison—Falls of Montmorency—Afloat again—
  Montreal—The Lachine Rapids—Toronto—Niagara—The
  Falls and surroundings—A perilous voyage—Fascination of
  the locality.

THE distance from Newcastle (or, as it pleases the
existing railway officials to call it, "Miramichi
Station") to Quebec is 422 miles, which is performed by the express in seventeen hours. Some
of the journey is extremely picturesque, especially
that portion where the line runs along the fine
salmon river, the Resticouche, and again where it
skirts the magnificent Gulf of St. Lawrence, here

about forty miles across. From the station called Bathurst, good fishing is to be got in the proper season, but before embarking on this sport, all the preparations possible should be made against the mosquito and the blackfly, which, from what I heard, and from the appearance of a certain lover of the rod I accidentally met in these parts, even thus late in the season—the middle of September— must be something awful, and must preclude any but pachyderms from enjoying themselves. As we proceeded on our journey, the names of the stations on the line speak of the aborigines and of the nationality of the early settlers. The stations "Assametquaghan," "Amqui," and "Sayabec," leave no doubt of their Indian origin; and " Trois Pistoles," " Isle Verte," and " Rivière du Loup," are as distinctly French. At the last-named station we leave the Intercolonial Railway system and get on to the Grand Trunk, which conveys us for 126 miles through a country of old French settlers to Point Levi, opposite Quebec, on the river St. Lawrence, whence a good steam ferry carries passengers across in about ten minutes to the town of Quebec.

What a charming, quaint old French town this is !—far more French than English, and built on such a steep hillside, that it's a wonder that the inhabitants are not always on the roll down the hill, and all of a heap at the bottom. It is picturesquely situated on the peninsula dividing the rivers St. Charles and St. Lawrence, and terminating with Cape Diamond 350 feet above their waters. The streets in the old part of the town are narrow and closed in by high houses. In hard winters, when the snow is

deep, the " way" (or what the Germans would call
the " Bahn ") on which the sleighs travel is so high
above the normal level, that the occupants of these
vehicles can look comfortably into the first floor
windows; what becomes of the front doors and " side
walks" (pavements), I cannot imagine, except that
they are dispensed with altogether during the winter.

Quebec was founded by Samuel de Champlain on
July 3rd, 1608, and was surrendered to Admiral
Kirk in 1629; it was returned to the French in
1632, and unsuccessfully besieged by Admiral
Phipps in 1690. After this came Wolfe's celebrated victory on September 13th, 1759. Since
then we have been left in possession of this bone of
contention. But I do not mean to do guide-book;
the past of this quaint old city is far too well known,
neglected as history is, or at any rate used to be,
in our English education. I will, however, mention
some of the " sights" which struck me most during
the few days I spent here.

First, the citadel, from which a magnificent view
is to be obtained of the city and its surroundings.
A couple of hundred feet below flows the grand
river St. Lawrence, boasting a fair amount of shipping, and entirely commanded from this position.
On the slope, between us and the river, is the
main portion of the town; the lowest part is, to a
great extent, inhabited by the French-speaking
citizens. On the opposite side of the river is the terminus of the Grand Trunk Railway—Point Levi,—
which system is in connection with those of the
Great Western and the Intercolonial Railways. Passengers to or from England pass over the Grand
Trunk and Intercolonial lines, embarking, or dis-

embarking, as the case may be, at Rimouski, where steam tenders ply between the shore and the ocean steamers.

The view up the river takes in the well-known Heights of Abraham, on which the gallant Wolfe achieved his memorable victory. The British force engaged in these operations against Quebec consisted of a fleet of twenty-two line-of-battle ships and twenty-one frigates, under the command of Admiral Saunders, and a land force of ten battalions of infantry and some artillery. The French had about 10,000 men, about half of whom were regulars, and the rest recently raised conscripts from the provinces, under the command of the Marquis de Montcalm. General Wolfe, finding that his small force of some 8000 men would be exposed to too great a loss in landing under the fire of the citadel, had it conveyed in boats up the river and past the forts, during the night of the 12th September. By aid of muffled oars and the darkness of the night, they escaped the observation of the French sentries, and landed about a mile above, at the mouth of a small ravine which is now called "Wolfe's Cove." It was not till the landing had been effected that the French garrison were made aware of the attack. Then followed a stubborn, hard-fought battle along the elevated plateau, of which the citadel forms the terminating point, a feigned assault from another direction having been planned and carried out to favour this, the real attack. The French lost about 1500 men. Their commander-in-chief was wounded and died shortly afterwards, and the two generals next in command were killed on the spot. The loss of those who should have led them in further efforts to repel the assailants, so paralyzed and demoralized the garrison that they surrendered the next morning. We lost about 600 men, and had to lament the brave hero who so successfully commanded our forces, besides many other gallant officers. A grateful country has erected a monument to General Wolfe on the spot where he fell, consisting of a mean, poor-looking column, with a fireman's helmet on the top, truly despicable in taste, and paltry in the extreme, to commemorate so great a hero.

To my civilian eye, the citadel still appears assailable from this side. Nature has made it so, and the science of war does not seem to have done as much as it might to counteract this natural defect in the position. The so-called "Heights" appear as elevated as the citadel itself, and if guns could be got into position on them, it would be a duel on equal terms. The present garrison consists of about 200 men of the Dominion Artillery; the right wing of which is English-speaking and commanded in English, while the left wing speaks French and is commanded in that language—an arrangement which might, I should imagine, lead to considerable difficulties and misunderstandings in action. They appeared a soldierlike lot, especially the right wing. The men enlist for three years, receiving fifty cents (2s.) per day, all found, and the service is popular. Being in garrison here, seems to be much the same as going through a School of Instruction with us, great attention being given to the scientific training of the men. The present armament consists of some Pallisser rifled 68-pounders, a few Armstrong 7-inch breachloaders, and a great many old 24-lbs. smooth bores and mortars.

I gathered here, as elsewhere, that so loyal are the people and so popular is the red coat, that as far as men are concerned, an ample supply of the very best description could be obtained from the Dominion, in case of the "old country" being involved in war.

Another sight well worth visiting, whether in summer or winter, are the Falls of Montmorency, situated about eight miles from Quebec. The distance is just right for an agreeable drive, and the Quebeckers seem to agree in this, judging by the crowds of people we saw enjoying themselves there. A good road crosses the little river or brook within a hundred yards of where it precipitates itself over a ledge of limestone on to the rocks 230 feet below. By the time the water reaches the bottom, it is pretty well all spray, having been broken up by the pointed rocks, which start out from the perpendicular face. It is well worth while, at the cost of a little fatigue, to descend the 305 wooden steps which lead to the pool at the bottom, and to have a look up from below at the magnificent falls. It is here that in winter the sport of "tibogging" is indulged in, on the mound of frozen spray which accumulates at the bottom of the fall. This amusement consists in a man seating himself on a shaped board with a companion behind him, on the top edge of the ice mound; the board is pushed over the edge, and down it shoots along the sharply inclined, smooth and frozen surface, being guided only by a small stick in the hands of the after-passenger. If the board—as it is always inclined to do—gets broadside on, a fearful cropper ensues. It sounds somewhat a dangerous amusement, but I am told it is not so, and that the enjoyment and excitement are intense.

Before turning homewards to Quebec, the curious platforms or stages formed by the layers of the calcareous schist rock, in the gorge above the road, should be visited. At this time of year, the colouring of the foliage is such as not to be believed by any who have not themselves seen the North American forest when the leaf is falling, and the hardwoods are all contributing their peculiar tints to the gorgeous, yet perfectly harmonious, masses of colour.

Quebec may be said to be standing still as regards growth of population. The census of 1871 shows even a slight falling off on that of 1861, the actual figures being 59,699 in 1871 against 59,990 in 1861, and the general appearance of the whole town quite conveys the idea of its having seen its most populous, if not its best days.

I had now joined my nephew Loyd, and as he was in the army, and his leave but short, we were very anxious to get to work on the happy hunting-grounds of the Far West, with as little delay as possible. Accordingly rapid travelling was the order of the day, and this we combined with seeing as much *en route* as we could. The distance by water from Quebec to Montreal is 187 miles, which is got over almost as expeditiously as by the land route. Travelling by steamer in America has certainly the advantage of being far more comfortable than any railway, so we gave the water carriage the preference. The service is performed by a fine line of paddle, or " side-wheel," boats, built on the American model, regular three-deckers, and very fast. They draw about eight and a half feet of water, and considering their size, seem very easily handled. The accommodation is capitally arranged, for, besides a large dining-saloon, and drawing-room, a great many good sleeping-cabins or "state rooms" are provided. We went on board at Quebec at five o'clock one evening, and the next morning at six o'clock found ourselves at Montreal, having in the meantime passed a comfortable and uneventful night. The St. Lawrence, up which we had steamed during the still hours of the night, is certainly a magnificent river, being often two miles in breadth, but as far as scenery is concerned I fancy the traveller loses nothing in passing over it in the dark. Besides the river proper, the lake called "St. Peter's" is traversed for about thirty miles. It is very shallow, but by dredging extensively the large ocean steamers and sailing ships are enabled to pass up through it to Montreal. The whole course is well lighted, and every precaution seems to be taken to make the navigation as safe as practicable.

A long day spent at this fine and fast increasing city enabled us to see something of its attractions, and to accomplish one very pleasing though short excursion, namely, shooting the rapids of Lachine on the St. Lawrence. A train by the Grand Trunk Railway at 7 a.m. is timed to arrive at Lachine (nine miles higher up the river) in time for the first down steamboat in the morning. Here you embark, and in a very short time the rapid water begins. The whole huge river goes bounding and swirling down a narrow channel, with rocks protruding in close proximity on each side, and as the fall, or

difference of elevation, is said to be eighty-two feet
in three miles, and most of this occurs in a very
limited distance, there is more reality about it than in
tourists' excitements generally. The little steamer
"Beaucharnais" is treated by the surging waters
very much as if it were a child's toy-boat, and four
men at the wheel and two at the tiller testify to the
necessity of additional care and precautions. But
as in many other cases besides that of the individual
who first ate an egg, the first man who tried this
amusement was the real plucky one. This pluck
or "grit" (as it is here aptly called) must have
descended on the hardy *voyageurs* who now so
merrily shoot these rapids on the small sections of
open rafts, which are disunited above and put together again below when the descent is accomplished.
We were only two hours absent from Montreal on
this enjoyable little excursion, which far exceeded
my expectations.

Before leaving by the night express for Toronto,
we drove through the city up to top of the so-
called "Mountain," a hill of trap rock rising 500
feet directly behind the town. It is devoted to the
public as a sort of people's park, and commands a
most charming view of the city and neighbourhood.

The rapid growth of Montreal is remarkable even
in this country. In 1829 there is said to have been
scarcely a wharf here; now great lengths of quays
line the fine river, and alongside of them masses of
shipping load and discharge their merchandise to
and from all parts of the world. The city is built
on an island formed by the St. Lawrence and a
branch of the Ottawa.

In the spring of 1849 Montreal was the scene of a

serious riot, during which the Parliament House
was attacked and destroyed. The cause of the disturbance was said to be that the mass of the people
believed the existing Parliament to be too French in
its composition.

This city can boast many very important buildings,
amongst which is a fine Roman Catholic cathedral,
called Notre Dame. A second cathedral is in course
of erection which is to be exactly similar in plan, so it
is said, to St. Peter's at Rome. From this it may be
inferred that the Roman Catholics are both very
numerous and wealthy. Nearly two-thirds of the
population of 110,000 are French-speaking, and
so most probably Roman Catholics. In Quebec, the
proportion is even larger; I was told, on good
authority, that in that city there were eight Roman
Catholics to one Protestant. Amongst the sights of
Montreal is a magnificent stone railway bridge,
which is, with the usual Canadian loyalty, called the
Victoria Bridge.

A night in a Pullman's "sleeper," and the morning found us far on the way to Toronto, which was
reached before midday. This city of 56,000 inhabitants is more English-looking than any I have
seen since I landed. The natives pride themselves
on their English-like customs and habits, and there
is said to be a strong Yorkshire element in this
place, which may account for a John Bullism which
exists here more than anywhere else in Canada, and
which shows itself in times of peace in a readiness to
come to blows among themselves, and when the war
cloud approaches, in no reluctance to have a turn
with their old enemies across the borders, utterly
disregardless of any disproportion of numbers. At

the time of the Trent affair this feeling came out most strongly, and many loyal inhabitants were greatly disappointed when the difficulty between the mother country and the United States was amicably settled. At that crisis a loyal enthusiasm burst forth all over Canada. The very idea of the old flag being insulted seemed to have raised a fierce enthusiasm far and wide, and a declaration of war would have been most popular, however much this town and the surrounding country itself would have suffered, at any rate at the commencement of hostilities.

From being situated on the shores of Lake Ontario, this fine and growing city has easy water communication with Montreal and other towns situated on the St. Lawrence and on the shores of the line of lakes, and with these it carries on a large and increasing commerce.

A short voyage of thirty-six miles, across the western end of Lake Ontario, in an old blockade-runner called the "Southern Belle," brought us to the town of Niagara, situated on the left and Canadian side of the river of that name where it runs into the lake. On board the steamer I fell in with a Colonel Denison, who had had command of the volunteer cavalry at the time of the last Fenian raids, a most enthusiastic and scientific soldier. He had just carried off the great prize of about 800*l.* offered by the Grand Duke Constantine of Russia, and open to all the world, for the best treatise on the employment of cavalry in modern warfare—a very great achievement for any regular officer, how much more then for a volunteer? I found him most communicative and full of information, and, as usual, anxious in every way to promote one's pleasure.

On the American side, opposite the old town, is Fort Niagara, over which floats the Stars and Stripes. It is still a fort, but no longer of any real importance in a military point of view. In former days this was the scene of many a hard fought skirmish. Nearly opposite and within easy range of artillery on the Canadian side, are the remains of the ancient earthwork of Fort Mississagua. At no great distance from here is the monument erected to the memory of the great hero of Upper Canada, Sir Isaac Brock. In 1841, some miserable wretches tried to destroy this tribute of honour to one of the bravest of men, but fortunately the attempt was only partially successful.

A short bit of rail, and we were landed at a small station about half a mile from the "Clifton House," which is a good hotel on the Canadian side, and from which a fine view of the great Falls of Niagara is obtained. Even before the railway station is reached clouds of spray and a dull roar proclaim the proximity to this colossal work of nature. The reader need not be afraid that I am going to attempt to describe its appalling vastness; it would be impossible for even the most gifted to do anything like justice to it. It must be visited to be appreciated, and then I cannot conceive how even the most sanguine can be disappointed. Even if looked at, as it were, from a money-making point of view (as one gentleman I met in America seemed to have regarded it, who asked me "if it was not a pity so much mechanical power was allowed to run waste")—even then, I say, the very rough guess rather than calculation of its powers which would result could do nothing but increase the feeling of

almost reverence for its mighty power. Dry figures
are only obstructions to enjoyment on such occasions,
so I will avoid them as much as possible; but it
may convey some idea of the grandeur when we
know that over the Horse Shoe Fall alone more
than fifteen hundred million cubic feet of water
passes per hour, and that the Fall is about 164 feet
sheer down, with a depth of over sixteen feet of
water on the ledge of rock from which it falls. The
American Fall is 300 yards across, and perhaps
about one third smaller than the Horse Shoe, being
separated from it by Goat Island, which is about
150 yards across; but no real ideas can be conveyed by such details, and it is all too unlike what
can be seen elsewhere, as far as I know, to admit
of comparing it with other waterfalls.

We spent the best part of two days here; but
that time is miserably insufficient and unsatisfactory;
every point above and below the Falls is well worth
visiting, for although, as might be thought, from the
short distance between the show places, that there
must be a great similarity between them, yet this
is not the case, and there always appears some new
view or some new combination of views at every
fresh point of observation.

The river is very swift for some distance above
the Falls, even before the so-called rapids commence. About a mile and a half above is a
ferry, and boats, through accident or improper
management, have been swept down even from that
distance above. Whatever goes over the Horse Shoe
Falls is generally found—or rather its remains are
—in the so-called " Whirlpool," about one and a half
miles below, but when anything goes over the

American Fall it is generally smashed up and arrested amongst the many rocks at the foot. The Rapids above the Falls are wild and grand in the extreme, whether you see them from Goat Island or from the mainland, or the smaller islands of "Cynthia" or "Log," on the Canadian side. One's ideas of rapids are altogether out of joint when one comes to see these; they are more like a strong race of tide at sea, or in some of the kyles on the West coast of Scotland, than anything else I have ever seen. Nothing could have a chance against them; all must give way before the tearing irresistible power, and be carried on in the foaming, surging torrent to the awful plunge.

Goat Island is reached from the American side, by a bridge to Luna Island (on which is placed, alas! a large paper factory), and a second suspension bridge hence completes the distance. It is well wooded, and very charming, abounding, especially on the side towards the Horse Shoe Falls, with beautiful peeps of the Falls and Rapids. The "Sister Islands"—connected with Goat Island by small suspension bridges—are also well worth visiting.

The view of the Falls from Prospect Point, in the Park on the American side, is certainly one of the finest and most extensive. Also from the very fine suspension bridge connecting the two countries, about half a mile below the Falls, a very comprehensive and instructive view is obtained. This bridge has a span of 410 yards, and is 256 feet above the surface of the boiling river below. It is a fine specimen of engineering skill, even for this country, which is full of scientific triumphs over great natural difficulties. It is worth while to cross in the ferry-boat underneath the Falls, which, by taking advantage of the eddies, can be rowed across by one man within a quarter of a mile of the Falls themselves.

A short distance below, the magnificent river again tears away at a terrific pace, as if it had not already had enough of it, and the rapids here are even more terrific and fascinating than those above.

> " The fall of waters ! rapid as the light,
> The flashing mass foams shaking the abyss ;
> The hell of waters ! where they howl and hiss
> And boil in endless torture."
>
> *" Childe Harold," Byron.*

It was down these fearful rapids that six years ago the little steamer, the " Maid of the Mist," made her wonderful voyage, merely to escape from the sheriffs' officer. It appears that her captain and owner, Robinson, was about to lose her for debt. On learning what was to happen Robinson told the engineer to get up steam, not informing him or any one else what he was going to attempt. Casting loose, away he started down the river, taking the helm himself. It is said that the puny craft was at times buried in the surging torrent, and that everybody thought she must be lost, but Robinson got her through all right and saved her from the myrmidons of the law. The strain on his nerves, however, was so great that he never got over it, and he died last year, by no means an old man. The little steamer had to pass through the far-famed " Whirlpool," and this part of her short but fearful voyage is looked upon as more wonderful than even the descent of the Rapids.

The water in the centre of the Whirlpool is said to be eleven and a half feet higher than at the sides, being forced up by the confining banks. The scenery in the neighbourhood is magnificent; the grand river, foaming and boiling as in a cauldron, is driven through a gorge of splendid limestone cliffs, wooded and green wherever there is sufficient hold for soil to accumulate. When we visited this spot the carcase of a wretched horse was being made sport of in the swirling eddies; at one moment it was thrown high up above the surface of the current; at the next, it was hidden from view in the boiling waters; round and round it spun, never apparently getting nearer the edge of the circular power of the Whirlpool, and how it was ever to escape out of the vortex of this awful trap, and to resume its dreary voyage down the rushing, roaring river, remained to us an unsolved enigma.

The gorge through which the river runs below the Falls is only 300 feet wide, whereas the breadth of water above them is said to be over a mile: this hemming in of the waters, together with the steep gradient, causes the striking phenomena of the Rapids and the Whirlpool, both worthy sequences to the glorious Falls themselves.

I should have liked to have lingered on here some days; the natural surroundings are so magnificent and grand, and I can quite understand any amount of enthusiasm about them; they had much the same effect upon my mind as the ocean or perpetual snow mountains. The sense of Nature's power is so ever present and overwhelming. One reflects how this colossal force has been exerted from the creation until now without any cessation; the same incessant flow of irresistible power has rushed on year after year, and season after season, perfectly independent of

our poor little outside world; and the thought that
they will so continue as long as the world lasts, fills
the mind with an overpowering sense of the great-
ness of Nature and the littleness of man.

I quite believe in the fascinating effect the Falls
are said to produce on beings of enthusiastic
temperaments. Amongst the many stories told of
such cases is one of a delicately-nurtured youth who
lived in the woods on Goat's Island for many a
month through the fierce heat of summer and the
intense cold of a North American winter, never able
to tear himself away from the sight of his beloved
Falls. One day his little hut was empty, and he
was found drowned in their waters.

We had much to do and see, however, and only a
very short time still at our disposal, especially for
my companion, so were obliged to be off, hoping
before we returned to England to have another look
at the Falls, which might then be in their winter
garb.

CHAPTER VII.

"And the palpitating engines snort and steam across the acres."—*Mrs. Browning, "Lady Geraldine's Courtship."*

    " These are the gardens of the desert, these
    The unshorn fields, boundless and beautiful,
    For which the speech of England has no name,
    The prairies. . . . .
                       " Lo, they stretch
    In airy undulations far away,
    As if the ocean in his gentlest swell
    Stood still, with all his rounded billows fixed,
    And motionless for ever."
                   " *The Prairies*," *Wm. C. Bryant.*

" Taking the cars," we hurried on by the Canadian Great Western express to the rising town of Hamilton, situated at the western end of Lake Ontario. Here are the head-quarters of the Great Western Railway, apparently one of the best managed systems in Canada. Our stay here was very short, and we were soon away again along the well-laid steel road to Detroit. The whole train is here taken on board a large steam ferry-boat, and in this manner the frontier between Canada and the United States is crossed. No custom-house officials disturbed our repose, and the night was peacefully passed in the Wagner sleeping-car, in blissful ignorance, it might have been, of having taken so important and vexatious a step, in a European's eyes, as entering another country, with its own customs and duties. Our meals are well served in a dining-car attached to the train, to which access is obtained between certain hours for breakfast, dinner, and supper. The passenger is thus able not only to fare well, but at his leisure.

About forty-four hours' incessant travelling from Niagara found us at that marvel of modern cities, Chicago; and truly it is a marvel when we consider that it is only six years ago since it was almost totally destroyed by fire, and that now it is not only rebuilt to its former size, but is superior in every way to what it was before the terrible disaster. Splendid wide streets, full of excellent "stores," public buildings, gigantic warehouses, and colossal offices, are to be seen in every direction. Nor do these edifices seem to have been run up in the cheapest and most expeditious manner, as we too often see at home, but they are apparently really good, solid, "square" buildings, on which both time and money have been spent. Notwithstanding the awful fire, the population increased in the decade in which it occurred, from 224,251 in 1866 to 407,661 in 1876, and the debt of Chicago is still very far less in proportion to its size than that of most large towns in the United States.

The main staples of trade seem to be grain, and live and dead stock. From its situation on Lake Michigan, a very large and prosperous shipping trade is carried on with the eastern cities, and this young "Queen of the West" is said now to interfere somewhat seriously in many markets with old-established New York, notwithstanding the many advantages which seniority must give to the latter. Here has been carried out to a large extent the essentially American idea of raising bodily not only the houses, but even the streets; and, strange as it may sound, this process has not unfrequently been accomplished without any interruption to the every-day work.

But I must not dwell longer on Chicago, or attempt to describe a city now so well-known. Our stay was of the briefest description, and in a very few hours we were steaming away again towards the banks of the transparent Mississippi and its muddy-complexioned sister, the Missouri. I cannot say that the railway journey across this great continent is particularly interesting, beyond the undeniable fact of seeing so much that is new and strange to our English eyes. Points of great novelty and interest there unquestionably are, but on the whole, the journey is wearisome and monotonous, until the long breadth of prairie beyond Omaha is passed, and the mountain ranges forming the back-bone of the continent are reached beyond Cheyenne. The Mississippi is crossed near Burlington, about ten hours from Chicago. It is truly a magnificent river, clear and rapid, and contrasts very favourably with the dirty, sluggish, and erratic Missouri, which is reached twelve hours afterwards at Omaha. Two sections of the iron railway bridge over the latter were under repair, having been literally blown down in a hurricane a short time ago. This scarcely sounds well for the stability of the structure, but nobody seemed to take much notice of it, or to think it signified.

Omaha, the capital of the State of Nebraska, has 40,000 inhabitants, and possesses some fair-looking edifices. Amongst the most imposing are the Roman Catholic Cathedral and the High School. According to the driver—who was conveying us to church during the few hours' stoppage here on a Sunday morning—the town is deficient in churches, for that it "had run into schools, and that the churches were awful mean."

Here are the head-quarters of the Platte Military District, which can muster all told about 1,000 troops. We came across here the first red Indians we had seen since entering the States. They were of the once formidable but now almost extinct Omaha tribe; not striking-looking individuals in any way, spare and diminutive in stature, and very dirty, and they looked, poor fellows, as if they would be more at home in their native blankets than in the worn-out civilized clothing which now covered them. Their reservation is but a short distance from the town, and the fifty representatives of the tribe—all that now remains—occupy themselves in fishing and shooting, obtaining thereby a bare and very precarious existence. My informant's opinion of Indians was very summary, and as it is shared in by most of the inhabitants of the west, I give it in something like his own laconic language. "The boys in blue," he said (i. e. the troops), "are too kind to them Indians; they want the settlers and ranchmen to deal with them; there is nothing for it but to shoot them down." Another western man said to me that he "never believed in an honest Indian until he was dead."

Omaha contained in 1865 only 4,500 inhabitants; in 1875 the population had increased to 20,000, a fair specimen of the manner in which these western towns grow when situated on the highways across the continent. The train stopped here three hours; when again under way we entered on a more recently "settled up" country, and in a short time were running along the valley of the Platte, but although this interesting and important river was often close to us, we very seldom caught even a glimpse of it. This part of the country is very productive, and realizes to sell from $3 to $10 (12s. to 2l.) per acre, which is considered a high price out here.

And now that we are fairly embarked on that great line of railway which especially unites the Atlantic with the Pacific, it may perhaps interest my readers to learn something about its origin and construction. The colossal project had been mooted many years before any steps were actually taken to carry it into effect. It might have remained in the future for many a year longer, had not the Civil War broken out, when it became most desirable, as a matter of national policy, to connect the Western with the Eastern States by more rapid communication than the old stage-coach lines. The Government of the day, being fully alive to the desirability of getting the railroad completed with the least possible delay, granted most favourable terms to the pro-

moters and constructors. I believe they guaranteed
the stock, and subsidized very largely in the usual
American manner of granting to the companies
every alternate mile of country passed through for a
depth or breadth of twenty miles. Two companies
set to work to construct the line; the Central
Pacific Railroad Company started eastwards from
San Francisco; the Union Pacific Railroad Company set out westwards from Omaha. The actual
work of construction began about the commencement of 1866, and the line was completed in May,
1869. As the Government subsidy was so very
liberal, the rivalry between the two companies
became intense as to which should construct the
largest portion and thus obtain the greatest share
of the country passed through. From Omaha to San
Francisco is 1,915 miles; but the Central Pacific Company, by taking advantage of the carriage by water
afforded by the Sacramento River from San Francisco, was enabled to make Sacramento their first
base of operations, and thus establish their starting-
point 140 miles nearer the other. The number of
miles to be laid was in this way reduced to 1,775
miles. Both companies had at first great difficulties
to contend with, but as far as I could judge the Central Pacific had by far the most expensive and difficult
portion of the road as their portion. The whole of
their rails, fish-plates, spikes, and other iron work
had to be brought round by sea from the Eastern
States to San Francisco, and they had to contend
with very great engineering difficulties at an early
stage of their career, in crossing the Sierra Nevada.
The Union Pacific had also at first to pay very dearly
for their materials; even their sleepers (or, as they

are called here, "ties") had to be brought from the far-off States of Michigan and Pennsylvania. But on the other hand they had more prairie to travel over, which may well account for the final result, namely, that of the 1,775 miles which had altogether to be constructed, the Union Pacific Company were able to place to their credit 1,085 miles before the rails met each other on 10th May, 1869, at Promontory, a station in Utah, fifty-three miles to the west of Ogden.

The work of construction was carried on by perfect armies of navvies and roughs, all of them armed, on account of the Indians and of one another, and, if half the stories be true, they had more to fear from themselves than from the onslaughts of the dreaded Sioux. As might be supposed, there were here gathered together desperadoes from all parts of the world, who, whatever were their crimes, were safe here from the hand of justice. The consequence was that, during out-of-work time, gambling, drinking, and every sort of vice used to be rife, accompanied as usual by quarrelling, brawling, and what is called out here "shootings." Vigilance Committees were formed wherever any small settlement was established on the line of progress, and endeavoured to maintain some sort of order and regard for *meum* and *tuum*, by a most liberal exercise of Lynch law. Two waggons, drawn up alongside one another, with the two poles placed upright and lashed fast at the top, would form an effective and speedily-constructed gallows. But notwithstanding these social drawbacks, progress was the order of the day; more than seven miles of railroad have been known to be laid in one day by the Union Pacific Company, and I see in that interesting and instructive guide-book by Williams, that even this has been ex-ceeded by the Central Pacific Company, who, on the 29th of April, 1869, laid and finished in twenty-four hours, fit for the locomotive to pass over, no less than ten miles of road. To feed these advancing armies was of course a matter of grave consideration, but fortunately the country passed through was generally covered with buffalo grass, on which the cattle did well, so that as long as they were on the prairies, as far as meat was concerned, all they had to do was to have sufficient herds moving alongside of them, and to see to the numbers being properly kept up. When the Rocky Mountains were reached, game played no inconsiderable a part in the com-missariat department. Men were told off to hunt, and elk (as the wapiti are here called) and deer, in addition to the prong-horned antelope of the prairies, were brought to the camps in great quantities. One mountain on the left of the line, beyond Laramie, still bears the name of " Elk Moun-tain " from the number of those grand animals which it supplied to the first constructors of the "U.P.," as this railroad is familiarly termed. But I must not weary my readers with more details on this matter; if they care to know more about it, I must refer them to that handy little volume to which I have already alluded, namely, " Williams's Pacific Tourist and Guide across the Continent," published in 1877 in New York, moderate in price, and well worthy of possession.

And now to return to our own experience of this line. For miles and miles we run alongside the old emigrant road leading to the fertile tracts of Colorado and to the other Western States and territories. The mind may here picture to itself the many fearful encounters with the Indians which this road has witnessed; the many scenes of desolation, despair, and woe in which the poor " played-out " emigrants have taken part on their way westward to the " promised land;" poor creatures! often bereft of their all by the Indians, or brought to a standstill by their stock failing, and left to die of starvation, thirst, and cold. The bleached bones of cattle and horses bear ghastly testimony to such episodes, and to the severe and disastrous struggles under which they have succumbed. Many a little mound of heaped-up earth and gravel may be observed on this dismal, dreary road, sometimes surmounted by a few bits of wood, sometimes without any mark at all, to denote the spot where a poor wayfarer has here at last found a resting-place for his weary, broken-down frame.

What the early emigrants must have suffered on their awful journey of many weeks', aye months', duration, it is difficult for us to conceive. Before their destination could be reached, hundreds of miles of dreary, desolate prairie had to be traversed, sparse in herbage, wanting in water, and infested with hostile Indians, who hovered on their flanks, always ready to take advantage of any want of caution, and to swoop down with devastating effect on the fated " outfits." Generally the emigrants travelled in large parties or caravans, sufficiently strong to present such a front that attacks were either not attempted, or were easily repulsed, and it is a source of great comfort in a hostile Indian country to know that the " redskins " will never attack if there is any likelihood of proportionate loss, which is regarded by them as bad generalship. But recklessness and disregard of ordinary precautions were very common amongst the early settlers, and, consequently, fearful scenes of massacre and misery are recorded. Nor did the Indians confine their attacks to the road caravans; for on more than one occasion they have been known to make fierce onslaughts on the, at first dreaded, railway trains. Plum Creek (a station 230 miles west of Omaha) was the scene, in 1867, of one of the fiercest of these attacks, when a party of Cheyenne Indians contrived to upset a goods train by removing some of the rails. The vans and cars were at once sacked, and the contents made off with. Both the engine-driver and stoker fell victims, burnt and scalded to death by the upsetting of the locomotive. But vengeance speedily overtook the perpetrators; armed parties of whites and friendly Indians were quickly on the track, and in a very short time came up with and shot down the offending redskins.

Nowadays the railroad is free from such dangers, and the traveller and emigrant can pass from one seaboard to the other, without the smallest risk of molestation by Indians. But it would seem as if security from the white " desperadoes "—as the roughs are here termed—is not quite so certain. Not a fortnight before we passed over this road the express train bound eastwards was stopped and plundered by a band of six ruffians, at a station called Big Spring, 361 miles west of Omaha. As this incident was most unusual and caused a good deal of sensation at the time, and as the attendant circumstances are characteristic of this far-off coun-

try, I will give a brief account of the occurrence.
My information is gathered partly from hearsay,
and partly from a small pamphlet recently published
at Omaha, entitled, " Hands Up."

The daily express train from San Francisco
(called " No 4" in the railway tables) is due at Big
Spring at 10.48 p.m. By it are often sent large
quantities of bullion and gold coin, the production
of the gold-fields of California and the mines of
Nevada. On the night of the 18th of September,
the express car, which carries the "treasure," contained three boxes of twenty-dollar gold pieces—each
box being worth about 4,000*l*.—and about 60,000*l*.
in bullion. When the train arrived at Big Spring
Station, six ruffians, who had previously overawed
"the station-agent" (Angl., station-master), quietly
took possession of the train. They wore black
masks, and were well armed with six-shooters, of
which they would no doubt have made a free use
had they been opposed in their operations. It is
difficult, however, to understand how only six men
could rob a railway train, which consisted of several
cars well filled with the rougher sex, without encountering some resistance from some one. It can
only be supposed that, the attack being in the
night, the passengers and officials were half asleep,
and that none of them knew how many "road
agents" were at work, and that no one liked to
encounter the first fire; but whatever were the
reasons, the results were that the express car was
robbed of the 12,000*l*. of twenty-dollar pieces—the
bullion being too heavy to pack—and the passengers
were relieved of their personal valuables. The tra-
vellers were systematically searched in their places

in the cars, all being compelled to hold their hands
up whilst one of the robbers searched their pockets,
another of the gang superintending the process
with a cocked revolver. Two of the wayfarers
happened to get out on to the platform for a breath
of fresh air, in ignorance of what was taking place
inside, and were promptly ordered back "without a
break" into the car. The sight of a levelled six-
shooter quickly convinced them that "the evening
air was unhealthy, and that they had business
inside." One of them, however, was not quick
enough in his movements to please the marauders,
and a couple of shots were fired at him, to "hurry
him up a bit," one of which grazed the side of his
left hand, the other lodging close to him in the
woodwork of the car. He was then relieved of his
watch and pocket-money. The only carriage which
escaped "tapping" was the sleeper. It appears
that the conductor of this car knew there was
something unusual going on, and shut the outside
door, which locked with a catch. The robbers tried
this door, but finding it locked, and the lights of an
approaching goods train fortunately appearing just
at the moment, they thought it advisable to be satisfied with their already ample booty, and to be "skipping." They quickly mounted their horses—which
were left hobbled near the small station-house—
and were soon away with the 240 pounds' weight of
gold, besides the other valuables. The station-
master seems to have kept his wits about him, for
as soon as he had got rid of his unwelcome visitors
he set to work to repair the telegraph wires and
apparatus, which they had taken the precaution to
smash, and was able to pass a message on to the

line to this effect, " No. 4 has been robbed at this
station of $60,000." This was "heard" (telegraphy
is worked by ear in America, instead of by sight,
as with us) at Cheyenne and Omaha, and was
at once acted upon, and 2,000*l*. reward was offered
for the detection of the perpetrators. A superintendent of detectives, noted for what is here termed
his " hang-to-itiveness," was soon on the spot,
and luckily selected a young fellow named Leech,
who followed up and stuck to his quarry quite
alone, with a pertinacity worthy of his name, and
with a courage truly remarkable. After striking
the trail, he found that the "band" had travelled
for some distance in company with some " cow
boys " (Angl., herdsmen), who were driving cattle
over the prairies. This slow rate of travelling
enabled Leech to make up for time lost in starting in pursuit, and in a very few evenings he
sighted their camp-fire. Dismounting and tethering
his horse, Leech crept cautiously on, and finding
all asleep, was able to get right in amongst them,
and to recognize the whole of the party without being discovered. He then got quietly back to
his horse, and sent the information to the authorities
from the nearest *ranche*. The next day he resumed
the hunt, and in the evening repeated the exciting
performance of stalking their camp-fire. This time
they were all awake, and discussing the whole affair
of robbing the train. They seemed not a little
astonished that no fight had been shown, but were
very well satisfied with the results; to use their own
gold-mining vernacular, they were glad " that it had
panned out all right." They then went on to swear
solemnly that if " corraled " (i.e. caught in a corral

or pen, like cattle), "they would not be taken alive, but would turn their toes up with their boots on."

Leech nearly got caught on this occasion through making a noise in getting back from his stalk, but was fortunately able to escape without being discovered. The next day he came suddenly on two of them refreshing at a *ranche*, and had to ride for his life. This scare led to the dispersion of the gang; they divided the gold, and separated forthwith. Leech kept on the trail of the leader, Collins, and another. A few days afterwards these two rode into the small station at Buffalo, on the Kansas Pacific Railroad, being then on their way to Texas. There happened to be a small detachment of United States cavalry near here, and the station-master suspecting who the new arrivals were, from the descriptions forwarded by Leech, put himself into communication with the sheriff and soldiers, who apprehended the strangers a short time after they had left the station. It is said that after they had surrendered, they attempted to draw their six-shooters, and that the sheriff and soldiers, on seeing this, shot them down in self-defence. But be this as it may, only their lifeless bodies were brought back to the station. They had with them in a grain-sack 4,000*l.* in gold coin.

Of the other four constituting the gang, I had only heard of one being accounted for before I left the country. He was shot down by the sheriff in Callaway county, Missouri, close to his own home.

I have entered into the details of this little affair as it illustrates somewhat forcibly what may still occasionally occur even on the highways of this far-off country. We might hear of the same sort of highway robbery occurring within the last few years in Spain, or even in some parts of Italy, but, be it said to the credit of the western frontier man, and of the determined courage of the detective element, I doubt very much if in either of these old countries the perpetrators would have been hunted down and brought to justice so speedily and so deterrently as in the present instance.

We passed the Big Spring Station early in the morning, and had no excitement to record beyond the fact that a short way further on, when looking out of my window in the "sleeper," I saw some antelope moving quietly off in the early dawn. I confess to a slight thrill as hopes of future sport passed through my mind.

From Omaha to Cheyenne the railroad passes nearly the whole way through the State of Nebraska, until within a very short distance of Cheyenne, where it enters the territory of Wyoming. Cheyenne is the capital of Wyoming; in it the Territorial Parliament holds its sessions, which were going on when I returned to these parts in the month of December. The journey from Omaha up to this point is decidedly monotonous; as a rule nothing is seen from the train windows but endless plains, stretching out as far as the eye can reach on both sides, and covered with a sparse vegetation of buffalo or prairie grass. But although the herbage appears so poor and thin, it is extraordinarily nutritious. On it, in years gone by, countless numbers of buffalo existed; now-a-days countless herds of well-bred cattle not only exist but fatten. Nor are these hundreds of square miles of prairie mere summer runs, for almost the whole carry cattle all the year

round. It would seem that the grass, instead of rot-
ting if left uncut, as with us, becomes self-made hay,
and as such affords excellent winter provender for the
cattle. I can only account for this by supposing that
it is due to the intense dryness of the atmosphere,
which arrests all decomposition. The head of cattle
possessed by individuals is enormous, sometimes
over 10,000 bear the brand of the same stock-
owner! As may be supposed, this cattle-trade is a
great source of traffic to the railway company,
who, I am told, convey over this line more than
400,000 head of cattle a year! Nearly the whole
are transported to Chicago, whence they are
sent to New York and other great eastern cities.
These vast, monotonous, bare-looking prairies are
already the great beef-producing regions of the
United States; and before many years are passed
it would seem as if they were destined to play a
very important part in the meat supply of our own
home market. The dead-meat trade is only in its
infancy; science has not yet been brought to bear
fully on the arrangements necessary to make its
transport an entire success; and yet there can
be no doubt—for experience has taught us this
—that American dead meat can be delivered in
perfect condition in English ports. What is the
reason then, it may be asked, why this trade has
not already assumed larger proportions in our im-
ports than it has hitherto done? In the first
place it is completely new, and, like every new
trade, requires development and organization, not
so much perhaps in its transport to this country
as for the speedy distribution from the ports of
debarkation. When these are perfected I feel sure

the consumer will never have cause to fear short supplies again, except perhaps in the improbable event of a war between ourselves and the States, and that further if dead meat importation becomes a perfect success, our own home meat growers may rest in peaceful security from the ravages of imported disease amongst their own herds and flocks, which will also ultimately benefit the consumer.

When the mountain ranges are reached, the plains which support these masses of cattle all the year round almost disappear. There are some tracts and "parks" enclosed between the mountains where the summer food is most luxuriant, but where it would be impossible to leave cattle during the winter on account of the depth of snow which lies in them for many months. Snow falls heavily too on the prairies, but the wind sweeps over the low ridges, and keeps the sweet herbage from being covered up, so that the stock is enabled to pick up a fair supply of food.

Great fortunes are made by the stock-owners, where experience is combined with industry and steadiness; but the life of the "cow puncher"—as he is called in western parlance—is one full of hardship and excitement, more especially when he is located in the frontier country. Amongst themselves they have to guard against cattle stealing and falsely claiming and branding, which latter is especially practised on the calves in the early spring. In such cases Lynch law is often resorted to as the most effectual way of discouraging such practices. When cattle are "run off" (Angl., stolen) a "band" of the neighbouring ranchemen is got together, and forthwith start in pursuit of the thieves.

The wild training of the pursuers enables them to follow up so closely that escape is very seldom effected; the marauders are generally run into, and often fired upon and killed right away.

Private " shootings " also occasionally take place, generally arising from disputes as to the ownership of stock. A cow puncher must at times be prepared to defend his own at the muzzle of the six-shooter, or submit to robbery at the demand of a bullying desperado.

Each stock-holder has his own particular brand, which, in the more civilized States, is notified in the public press, and which it becomes penal in the courts of law to interfere with in any way. When cattle are sold the brand has to be crossed out,—I believe by the vendor,—and the brand of the buyer substituted. The young stock is branded as yearlings, and is then allowed to roam the prairies. If the country is quiet the herds are not gathered up more than twice or thrice every year.

When moving stock from one part of the country to another for sale or any other purpose, the stockman has often to spend both day and night in the saddle, not daring to leave his charge, which are in the habit of attempting to break away back to their old pastures, or if in an Indian country are liable to be stampeded and " run off " by the wily Redskin. From being so much on horseback he becomes a most hardy and skilful horseman. One man I met had ridden on an average sixty miles for thirteen consecutive days.

Notwithstanding the temptations of the life, I have universally found the so-called "cow punchers" honest and straightforward in their dealings, and always good-humoured and ready to share with any chance traveller the best they possess. Rough they are, and one cannot say too much in condemnation of their fearful swearing; but I have met first-class stock-holders, quite at the "top of the heap," and bearing a great reputation amongst their fellows, whom I never heard utter an oath. This proves that the business can be carried on without the usual extravagant indulgence in bad language, notwithstanding the assertion that driving cattle is the most provoking of human trades, making swearing inevitable. I am sorry to say, too, that this habit is not confined to the "cow punchers;" for the miners and every other class of the western community are more or less impregnated with it.

There is one good quality of these frontier stockmen in which, I am told, they greatly surpass their brethren of California, and that is, they will stand by each other in trouble, and come from any distance, put themselves to any inconvenience, or run any personal risk, to render assistance to one of their own calling. This trait used to be severely tested in earlier times, when herds were so often run off by Indians; and at the present time, towards the Sioux country, they have still occasional opportunities for displaying it.

Some of them have led such a wild life from their earliest infancy that they cannot exist without its excitement. They cannot settle down to a quiet and more civilized existence, but must follow as the Indians retire, and continue their frontier career. One man I met, of Scotch origin, had made his fortune and become the possessor of a good farm in the more settled portion of Oregon; but this was too

quiet for one of his adventurous and roaming dis-
position, so he had just brought over from this
peaceful district a large quantity of his own cattle,
and had located himself in a *ranche* on the Sioux
frontier, where, perhaps, next spring he may have
a good opportunity afforded him of distinguishing
himself in Indian warfare, and losing some of his
cattle, to say nothing of "getting his own hair
lifted," as scalping is termed in western phraseology.

I must now return from this long digression on
stock and stockmen, brought about by the large
herds seen from the train windows between Omaha
and Cheyenne, and will say a few words about
another quadruped, of much smaller dimensions,
but of very great interest to the stranger like
myself. I mean the perk little prairie-dog. These
little fellows are to be seen close to the track, sun-
ning themselves outside their burrows, exactly like
our common rabbit (which are called out here by
the expressive name of " cotton tails "). The train
approaches, and away scuttle the little dogs for the
nearest hole; not quite so rapidly as our little
coneys, having more the " lope " of a hare, but still
losing no time about it. They appear to arrange
their colonies of burrows or holes, which are called
here towns or villages, in much the same fashion
as ordinary rabbits. In colour they are lightish
brown, turning to grey underneath; the head is
round and full, and more like that of a guinea-pig
than a rabbit. I am told that they are not difficult
to tame, and that they make very good domestic
pets. They are said to be good food, but on this I
cannot speak from personal experience, the country

I hunted being at a greater elevation than these little animals care to inhabit.

I am told that prairie dogs do not exist on the western slopes of the Rocky Mountains, their place being occupied by the ground squirrel. It is extraordinary how small a thing helps to break the monotony of a long journey, whether by sea or land, and one thanks the cheery little prairie dogs for the living interest they afford to the often monotonous, lifeless landscape.

Soon after we had passed Sidney, with its land and law offices and drinking saloon—the three most prominent buildings in a frontier town,—we reached at last Cheyenne, called in the guide-book "The Magic City of the Plains." The station is large and roomy, and, as usual, entirely constructed of wood. This town is 516 miles from Omaha, and about 1,400 miles from San Francisco, and is situated at an elevation of more than 6,000 feet above the level of the sea. It is said to be healthy, and now quite orderly; but, like Denver and all other frontier towns, it has had its period of almost inconceivable rowdyism and disorder. It has entirely passed through this unenviable stage, and is now developing itself into a permanent and solid position and occupies a prominent place amongst the western towns. In early times it had the reputation of being more full of desperadoes and outlaws than any other town in these parts. It scarcely existed in 1867; but in 1868 it became the winter terminus of the Union Pacific Railroad, and forthwith the population amounted to 6,000. Every sort of villainy soon prevailed; dancing, drinking, and gambling saloons abounded, and brought with them the

usual brawling and "shootings." I have heard that
as many as seven dead bodies have been found in the
morning in a single dancing saloon! Vigilance committees were formed, and Judge Lynch ruled in full
power. I believe theft was even more summarily
and promptly punished at these tribunals than life-
taking. All this is now in the past, and trade can
be carried on with a fair amount of security. Such
a wholesome dread has been established that there
are now only three public guardians of the peace;
but the fact is, that all the citizens are, as it were,
private officers, for they are known to be ready to
take their personal share in maintaining order.
Certain regulations have been framed which are dis-
regarded at much risk, amongst which is one that
no six-shooter be carried in the streets. Rough and
prompt justice quickly follows any breach of the peace.
However uncivilized this state of things may seem, it
has been forced into existence by the presence of a
large proportion of the greatest ruffians who perhaps could well be found; and now, notwithstanding
this, the streets can be walked in safety, and even
the jewellers can display their alluring wares with
the same amount of security as in Bond Street.
A great discouragement to burglary is that the invaded party does not scruple—as he might in more
civilized countries—to shoot down any suspicious
trespasser on his premises. The result is that the
desperado knows that he follows this trade with his
life in his hand, and thinks twice before doing so.

I learnt much about the place from an intelligent
Highlander, who had been settled here from early
days, and was carrying on the trade of a goldsmith
with considerable success, in spite of which he

looked forward to the time when he should have realized a sufficient competence to enable him to return to his native land, a feeling not uncommon among emigrants, especially amongst those of Celtic origin.

Cheyenne is a military post of some importance; there are generally six or eight companies of infantry quartered here; but at the time I write there were not more than 100 men, six companies having been sent out in pursuit of the Nez Percés Indians, who had been giving trouble in Oregon. It is not believed that the troops will fall in with the aborigines, and hardly to be hoped that they will; for the common belief is that when the "boys in blue" are matched against the wily, well-armed Redskins, the usual result is that the soldier gets "whipped." From what I have heard, drink seems to be the curse of the soldier, as well as of many others in these parts. For the accursed whiskey he will frequently "trade" his kit and not unfrequently his rifle too.

From Cheyenne a stage coach runs in twenty hours to Deadwood, in the Black-hills of Dakotah, about 200 miles distant. This is said to be one of the richest mining districts discovered of late years. At present the journey to it is not made without a shade of excitement, as of late the coach has been robbed—or, to use the native phrase, "the stage has been tapped"—pretty frequently. On these occasions passengers and "treasure-box" have alike been lightened of their valuables. A short time ago it happened that two soldiers were "on board" for extra security. The stage was attacked and the soldiers thought it prudent to "skin out" (Anglicé, bolt); the only person who made any resistance was the unfortunate driver, who was shot through the leg.

I am informed that the Black-hills mining district is situated in the Indian reserve, guaranteed to the unfortunate natives by treaties with the United States Government; but when minerals were discovered and the country was wanted for the whites, the wretched redskin had to go, treaty or no treaty. This is only one of the many cases of similar treatment on the part of the whites, and the natural consequence is, that great ill-feeling prevails between the two races. In the case of the Black-hills of Dakotah, the dispossessed happened to be the warlike Sioux, and a long and sanguinary war ensued, which led to the retreat of the largest portion of the tribe within the Canadian frontier, under the leadership of their great medicine-man, "Sitting Bull." The remainder of the tribe are said to be subdued and ready to come into the posts assigned to them by the United States Government; but whether this will be a permanent peace is another matter. The Indians are extremely cunning; they readily consent to be supported, themselves and their families, during the hard months of winter, but not unfrequently with the full intention, when the spring returns, of resuming hostilities against their hereditary enemies. But more by-and-by on this Indian question. As to the Black-hills themselves, there seems to be but little doubt that they are destined to be a rich and populous mining district, though there are great differences of opinion as to the value of the discoveries already made. The richest lodes of ore are said to be near the rising town of Deadwood, and to bear much resemblance to the famous Comstock Lode of Nevada. The United States Government appears to have given up any idea of dispossessing the white miners from the territory, " reserved " though it be, and so there exists but little doubt that the district will soon be opened out by the indefatigable " prospectors "—as the mining explorers are here termed— and the population which will soon follow them. Should the Indians themselves interfere, it will only hasten their total extinction ; for although the western miner is quiet enough when left alone, yet when interfered with he is more determined and vindictive than even the ranchman or cow puncher. Woe betide the tribe of Indians who molests the miner ; his brother miners will remember it ever after, and however busy or prosperous a mine may be, should a chance of revenge offer, the whole mine will turn out, and dire will that vengeance be.

Later on, I came across some very good specimens of auriferous quartz and small nuggets from this district, but what are the real prospects I am unable to say. Had our time allowed of it, I should have much liked to have visited the mines and judged for myself, but the journey would have been long and tiresome, and we were anxious to get on to Denver and the mountain ranges of Colorado.

From Cheyenne to Denver, by the Denver Pacific Railroad, is a little over 100 miles, and takes about four hours to accomplish. The country passed through is at first monotonous and uninteresting, except to a stock-owner's gaze ; but after a while the fine range, of which Long's Peak is the highest point, comes into view, and lends at once charm and interest to the journey. A few small

stations are passed on the road, the most important
of which are Greely and Evans, the former situated
on the Cache la Poudre river, and in the midst of
one of the finest corn-growing countries of the
world. Although containing over 2,000 inhabitants,
it is said to be a strict temperance town, no "drinking saloon"—answering to our public-houses—
being allowed in it; and the inhabitants are satisfied
and well to do. We are now in the newly-formed
State of Colorado, of which Denver, prettily situated
on the plain about thirteen miles from the base of
the mountain range, is the capital. From its elevation of 5,224 feet above the sea, the air is light and
bracing, and on this account it is much resorted to
by invalids. The State generally is said to be a
most salutary climate for all chest complaints, when
not in a too advanced stage, for although in winter
the cold is very severe, yet it is always a dry
cold, and even in mid-winter, bright days may be
looked for with a tolerable certainty. The storms,
which are at certain seasons pretty frequent, pass
quickly over, and then all is left as dry and bright
as before. Denver contains some 16,000 inhabitants, is cheerful and gay, and full of tempting
shops. Its frontier character has quite passed
away, and it now seems to be as safe and comfortable a place of residence as any European town.
From its convenient situation it is much used as a
starting-place for hunting expeditions, and possesses
some excellent gun and other stores, from which all
the necessaries of an outfit can be obtained.

VIEW OF LONG'S PEAK IN ESTES PARK.

From a sketch by A. P. V.

CHAPTER VIII.

"In these plains
The bison feeds no more. Twice twenty leagues
Roams the majestic brute, in herds that shake
The earth with thundering steps—yet here I meet
His ancient footprints stamp'd beside the pool."

"*The Prairies,*" *William Bryant.*

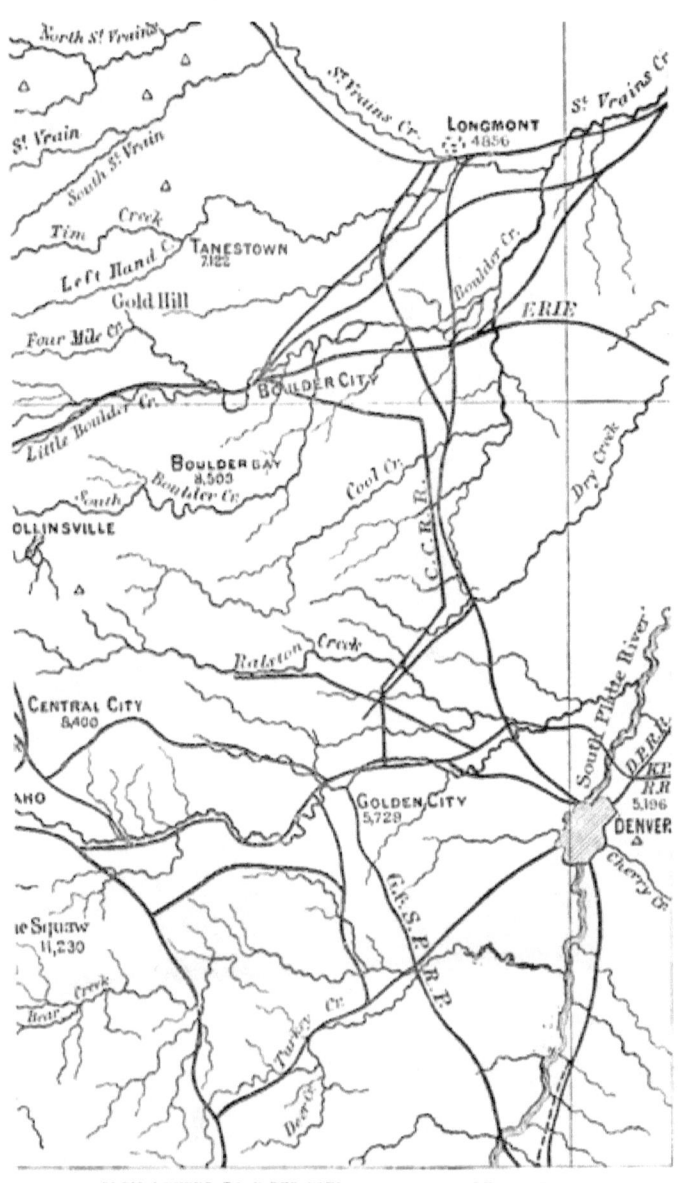

FROM DENVER TO ESTES PARK.   [From a Government Map.

WE did not linger long in Denver, but were soon
away again for Longmount, *en route* to Estes Park,
where we meant to commence hunting operations.

As far as Longmount there is a railroad which
runs for about sixteen miles over the prairie, until
the junction for Golden is reached, whence a three
foot guage line runs up a narrow glen for twenty-
one miles to Black Hawk.

In this valley metalliferous mining is carried
on to a considerable extent, and nearer Golden,
where the geological formation is lignitic, extensive
smelting works are established. This lignite is
very different in appearance from the "Braunkohle"
of Germany, being blacker and denser, and often
resembling at a distance bituminous coal; but the
amount of ash and moisture, as shown by the
analyses given in the Government Survey Reports
for Colorado, by Professor Hayden, proclaims it to
be a very inferior fuel to even a low-classed bituminous coal. The average of four analyses gives
$13\cdot38\,\%$ of water, and slightly under $4\,\%$ of ash,
whilst the volatile matter, or gases, in two analyses
were $36\,\%$, and the fixed carbon or coke $46\cdot50\,\%$.
The average thickness of the main seam is put down
at five feet; but this appears somewhat difficult to
arrive at, as the thickness varies from a few inches
to eight or ten feet. The smelting works of Mr.

K

Hill are carried on here; but to what extent lignite is used in the operations I was unable to ascertain. I was told, however, the pine-forests of the neighbouring hills were almost exhausted, and that before long the proprietors of the smelting works would be obliged to bring bituminous coal by rail from very distant parts at a large cost. The ores here dealt with come from the George Town, Black Hawk, Central City, and many other mining localities lying up in the mountain ranges to the westward. They are principally lead ores, more or less rich in silver and gold, and are found in lodes in the old formations of gneiss and schist. The ordinary concomitants of a good mining district, volcanic rocks, are not wanting. They are here granite and the more recent porphyry, and hornblende. Both the sedimentary and igneous rocks are stated to vary much in character, and to afford ample scope for a more defined and closer mineralogical nomenclature.

The main systems of lodes run due east and west, whilst some of the smaller vary to about from north-east to south-west. The hornblende dykes run north and south. In some places the granite masses enclose the more recent porphyry. The lead is generally in the form of the sulphuret, as galena, containing more or less silver. Silver is also found as native, and in various combinations of its own, as chlorides, sulphurets, and, I believe, alloyed with the comparatively new metal tellurium. The matrix, or vein matter, is said to be generally quartz. The system adopted here for valuing the ores is the same as in other parts of the States, and differs materially from our English custom. With us an ore is said to contain so many per cent. of

lead, copper, or any of the less valuable metals, and
if silver or gold are present, so many ounces of those
metals per ton of ore, from which the purchaser can
make his own calculation as to value, whereas in
this country the ores are, as it were, at once money
valued by the assayer. An ore is said to be worth
$100 or $200 per ton, as the case may be, according
to its contents with certain well-known deductions.
The American system would certainly seem to have
the advantage of being easier understood by the
general public.

It is stated in the Government Geographical Survey of Colorado, 1873, that Mr. Hill's scale of payment for ores delivered at his works is as follows :—
" Ores containing per ton $50 he charges for smelt-
ing $35, and pays $15; ores containing per ton
$100, charges for smelting $40, pays $60; ores
containing per ton $150, charges for smelting $45,
pays $105; ores containing per ton $200, charges
for smelting $50, pays $150; and in addition to
this $1 50c. for every per cent. of copper in 2,000
pounds. All the prices of this schedule are in
currency."

I believe the miners' wages until lately were often
as high as $4 per day (= 16s.), but there is now a
downward tendency. It is very difficult to make
anything like a correct comparison between the
actual benefit received by the miner here in Colorado
and in the old country, the rent of houses and all
the ordinary commodities of life, with the exception
of meat and flour, being so much higher here.
There must be, moreover, so many social drawbacks
in a miner's life here, and which must necessarily
continue for a long time to come. But, as I shall

have to speak hereafter on the subject of mines and miners, no more for the present.

From Golden we had still thirty-seven miles to travel to Longmount, and the speed of the Colorado Central Railroad being anything but express, two and a half hours were required. The track runs northwards, skirting the foothills, with the higher mountains visible beyond. Boulder City is passed on the way, which, like Golden, is the county town of a large mining district extending far into the mountains, and of which a place called Caribou is the "mining camp." The term "mining camp" is very common out here, and means the head-quarters, or centre, of a mining district. The famous Caribou lode occurs in syenite, a sort of granite in which hornblende takes the place of the mica of ordinary granite. The mining camp of Caribou is spoken of as intensely cold in winter, which is scarcely surprising considering that it is nearly 10,000 feet (9,905 feet, speaking accurately) above the sea level.

We reached Longmount soon after midday, and, although we were now in October, the sun was striking down with a fierceness as great as on the hottest day of midsummer in England, and clouds of hot dust swept along the roads and streets, making the place anything but agreeable. We consoled ourselves, however, with the thought that in a few hours we should escape from these miseries, and be inhaling the delicious breezes of the higher foothills. But we reckoned without our hosts; for although we were only 35 miles from the ranche at Estes Park, and seven hours' daylight still remained, the livery stable-keepers refused to undertake the

journey; they pleaded that the season was over,
that their horses were tired, that the road was bad,
and finally, that there would be a "stage" on the
morrow. All expostulation was useless; they were
in command of the position and were immovable.
In vain we declared our willingness to ride there on
horseback, but no, they would not let even a pony
out of their stables; so there was nothing for it but
to resign ourselves with the best grace we could to
spending the rest of the day in this most uninviting
city, town, or village, or whatever other title they may
please to give it. Being situated on a bare, parched-
up prairie, hot, baking sand lay inches deep in its
streets, which was to-day set into rapid motion by a
strong whirling breeze, and persistently made its way
into one's eyes, ears, and hair. Certainly that afternoon was one of the most unpleasant I ever spent,
and we wished over and over again that we had never
left our comfortable quarters in Denver. The place
was to-day by the way of being unusually lively, as
an election for a sheriff was going on, which crowded
to repletion our miserable little pot-house, rejoicing
in the dignified appellation of the "Hôtel St. Vrain."
How we panted for the mountain breezes and the timbered ridges, apparently so close at hand—but really
twelve miles off, when measured only to the base of the
foothills,—and what would we not have given to have
been transported on to the top of one of those many
peaks, of which—as we were told by a geographical
memorandum at the back of an hotel card—there were
no less than forty-three upwards of 14,000 feet above
the sea level, the highest being Blanca, 14,464 feet.

But it was no use chafing over our misfortunes;
we tried to practise equanimity, sauntered about a

little, and, when driven in by the blasts of hot sand and the stifling heat, did our best to pass the time in the miserable hostelry.

Longmount boasts a daily paper, and judging by the paragraph in which it announced the arrival of our poor selves, it is not wanting in enterprising imagination. The paragraph ran as follows :—

" Members of the English Parliament and other English notables passed through here on their way to Estes Park. Their baggage consisted of eleven guns, sixty-two pairs of blankets, several dogs, ammunition, and a great variety of camp equipage, paraphernalia, &c." (*Longmount Post*.) ! !

Now, as a matter of fact, our party, all told, consisted of myself and L., Sandie (stalker), and L.'s servant ; we had one pair of blankets each, six guns all told, and two dogs between us. Our " great variety of camp equipage " was one tent and two camp bedsteads, which, together with our four selves and " paraphernalia," were all packed comfortably next morning into one not over large vehicle. So on the whole this spoke well for the Longmount powers of " tall writing." But I am sure every excuse should be made for the fearful *ennui* of enterprising minds doomed to pass an existence in this wretched place.

After trying in vain to take an interest in the sheriff's election—for no one seemed to care the least about it, or to be able to give us any information—we at last gave up and turned in at a very early hour, and at an early hour turned out again, relieved beyond measure with the prospect of getting away from this wretched little town. The vehicle, a sort of brake, called here the " hack," was ready

for us about 7 a.m., and soon afterwards we were
shaping our course across the plain towards the base
of the foothills. It was a miserably cold morning,
which we felt the more after the excessive heat of
the previous days, but the air was light and invigorating. Passing by patches of cultivation, from
which magnificent crops of wheat had been taken
in the fall, we at last reached the mouth of the
cañon, or glen, up which our road lay to Estes Park.
Close by here were some very ducky-looking lakes,
which are the resort in the early part of the winter
of immense flocks of geese and other sorts of wild
fowl, attracted here to feed in the long wheat
stubbles. If a good harvest specially brings these
wanderers, there ought to be a rare lot of them this
autumn, for they tell me the corn crop had been
most abundant, averaging as much as forty bushels
of wheat per acre, and this grown simply by irrigation and without a pound of manure.

After entering the cañon, through which runs
the little stream called the St. Vrain, the scenery
became very beautiful. The foothills through which
our road lay were luxuriant with a varied vegetation,
most refreshing to behold after the monotony of the
plain. The two most common conifers were the
yellow pine (*pinus ponderosa*), which grows to a
height of from seventy to one hundred feet, and the
balsam pine. Of other trees there are some very
fine specimens of that peculiar poplar called the
cotton wood (*populus balsaminifera*), and the small
birch, and the dwarf or scrub oak (*quercus alba*).
Here and there were great masses and slabs of
granite, or, properly speaking syenite, cropping out
through the dense forest growth, and adding im-

mensely to the charm of the scenery, which put me
much in mind of the Esterelle mountains in the
south of France, but here, the high range beyond is
nearer and higher than the Alpes Maritimes, though
not at this time of year covered with snow.

I cannot say much of the road itself. In those
my early days of inexperience I thought it pretty
nearly as bad as a team could be got over; now,
perhaps, after some little trial of the tracks of the
West, I might think more charitably of it. We
had, however, a capital man at the " lines," and we
came to no grief, although some of the very abrupt
and sudden dips must have sorely tried the stability
of our machine. How wood and iron can be put
together to withstand such jars and jerks as we
came in for, I cannot conceive. Certainly our
American cousins do understand carriage building,
and their hickory wood, of which their best vehicles
are built, must be the toughest of material. But
although the road is so infamous, the toll-gate is
there, making its modest demand for $3 (12s.) for
our one conveyance !

Higher and higher we get as we slowly perform
the journey by the simple but sure process of more
ups than downs, until at length we reached the
ridge above Estes Park, and looked down upon this
lovely basin with the grand encircling mountains
beyond. The beauty of this view must be seen to
be appreciated; even such an artist as Bierstadt,
who is certainly the happiest I have seen in depict-
ing American scenery, could not do justice to this be-
witching *coup-d'œil*. The " Park " lies below us, like
a well kept pleasure ground, about a couple of miles
in breadth, and ten or twelve miles long. Running

SCENE IN ESTES PARK.

up from it into the range are many little glens, some pretty long and broad, others mere "gulches," but none extending more than six or eight miles before the mountain sides are reached. The encircling range on the left of our view can boast of Long's Peak, which is 14,271 feet above the sea level, and the highest point in the park; but the peaks opposite are within a thousand feet of it, and have equally enchanting outlines. The loveliness of the scene is much enhanced by the brightness of the green of the park itself, which, although in marked contrast with the grim and sombre crags of the mountains beyond, seems to pass away to them in perfect harmony through the medium of the pine-covered sides. The trees grow as high up as a 12,000 feet elevation, beyond which are the bare ragged masses of volcanic rocks towering up two or three thousand feet more. Truly, the introduction to Estes Park is a lovely one.

The sun was beginning to get low when we "made" the little nest of wooden erections rejoicing in the general appellation of the Estes Park Ranche. What a charming spot on Dame Nature's face it is! what must Estes, the trapper—who only died last year—have thought of his discovery? At that time he was a solitary trapper, probably in constant dread of the Indians, who ranged undisturbed over these happy hunting-grounds, and who, no doubt, looked upon a white as a dangerous interloper, to be disposed of as speedily as possible. In those days they must have had a real good time of it, for the quantities of old bison heads and magnificent wapiti horns which lie scattered about even now are really marvellous. And they had

their little excitements too, for there exists now in
the park the undoubted sites of more than one
sanguinary battle.

THE BLACK CAÑON AND RANGE IN ESTES PARK.
From a Sketch by A. P. V.

The charms of Estes Park are so well-known and
appreciated by the inhabitants of Denver and the
plains, that for many years past, during the late
summer and autumn, the small accommodation
afforded by the ranche and huts was always filled
to overflowing. To meet the requirements of the
tourists and to attract still more, a very commo-
dious and well-furnished hotel has now been started
by the Estes Park Company, about a mile higher
up the park than the present ranche. This hotel
was only finished and opened on the 1st of July of
this year, and was closed about the middle of
September, when the tourist season was over; but
I hear that it was never empty from the day it

opened to the day it closed. In its neighbourhood
are two chalybeate springs, called the " River" and
the " Ranche" springs, containing—besides the
bicarbonates of lime and magnesia in important
quantities—4.8565 grains in the River spring, and
2.2746 grains in the Ranche spring, of bicarbonate
of iron per gallon—of 231 cubic inches—of water.
But, I expect, as in many other health resorts, that
more good is got out of the early hours, and the
rides and walks in this fine pure air at 7,500 feet
above the sea, than from drinking the waters, however medically good they may be.

I had telegraphed ten days before from Quebec
to Mr. Whyte, the resident partner of the Estes
Park Company, to ask him to be kind enough to
get things arranged for our hunt, so that no time
might be lost after our arrival. Unfortunately, in
consequence of the lateness of the season, the usual
means of communication with the outer world had
ceased a fortnight before, and it turned out that our
own trap was the first opportunity which offered,
after the arrival of the message at Longmount, of
sending it on; and, worst luck of all, Mr. Whyte
himself had left that very day for Fort Collins,
thirty-five miles off.

Things looked dark and a provoking delay seemed
inevitable, but Mrs. Whyte was most kind, and
proved herself equal to the occasion. By her
orders a messenger was despatched at once on
pony-back after Mr. Whyte, and a little wooden
hut was speedily got ready for our own sleeping
quarters. We were supplied with excellent meals
at the Ranche, now used as a small hostelry, and
kept by a Welshman, called Griffith Evans, and his

wife. As "Griff" will occupy a prominent position in many of our future operations, and is a known character in these parts, not only as what would be called in Canada "quite a mighty hunter," but also as a very early and leading settler, I will here say a few words about him.

Although he had emigrated when a mere child, and was now considerably past the prime of life, and had never been home since, yet "Griff" loved Wales and everything Welsh with as much warmth as if he had left his native hills only a few months before. Nothing pleased him so much as to talk of Wales, of his parents and family, of what he remembered of his father's old home; of how he went errands to the Penrhyn slate quarries, and got into trouble for taking part in the "squailing" of a hare: so he had evidently had a sporting turn from early boyhood, which did him good service in after-life. His family had first settled, I think, in the State of Wisconsin, at that time a very uncivilized frontier territory. Here he had been able to practise the art of hunting in combination with his farm employments, and such an adept did he become in the use of his rifle, that few could beat him at this national pastime. Changes occurred in family matters, and eleven years ago he advanced with civilization, and was one of the earliest settlers in the locality where we now found him. Such was the quantity of game in these parts, so short a time as only four years ago, that Griff was able to support himself and family almost entirely by the produce of his rifle. He used to send the meat down by waggon to Denver, and sell it for what it would fetch in the open market. In two months, he tells me, he killed in this locality 112 black-tailed deer, seventeen wapiti, and twenty-six mountain sheep (*ovis montana*). I think he had one man hunting with him as his partner, but even so the sport was wonderful. Now, alas! things are different—many squatters have come into this paradise, and the game has been to a great extent destroyed and driven off; and this last misfortune has been hastened by the habits of many American hunters, who delight in letting off at all distances and at anything they may chance to come across. Besides being a capital shot and an experienced hunter, Griff Evans was well up in his present work of superintending cattle, which he was now doing for the Estes Park Company. Whatever his failings may have been, he was certainly a most cheery companion, most thoroughly well-informed in all matters connected with a western life, and one of the best hunters I came across in my trip.

On the strength of Wales and a common love of sport we soon began to understand each other, and and got on swimmingly. But unluckily for us Evans's abode had been lately invaded by a great destroyer of comfort, for it chanced that a day or so previous to our arrival a family of skunks had taken possession of the space between the flooring boards and the earth. An attempt had been made to dislodge them, which had been resented, and the weapon of defence nature had provided to these little animals, namely, of emitting a most fearful smell, had been used most freely and effectively. The final result of the conflict had been to make Griff " quite sick," and the principal room of the Ranche perfectly uninhabitable. Let the reader who has never fallen foul of this wonderful provision of nature take the advice of one who has been unfortunate enough to do so more than once; let him make the longest *détour*, put up with any insult or inconvenience, let him in fact do anything sooner than offend one of these mild-eyed, sleek little creatures. Think not of obtaining a specimen for preservation, nor of their long, glossy, tempting fur, for the chances are it will be spoiled in the act of getting it, and you will be sickened. Anything so loathsome, so sickening, so pungent and pervading as that smell I never came across. Curiously enough dogs have the same opinion of this odour as human beings; for, after having been once subjected to it, be they never so big and savage, nothing will induce them to encounter it again. They will very often sicken for some days afterwards, refusing food and moping away, as if they knew, poor beasts, that they were now no longer welcome even to their own masters.

This little brute (*mephitis mephitica*), who is thus able to cause discomfort to all around him, is in shape like a pole-cat or marten, but about twice as large as the latter. Its fur is of a rich dark brown, with occasional streaks of white; the hairs of the tail long and bushy, and more freely mixed with white. It is said that if the animal is killed suddenly no stench will be emitted; but on two occasions when we tried this experiment it signally failed. In these instances death might not have been absolutely instantaneous, but it was meant to be so. The first time the animal was shot apparently quite dead, but a fearful smell ensued. On the second occasion he had been caught in a trap, when, oddly

enough, no smell was emitted; an attempt was then
made to kill him instantaneously by a blow on the
head with a heavy club, and so to elude the smell;
but this was by no means successful, and we were
again treated to the loathsome odour; so bad was it
that my men were glad enough to throw trap and
all into a neighbouring stream. I once stopped at
a dairy ranche, where, a short time previously, I am
afraid to say how many tens of gallons of milk had
been utterly spoiled by a skunk having emitted his
stench in the cellar in which the milk was kept.

It is said that the bite is very poisonous, the
effects resembling that from a mad dog; but this
I can hardly believe, as I am told that some of the
hunters make pets of them, taking care to remove
the gland in which the fetid secretion is retained.

These little animals live in burrows or under old
buildings, like rats, and are carnivorous in their
tastes. One morning at Estes Park we were amused
by seeing a large skunk dragging along a full-grown
fowl which it had killed; it was followed by a small
pack of different descriptions of dogs, varying in
size from a bloodhound to a terrier, and having
amongst them a large and savage black retriever;
all joined in a chorus of anger, but not one dared
to attack. Having arrived at its hole under the
old ranche, the skunk found the fowl too big to be
pulled into it. How it would have got over the
difficulty must remain unknown, as one of the
bipeds of the establishment appeared on the scene,
and the skunk had to abandon his prey, falling a
victim to a charge of small shot.

One day I was fishing in the "Big Thompson"
River, which flows through the park, when my old

retriever, "Sailor," pointed a small bush. Not knowing what was likely to be inside it, I told him to fetch it out. In he went, a fearful struggle ensued, followed by the most powerful emission of skunk odour conceivable. I retreated at once, and called out the old dog, but too late to be of much use; he came out in triumph with the dead skunk in his mouth, but, poor old fellow, the only reward for his bravery was to be banished to the smith's shop, as, notwithstanding constant baths in the river, he was perfectly unendurable for many a day.

We spent some time hunting in the neighbourhood of the ranche, and very enjoyable it was. The scenery was very beautiful, and our quarters thoroughly comfortable; the weather a little cold, but by no means disagreeably so, for although the thermometer registered as low as 17° of frost in our sleeping huts, it was so dry and still that we experienced no inconvenience from it. Although now getting late in the autumn, it was too early for game in these comparatively warm and sheltered regions. Until the weather has settled into winter the wapiti and black-tailed deer prefer hanging high up about the timber line, and not till they are actually forced by the extreme cold will they leave their mountain fastnesses, and retreat downwards towards the habitations of their greatest foes, the human race. The black-tailed deer come down first, but generally do not linger on the road until they reach their permanent winter quarters.

As it was plain, from a series of blank days that no game had yet arrived in this immediate locality, we determined if possible to cross the

range of mountains, and to get over into North
Park, which was said to be the summer and autumn
haunt of the deer tribe. It was now getting late
in the season for this expedition, so, if attempted,
it must be so without delay. Mr. Whyte thought it
very desirable that we should first make an experi-
mental camp at no great distance from the ranche,
in order that we should find out for ourselves our
particular wants and requirements. Accordingly
one lovely day we took our two hunters, Messrs.
Row and James, and our two servants, and accompanied by Mr. Whyte himself, started off for Horse
Shoe Park, a beautiful branch glen about seven

CAMP IN HORSE-SHOE PARK.
From a Sketch by A. P. V.

miles from the ranche. Here, in the midst of the
grandest scenery, and by the side of a tempting
little trout stream called Fall River Creek (pronounced "crik"), we made a most enjoyable camp.

L.

The towering snow-covered peaks of the range surrounded us on three sides. From it, on our east side, tumbled a foaming torrent, called the Roaring Creek; immediately above us to the east rose a splendid rock of syenite, starting up from the valley almost perpendicularly to the height of at least 1,500 feet. The serrated ridge of the

SHEEP ROCK IN HORSE-SHOE PARK.

From a Sketch by A. P. V.

Range itself must have risen 6,000 or 7,000 feet above our position, and from our plateau to within some 3,000 feet of the top, a dense growth of pine timber covered the sides. It seemed as if game must abound in such hunting-grounds; such rocks for wild sheep, such timber for elk (wapiti) could surely not be surpassed; but, alas! however favourable the locality, the raw material was wanting, and two days of fruitless hunting convinced us of the hopelessness of continuing in our present camp, and we accordingly returned to the ranche.

We now set to work to supply our requirements and make final arrangements for attempting to cross the Range, and the second day after our return found all prepared. But for this expedition all our packs had to be conveyed on pony back, so that we had to press into our service five bronchos, some of which were to carry packs for the first time. The process of loading, therefore, was both tedious and temper trying.

The first problem in packing was to divide the weight with due regard to the individual capabilities of each animal. This being done to the best judgment of the bipeds, the quadrupeds did not often agree with the decision arrived at by their betters, and the results were continual misunderstandings between the two. These disagreements delayed us much, but at last all the packs were " on board," and secured as fast as our men thought possible; for they knew full well that the track was miserable and the fastenings would be sorely tried. The pack train being ready we mounted our " bronchos " and started off in good spirits and in brilliant weather; but this latter was destined soon to undergo a remarkable change, and our spirits as quickly followed suit. It is true that the night before, when coming back from hunting, I had seen much lightning, which

I knew in Scotland would have portended, at this season of the year, bad weather; but here, being a stranger and quite ignorant of the weather signs, and nobody prophesying a storm, I thought no more of it, and now started away quite unsuspicious of what was in store for us. We had not been an hour on our journey before it commenced to "storm;" at first only a slight rain fell, but as we ascended into higher regions this changed into snow and increased in denseness until we were enveloped in a regular snow-storm. Now commenced our difficulties; the trail was "mean" in the extreme, being indistinct and rough, and so narrow that it was scarcely possible in many places for the pack animals to get between the timber. The poor pack beast I had charge of was rolled completely over by the pack fouling a tree, and there he lay until three of us had dismounted and relieved him of his load. As soon as he had recovered his feet and got back on to the track, the process of loading had to be gone through once more. Then some of the packs worked loose of their own accord, and had to be repacked right away; and some of the animals, being young and not liking the weather and a mountain scramble, endeavoured to get off the trail and return to the ranche. All these little episodes were causes not only of great annoyance, but worse still, of disastrous delay, and it was pitch dark before we reached the first spot suitable for camping. Well, making camp under such circumstances is not enviable. It was very dark, snowed heavily and unceasingly, and the ground was rough and broken. We ourselves were wet through from the previous rain, and the temperature was Arctic.

However, all worked hard and willingly, and by dint
of perseverance we got at last the two tents pitched,
the bronchos unloaded and turned loose, and a
blazing fire of gigantic logs of pitch pine. After
a supper of soup made of salt bacon, and fried
rashers of the same, with fresh baked bread, we
turned in, and were soon oblivious of the misadven-
tures of the previous evening and our lessening
prospect of crossing the Range.

The next morning, although still snowing, the
weather looked a trifle better, but the snow lay very
thick in our camp, which was between ten and eleven
thousand feet above the sea. Occasionally through
the mist we were able to see bare ragged peaks of
rock frowning down upon us from above, starting, as
it were, out of the mass of forest which surrounded
us, and which reached to within a couple of thousand
feet of the highest points. Except where the naked
rock protruded, all around was covered with a
virgin white layer of fresh fallen snow nearly a foot
in thickness.

As may be imagined it was not sultry up here. In
the night the thermometer in our tent had registered
25° of frost, but the air was dry and there was no
wind, so that we did not feel it as much as might be
expected. Our two hunters held different opinions
as to the weather prospects, one of them was a
Canadian by birth, superior in education and position
to the other, and besides—which no doubt told more
in his favour with his partner than his educational
attainments—he was one of the best hands with an
axe I have ever seen; it was really a pleasure to see
him use one of the ordinary long-handled axes, every
stroke seemed so easy yet so effective. The other

hunter was a native of the States, and had served all through the civil war without getting a scratch. They were both most willing and obliging and full of anecdote, which helped to while away the weary hours of two whole successive days spent in camp, for our sanguine hunter was wrong, and the storm recommenced in earnest about midday and continued with but little cessation for three whole days.

The third morning broke somewhat better, and we determined to try and have a hunt. L—— went eastward with Row—the oldest hunter—and his servant, whilst I took my chance in the opposite direction with the other hunter and Sandie. First of all we toiled up to above the timber line on to the bare ground beyond, and carefully searched for tracks all the natural passes which wapiti or deer would be likely to use in moving down to the lower grounds. But all of no use; not a sign was to be seen, although we hunted hard for the whole day; and stiff work it was tramping along through two feet of fresh fallen snow, sometimes on the level, but more often on the steep mountain side. When all chance seemed over, and we were making for camp as fast as we could, we were most unexpectedly rewarded with a sight of game. My hunter, James, was leading the way almost on the identical track of the morning, when all of a sudden I saw, I should say about 100 yards off and right in front of us, something, which could not be a stone, and which I thought must be an animal. I looked at it intently, and at last made it out to be a bear! To stop James, to unbolt and cock my rifle, was the affair of a moment, but Bruin had picked us up, and was off at a good round shuffle through the

thick timber. Two barrels were let off in his
honour, but with no result; and, although we put
the two dogs "Ned" and "Sailor" at once on his
track, they very speedily returned, having no doubt
come to the conclusion that the old "anchorite
monk of the desert" was not to be trifled with. It
was now late, so we gave up any thoughts of
pursuit until the morrow, and got back to camp as
quick as we could.

The next morning our hunters again held different
opinions as to the chances of a successful pursuit
of the bear; Row, the oldest and most experienced,
strongly asserting that to track him would be
useless, for that he would be many miles away
before he would think of stopping. However, the
majority of us were keen for the hunt, and leaving
Row behind, with L——'s servant, to get together
what horses they could, and move camp down to
the ranche again—the weather continuing hopeless
—we started for the place where we had left the
track on the previous evening. This was in a gorge
called the Roaring Branch Gulch, and rare ground it
was to travel over. A very steep hill-side, covered
with quantities of detached rocks and boulders,
ranging in size from a football to blocks as big
as a cottage, the latter forming minor precipices
of from twenty to thirty feet in depth; all were
covered over with snow, and overhung in many places
the Roaring Branch torrent tearing along 2,000 feet
below, so that it was a matter of no small difficulty,
not to say of danger, to follow Bruin along his
erratic course. We were all well armed, as, although
not large, these range grizzlies partake of all the
well-known ferocity of their better fed brethren of

the plains. Sandie led the way, and his Highland training and brawny legs proved of great service to him in this fearfully broken ground. There was but little difficulty in keeping the trail, no fresh snow having fallen since the previous night. It was a fine bright breezy morning, but very cold; the thermometer having registered 23° of frost during the previous night, and the air was clear and invigorating in the extreme.

After about an hour's tracking, Sandie spied a fresh earthwork thrown up on our line of march. Concentrating our forces, we advanced cautiously, and found that it was the *débris* from a cave which our friend had been at work at during the previous night. He had evidently found the temperature so severe and uncongenial that he had made up his mind to construct winter quarters, and to retire into them with as little delay as practicable. The progress he had made in his tunneling was so good that we could not, at first, see the far end, and it was a matter of doubt whether he might not be in actual possession. Being all of us as keen as mustard, we advanced in line to the mouth of the cave with our rifles at the ready. Had Bruin been at home and charged out, it is a matter of considerable doubt whether he would not have routed the attack and escaped uninjured. He would have had all the advantages of the defence, besides the nature and lie of the ground in his favour. Fortunately, as it turned out, he had not sufficiently progressed with his work to suit his taste for a permanent winter abode; or he had wished to have one more look this fine morning at the outside world before " holeing up " for so many months of seclusion

and darkness; or possibly he had felt hungry and
had wished to have the chance of one more meal.
At any rate, whatever his reason, he had left; and
we had nothing to do but to resume our toilsome
tracking. The falls we got were many, and
curious from the grotesque positions in which
they often placed us. Luckily no one came to
any real harm, and all went on cheerily enough.
We had not got more than a quarter of a mile
beyond Bruin's earthwork, when I saw Sandie,
who was about a hundred yards in advance,
beckoning and gesticulating frantically and pointing his rifle down the hill. To run or tumble
over the distance which separated us was a matter
of a few moments, and lying down breathless beside
him—as I had so often done before on the Highland hills—my eye at once took in our sought-for
friend, poking about quietly amongst some boulders
of rocks about 120 yards below us. Pulling myself
together, away went one barrel, with no effect
beyond making Bruin turn his head upwards to
see what was up. Concluding that I had fired
over him, I aimed lower with my second barrel,
and the expanding ball entered just between his
shoulders, passing downwards into the region of the
heart and lungs. The little express had done its
work well, and poor "ursus ferox" (or " horribilis ")
ceased to exist without a groan. As may be imagined, a shout of triumph filled the air, and we
emulated each other in tumbling and scrambling
down to where the prostrate body lay. The dogs,
too, were brave enough now that their foe was incapable of defending himself; they bayed and would
have worried to any extent, but this latter process

I objected to out of respect to the hide, which was, though small, a remarkably good one. He was pronounced to be a four-year-old bear, but by no means large. It appears that these Range grizzlies, owing to the difficulty of procuring food in the high altitudes they frequent, never attain to any great size; but to meet the severity of the climate, nature has provided them with a much thicker and warmer covering than their brethren of the plain. The carcase was soon stripped of this appendage, and, laden with it and with the head and some steaks and fat, we started towards the ranche at Estes Park. On our way down the Roaring Branch Gulch we came on fresh signs of sheep, so fresh, indeed, that I doubt whether we had not disturbed them when operating on the bear. Nothing, however, could be seen of them now, even with the aid of our glasses, and as it was getting late and we had a long way before us, we had reluctantly to push on.

On arrival at the ranche we found that all the bronchos had been recovered except three, but that the men had only been able to bring down one very small pack from our old camp. The next day the weather was a little better, and taking advantage of this, we sent up some men with the bronchos, and were enabled to get home nearly everything—and only just in time, as a heavy fall of snow again commenced, which might have prevented their removal for the rest of the winter. Besides the bear, I had been fortunate enough that same day to get a very good "sable,"—or, as they are called here, "marten,"—*Mustela Americana*, whilst in active pursuit of a terrified tree-squirrel. A good marten's skin, such as that I got, used to be worth out here

S12 or S15 (2*l.* or 3*l.*), but now all furs are considerably down in value, and it is hard work for the "fur-hunters" to make a livelihood.

The weather still continuing bad, and few signs of game to be seen, we determined to take Griff Evans's advice, and to strike away by way of the plains for certain game regions to the northward. Griff, who alone was to accompany us, spoke much of a locality called "Rock Creek," of which he had no personal knowledge, but had heard good accounts. To get to this district we should have to turn the Range by going down on to the prairie, and heading up into the foothills again further to the north, and then crossing the main Range, where it was lower.

Having hired from the Estes Park Company a wagon and a team of horses, and some ponies, and bronchos, for riding and packing, with the necessary saddles and fixings, on the 20th of October we started away once more on our wanderings. Our course lay in a south-easterly direction, through the beautiful foothills, to the little town of Fort Collins. The road in itself was miserable, although dignified by the title of "the county road;" and its difficulties were increased by the covering of snow which now lay over everything even at this lower elevation. It was lucky for us that Griff had made arrangements for the Estes Park Company's team of mules to help us over the first part of the road. Had it not been for them, our small horses must inevitably have knocked under, and we should have been very much delayed in our movements. On our road down we saw tracks of black-tailed deer, but being keen on bigger game, we were not to be tempted, and continued our course for the plains. Two settlers' abodes were passed among the foothills; one of these was inhabited by a man named Fogg, a native of Cumberland (England), who had emigrated many years ago, and had since seen much military service against the Indians. Some refreshments and a chat with the old fellow helped us on our road, and we soon afterwards got down to the prairie. A little farther we came on a large farming establishment, which I found belonged to an old Mexican, by name Marianna, who had in early life made a good fortune by farming, breeding stock, and horse-racing. He had, however, within the last few years lost his daughter, who had assisted him much in his worldly affairs, and since then all had gone wrong with him; so that now, poor old fellow! he was said to be in a very bad way.

From Marianna's to Fort Collins is not more than twelve miles, and as it was now getting late, and we were told the road was straight and easily "made," L. and I determined to desert the tired team, and "make the best time" we could hither on our ponies. Our sailing instructions were to steer north, and to keep the trail. The night being clear, and the track said to be quite straight, we thought we should have no difficulty in obeying, but along a flat prairie it is by no means easy to keep an ill-defined track at night, which we found out to our cost, for when about two miles from Collins, we got off it, and had a near shave of passing the night *al fresco*, without fire or food. After some trouble, however, we struck the road again, and eventually arrived at Collins some hours before the waggon.

Although this is "the county town" it is but a

small village. The inn or "house," however, was
both clean and comfortable, and we slept well between the sheets the last time for some months.
Here we purchased stores for some weeks, and on
the morrow left in a northerly direction. We
entered the foothills again about four miles from
Fort Collins, and soon after passed the little village
of La Porte, on the Cache la Poudre river. This
little settlement was in old days an important post
of the French Canadian trappers employed by the
Hudson Bay and American Fur Companies. One
of these veterans, by name Jim Baker, is still alive,
aged sixty-eight, and living with his Indian wife on
Snake River. Many curious stories are told of the
old fellow's wonderful skill in trapping. He is said
to be able to trap a beaver by any foot he may
choose, whereas nowadays many of the would-be
trappers can scarcely catch a beaver at all. In early
days, when civilization first advanced into this part
of the country, it found here some old hunters who
had adopted Indian customs and married Indian
squaws. Most of them abandoned their unfortunate
partners, but to the credit of human nature, some
few stuck to their coloured helpmates, and amongst
them was old Jim Baker. He has now a large and
thriving family, and is much respected by all his
acquaintances. In early days he and sixteen other
trappers most gallantly defended themselves against
nearly all the warriors of the powerful Ute tribe at
a place called Battle Creek in Wyoming, and eventually beat them off with considerable slaughter.

One little incident I heard of old Jim is so
characteristic of the determination, independence,
and moral code which possessed these early trappers

that I cannot help giving it. Some years ago a party of Cheyenne or Sioux Indians made a raid into these parts, and carried off a lot of cattle, amongst which were some belonging to Jim Baker. The ranchemen and settlers at once assembled to arrange for the pursuit of the marauders. Whilst so engaged old Jim passed by with his pouch, blanket, and long heavy rifle over his shoulder. On being asked by some of the assembled friends where he was bound to, "After Injuns," was his brief reply. He would not join in the general pursuit, preferring to have his hunt alone and on his own account. Nor did he return until he had killed an Indian for every head of cattle taken from his herd!

COLORADO
1877.

CHAPTER IX.

"Man hath no part in all this glorious work,
    The hand that built the firmament hath heaved
And smoothed these verdant swells, and sown their slopes
With herbage, planted them with island groves,
And hedged them round with forests."
                            "*The Prairies*," *Wm. C. Bryant*.

A FEW words now on the geology of these parts.
In Estes Park, and in the greater portion of the
foothills, we had to do with the old volcanic and
metamorphic rocks, such as granite, gneiss, and
quartz schists, of which the mountain ranges are
mostly composed. These formations furnish grand
outlines and precipitous gorges to the wildest type
of nature's pictures. Travelling towards the plain
or prairie,—as we did from Estes Park towards Fort
Collins, when following the line of the Big Thompson
River,—these classes of rocks are left behind, and
with them the serrated ridges and bold faces of

the mountain scenery. As soon as the sedimentary rocks are reached we come on the flatness of the prairie landscape, proclaiming the quiet peaceful times when these level beds were deposited from the then existing boundless seas. The sedimentary or stratified formations are represented by rocks belonging to what are here termed the Jura Trias and cretaceous groups. Generally speaking, the Trias rocks lie skirting the metamorphic, and between them and the cretaceous and post-cretaceous which underlie the greater portion of the prairies and plains. The rocks in Rattle Snake Park— through which we passed between Estes Park and Fort Collins—are sedimentary, and belong to the Trias group. After this we re-entered the metamorphic rocks for a short distance before finally passing into the cretaceous formations of the prairie.

It seemed as if in this wonderful climate there was the same marvellous luxuriance of growth on all kinds of soil. In the mountains and foothills the coniferæ attain such dimensions as are scarcely to be equalled in any other part of the world. Lower down, on the soils formed on the cretaceous rocks, crops of wheat are grown, surpassing in quality and abundance those produced in any other land. Pass on to the prairie overlying the same rocks and those of the post-cretaceous periods, and you have a rich short grass not to be excelled anywhere in meat-producing qualities. It is as if all geological formations came alike to Dame Nature for creating productive soils in this favoured clime ; and this is perhaps the more striking when we come to consider the vast extent of country with which we are dealing. The State of Colorado is said to contain an area of 106,500 square miles, or 68,144,000 acres; about four-sevenths of this vast extent is said to be mountainous regions, whose snowy summits form the "Great Divide," or watershed of the continent; the remaining three-sevenths—nearly 30,000,000 acres—embrace the corn-producing lands of the State. A great deal of this is already growing the very finest quality of wheat, and, no doubt, when irrigation is further carried out, much more will be put under the plough, and add to the important part Colorado is already playing in the supply of bread-stuff not only to the continent of America, but to the fast-growing populations of the old world. There seems to be no want of water in these regions, a good supply coming from the many streams, such as the Cache la Poudre, Big and Little Thompsons, St. Vrain Creek, and other rivulets, which debouch from the mountains on to the plains. These waters are already largely used for irrigation, but there is no doubt that in the future they will be still more so. The whole question of corn production on the plains out here resolves itself into irrigation, and where water can be insured grand crops of corn can be counted on with almost a certainty. This all-important commodity is said to be now more abundant than it was formerly, which probably arises from the changes made by the process of settling in the timber-covered portions of the country. The Mexicans and Indians assert that the Americans bring rain with them, and this assertion is as it were confirmed by the observations noted in the Government Reports. Harvesting operations generally take place in these parts about the beginning of August; thirty-five

M

bushels of wheat per acre may be said to be an average yield.

To resume our journey northwards from La Porte, where we leave again the sedimentary rocks of the plain, and strike the volcanic and meta-morphic rocks through which the charming little river, the Cache la Poudre, has found its winding way. Here we came across large herds of cattle, which seemed to be thriving on the very sparse tufts of short buffalo grass. There must certainly be something wonderfully nutritious in this herbage. To my English eye it appeared both thin and dry; but the proof of the pudding is in the eating, and cattle, even when herded thickly on it during the winter months, hold their own fine summer condition.

We were much interested in meeting to-day a waggon laden with black-tailed deer, coming from the neighbourhood of Livermore, and destined for the Collins market. They were in size between a red and a fallow deer, and appeared to be in capital condition.

The first night after leaving Collins we brought up at a wooden erection, which was pleased to call itself "The Forks Hotel." There was no accommo-dation either for sleep or food in this edifice, only a sort of bar where certain drinks could be obtained. The night was bitterly cold, and as timber for our camp-fire was scarce, we betook ourselves for rest to a sort of hay-loft. The hay would have been a comfortable bed enough had it not been of a peculiarly prickly description, so that our clothes were perforated with the greatest ease by the sharp points it contained. This was, moreover, no mere temporary inconvenience; the pricks broke off and remained in our garments, and made themselves afterwards felt at the most unexpected and inconvenient moments. I concluded this pot-house took its name from the fact that two roads or trails branched off at this spot; the one leading towards a place called Tyseiden, the other heading more directly into the mountains towards Livermore. We selected the former as being more in the direction of North Park, which we now sought to reach, instead of Rock Creek. We had been led to abandon the latter for want of good information, both as to its exact whereabouts, and the sport we were likely to have when we got there.

None of our "outfit" had ever been in this country before, so we were obliged to shape our course by such directions as we could gather from passers-by, and from any ranches we came across. Our first instructions were to take a northerly course, passing by "Tyseiden" and "The Dirty Woman's Ranche;" but, perhaps from keeping too far to the north, we contrived to miss these landmarks, and had to follow a small and rough trail through a beautiful country, with scarcely a habitation of any sort or kind. At the close of the first day we found ourselves on an extreme point of the great Laramie plain, where we had to make camp for the night. From what I heard afterwards, I gathered that the trail we used was what is known as "The old Cherokee trail," made formerly by that tribe of Indians when on their yearly marauding incursions from the south. We calculated we made about thirty miles this first day, and that over a very undulating country, well covered with thick timber.

Although our camp was on a so-called " plain," we were as high up as the top of many mountains. The weather was bitter, and we felt the cold the more owing to the keen wind which blew off the snow-covered range on to our exposed position.

Laramie Plain is an undulating, treeless, elevated plateau, from sixty to ninety miles in length from south-east to north-west ; and from fifty to seventy-five miles in width from north-east to south-west.   It is said—in the Government Geological Report, 1870, —to contain 6,750 square miles, or about 4,500,000 acres, which are drained chiefly by the Medicine Bow Creek and Laramie River, both flowing into the North Platte.   On the east and north-east sides, it is bounded by a high range of syenite mountains. Like the prairie further south, the plain itself is, I fancy, entirely composed of sedimentary rocks, belonging probably to the Trias and cretaceous formations.   Not many years since this plain was a favourite hunting-ground of the Sioux and Cheyenne Indians, but the whites have now driven them northwards, never to return.

The next day we were lucky enough to fall in with a ranche-man, who happened to be looking for strayed cattle, and whose search pointed towards the North Park.   Under his guidance we soon left the plain, and turned towards the mountains in a north-westerly direction.   The country was well wooded, and looked exactly suited for black-tail deer ; but we were keen now on larger game, and looked forward to being in a wapiti country before long.   Fortune favoured the cow-puncher in his search, for we came on his cattle within a very few miles ; but we suffered from his good luck, as

we were again left to our own ideas. We now tried
to find a certain ranche, kept by what they call here
a "Dutchman" (Angl., a German) named "Singen-
borger," whom it was thought probable we should be
able to induce to guide us into North Park. After
some trouble we found the ranche and the old
Prussian Pole; but his wife had gone down to buy
stores for the winter, which prevented the old fellow
from coming with us, as there would have been no
one to feed the milk-stock. He was a cheery old
bird, had spent most of his life in Mexico, and had
lately married an American, who had brought with
her six "lomachs" of boys, by which I supposed
him to mean six "lumps" of boys. The old
fellow's ranche was well situated, but he found the
climate too cold, and he meant to return to Mexico,
with or without his bride, as might suit her best. He
could speak six languages, his "American" being
of the choicest frontier description. We learnt from
him the good news that North Park was only one
long day's drive from here, for that he had done it
himself in that time. Getting sailing directions
from him we resumed our journey, and soon re-
descended to the Laramie plain, having in our
march crossed over a spur of the foothills. We
made but a short distance to-day, in consequence of
the delay caused by one of L.'s rifles being lost out
of the waggon. On one of our party riding back,
it was found in the hands of the stockman who had
been with us in the morning, and who did not now
like parting with it.

The next morning we made an early start, hoping
to get into North Park before nightfall, but we
either missed the trail, or the distance was far

greater than our friend the Dutchman made it out
to be; at any rate it was well into the afternoon
before we got even into the valley of the Big
Laramie River, beyond which lies the main "divide"
into North Park. Here we came across a ranche
kept by two Swedish brothers, and arranged with
one of them to horse our waggon, and to come on
with us himself into the park. We were now able
to send back the mules and teamster we had
brought from Estes Park, and which we could not
hitherto have done without. That night we brought
up at a ranche on the Laramie River, belonging to a
late captain in the United States army, where the
accommodation was rough, but hearty. Amongst
the inmates of the ranche was the deputy-sheriff
from Laramie city, who was in search of witnesses
in a case of "shooting," which occurred a few
weeks ago at a "Tie Camp" in this neighbourhood.
It appeared that a lot of men employed by a contractor were camped out, cutting sleepers for the
Union Pacific Railroad. A lad named Cowan, only
seventeen years of age, thought he had been ill-
treated in the matter of wages, and pulling out a
six-shooter, shot the contractor, by name Tim Ryan,
dead on the spot. Upon this, the contractor's
clerk seized the heavy stove-poker and dashed out
Cowan's brains there and then. A woman was the
only witness, besides the clerk, of the occurrence,
and it was to *subpœna* her that the under-sheriff had
come here.

This little episode caused much discussion, and
led to many a wild tale of western life. I remember one, of a young fellow, who was said to
have been a marvel of strength and good looks, and

although a gambler and utterly reckless, yet looked up to by his lawless companions as "straight" in his dealings. He went by the *soubriquet* of " Wild Bill." Once in a gambling saloon in Montana he was set upon by three brother rowdies, and disposed of the whole three with his bowie knife. Eventually he lost his life while playing cards somewhere in the Black-hills of Dakotah. A man he had been gambling with had lost heavily to him, and avenged himself for his losses by shooting " Wild Bill" through the back of the head, as he sat playing with another set. Such was the public indignation against the perpetrator that he was lynched there and then without further ceremony.

The next morning broke heavy and lowering, and we felt a great amount of uneasiness about the weather. However, but one more divide and we should be in North Park, the long sought-for hunting-grounds. We followed the Laramie River on first starting from here for about three miles, and then struck up westwards into the divide ; the ascent was gradual, and the road fair, though there was still a thick covering of snow from the recent storm. The highest part of the pass or divide was about 10,500 feet above sea level, so well within the timber line, which is here about 12,000 feet. We travelled steadily all the morning, seeing tracks of both wapiti and black-tailed deer; but as we were anxious to make a ranche called " the old man Pinkham's " before dark, we pushed on till we were almost within sight of it. On the slope into North Park we were greeted with the sight of a herd of antelope, and this was more than we could resist after so many weeks of disappointment. The bronchos

were tethered whilst L—— and I, accompanied by
Griff and Sandie and "Ned," started for a stalk. The
antelope were evidently suspicious that all was not
right, and very shortly began to move up the hill,
to a bare place beside a wood, where it was very
difficult to get quietly in upon them. With some
toil we got round and above them, and were settling
down to a quiet shot at 100 yards or so, when up
went their heads, and we knew quick shooting was
now our only chance. We both fired and wounded
three, only one of which, a fine doe, did we succeed
in securing, and that only after much tracking. This
was my first acquaintance with that pretty graceful
little animal the prong-horn antelope (*Antilocapra
Americana*), which still abounds in some parts of
the Western States and territories, though far less
numerous than it used to be. Its powers of sight
and smell are very acute, though perhaps not so
keen as those of the black-tailed deer. The bucks
and does herd together, in bands of from two or
three hundreds and more; when fired at and
frightened by a near shot—especially when they do
not see whence the danger comes—they will frequently run round in a half-circle, and thus afford
several chances. Their meat is excellent, I think
second to none I came across. A good buck will
weigh as much as 70 lbs. "clean." They "run" in
October, but soon recover condition and become very
quickly fat and in good order. The males alone
have horns, something like those of the chamois,
which they "shed" about December; the outside
shell of the horn comes off, leaving a soft core exposed, on which the new shell forms. They are
very swift for a short distance, but can easily be

run down by a good grey-hound. They migrate long distances at different seasons of the year. During the summer large herds frequent North Park, but as hard weather approaches they commence to move down the valley of the Platte, seeking winter quarters on the lower prairies. They are essentially inhabitants of the open plains and are never to be found of their own accord in heavy-timbered districts.

This little bit of sport delayed us in getting to "old man Pinkham's," the more so as we endeavoured to follow up the wounded; but in vain, with the exception of a doe, which "Ned" tracked in some timber, and "jumped" and secured. I was

PRONG-HORNED ANTELOPE (*Antilocapra Americana*).
From a Sketch by A. Bierstadt.

much astonished at the tenacity of life which these little creatures possessed; for although not more than a quarter the size of our Scotch red deer, they take quite as much killing, and unless struck in a vital part, even by that destructive little express bullet, there is but a poor chance of getting them without a dog.

At the ranche we found quite a party; there were a certain "Judge" Brown, and another lawyer from Laramie city, and two miners, all on their way to a silver lead mine on the range, which the miners were in hope the judge and his companion would buy. Then there was the old man Pinkham himself, a frontier man of some sixty summers, and his partner, originally a tailor I believe, who had preferred this wild sort of life to sitting crossed legs on bench working his needle. The ranche was well built of logs by old Pinkham himself single-handed. It possessed a single room about thirty feet square. The great pride of the old man was a chimney corner he had just erected, which was universally declared to be "elegant" and "high toned." In it blazed some huge logs of pitch pine, cheerful to look at, and to feel the glow of too, when we first came in, but, as the evening advanced and outside air grew scarce, the atmosphere became stuffy and overpowering. Besides the grand fireplace, the room boasted a small cooking-stove; and at this the respective cooks of the three outfits were accommodated in turn. After a good supper on antelope meat, we looked about for convenient positions for our bedding and blankets, but as we were in all thirteen men, two dogs and several cats, space had to be economized; however, we soon shook into places, and were speedily in the land of dreams, as attested by deep-toned snoring on the part of some of our comrades. This did not interfere with well-earned sleep, and, curious as it may now sound, I often afterwards wished myself back again under old Pinkham's warm and hospitable roof.

The next morning I induced one of the miners, Jim, who was said to be a good hunter, to come with me after antelope. The weather was dull, and there was every appearance of more "storming." We had not got far from the ranche before we sighted a "band," consisting of three bucks and about a dozen does. Jim made a capital stalk, and we got within about one hundred yards, when I killed the best of the bucks, which Jim pronounced to be an old one, and to weigh, when "dressed," about seventy pounds. Another stalk did not come off so happily, as they picked us up and got away without a shot. Later on in the day I had another chance at a buck, but as he was galloping at a great rate I missed him clean.

When heading homewards in the evening from the somewhat isolated hill opposite the ranche, Jim happened to look back and saw we were being followed by a large grey wolf; as soon as we halted he halted too and sat down watching our movements, keeping at the respectful distance of about four hundred yards. We thought that the best chance to get a shot at him would be for me to creep away from the men and dogs—the latter probably being the object of his curiosity and greed—and by making a *détour* below the hill to come in behind him, whilst he was absorbed in watching. Such was our plan, and the wind suited it well, but the cunning beast was too crafty for us; he must have detected me parting from the others, for when I got round he had disappeared. This was a fine specimen of the big grey "timber" or "buffalo" wolf (*canis lupus occidentalis*). They are generally about four or five feet in length, and stand as high as a deer-hound, but are heavier in build. They are not to be confounded with the coyoté, or prairie wolf (*canis latrans*), which are not above two feet in height and three feet in length, and are lighter in make, resembling much the eastern jackal. The "timber wolf"—so called from being generally found in the forests—is a very powerful but at the same time cowardly and suspicious animal. He is generally either alone, or in company with only one or two others, whereas the coyotés are often in small packs. He is to be found in close attendance wherever buffalo hunting is going on, hovering about and ready to pounce down and feed on the carcases, and to attack the wounded as soon as he can do so with safety. The fur is long and thick and much prized by the hunter. I am told that no dog, however large and fierce, has a chance in a fight with the timber wolf, the jaws of the latter being of such immense power and armed with so formidable an array of fangs. Although pretty numerous in some regions, they are nowhere so common as the coyoté, which abounds throughout the prairies and ravines of the Rocky Mountains. Scarcely a night passes on a hunting expedition but the coyoté's unearthly barking and yelling are to be heard; and they possess the power of varying the noise in such an extraordinary manner that you can scarcely believe that such different sounds can proceed from the same animal. Although very shy, I don't think the coyoté is so "sus-

picious" as the timber wolf, at any rate he is not so
canny, as the following anecdote will show.   It was
related to me by an eye-witness, a hunter in the
Sweet-water country with whom I afterwards stayed,
and whom I had every reason to believe.   It appeared that he had seen one of the large timber
wolves prowling about in the neighbourhood of his
ranche, and had set a trap for him by poisoning an
antelope carcase with strychnine.   After making this
arrangement, later in the day he saw the old wolf
loafing on towards the bait, and made sure that he
would fall a victim during the night.   But nothing
was to be seen of him the following morning, dead
or alive.   In the evening, however, the wolf appeared
again, but this time accompanied by a coyoté.   They
approached the bait together, but when close by,
the old wolf dropped behind and allowed the coyoté
to take the initiative in attacking the carcase.   In
a short time the poison began to tell, upon seeing
which the wily old wolf made off, convinced no
doubt that it was, in western parlance "no meat for
him."

The fur of the prairie wolf, although good, is not
so valuable as that of his timber cousin, a single well-
dressed hide not fetching more than a dollar at the
trading stores, whereas a good grey wolf is worth
twice as much or more.   I was often told that in
poisoning coyotés the males alone were killed ; but
this theory was quite upset by the fact that the first
two we got were vixens.

I enjoyed the day's hunt with Jim amazingly ; he
was far better informed than most of his class in
his own particular vocation of mining, and was
moreover a real good hunter.   The mine at which

he was then working—and in which I was told he was a part owner—is about thirty miles south-west of old Pinkham's ranche, and is situated over 11,000 feet above the sea level, on the "divide" which separates the North from the South Park. Jim tells me the ore is of great value for silver and lead, and that the miners—probably all part owners—make about $12 per day (= 2*l.* 8*s.*)! The ore is sent down to Georgetown, near Central, in Colorado, where it is smelted. This undertaking is but small at present, employing only about a dozen men, and these are, as usual, anxious to realize their shares.

As is often the case with these mines situated in the game countries, the men are fed to a large extent on venison killed in the locality, one of their number being told off to do the hunting. Jim had got an amusing story of an incident which had befallen their hunter a short time ago. It appeared that bears were pretty numerous up there, and the hunter was afraid that these inquisitors would make an onslaught on some wapiti meat he had just procured for winter use. To prevent such an occurrence before he was able to secure it in one of the log huts, he thought the safest way would be to make his own bed on the top of it, and acting on this plan he arranged his blankets and settled down for the night. He dreamt that he was in an orchard near his old home, in an Eastern State, and that a bull-dog had fixed him in the act of robbing the trees. Awaking suddenly from his dream, he found that an old bear was shoving him about to get at the meat underneath. Jumping up, he seized his rifle, and "in the scare" fired "right away." He then ran to the nearest tree, which he endeavoured to climb, and thought he was doing so too, but when found by some of the occupants of the neighbouring huts, he was embracing the trunk, but not off the ground. Fortunately for him Bruin was scared too and had made off, passing close by him, but not molesting him. I give the story just as I had it, and am inclined to believe it myself, from my informant's manner and its general acceptance, and considering, too, the well-known prying and predatory nature of the bear.

And now to say a few words about the physical character of these happy hunting-grounds which we have at last reached. North Park is oval, or rather quadrangular in shape. It is about fifty miles from east to west, and over thirty from north to south, thus having an area of over 1500 square miles. High mountain ranges encircle it, except on that side in which is the cañon of the North Platte. There is abundance of water all over the park, the smaller streams flowing into the North Platte, which drains the whole area. Excellent grass is to be found all over it in the summer time, affording a most fertile run for cattle, but the weather is thought to be too severe for them after the month of September, and they are then moved away to milder localities. They tell me that nothing can surpass the condition of the cattle after a few months' feeding in the summer time on the luxuriant herbage. Large crops of hay are taken off parts of the park, without going to any trouble whatsoever beyond the actual cutting and making.

Geologically, I believe, the park itself is a basin of sedimentary rocks belonging to the tertiary and cretaceous periods, enclosed by metamorphic and more recent volcanic rocks, which form the mountain ranges.

Not long ago (in 1870) this locality was the scene of one of those dreadful massacres by Indians which one hears of occasionally in travelling through this frontier country. A party of miners were at work in the park on a mountain called Mount Independence, about ten miles south-west of Pinkham's ranche, when they were visited by a party of Ute Indians under a chief called "Colorado." The tribe was supposed to be friendly, but Colorado informed the miners that they should have "two sleeps" (i. e. two nights) to leave in, and that if they had not left by that time they should be killed. The miners were badly armed, possessing only a few inferior revolvers and their tools. The older men counselled "skinning out" at once, and leaving it to the United States troops to settle accounts with the Utes, but the young bloods rebelled at this advice, and determined on awaiting the attack. Fortunately many left that same evening and escaped the massacre which was perpetrated the very next morning by an overwhelming number of Indians. Of nine miners who braved the Indians, only two escaped to tell the tale. Since then no Redskin has been allowed by the whites to exist in North Park. Should one be seen, miners and ranchemen at once turn out and hunt him away, as if he was a wild beast. Last year a party of eight Utes came to hunt in the park; but only seven left it alive, the eighth was found with a bullet hole through his body.

And now to return to our own movements. The next day we had settled to move up the park towards a little stream called the Canadian Creek. The morning was fine, so notwithstanding a threatening appearance in the sky, away we started. I rode ahead with Evans and Jim, having induced the latter to give me the benefit of his company for the early part of the day, after which he was to start across the park and rejoin his partner and Judge Brown and friend, on their way to visit the mine. About nine o'clock the day changed, and a heavy snowstorm set in. No hunting was to be done, so all that remained for us, was to await patiently the arrival of L. and the rest of my outfit. Whilst so waiting by a good fire we had kindled to keep off the cold, a buck antelope hove in sight on a ridge about 500 yards above us, and a lucky shot from my express brought him to book. Soon afterwards the "young captain" (as L. was called by Jim) and the rest of the party arrived, and Jim bade us adieu. It was now "storming" heavily, and it turned out afterwards that Jim never "made" the rest of his outfit that night, but had had to camp out as best he could by a fire of sage bush.

In the midst of this despairing weather we had a gleam of amusement in watching Evans "snake" down the carcase of the antelope by a lariat made fast to one of the bronchos. The pony, strange to the work, objected most forcibly, and whirled little Griff round and round in the snow, but he was a determined fellow, and held on most gallantly. After a desperate struggle, the broncho seemed reconciled, and Evans strutted down towards us, leading the pony by the bridle, no doubt complimenting himself on his victory. All of a sudden he discovered amidst shouts of laughter from below, that the

N

antelope's head had slipped out of the noose, and that the beast was left behind on the side of the hill; to his infinite disgust Griff had to remount the brae and once more attach the carcase. At length the antelope was dragged to the bottom of the hill and packed into the waggon, and we were able to resume our line of march. Within a mile of this we found that we had lost the track in the snow, which was falling very heavily. Nothing remained for us but to steer for the nearest timber we could see, and make camp. Fortunately, within a short distance we struck some cotton-wood trees on the banks of a frozen stream, where we established ourselves for the night. It was very cold, our thermometer going as low as it could go, which was about 5° below zero, and how much further it would have gone had it been able, we did not know, but probably the cold was not much greater than the thermometer marked.

The following morning promised well, and Griff went out to "prospect," and find, if he could, the road which was said to lead up the park, but which we had failed to strike the previous evening. After some hours he returned somewhat enlightened as to our position. He had had an adventure too, having come across a wolverine, but being unarmed, and the beast giving unmistakable signs of showing fight, he had not been able to bring him to bag. Griff, when he first saw the beast, had thought of dismounting and doing battle with a "club," but on consideration he deemed discretion to be the better part of valour, and reluctantly turned his back on this pugnacious little animal.

The wolverine (*gulo*, or *ursus luscus*) with its

many local names, such as the "skunk bear,"
"corky-jo," "gofordog," &c., is now becoming
rare even in the most mountainous and unfrequented
regions.   In shape it is like a marten cat, but attains
the wonderful weight (as I am told) of 100 lbs., and is
so ferocious, and can use its formidable claws with
such effect, as to be a match for a small bear. It is said
to throw itself on its back, and to rip open the under
part of the body of its antagonist by a blow of its
muscular and keen-armed paw.   The body is of a
light grey, turning to black at the muzzle and at
the extremities.   Hunters relate wonderful stories of
its ferocity and great muscular strength, even when
in captivity.   The celebrated Jim Baker is said to
have kept one at the same time as a cinnamon bear,
and that the wolverine always "whipped" the bear
over the food.   It was a matter therefore of great
regret to us all that Griff had been unable to bring
in so great a prize.   If he had only had a six-shooter
with him, the affair would have been soon settled.

A WAPITI ROARING.

From a Sketch by A. Bierstadt.

CHAPTER X.

"The bounding Elk, whose antlers bear
  The branches, falls before my aim."
"*The Hunters of the Prairie*," *Wm. Cullen Bryant.*

THE next day broke as badly as possible, and it being now late in the season (October 29th), and L.'s leave getting short, he deemed it prudent to depart for more civilized and warmer regions, fearing lest the snow should fall so heavily as to prevent his egress from the park. Accordingly, very much to our mutual regret, we parted. With him went my Highlander—Sandie—and my poor old dog "Sailor." The latter I was glad of the opportunity of sending home, the weather having become too cold for his thin skin, and the poor beast did nothing but shiver. Sandie was a great loss to me, and just as I was in hopes of good sport amongst the big game, it was most provoking to lose him; but he had not expected I should be away so long, and had taken a farm in Scotland, to which he was obliged to return.

I must confess to feeling low and lonely, left here so far from civilization, without a human being as a companion save Griff Evans, a comparative stranger, who had moreover never been in these parts before, and knew nothing of the country. I thought, however, that after coming all this way I was bound to persevere, and I had great and just confidence in Griff's hunting and campaigning qualities. This was not misplaced, for so long as he and I were alone together we did remarkably well, and I firmly believe that if we had continued alone, my sport would have been better. But there came a day when he was induced to ask me to take on others, and after that there was a great falling off both in sport and comfort. But I must not forestall.

As soon as all was arranged and it was decided that L. should take Martin, the Swede, and the team to convey his party and *impedimenta* to Laramie city, on the Union Pacific Railroad, Griff and I started for our first day after wapiti. We made for some likely-looking timber about ten miles up the park, and although we killed nothing, the day was not without much enjoyable excitement. We were both mounted on "bronchos;" Griff leading, piloted the way through the thinnest parts of the forest, examining most carefully the fresh fallen snow for signs of game. After some hours hunting he suddenly pulled up, and pointed to some very large fresh tracks, which he said were those of a "bull elk" (i. e. stag wapiti). Dismounting and making our ponies fast to a tree, we took up the track on foot. This was real excitement, Griff following the track cautiously and carefully, while I was all eagerness close behind him, with rifle ready for a snap shot, in case we "jumped" the bull. My companion pronounced the track to be quite fresh, in fact, only made within an hour or so, and as the beast was walking and browsing, and the wind all right, I was very sanguine, and had a full feeling about the heart at the idea of a shot at one of these magnificent animals.

We had not followed the track more than half an hour when Griff started back, and at the same

moment I caught a glimpse of a magnificent stag
crashing through the thick timber. Crack goes my
rifle, but with no apparent effect beyond perhaps
hastening the beast's movements. Down go my
spirits, to be raised again very speedily by a drop of
blood on the virgin snow; at any rate I had hit him;
but was the wound mortal? and shall we get him?
were the next questions I anxiously put to myself.
Taking the track, with " Ned " straining at the
leash, we plodded on and at last " jumped " him,
but not in view, owing to the thickness of the
timber. With Evan's approval I decided, as it
was getting late in the day, to slip " Ned " on the
track, with the hopes of getting a bay. Off he went
at full tear, and very shortly we were greeted with
his well-known bark, plainly telling that he had
come up with the elk. Instead of remaining
stationary, however, which would have assured us
of a bay, the bark grew fainter and fainter, too
clearly showing that the bull was not sick enough
to bay, and that he had refused to stop and was
pursuing his onward course. Old " Ned " had been
trained on red deer, which readily bay when tackled
by a colley; but these great, big brutes are too
impulsive and impatient to stop, and the only
chance of baying them is for the dog to snap their
heels, when they will turn round to defend themselves. This is the case too with bears and other
wild animals, and should be remembered when
training a dog for work out here. I found this out
one day when watching " Ned " run a wounded elk,
when it happened that the whole chase was full in
view. I saw him run up in front and head the elk,
barking violently, but without the smallest apparent

effect on the animal, which eventually got well away and was never brought to bag.

But to return to the present occasion. When "Ned" rejoined us exhausted and tired, having evidently had a long run, it was so late in the day that we had to give up further pursuit, and had only to make for our bronchos, and get back to camp as quickly as we could. Fortunately the night was pretty clear, for most of our ride was in the dark, and Griff knew nothing of these parts; he was, however, very good in wood-craft, and had marked the country well, so we got back without a hitch.

What a fearfully depressing thing a deserted camp is! a lonesome overpowering stillness reigns, where a few hours before all was active, stirring life. Such feelings of depression assail us more strongly on a return from a long day's unsuccessful hunting, tired, cold, and hungry, than when we have something to show for our labours. And to add to our present trials our party before leaving in the morning had neglected to bank up the camp-fire, or to cut any firewood; consequently directly we got in, we had to go out and seek for wood in the dark, and then to set to work and "chop" it. Fortunately some cotton-wood trees were not far off, and we managed to get a fire pretty soon, for the weather was bitter and we felt the necessity of speedy warmth. To add to my own discomfort, I found that the bag which contained my change of clothes was locked, and no key could be discovered for "quite a while." Whilst I was engaged in the search, Griff had been most successfully occupied with the supper. Our fare was antelope venison

and fresh baked bread, and right good they were.
We thoroughly enjoyed the repast, and having done
ample justice to Griff's cooking, and being well
tired out, were very soon curled up for the
night.

The following day was a most glorious one for
hunting, but as we had decided on moving camp
some seven or eight miles further up the park to
be nearer the best elk ground, the greater part of
it was spent in this operation. The work was hard
and took a long time, as there were only two of us
to strike the tent, and then pack and drive the
laden bronchos, so that the sun was nearly down before we got to the spot we had selected on the previous day, on the bank of a creek or stream, close to
where it escaped from the mountains. Near here
we thought from appearances there would be both
good grazing and plenty of wood and water—the
main essentials of a good camp.

Whilst Griff unpacked the bronchos and pitched
the only tent we now had with us, I thought I
should have time before sundown to take a quiet
hunt with " Ned." Leaving camp, I made for a
neighbouring pine-clad ridge, where, as I expected,
I soon found fresh elk tracks ; it was too late, however, to follow them, and, after making a *détour*, I
headed back for camp. On my way hither I came
across an ungainly-looking creature, which I soon
made out to be a porcupine, and with little trouble
I got a shot at and wounded it. Unfortunately
" Ned " did not " down charge," but, despite my
loudest shouting, went straight at the brute, and
severely did the poor old dog get punished for his
disobedience. A yell of pain, and a very precipitate

retreat showed that the porcupine had made good use of its natural means of defence. Poor " Ned " was stuck full of quills—his mouth, cheeks, and fore-legs appearing like a pincushion. With some diffi-culty I got him back to camp, and then, as may be imagined, we had truly a nice job to extract the quills. Luckily I had some nippers, and with these, and with the aid of Griff Evans's firmly-planted incisor teeth, we contrived to get most of them out of the lips and cheeks of the poor suffering dog. By the time we had finished with his head we had had quite enough, and, thinking that he would be able to take them out for himself from his paws and legs, we were glad to leave these for his own treatment. But it appeared afterwards that his patience was not like ours, and instead of extracting the quills whole, he had bitten them off short, and consequently the points worked in, and made him lame for many a long day.

This porcupine is not the same variety as the South African and Indian (*Nystrix cristata*), but is, I believe, the urson, or Canadian porcupine (*Erethizon dorsatum*). Its flesh is said to be very fairly good, and in request among the Indians. It is supposed by many that they possess the power of shooting out their quills clear of the body, and it would seem as if Longfellow shared in this opinion, for he writes in " Hiawatha : "—

> " From a hollow tree the hedge-hog
> With his sleepy eyes look'd at him,
> Shot his shining quills like arrows."

But from what I saw and heard from others, I think this is a mistaken idea ; the fact is that the quills can be very easily detached, and being very pointed and sharp, the moment anything comes in contact with them, they are left sticking in that object. If not removed at once they work in with wonderful quickness, and cause great suffering, and even danger.

But to resume—during my absence Griff, after making camp, had discovered that the spot we had fixed on was a complete swamp, and that there was nothing for it but to move! Truly a delightful prospect! bad enough for a weak-handed party in broad daylight, but with the light fast failing, and a second time in the same day; it was really enough to make one sit down and greet. But it had to be done, so to work we set. First of all we had to lay hands on those ill-conditioned and mule-like bronchos, who evidently considered that any further call on their services was most unwarrantable and not to be endured, and resisted to their utmost; but Griff's blandishments and tact at last prevailed, and my own especial pony, who seemed to be the ringleader in the obstruction, was at length caught and bridled. With her the resistance ceased, and the other two soon gave in. Then we had to repack, and as the distance to the new camping-ground was only a few hundred yards, we naturally thought it unnecessary to make the packs very secure. Unfortunately, in that short distance we had to cross the creek, and all the things which could possibly fall off took the opportunity of doing so, generally at the exact moment when they were over the rushing water. Amongst them was my box of rifle cartridges, and a nice soaking it got. By this time it was dark, and we

had to grope about for everything in a most dis-
heartening and wearisome manner; but with all our
endeavours we failed in recovering that night all we
had lost, and some things were never found at all.
We were completely beat by all these trials and
exertions, and at last we found ourselves, as Griff
called it, "quite played out," and that before we
had begun to get our second camp made. We were
so exhausted that we could scarcely collect enough
wood for a fire at which to warm ourselves
and cook some meat, without even attempting to
repitch the tent or unpack any of the things.
Fortunately the evening was fine, though bitterly
cold; what was now to be done? we must get some
shelter and warmth for the night somehow. As
it happened, on our way up in the morning we had
met a young trapper whom we believed to be living
in a hut somewhere up this creek, but where we had no
idea; supper had, however, refreshed us much, and
we thought the best thing we could do would be to
try and find him out, and get shelter with him.
Following the creek for about a quarter of a mile,
we most luckily came on the hut, at the door of
which we knocked loudly, but for some time
without any answer. At last a sleepy voice re-
sponded, and we raised the latch and went in. A
curious sight awaited us, which by the fitful blaze
of the waning fire we could just make out. The
interior of the hut seemed to be about twenty-five
feet square. On one side were arranged against the
wall two "bunks" or berths, in one of which slept
a woman; in the other, the young trapper. On the
earth floor, beside the woman, were five little children rolled up in blankets like so many mummies;

no article of furniture was visible, save a broken
chair or two. Griff soon explained our business, and we were at once asked by both of the
adult inmates to make ourselves at home in the best
way we could, which we forthwith proceeded to
do. Griff had brought up our blankets, and we
were soon deposited at full length on the mud floor,
too thankful for the shelter and warmth. After
the hard day's work I looked forward to having a
good sleep; but this was not to be, for soon after
I had laid down such an attack of acute cramp
seized me that I was forced to spring up and
elongate my lengthy limbs to their utmost,
to the great astonishment of the rest of the
party, who were awoke and could not make out
what ailed me. This occurred twice during the
night, causing the sharpest suffering, besides de-
priving me of much-needed rest. At early dawn
the children began to crawl about, and would no
doubt have proceeded to a closer investigation of
the "strangers" had it not been for "Ned," who
slept by me, and showed unmistakable signs of not
appreciating a nearer acquaintance with the little
ones. I must confess that this was much to my
inward satisfaction, and, as I found out afterwards,
to Griff's also. But I could not help feeling sorry
for these poor little creatures, such bright, happy
little beings, but so wretchedly clothed, and some of
them suffering from such racking coughs.

The poor woman's lot was a hard one. It
appeared that her husband, named Rose, had been a
preacher somewhere down the Platte. Unable to
make his livelihood at his calling, he had entered
into partnership with the young trapper, Curly

Rogers, and had migrated in the summer to this hut, in the neighbourhood of which, he was told, there were plenty of furs to be got. During the summer they had been just able to get along, but had saved nothing. Rose was now away at Laramie city, selling a small quantity of furs, and buying stores for his wife and family. He had now been gone some time, and had it not been for his partner, I don't know how his poor family could have existed.

As we shall have much to do with this said partner, I will give his description now. Curly was a native of the State of Michigan, but had been out west since early childhood. Though, after the manner of the country, called a "boy," he was about seventeen years old, and looked more ; he was light-built, hardy and keen, and, although rough in manner, and not a first-class trapper or a good shot, was yet a very useful man about camp. He possessed the pleasing quality of being always cheery, and I never saw him out of temper. On the present occasion he showed anxiety to be useful, and, now that this most miserable night was over, Griff suggested that he should be engaged to come with us, which was arranged.

At the break of day we returned to our own baggage, and got some breakfast. After which Curly showed us the best place for a camp, which had evidently been often used for the same purpose before. Things looked better, and all seemed straight sailing now, so after breakfast Curly and I started off to hunt for elk, leaving Griff in camp to get the tent pitched and the other things a little in order. Curly thought our best "show" (Angl., chance)

was on the mountain sides down the park. He had
seen yesterday fresh tracks of elk thereabouts, and
did not think they were far off, so thither we bent
our steps.

Not long after we had taken the brae and got
into the timber our ears were greeted with a cry
peculiarly strange and quite unlike anything I had
ever heard before; it put me in mind of a large
penny whistle, on which a proficient was prac-
tising his scales. Anything more unlike the roar
of a gigantic stag I could not have conceived;
such, however, it was—the roaring, or as it is here
called, the "whistling" of a bull elk (stag wapiti).
Once aware of the cause, the sound had a wonderfully exciting effect on my nerves. It was very
weird, wild, and peculiar, but I certainly should have
expected louder things from so colossal an animal.
As the beast seemed to be at no great distance
we now proceeded with the greatest caution, peering
into every hollow and opening, and using the glass
freely. At last, on looking over a low ridge, as
pretty a sight broke on us as it is ever the lot of the
hunter to enjoy. In a small hollow about 500 yards
below us, was quietly grazing a "band" or herd of
about thirty wapiti; about twenty-five of which
were cows (hinds), the remainder bulls (stags).
Amongst the latter was one decided master stag,—a
real "boss,"—and three or four small ones, which
were being driven away by the "boss" whenever
they approached the cows. I sat watching them
for some time, with my glass, as they fed up a slope.
They moved and behaved in every way exactly like
our own red deer, in fact, I almost knew what they
were going to do next, from having so often and closely

observed the latter under similar circumstances. How I enjoyed this my first intimate acquaintance with wapiti! and how keen I was to have the big bull and none other! *Dis aliter visum!*

As soon as the last of the herd had fed over a small ridge we followed on very carefully, and, the wind being right, we were able to crawl in right amongst them. They were lying down close on the other side of the ridge; the cows were all around us, some of them within thirty yards, and lying quite "canny." I could see the smaller bulls plainly enough, and within easy shot, but where was the big bull? The old villain—as so often happens in deerstalking—had taken himself off, and was lying down somewhere out of sight. My young and keen friend Curly was all for "getting a stand on" (Angl., having a go in at) the cows or small bulls, but I restrained him, hoping there might still be a chance of the big bull. A puff of wind came, and betrayed us to some small outlying bulls which we had not observed. Away they went, and being in sight of our lot communicated to them the scare, and very "good time they all made" of it, considering their great size and weight. I had hoped that in the first scurry I might get a sight of the big bull, but he never showed again, and the band got off without a shot, very much to Curly's disgust. He acknowledged, however, afterwards that I was right in not shooting the cows or small bulls, and that my ill-fortune was due to bad luck, and not to bad hunting. We then tried to follow the band, but in vain. They were quickly amongst the thick timber and well away for the main divide.

Later in the day I got a long snap-shot at a bull

elk going through the timber, but without success,
and eventually we returned homewards once more
with heavy hearts.

The day, which had been beautiful, changed towards evening, and it began to "storm" heavily
before we had got far towards camp. It was a long
and tiring trudge back, but when we got there we
found that Griff had got all fixed up in "elegant"
form, and I passed an excellent night after a capital
supper.

The next day after breakfast we found to our
dismay that all the bronchos had "skinned out"
(Angl., bolted); the food had been too scarce,
covered as it was with so much snow, and they
had made for clearer ground. I did not want to
lose a day's hunting by this untoward event, so
leaving Griff to track and recover them, if he
could, I took Curly with me and started off for
the high timber on the mountain-side behind our
camp.

It recommenced storming very soon after we
started, and, as there was already nearly two feet of
snow on the ground, the travelling was very
fatiguing. Here and there sharp ledges of the
volcanic rock protruded through the snow, the intervening spaces being filled up by drifted masses;
the falling into these was mercifully soft—for fall
we did, and that pretty often.

Not very far from camp we struck on two large
bull-elk tracks quite fresh, leading straight up the
mountain. With the wind as it was—pretty nearly
in the direction they were travelling—we ought to
have known better than to have attempted to follow
them; but our blood was hot after our hunt of

o

yesterday and up we went. What a climb we had
of it! The mountain-side was steeper than any
house-roof I ever saw, and the footing almost as
difficult; and after all we never even saw our game.
Time after time we came to where they had stopped
only a few minutes before, and probably looked
down on us in our labours, and then had quietly
continued their own comparatively easy ascent as
soon as we got within dangerous proximity. This
wild-goose chase we continued until the timber line
was nearly reached (12,000 feet), when we came
to the conclusion that they had made up their minds
to cross the divide into the Laramie Valley, and
decided upon abandoning the severe and disheart-
ening stern chase.

On our way back Curly showed me where he
had successfully " set a rifle trap " for bear during
the past summer. It was made by securing a
loaded rifle at full cock to a tree, with the muzzle
pointed at an elk's carcase. Round the bait was
stretched a cord about a foot off the ground made
fast at one end to the trigger of the rifle, so that
nothing could meddle with the carcase without
setting off the rifle. By this arrangement Curly
had killed one bear and severely wounded another.
A fine golden eagle had also fallen a victim, and
lay now untouched, where it fell, but too far gone
for preserving.

When we got back to camp we were relieved to
find that Griff had recovered the ponies. He had
found them about four miles further down the park,
beside a swampy creek which had barred their progress towards better pastures.

The next day I took Griff with me for a hunt, and

worked the ground to the southward. After some little time we struck and followed the trail of a couple of bull elk, and presently found them feeding in the timber; but luck was still against me, for, as we were getting well in for a quiet shot, one of our miserable ponies—which we had dismounted and left some little way off—suddenly appeared on the scene and put the deer away at a gallop; a scrambling, running, hurried chance was all I got, and this I missed.

But we were not destined to go back to camp meatless, for shortly after this we came across the fresh tracks of a small band of elk, which we followed into the thick green timber we had hunted on the first day. Very soon after entering this they seemed to have dispersed and broken into small groups in a very unusual manner. Under these circumstances it was most difficult to do any good with them, as they were continually " on the lope" and scaring one another. Eventually we came across a very fine old cow elk alone, which we at once made sure of, the meat of the cow being thought very superior and a great delicacy. Evans had got my large eight-bore gun loaded with spherical ball, and not thinking that I had seen the animal as well as himself fired at the same moment as I did; his bullet entered the neck, and on its way thither cut down a small fir-tree. My express, too, had shot truly, striking the elk just below the shoulder; both were fatal shots, and the poor beast never stirred from the spot. So at last we had got some elk meat, and of the finest quality; but I am free to confess that I should have much preferred a bull, with less good meat and a head with horns.

The next morning I was out early with Evans on
the mountain-side to the northward of the camp.
We soon struck elk tracks, and as they were fresh
we followed them on.   After some time it became
evident that we were quite close on a band of bulls,
and as the wind was all right and the trail lay
through timber more or less dense, we did not know
the moment we might "jump" them.   This excitement continued all the afternoon, until it became so
dark as to compel us to think of making back tracks
for camp.   Before doing so, however, feeling that
the band could not be far off, I ascended a little rise,
and fired off my rifle to see if it would disturb anything within sight.   It was a "happy thought" of
Griff's, for scarcely had the sound died away before
there appeared on a small hillock about three-
quarters of a mile off a band of eight magnificent
bull elk, a glorious sight indeed.   There they were,
grand beasts, behaving just like a herd of red
deer stags, running after and poking each other and
playing about on the top of the bare knoll like so
many great kittens.   They were but little scared,
for they had not seen us, and did not seem to have
any idea what the alarming sound was, or where it
had come from.

We sat watching them for some little time, full of
wishes for a couple of hours' more day-light, but
it was now getting hopelessly dark, so the best
thing we could do was to leave them in quiet possession, and hope that we might find them on the
morrow ; we turned our weary footsteps to where
we had left our ponies, and thence had a ten-mile
ride in intense cold to camp.   This ride was very
nearly a bad business for me ; my feet—shod in

English shooting-boots—had got damp in the snow, half melted by the rays of the sun, and during the ride home had got partially frozen; they were quite benumbed at first, but after many and vigorous rubbings with coal-oil (paraffine) and keeping them in a compress of the same, pain set in, and no further harm resulted than the loss of skin, and more or less pain for many subsequent months. It was a lesson to me, however, which I did not forget. Henceforth I wore nothing but " gum boots,"—that is, boots made of indiarubber, which I had luckily sent for by L. to Laramie,—and with the most satisfactory results.

As may be imagined, the next morning was like that of the 1st of September in old Eton days. Very early was our start, and " You bet, Sirree," no time was lost in getting back to where we had seen the band of bulls the previous evening. We then soon " took the trail " and followed it some little way, but finding it was leading us up towards the ridge of the divide, we thought it would be more advisable to try and find them by sight. After some hours " speer-ing " about the open spaces in the timber, we were gladdened by the sight of the whole band quietly feed-ing on a very steep part of the mountain-side. They were undoubtedly our friends of the previous evening, the same in number and with the same remarkably fine heads, one in particular making my heart flutter.

Now came the real excitement of the stalk. Leav-ing our bronchos well hidden in some thick timber, we sat down, and, " made propositions " as to how the stalk was to be made, how the wind was there, &c., &c. Griff showed himself an old and experienced hand, and having settled our plans, away we started.

At first some thick timber hid us well from view, but after getting through this, between it and the base of the steep hill on the side of which were the elk, we had to take the open. The quantity of loose stones and dead timber afforded

"MY FIRST WAPITI."

From a Sketch by A. P. V.

us some shelter, but being covered with snow they made the travelling difficult and tiring, and I was glad enough to get on to the firm ground of the hill-side, steep as it was. Having toiled up this to a level at least as high, if not higher, than where the elk were, we took advantage of some scattered

undergrowth to reach unobserved a ridge of broken
and rocky ground, which abutted on to the edge of
a very steep gorge, or "gulch." Arrived here at
last, we knew the deer were on the opposite side of
the gulch, but could not be certain of their exact
distance or whereabouts. Cautiously peering along
the edge of a rock, I saw within 150 yards of
me a magnificent bull elk, the nearest of the
band. Under ordinary circumstances I should have
been well satisfied to have got such a chance, but I
had seen a monster head with the band and knew
that this was not it, and my heart was set on possessing that if possible. As is so often—one may
almost say always—the case in deer-stalking, the
largest beast was not the nearest. On the present
occasion I soon made out my grand head, bent in
feeding about fifty yards or more beyond the nearest
of the herd. But there was no chance of getting
any nearer; the gulch was too bare of cover to get
into without being seen, and the nearest elk commanded it completely. Nothing therefore was to
be done but to settle down for a shot from where I
was, and "tak' him noo." How it came on to storm
just at this momentous crisis! the keen wind blew
the frozen snow into my eyes and face until they
smarted again with pain, but the excitement was too
intense to think of such trifles at the time. My one
thought was to get the big head, and I did not care
what I suffered so long as I could draw a steady bead
on my beauty. Getting myself into the best position I could, I pulled off as steadily as for a bull's-
eye at a thousand yards. Bang went the rifle, but
the big brute never stirred; a moment more and he
moved forward a yard or so, but in that short move-

ment I was able to see that he had got the ball
well, and at once turned my attention to the first
bull, who was standing quite still, trying to make
out what caused the alarm. Taking him with
my second barrel, I had the satisfaction of hearing him tumble into the gulch, setting all the
stones rattling as he fell. Reloading, I fired
again at the large elk, who was now bolting away
with the rest of the herd; whether I hit him or not,
I do not know, but he disappeared with the rest.
Without stopping to gralloch, or even look at the
second beast, we started off in pursuit of the " boss."
There was no difficulty in taking his track in the
heavy snow, he was bleeding so freely; but we
were rather too rash in our pursuit, and rushed into
sight as he lay about 300 yards off, and away he
bolted again. He now left the trail of the rest of the
band, and turning down the hill laid down amongst
some timber. I was then able to stalk in pretty close,
and to give him the *coup de grâce*, but not without
some trouble, as the vitality of the elk is very great,
and as long as life is in them care must be taken not
to give them an opportunity for a charge.

This was truly a magnificent beast! such a grand
head of fourteen points; and what splendid points
they were! the largest of them measured twenty-
eight inches in length! The circumference of the
horn round the coronet was twelve inches, and the
greatest " timber " (Angl., beam or girth) was half
an inch more. It was a very regular head, which is
somewhat unusual in wapiti, the horns very often
having curious growths and excrescences, probably
arising from injuries when soft and young. After
gralloching the big beast we turned back to the

other, which proved to be a very fine one, but his

A "RIGHT AND LEFT."

A LARGE SCOTCH RED DEER HEAD.
Drawn on same scale as Wapiti above.

points were a good deal damaged by the fall into
the gulch. Griff judged the weights to be about

600 pounds each (over forty-two stone) when "dressed" (Angl., clean).

We had a long pull back to camp, and encountered some very severe squalls of wind and snow, but what did the weather signify after such sport?

We had a little excitement, too, on the way in the shape of a strange camp fire about a mile off our track, and some little distance out on the plain. Judging from its position, so far away from the timber, Griff did not think it was likely to be a white man's camp, nor was it likely to be Indians here in North Park. We did not care, however, about investigating further, being only two of us, and curiously enough we never heard afterwards a satisfactory explanation of the unwelcome vision.

Elated with yesterday's success, I was away early next day with Griff to the southward of our camp, and after some hours' hunting sighted on the outskirts of some timber a little band of elk, consisting of one good bull and a few cows. They had evidently seen us, and were uneasy, so leaving Griff with the ponies to keep their attention, I proceeded to stalk them by myself. From the commanding position they occupied I was unable to get nearer than about 250 yards, and then, seeing that they were about to move, I took a quiet pull at the bull. My first barrel missed him, but he stood still for a moment, and with my second I had the satisfaction of seeing that I had decidedly scored. Off they all started, the bull with the rest, but after following the track some little way, we found that he had parted from the cows. This is generally an unmistakable sign of a severe wound, and so it proved to be in this case; for although I had a long piece of tracking, I got him at last, after having "jumped" him four times, each time, except the last, with scarcely a chance of a shot. The head was a good one, though nothing like those of yesterday, nor was his body so heavy.

The next day was spent by Griff and the Swede, Martin—who had now rejoined us after taking L. to Laramie—in getting the heads, &c., to camp. When this was accomplished it was too late to move camp, as had been our intention, for the weather had now become so severe and threatening, that we deemed it advisable to get down to a less elevated region, lest such a fall of snow should come as might cut us off from civilization. If this had happened we should have been obliged to abandon the waggon and our poor horses, the latter to perish of cold and hunger, while we ourselves would have had to to get out, on snow-shoes, as best we could.

The next morning we made a very early start with all our goods and chattels from our encampment on the "Big Sandy," as the creek was called. Although the weather was intensely cold, and further delay was full of risk, I was very sorry to leave; I had had such capital sport in this locality, and we had become so comfortably settled. I had grown quite fond even of the poor "Whiskey Jacks" ("Clark's crow," *corvus* or *picicorvus Columbianus*), which so often associate themselves with camp life in the Rocky Mountains. In shape and size these busy birds are more like magpies or jays than crows, and reminded me much in their behaviour and movements of our black and white friends in the old country. The plumage is a sort of drab grey of various shades. We had always from three to five about our camp here, taking a most lively interest in all our proceedings, and ready to come down and peck at any scraps which might be thrown away while the cooking or feeding was progressing. Finding they were not interfered with, they became so tame that they used to perch and sit within a few yards of us. Their notes were lively and cheery, and any noise was welcome in these lonely wilds. The poor birds are often shot at by way of practice for the six-shooter, and then become wild and canny. They are found only in elevated regions, rarely descending below a 3,000-feet altitude.

It was now the second week in November, and the cold was getting more severe every day. The winter storms had begun in earnest, and the weather in which we moved from the Big Sandy to Old Man Pinkham's was truly a caution. Almost from the very commencement it stormed, and we had to fight the whole of the way against a cutting snow, propelled by the keenest north-east wind. Griff would not stop for baiting or rest in the twenty or twenty-five miles, fearing that the horses would freeze. At times we could not see at all, the driving frozen snow was too blinding and cutting, and the cold was so intense that it was all we could do to keep ourselves from freezing. As it was, I lost the skin off my ears, although they were well tied over, and Griff was knocked up for many a day afterwards. When about six miles from Pinkham's we passed the minister, Rose, in a little open cart drawn by a mule and a pony, in which were his wretched wife and the four small children, rolled up in some scanty bedding at the bottom. How that poor woman and her infant offspring ever got through that awful day I cannot imagine; but they did, and moreover, two days later, crossed the Divide into the Laramie Valley, in the warmer clime of which they intended to pass the winter. One of our wheelers, Nell, "played out" (Angl., "broke down") within two miles of Pinkham's, and we were obliged to leave her to weather that night as best she could. I was very sorry to do so, but we could not help it; for no one could stand the cold to stand by and coax her on, through such a storm as this. We hardly knew whether the poor beast would be alive in the morning, but contrary to the prevailing opinion of the inmates of the ranche, she was alive, and able to walk in to the shed which served for stables. She seemed, however, never to recover from the effects of that journey, and was not of much use during the rest of our hunt.

The next four days we remained at the ranche for the benefit both of ourselves and of the stock, and I was here able to lighten our load by leaving the wapiti heads and hides, to be sent from here to Laramie city, thence to be "expressed" eastwards for preservation. It was a great amusement to me superintending the packing, and talking over the trophies, and I will take this opportunity of saying a few words on this splendid representative of the deer tribe, of which I had now got such good specimens. The wapiti (*cervus Canadensis*), usually misnamed out here the "elk," is essentially the red deer of America, as the caribou is the reindeer, and the moose the elk, only with the wapiti the similarity with the European representative, except the size, is even more marked than in the case of the other two.

As far as I could ascertain, its habits are identical with our red deer. The "bulls" (or stags) go with

WAPITI FEEDING.

From a Sketch by A. Bierstadt.

the "cows" (or hinds) till the rutting commences, about the beginning of October. This season lasts about six weeks, after which the bulls keep by themselves in small "bands" or herds. As I have on other occasions observed of deer in foreign climes, they recover their condition very quickly after the rutting season is over, which is doubtless owing to the superior quality of pasture compared with that which our own red deer can obtain, and it is a merciful provision of nature that the spring is far advanced before their constitutions are called upon to bear another strain in growing their colossal horns, which do not become sufficiently hard to allow of the velvet being shed

WAPITI ON THE PRAIRIE.

(From a Sketch by A. Bierstadt.)

Chapter IX., page 205.

before the beginning of August. From this time to the commencement of the rutting season, the bulls are in their best condition. In colour they are a rich reddish brown, with very dark, almost black, points. A full-grown bull will stand from fifteen to sixteen hands in height, and will weigh about forty stone " clean," and a good cow will weigh nearly thirty stone. The meat of the cow is considered of finer quality than that of the bull, and remains good all through the winter.

Wapiti are, I believe, easily domesticated, but when in that state the bulls are said to be very unsafe during the rutting season. I heard of a man in the Eastern States being caught when crossing an enclosure in which some were confined, and having been rescued with the greatest difficulty from the attack of a savage stag. Good mocassins, or rather leggings, are made out of the skin of the hind leg, peeled off for a few inches above and below the hocks, the bend of the hock forming the heel of the boot. I found the wapiti as difficult to stalk as red deer, but I believe when in large herds they are not so wary, and do not get under way so rapidly, as when alone, or in small lots. When in motion they are not so swift as smaller deer, and on this account it is sometimes easy, when they are massed together, to obtain what the hunters call "a stand," that is, a chance of firing an unlimited number of shots into the brown before they can get sufficiently far away to be out of shot. I have heard of as many as seventeen of all sorts and kinds—bulls, cows, and calves—being killed in this way on one occasion by a single repeating rifle—an unsportsmanlike proceeding

well calculated to hasten the extermination of this
the handsomest of the deer tribe.

Old Man Pinkham's had been somewhat trans-
mogrified in the short time since we were here on
our way up the park. The "old man" was away on a
hunt after what are called here "bison," in distinction
to the buffalo of the plain, but of this hereafter.
The ranche had been turned into a sort of inn, and was
"run" (Angl., conducted) by a Frenchman and his
wife. The solitary room had been divided in half
by a thin board partition, to make it, I suppose,
rather more private for the wife; but the numbers
who slept under this roof were such that very little
privacy could be secured even under these new conditions.

Here I parted with the Swede and engaged a man
from La Porte, on the Cache la Poudre, by name
Edward Herridge, together with his waggon and
team of horses. "Edd," as he was called, was a
native of Devonshire, but had emigrated here when
only a few years old. It would seem that from
earliest boyhood he had been a regular *Weltkind*,
having run away from his parents when very young,
and since then spent his life in wandering on horseback—or "packing," as he called it—through most
of the Western States. He had gone through a
very varied experience of hardship and excitement,
and although still a fine and well-made man, and
only about thirty-five years of age, yet from the
many serious accidents which had befallen him, and
from the hard life he had led, he was much weak-
ened both in physical strength and constitution.
He and Griff now formed my paid retinue, but
besides them I had two volunteers, friends of Edd,

who were anxious to see the country I was about to
visit, and in return for being fed by me rendered
such services as cooking and camp work, besides
occasionally assisting in the hunt. These two men
were called Lee and Hank. The former was a well-
made, active young fellow of about thirty, who had
originally been brought up in a druggist's shop
" down east," but had preferred a wild western
life of sometimes mining, sometimes hunting, to the
tame routine of civilization. He, too, had seen
some wild work. In self-defence he had been
obliged to shoot two white men, one in a card row,
the other about a cow. One of these unfortunates
was killed on the spot ; the other still lived, and, it
was believed, waited for revenge. He was a good-
natured, obliging fellow, and I never had any occasion to find fault with him. The other volunteer,
Hank, although under thirty years of age, had
already seen more roughing and hardships than fall
usually to the lot of even a frontier man. He had
done a great deal of what is called " freighting," that
is, carrying goods for the Government or private
traders from the railway stations to outlying posts.
In his wanderings he had seen much, and had it not
been for his excessive use of the strongest western
phraseology, he would have been a very entertaining
companion. Hank was our cook, and a very good
and enterprising one he was. So after Curly Rogers
left us, on Cow Creek, a little further down the
Platte, we mustered five hands all told, and this
was our strength through my subsequent hunting
campaign.

For nearly two months from this time I did
scarcely anything but hunt. Those, therefore, of

my readers who do not care for this amusement would do well, according to Bacon's advice, to taste and not digest the pages devoted to my sporting adventures, until Rawling's Spring, on the U.P.R., is reached.

Whilst my stock and outfit were recruiting and refitting at Pinkham's, I went up the park with my new acquaintance, Hank, to fetch down the first elk I had killed. The weather had been so intensely cold that there was no fear of its having been spoiled by its lengthened sojourn on the hill; in fact, so severe was the frost now, that all the meat required for cooking, had to be chopped with an axe. So far from being detrimental to the quality, this freezing process appeared to improve it both in tenderness and flavour, and to make it far better than the same meat killed during the warmer season and eaten fresh; I found that this was a fact well known to hunters.

We had about eleven or twelve miles to drive from Pinkham's before we turned off the plain towards the mountains where the elk lay. The snow being very deep our progress was slow, and it was late in the afternoon before we reached the stream which we had to follow towards the high ground where we were to camp for the night. Arrived here we took the horses out, made a fire, and cooked some meat. Whilst Hank was so employed I thought I would have a little hunt in the surrounding timber. I soon struck some fresh tracks, and, keeping a sharp look-out, was speedily gratified by seeing four large bull elk browsing in an open place about half a mile off. Unfortunately, they were in a very commanding position, and I

soon saw that the most I could do would be to get
a long shot from the opposite ridge, and that that
could only be done if I could get unseen into the
hollow below. Marking the ground carefully, I proceeded to carry out my ideas; but when I got on to
the nearest ridge I found the distance from the elk
was further even than I had expected, and that they
were still at least two hundred and fifty yards
off. Seeing, however, that I could not get any
nearer, I determined to make the best of it, and,
picking out the bull with the finest head, I waited till
he gave me his broadside, and then pulled off
steadily. Away dashed the four big beasts into the
thick timber, every one of them apparently uninjured. Faithful, however, to a good old practice, I
went to the spot and took their tracks, to satisfy
myself that I had not scored. I had not gone very
far on the trail before an occasional crimson shilling
lay on the pure white snow, and then a little
further on a large splotch of gore showed that the
deer had received a fatal wound; then a few hundred yards more, and my eyes were greeted with
the sight of the grand beast lying on the snow.
He was not quite dead, however, for he quickly
jumped on to his legs, and I, as quickly, put a tree
between him and me; but he soon fell again and
died without another shot. He proved a very fine
beast, with a magnificent head of thirteen points.
After discussing with Hank an appetising meal of
antelope venison, we proceeded to gralloch him, and
then set out to look for the small log cabin which
was described as being somewhere in this locality,
and in which it was our intention to pass the night.
We searched for it as long and as closely as we could,

for the weather was fearfully cold, and we neither
of us fancied an *al fresco* camp in such threatening
weather; but no hut could be found, so, when darkness came on, we had to seek the waggon, and make
the best arrangement we could for a night in the open.
Another meal of fresh-baked bread and meat and
tea, and then we settled down for the night. With
my Old Country prejudices against sleeping on the
ground, I preferred the waggon covered over with
the sheet, whilst Hank—a very old campaigner—
spread his blankets on the frozen ground, close to
the immense pitch-pine fire, and I feel pretty sure he
had the best of it; for the wind certainly did come
up through the chinks and cracks of that mean
old waggon, and mighty cold I was before the
morning broke. Hank appeared comfortable enough
when he aroused from his slumbers, and had no
complaints to make. On the contrary, he was full
of congratulations that it had not stormed during
the night, and that it had been so fine and quiet.

Besides being a good cook, he was a very cheery
fellow, and whiled away the time pleasantly enough
during meals with stories of his experience in
freighting, of which he had done much to and from
the mines and the Indian "agencies." These "agencies" are Government posts, at which the Redskins
reside during winter, and where they are fed and
clothed by the Government on condition of good
behaviour. According to all accounts, the robberies perpetrated by the officials of these posts at the
expense of the Indians have been scandalously great,
and this is, I believe, one of the principal sources of
the hostile feeling which now exists between the two
races. The Indians have been promised so many

A SIOUX CAMP NEAR LARAMIE PEAK.

(From a Sketch by A. BIERSTADT.)

Chapter IX., page 213.

thousand blankets, or whatever else it may have been, by the Government on certain specified conditions, which the Indians on their part generally honourably carry out. And so, too, would the United States Government were they not baffled by their *employés*, who, after the money has been voted by Congress, subject it to a regular system of blackmail as it were, on its way to the Redskin. Of the rascality practised, every one who travels through this country and comes in contact with the frequenters of posts, will probably hear enough. It would appear as if the Indian Bureau from top to bottom has been mismanaged and corrupt. Even after the blankets and clothing have been purchased and sent to the agencies, the Indian rarely gets them without paying for them, nor, when paid for, are they of the quality intended by the "White Father." I have been told too that goods sent as free gifts by Government are often sold by the officials to the Indians actually before they have been unloaded from the waggon in which they have been brought to the post, and that a single blanket is not unfrequently cut in half and sold as two.

So much for dishonesty; now for mismanagement. Last year, I heard from a man who freighted for the Government to the Red Cloud Agency in the Blackhills, that at the time the United States were at war with a portion of the Sioux, under the leadership of the famous "Sitting Bull," by some means or other the squaws at this Sioux agency were enabled to draw rations for 13,000 mouths, whereas there were not half that number of Indians here. The surplus, however, was useful to the Indians, as it assisted to support "Sitting Bull" and his band in their difficulties with the troops, and as a climax, it is said to have been conveyed to the warriors on horses stolen from the whites ! The horses " run off " by Indians last year in that district alone amounted to no less than ten thousand ! So said my informant, and I can quite believe it, judging from the many stories of similar purport which reached me from all sides. It is alleged that the number of the United States troops is so miserably small, having regard to the posts they have to occupy, that the local commanders are afraid of dealing out even justice to the white and the Indian alike. The whites complain that if Indians steal their horses or stock near a post where the troops are few and the Indians numerous, they get no redress from the commandant from his fear of creating a disturbance, and are obliged to put up with the loss. My informant himself was engaged in " freighting " to a Government agency, when, on one of his journeys, he was met by some Indians at a short distance from the post. One of them claimed one of his horses, my friend objected, and the case came before the commandant. The Indian stated that the horse had been stolen from him two years before ; the white man proved that the horse had been in his own possession over three years. But the Indians were numerous and independent, and the troops but few ; so it was thought politic to decide in favour of the Indian !

Such cases naturally create and keep up a very sore feeling on the part of the white settlers towards the Indians, and one hears frequent vows of vengeance to be taken on the Redskins should this system continue. I am not going to dogmatize on the Indian question. My stay in the country was too short to enable me to get more than a cursory insight into the case as between the United States people, the Government, and the Indians. As far as I could gather, I believe that Congress, as the representatives of the people, mean to be just and fair in their dealings with the Indians; but that their intentions have been hitherto most extensively thwarted by the slackness and corruption of the Indian Department or Bureau. The poor Indians are the chief sufferers by this; a great deal of the money voted to ameliorate their conquered condition feathers the nests of the officials and subordinates. No wonder then that they cease to believe in the white man's promises.

There is another cause which has created much ill blood between the two races. Certain parts of the country are assigned to different tribes on condition of their resigning their rights to their natural possessions which may be required for settling or other purposes. These assigned districts are called " reservations," and are guaranteed by the United States Government. It often happens that in a short time the population of settlers has increased largely and that it has overflowed into the assigned districts, perhaps from stock runs or minerals having been opened out. In either of these events the Indian must go, *nolens volens*, and the Government will scarcely have a voice in the matter. Naturally enough, this process of expulsion will not be carried out without strong remonstrance on the part of the Indians. They rightly look upon it as a breach of faith, and set themselves to work to oppose it by force. Then follow massacres—whenever a white man is killed it is called a "massacre"—reprisals, and all the horrors of Indian warfare. Troops are collected, and a campaign takes place, in which not unfrequently, being inferior in numbers and no better armed, the soldiers are at first severely "whipped." A bad precedent is thus established, and the well-armed, independent, and brave Indians are encouraged to resist and prolong a miserable war which can have but one issue. This system, together with the frauds committed against them in the matter of supplies, has created a feud between the mass of the Indians and the whites which can, it is feared, only end with the extinction of most of the 320,000 Indians now still existing in the United States territory.

Very disparaging comparisons are often made as against the United States Government, in contrasting our management of the Indians in Canada and theirs here. I dare say there is a great deal of truth in what is said. For instance, the Dominion Government does not—as has actually happened with the United States Government—undertake to supply the Indians with good cattle, worth $40 each, and allow a contractor to give them Texan brutes worth $11 each, which the Indians are obliged, in self-defence, to shoot the day after delivery. But, on the other hand the flow of settlers into Canada is very different from that into the States; consequently lands in Canada are not so keenly desired, nor have mining discoveries been made there, possessing the same force of attraction as in the States. The Dominion Government has not therefore been brought into the same immediate contact with the Indians, nor consequently had the same difficulties to deal with. When the time comes that

this Government shall require for her white settlers
tracts of country now occupied in perfect freedom
by tribes as warlike as the Sioux of the north or the
Commanches of the south, then will commence her
Red Indian difficulties. Let her profit by the experience and misfortunes of the States Government,
and let her, under all trials and difficulties, continue
to practise that unswerving good faith in her inter-
course with the natives which has hitherto redounded
at once to her honour and security. If this policy be
adhered to, we may hope that the lamentable feeling
of hatred and mistrust now existing in the States
between the two races, will never be aroused to the
same extent in the Dominion. It may perhaps be
doubted whether, even under conditions the most
favourable, the entire extinction of the Red Indians
can long be delayed. It would appear as if,
wherever the whites and the red men of the West
are brought into contact, diseases and the accursed fire-water do their work and carry off the
Indians with fearful rapidity. Maladies which are
not fatal to the white man attack his red brother
with the virulence of the plague; hence the Indians are diminishing so rapidly that, without any
extraordinary causes, we shall soon have them only
known and handed down to us by the works of
historians and novelists as the most pugnacious and
enduring, but at the same time the most cruel and
cunning, of nature's warriors. Attempts have been
made to induce them to take to agriculture, and, I
believe, in some cases with partial success; but, as
a rule, they are too fond of their wild, marauding life
to settle down to peaceful labour, at any rate so long
as they are able to procure meat and hides sufficient

for a bare subsistence, and **for** the purchase
of rifles and other necessaries only to be procured
from the posts and settlements. Some few tribes,
such as the Shoshones, appear to be too lazy to
follow any sort of active life; they would rather
exist from hand to mouth, and pass a miserable
and precarious existence hanging about the haunts
of the white man. But these are the exception; the
vast mass of the Red Indians prefer the wild but hard,
trying life of the war-path and the hunt with all their
attendant uncertainties and dangers. If, perchance,
there exists in some of them any portion of the
energy which has enabled the native Indian of the
east of Canada to adapt himself **to** civilized life
so as to appear in some departments **of** industry
a worthy opponent of the white, **it** lies very
deep, and has not yet been "tapped;" for even in
the older States, where labour is very highly **re-**
munerated, and where any sort would be welcome
and well paid, he is an incorrigible loafer, and
seems **to** prefer a life of loitering, begging, or
pilfering to the slightest regular exertion. I am,
however, bound to add that I have had but few personal opportunities of acquainting myself with the
characters of the Red Indians, and that most of my
information is derived from conversations with
settlers and hunters, whose opinions were certainly
not exempt from prejudice.

One cannot help feeling very sorry for the unhappy
Redskin, and conscience suggests that matters might
have been very different had one's own race behaved
more wisely and justly towards him. It would seem
to be now **too** late for regrets, and that the only
problem remaining is how to make the process of

extinction as painless as possible. Let us hope that at any rate in future, those spots of refuge on his native soil will be strictly respected, and that he may be allowed to pass away quietly on them, protected as far as practicable by his "White Father" from the headlong and dispossessing energies of the irresistible settler.

CHAPTER XI.

"Oh, no life is like the mountaineer's ;
      His home is near the sky,
  Where, throned above this world, he hears
      Its strife at distance die.
  Nor only thus through summer suns
  His blithe existence cheerly runs—
      Ev'n winter, bleak and dim,
      Brings joyous hours to him ;
  When, his rifle behind him flinging,
  He watches the *wild deer* springing,
And away, o'er the hills away, re-echoes his glad 'hurra !' "

  T. Moore, " *Evenings in Greece.*"

The log cabin—Return to Pinkham's—Encampment on the
Platte—More wapiti—Bad hunting—Disagreeable adventure
—Independence Mountain—The deserted cabin—Sad history
—After Bison—" Drummer "—A spoiled stalk—No luck—
The Mountain Bison—Magnificent scenery—Doleful prognos-
tications—Encouraging gossip—" Back tracks "—Indian ex-
periences—" Bill Wale's "—Old quarters—On the move—A
puma's " cache "—The beast himself—Exciting hunt—" He's
our meat "—Great joy—A severe walk—On Beaver Creek—
A wounded wapiti—" Curly's " misbehaviour—Awful wea-
ther—A red-letter day—Almost a tragedy—Hunting for
" Griff "—Ned's " sport "—Men's amusement—Clothing—
Stimulants—A welcome return.

It was easy enough the following morning, in the
bright light of day, to find the hunting cabin, useless to us now, but looking very comfortable as I
recalled the miserable night I had passed in the old

waggon. We observed that close round the cabin door a wolverine had been prowling that very night; the tracks were quite perfect in the snow, and he seemed to have had a mind to go in at the open door. Perhaps I might have had a shot at him had we passed the night there; who knows? and I thought with regret of having for a second time missed the opportunity of getting a specimen of this quaint animal.

We got back to Pinkham's that evening, and passed almost the whole of the next morning in skinning, salting, and packing the remaining wapiti heads ready for "expressing" eastwards. This work finished, the next morning we "pulled out," and encamped on the Platte, six miles below Pinkham's, just at the entrance to the cañon through which the river passes out of North Park. The snow was so deep that our teams had had enough for one day by the time we reached this spot, and we were anxious ourselves to have a hunt amongst the neighbouring rocky ledges and forests. The Platte is here about fifty yards across, but it is by no means so voluminous as one would expect from the immense area it drains. It is a very curious thing that this river never seems to get any larger as it flows onwards, a fact much commented on by the natives, amongst whom it bears a very bad reputation for the shifty, treacherous nature of its fords. Both these traits may arise from the porous or absorbent nature of the soil over which it flows. Another peculiarity it possesses is that neither it nor any of its tributaries contain trout, whereas the South Platte and its streams abound with them—an interesting problem for naturalists.

A few hours' hunt after making camp enabled us

to find a band of elk, consisting of thirty cows and a
large and a small bull.   It was too late to attack them
that evening, so we returned to camp, having marked
well their whereabouts, which was a sheltered gulch
or dingle running down to the frozen river—and a
nice mess Edd Herridge and myself made of it when
we did "go for them!"   Early the next morning
we looked for them where we had left them, but they
had moved away in the night, and it was some little
time before we "struck" them again, on a bare ridge,
surrounded with pine forest.   We then took counsel
together and arranged how they were to be got at ;
but, unfortunately, Edd was somewhat precipitate in
his movements, and I was not cool nor decided enough
to make the best of the chance I got.   The stalk
was well conceived, but badly executed ; for, after
having got well within shot of the herd, they made
us out before we could see the bulls, and went off at
a gallop.   All I could do was to let drive at about
eighty yards at a fine cow, as we wanted meat for
camp, the bulls not being then in sight.   In consequence of the lie of the ground, after the deer had
once started, we could not see them again until
about 300 yards off, when they were all disappearing
into the thick timber.   Edd had got his American
"Sharp" with him, and after I had once fired, commenced a veritable file-fire, but the result of this
expenditure of powder was—I am ashamed to say
for my own part—none killed ;   four separate
tracks gave proof on the snow that this number of
poor beasts were wounded.   We followed the trail
for miles, but without coming up with any ; then
Edd said he would return and see if he could find
any fresh game near where we had discovered the

herd in the morning. Here he got a cow elk, which
Griff and I strongly suspected was the one I had
fired at first, as it was so close to the spot of our
first onslaught.

I followed on the tracks of the wounded deer with
Curly Rogers, until it began to storm and became
so dark that we had to make back tracks towards
camp as fast as we could. Neither of us knew
the country, and we were foolish enough to try
to get back on the frozen river through the cañon.
The ice in some places was very thick and strong,
but in other places, where the current was swift,
it was rotten and treacherous, but we got along
pretty well until we reached a spot where almost
perpendicular rocks jutted out far into the bed of
the stream. These rocks were smooth, slippery
granite, with scarcely any foothold. Curly was
afraid of the ice near them, the current being evidently very strong, so he counselled climbing the face,
to cut off the small promontory. I was willing,
but tried it in vain. I could get no foothold with
my "gum boots," and kept slipping back time after
time. Curly, shod in moccasins, was able to manage
it, but I had at last to give it up. There was then
no other course open for me but to try the ice. It
was getting quite dark now, and Curly had just said
that if we did not take care we should not make
camp that night!—a pleasant prospect with the
thermometer anything below zero, and no food or
blankets! On to the ice I went; at first it bore me
notwithstanding portentous crackings, but just as I
thought I should manage it all right, crack it went,
and in a moment I was in the freezing water. Fortunately it was not very deep, and by struggling

through the ice I reached the shore. Here I found Curly awaiting me; he had heard the crash and was on the alert. Now came the only real danger, namely, freezing. I thought the best thing to do would be to take off my long boots, empty out all the water, and substitute for it the contents of a flask of brandy, with a small deduction for the internal use of Curly and myself. Curly evidently thought that it would have been far better if the whole had gone down our throats; but my previous experience of freezing made me very careful to save myself, if possible, from a repetition. A sharp hour's walk then brought me to camp not much the worse for the adventure.

I was out early the following morning on a quiet hunt by myself, but saw nothing except the fresh tracks of a small puma, or of a lynx. Whilst I was hunting half my party were moving camp to an old log cabin on Independence Mountain, about eleven miles from our present encampment, and in the neighbourhood of which we hoped for elk. When I got back from my morning's work I had an excellent lunch of elk's brains fried with eggs and bacon, and then set off alone on my broncho, following the tracks of the waggon wheels. I reached the cabin in good time, and found Griff and Curly comfortably housed in this solitary abode. The hut consisted of a single room about twenty-five feet long by twenty feet broad, remarkably well and substantially built of fine round logs. When it was built and by whom no one now knows, but it is supposed to have been the work of a party of miners, who had selected this pine-clad slope to supply them with the lumber necessary for their operations, and it was thought that about the year 1872 they were all massacred by Indians. This was about the date of

"THE MINER'S LAST ABODE."

From a Sketch by A. P. V.

the larger massacre of which I have already spoken, and which occurred on this same mountain. The only clue to the occupation of the original inmates were the remains of a small smithy close by, and the weird stumps of felled timber in the immediate neighbourhood of the hut. Such is life in these wild parts! All record or memory of even who or what the poor fellows were has died out in this short period, and their well-built dwelling alone remains, a welcome resting-place for occasional hunting parties or chance miners! It lies well for the latter, being on the way between the Hans Peak Mines and Laramie city, from which it is distant some sixty miles. Each successive party had left the cabin in a little worse condition than they found it ;

it was in consequence gradually getting out of repair, and no one appeared to have even swept it out, for it possessed a most uninviting floor of thick dirt. However, a log hut in any condition was not to be despised in so severe a climate and season; and too glad were we to avail ourselves of its shelter from the intense cold. Amongst various relics left by past occupants were the remains of a head of a mountain sheep, suggesting that these animals existed in the neighbourhood, and kindling hopes and thoughts of coming sport. From this hut I managed only one day's hunting, which resulted in a couple of long and fruitless shots at two bull elk, who had got our wind and were on the move.

Having been told of two herds of mountain bison on the western side of North Park, and E. Herridge having stated that he knew their whereabouts, which was only a day's journey from here, I was tempted to delay and have a hunt for them—a somewhat risky proceeding, as it was now the middle of November, and we had to pass over two divides to get back into the western part of the park. If a fall of snow took place whilst we were in the park, we should have great difficulty in extricating even ourselves; waggons and all *impedimenta* would certainly be lost, and we should be lucky to save the horses. Under these circumstances I determined to go lightly equipped, and to take with me only the lightest waggon and as little as possible in it, with Edd and Curly Rogers to cook and do camp work; the rest of the outfit were to await our return at the cabin.

The drive was a lovely one. After crossing the divide above the cabin, we followed up a magnificently-timbered valley, which at one point narrowed to a gorge or cañon, widening out again a little higher up into two broad glens. The snow was deep, and we had to mount considerably; consequently our progress was so slow that when camping time came we were still some way from the bison country; but an early start next day brought us by one o'clock down far enough into the park to be able to take a hunt that evening.

Whilst making camp, two bull elk were seen walking quietly over a high ridge above us. I at once started in pursuit, leaving the two men to finish the operations. A steep climb brought me to the spot where they had crossed the ridge, and as the snow was fresh and heavy, I had no difficulty in tracking them. When I had last seen them going out of sight they were browsing and walking quite cannily, and the wind being well in my face and the travelling very quiet, I felt sure of soon getting shot. But the best prospects are often doomed to disappointment, and so it was with me on this occasion. Edd Herridge had a bloodhound which he valued much, named "Drummer;" this brute was reported to be a most wonderful sporting dog, but I never saw him do anything except disturb a whole district. My dog "Ned" had evidently the same antipathy to "Drummer" as I had myself, as, although a much smaller dog, he could not help fighting him about once a week, when poor "Ned" always got the worst of it, which did not in any way interfere with a renewal of hostilities on "Ned's" part within a very few days. Well, I had not gone far on the track when I was joined by "Drummer." He was such a nasty-tempered brute that his master him-

self did not much like offending him; so after trying to drive him back to camp, and his refusing to
go, I did not think it necessary to take rougher
measures, but determined to trust to his reputed
training. We proceeded on the track quietly enough
for some time. It was evident we were close on the
elk; the old dog's eyes glistened, and he showed
anxiety all over. Once or twice he attempted to
push a little in front of me, but a gentle reminder
with the rifle barrel on his head brought him back
again. Every moment I expected to see something
of the fine beasts; every fresh bit of ground was full
of excitement; my nerves were at the utmost pitch
of tension, but withal I felt very deadly. All of a
sudden, with a bound and a rush, the old villain of
a dog shot past me, and in a minute more I heard him
"jump" the elk, and commence his useless yelping.
The scent had become too hot for the old brute, and
he had been unable to resist it any longer. What
my feelings were may perhaps be imagined. At
first I felt inclined to send the contents of my rifle
after him, but luckily restrained myself from so
useless a proceeding.

In the afternoon we made a careful survey with
my stalking-glass of the plains frequented by the
much-coveted bison, but not a sign was to be
seen of them. They had evidently moved off to
winter quarters, and where those were, Edd had no
notion. Everything was hard frozen, and covered
with snow too deep, no doubt, for any representatives
of the cattle tribe. I was very anxious to get one
of these so-called mountain bison, to compare with
the buffalo of the plain; but from all I heard afterwards, I became satisfied that they are one and the

IN NORTH PARK.

(From a Sketch by A. P. Vivias.)

same beast. It is probable that these two small
herds of about sixty each had been driven in days
gone by up into the mountains by some accidental and
exceptional scare, and had not afterwards returned
to the lower grounds. Living much in the timber,
they are seldom exposed to the sun, and consequently
their coats become darker than if they lived on the
shadeless prairie, while nature provides them too with
longer hair, to meet the severer cold of these elevated
regions. These are the great differences between
them and the so-called buffalo; they are said to be
smaller, but if so this arises probably from a scarcity
of food, as is the case with the mountain bears.

When we had satisfied ourselves that the bison
had " skinned out," we made for camp in a somewhat depressed state of mind. But my want of
success in hunting had been much compensated by
the magnificent scenery I saw this day, unsurpassed
by any it had been my fortune as yet to come
across. The views from the ridges were very grand.
Within a very short distance to the west, started
up a grand range of mountains attaining a height
of at least 13,000 feet. Dense pine-forests clothed
them to within two or three thousand feet
of their summits, beyond which the pure whiteness
of the snow was only broken here and there by
serrated masses and peaks of volcanic rock. This
range seemed almost to join on to the more distant
range to the south-west, called the " Rabbit Ear "
(or " Rabbadere ") Range, which is here the main
divide of the continent. Away to the north
stretched the mountains we had travelled along,
in which was Mount Independence, and further
to the north and west was the so-called Hans

Peak Range. The boldness and abruptness of the outlines were very striking. The whole scene was wrapped in that profound and indescribable stillness which so often accompanies intense cold. Heavy banks of cloud were heaping up to the westward, which, although they added beauty to the magnificent sunset, betokened in E. Herridge's opinion a coming storm. Keenly anxious was he to "pull out," and get back to the cabin on Mount Independence; and now that I was satisfied that there was no chance of bison, and that it would be only foolhardy to remain longer, with two "divides" between us and civilization, I felt I ought to accede to his wishes.

Soon after dark it began to snow a little, which led to the most doleful stories from Edd of sudden falls, from two to four feet in depth; of how last year a trapper in this district only got out by abandoning his waggon, and packing what he could on his horses; of how two years ago, in the neighbouring Hans Peak Range, two trappers, being caught by an unexpected fall of snow, only escaped themselves on snow-shoes, and lost all their goods and chattels, and had to shoot their horses to save the poor brutes the misery of dying of starvation.

Then he had another tale with a very sad termination, of two trappers who had taken in provisions, and arranged to spend the winter hereabouts, to hunt for furs, and who had calculated on being assisted in their commissariat with the flesh of the beaver they caught. Their trapping not proving very successful, they began to get short of food. They then settled that one of them should get out on snow-shoes, whilst the other remained behind, subsisting on the provisions still left. The man on whom it fell to make the attempt to reach civilization eventually did so in a very exhausted condition; and whether he thought his partner had sufficient food to last him till the coming spring, or whether he could not get back to him with fresh stores, Edd did not know, but, at any rate, he did not return until the trails were open in the spring. He then found that his poor partner had not been able to hold out, and had died of cold and hunger.

Undoubtedly such stories did not encourage delay, so early next morning camp was struck, and we turned our faces once more towards the old miner's cabin. We passed on our way near the scene of the Mount Independence massacre of 1870, and this led to Edd recounting some of his many Indian adventures. On one occasion, he had been saved a skirmish with the Indians in the Black-hills of Dakotah by breaking his leg, in consequence of which he had been unable to continue his journey. The Indians "ran off" the horses of his outfit, but the "boys" were too quick, and shot seven of the marauders before they could get away.

On another occasion he was "packing" across the country with another "boy," when they were followed late one evening by Indians. They were able to pitch their tent in a very narrow cañon, which could only be approached on one side. The next morning the Indians attacked, and commenced a heavy fire into the tent. Being, like most Red-skins, singularly afraid of losing their lives, they did not dare to come to close quarters, and Her-ridge and his partner, by lying flat on the ground until the Indians had done their shooting, escaped unhurt.

Another of his stories showed how pluck and presence of mind may desert even these frontier men when most needed. Herridge, with a man named Bill Wales, and another, was "packing" through the Sioux country, when two warriors of that tribe suddenly appeared, galloping towards them. Herridge thought they might be the advance-guard of a party, and that there would be more following, so counselled taking up a position behind some big rocks, where they could defend themselves to advantage. Bill Wales, who was a sort of desperado, was, on the contrary, for fighting, and said, at any rate he meant to have some fun. Herridge and the other man having vainly endeavoured to dissuade him, ensconced themselves behind the rocks, and watched the issue. Bill was an experienced hand, was well mounted, and well armed with an American Henry rifle and two six-shooters. His right game was to sit still, and to await quietly the attack of the Indians, shooting them down as soon as they came within sure range. But when the critical moment arrived, his nerve apparently forsook him, and he wheeled his horse round and galloped away. The leading Sioux quickly and easily rode alongside, and shot him dead without the slightest trouble. He then scalped him, and rode away with the ghastly trophy, and Wales's horse and firearms. Edd and his partner were witnesses of the whole proceeding, but did not dare take any part in it, nor did they think it prudent to leave their natural fortress till the following morning. They were so struck by the easy way in which the Indians overtook Bill Wales, that they measured the next day the strides of the respective horses, and found that of the Sioux to be twenty-two, against twenty-one feet covered by Bill Wales's, which was a remarkably fine animal.

Fortunately for us the threatened storm still held off, and very little fresh snow having fallen since we passed over the track, we were able to reach the cabin in good daylight. Hank had got us ready a most excellent supper, consisting of soup made of the ribs of the fat cow elk, fried slices off the haunch, and, as usual, capital bread. My appetite in these parts was scarcely credible; I was able to consume this very day, with the greatest comfort to myself, no less than six meat meals. The frozen venison is such food as I have never come across in civilized parts. It has a flavour and juiciness which no domestic meat I have ever tasted possesses, and it is as tender as well-kept Welsh mutton.

It being now the end of November, the cold intense and the snow very deep, my men thought it probable that the bands of elk and deer would by this time have moved down the Platte to lower regions. We therefore decided to follow their example, and settled on a stream called Beaver Creek, about fifteen miles further north, for our first camping-place. As, however, some of our stores were running short, we settled that Evans should drive the lightest waggon back to Pinkham's Ranche, get what was required, and rejoin us there, where we would remain encamped until his return. As it turned out afterwards, this was a risky proceeding so late in the year, but as Griff proposed it himself, and the rest of my outfit

offered no objections, it never entered into my head
as being in any way dangerous.

I was always glad to escape the tedium of riding
alongside the waggon when moving camp, and as the
range between Mount Independence and Beaver
Creek was well covered with timber, and very likely
for elk, I determined to hunt the way on foot, taking
the boy Curly with me to assist in finding the new
camp in the evening. On leaving the hut we struck
up at once into the timber, and within a couple of
miles crossed the deep cañon, through which the
torrent called "Big Creek" flows. What a pity it
is that the old Indian names are lost. These
wretched, commonplace appellations, such as Horse
Creek, Cow Creek, Sand Creek, given in early times
are repeated over and over again, and mountains,
settlements and mining camps alike enjoy the same
miserable disregard for practical, not to say eupho-
nious, names.[1] Not long after starting, we came

---

[1] The following extract from a supposed colloquy between two
old mining "prospectors" on meeting after a long separation,
written by Dr. Degnool, gives an admirable idea of western
nomenclature and phraseology :—

> "But where ye been, Jim, ever since
>   We left the Stanislow,
>   And pull'd up stakes down there at Dent's,
>   Now eighteen years ago ?"
>
> "Wal, since the time that we put out
>   On that stampede from Stoney,
>   Been mos' the time knockin' about
>   Down into Air-e-zony (Arizona).
>
> "Only been back a month or so,
>   And thought I'd take a tramp
>   Through the old diggins, 'long with Jo,
>   Who stops at ' Nigger Camp.'

on a mound of snow, in which it was evident
something had been "cached" or hidden by a

> " Started from Alpha on our trip,
>   And passed up the Divide,
>   Through ' Tangle-Leg ' and ' Let-Her-Rip,'
>   ' Red Dog ' and ' Whiskey Slide.'
>
> " Then after leaving thar we went
>   Down by the ' Tail-Holt-Mill,'
>   'Crost ' Greenhorn Mountain' to ' Snow Tent,'
>   And up to ' Gouge-Eye Hill.'
>
> " From ' Gouge-Eye ' down to ' Esperance,'
>   ' Slap Jack ' and ' Oro Fin ;'
>   Through ' Deadwood ' over to ' Last Chance,'
>   ' Root Hog,' and ' Lost Ravine.'
>   *   *   *   *   *
> " Then came along to ' Poverty,'
>   ' Dead Broke,' and ' Bottle Ridge,'
>   By ' Hangtown,' ' Poor Man,' and ' Lone Tree.'
>   ' Garotte,' and ' Smash-up Bridge.'
>
> " Through ' Nip and Tuck ' and ' Old Bear Trap,'
>   ' Coon Hollow ' and ' Fair Play,'
>   Along by ' Scorpion ' and ' Fir Gap,'
>   ' Kanaka ' and ' El Rey.'
>
> " We stopped one day at ' Never Sweat,'
>   Another up at ' Ophir,'
>   Then moved our boots on to ' You Bet,'
>   And struck across by ' Gopher.'
>
> " To ' Sucker,' near ' Grass Widow Bend,'
>   Whar, as 'twas getting late,
>   We brought our journey to an end,
>   Down by the ' Devil's Gate.' "

Then in this striking little poem Jim goes on to inquire after
common friends :—

> " Wal, Dan, you've been about some, too—
>   But tell me, if you know,
>   What has become of Ned McGrew ?
>   And whar is Sleepy Joe ?

wild animal.   On further examination we found
the fresh tracks of a large "mountain lion," or
puma.   As they were what is termed in western
parlance "burning hot," I was for trying to overtake
him by following on; but Curly, like all the hunters
I came across, was strongly impressed with the
common opinion that it was hopeless ever to try to
overhaul a mountain lion, that they were continually
on the move, always slouching and travelling and
watching, and he thought nothing was to be done.
In a very disconsolate mood at having been so near
this rare and much prized animal, I sat down on a
rock, and began to spy with my glass the barren
spaces in the timber for anything I might see.
Whilst so employed, I was surprised by the small

> " And Poker Pete and Monte Bill,
>   And—I forget his name—
> What used to run the Whiskey Mill,
>   And keep the keno game ? "
>
> " Well, as for Ned, can't 'xactly say,
>   But 'bout the t'other three.
> The last, we heard, were up this way
>   A hanging on a tree.
>
> " Went into the Road Agency,
>   Along with Texas Jim ;
> The Vigilants of Montany (Montana)
>   Likewise also got him.
>
> " Sleepy was drown'd at ' Upper Dalles,'
>   And so was Al La Tour,
> Went in a skift over the falls,
>   And we didn't see 'em no more.
>
> " Some think that Ned was eat by bears,
>   And I most think so, too,
> 'Cause didn't one gobble up Nick McNares
>   On the trail to Cariboo ?'

greyhound Curly had with him making a sudden
dash away from us. " Hulloa, Curly, what does she
see?" " Don't know ; maybe it's the mountain lion,"
and so sure enough it was. About 300 yards off
this object of my greatest ambition was quietly
sloping away from us through the timber. I opened
fire at once, but after a few shots I soon found that
I must try and get nearer if I wanted to hit him,
for the bullets were cutting up the snow very short.
Curly's dog soon overhauled him, and actually made
a snap at his tail before the lion seemed aware of her
presence ; but once was enough, for the beast
immediately wheeled round, showing such a front of
teeth and claws that the greyhound retreated, as fast
as she could, for our protection. I then put " Ned "
on, and he and the greyhound again came up with
him. The dogs barked at him, but on the same formidable front being presented, they both turned tail
and sought safety with us. All this time I was not
idle. I was running as hard as I could through
three feet of fearfully heavy snow, trying to get near
to an isolated piece of thick timber, for which it was
evident the lion was making. I thought he would
not rest there, but travel through it, and that I
might get a chance at him as he broke on the other
side. So it turned out, but he passed so quickly
through the thick timber that I was still about 250
yards from the edge of it when he reappeared on the
other side. He did not give a good broadside, not
being more than half on to me, but there was no
choice in the matter ; I must take this chance or none,
so sitting down and pulling myself together as well
as I could after the run, I opened fire. All the
shots dropped short, although I kept giving more

and more elevation, until about the sixth, when I had the satisfaction of seeing one of his forelegs drop helpless, with a wild lash of his long tail. His pace now quickened from a trot to a canter, and he soon disappeared over the neighbouring ridge of the Big Creek Cañon. Then came a shout from behind, "Hurrah, he is our meat," from the breathless Curly, who had followed close on my heels. I, too, felt very sanguine of eventually getting him, as the leg appeared to be broken very high up, and the ball had probably entered the fore-part of his body. Moving quickly on, we made straight for the place on the ridge where he had disappeared. Here all was bare rock, the strong wind having swept the ridge clean of snow. On looking over we could at first see nothing of the lion, nor could we take up his track, and I was just going to put "Ned" upon his scent, when I suddenly espied the bullet-head protruding over a rock about eighty yards below us. He was keeping a sharp look-out below, but, singularly enough did not seem to apprehend danger from the very direction in which he had received his hurt. Crawling cautiously forward until I opened his whole body, I took a quiet, deliberate shot, and put the ball in just in front of his loins. This completely paralyzed his hind quarters, and he rolled off the rock like a rabbit. Down we rushed, expecting to find him lying dead beneath the rock ; but not a bit of it, the game was not up yet. He had pulled himself together, and was sitting on his haunches below the rock, looking awful in his ferocity, growling and snarling, and showing his teeth, and making the claws of his forefeet start out in a most suggestive and unpleasant manner. It was a sight worthy of Landseer's brush, and such a backing of wild scenery

as would have warmed the heart of that great painter.
The skin was so beautifully clean, and the specimen
such a perfect one, that I felt sorry at having to give
him the *coup-de-grâce* by shooting; but although
paralyzed as far as any aggressive movement was
concerned, he still possessed one formidable fore-leg
uninjured, besides a fearful mouth, and when
approached he took care to show he meant to use
both. I was looking out where to shoot him with
least injury to the skin, when Curly wanted to try
if he could not kill him with a " rock " (Angl., stone).
I had no objection to the attempt, although I looked
upon it as a perfectly useless proceeding; but the
" boy" was all game, and having selected a couple of
large stones, he approached as close as he could, then
delivered the first of these missiles with unerring
aim, striking the beast a tremendous blow between
the eyes. An enraged and bitter growl was the only
result. Nothing daunted, Curly hurled the second
stone, which took effect on the point of the nose.
For a moment the eyes closed and the head dropped,
and like lightning, Curly's keen knife was buried in
the lion's throat. It was out again in a second, and
lucky it was so, for the beast quickly recovered; but
the knife had done its work, the jugular was cut,
and life's blood was ebbing slowly but surely away.
He proved a magnificent adult male, measuring eight
feet six inches from nose to tip of tail, and weighing
about 150 lbs. We took the skin off there and then,
but the operation occupied two hours, and precious
cold work it was after our hot chase. When finished,
Curly shouldered the hide, and I the two rifles, and we
made the best of our way off the range to the plain
below. We were at least fourteen miles from the

nearest place at which our outfit could have made a
camp, and it was quite possible they might have found
it necessary to go still further before a good supply
of fuel was struck. The snow was very deep, and the
travelling very heavy. My light companion, shod
in mocassins, made easier work of it than I did,
but by the time we had reached the lower plains he
had had quite enough of carrying the skin, and
suggested hanging it on a tree till the morrow, when
a pony could be sent back for it. My only objection
to this was lest the mischievous coyotés might get
hold of it, but Curly assured me that the lion was
the "boss of the country," and that all other animals
would take good care to give the scent a very wide
berth.

The cold became so piercing that Curly got
"scared" at being frozen, and as soon as he was relieved
of his burden made off for the new camp, leaving me
to follow on his track as best I could. This was
easy enough in the heavy snow as long as daylight
lasted, and luckily before it got very dark I had
struck the trail made by our waggon. I must confess that I was well-nigh "played out" before I
reached camp, between seven and eight o'clock that
night. But I had had a great day's sport, and after
having got through a prodigious supper, I almost
forgave Curly for deserting me. I found that he
had arrived a very short time before me, and had
already narrated the events of the day to the rest of
the men. They were greatly surprised at my luck;
none of them had ever killed a "lion," and on my
expressing some regrets at not having had time to
follow a bull elk I had seen on my way home,
Herridge said, "Why, a lion is worth forty bull elks."

I may add that the American puma (*felis concolor*) is considerably larger and more tawny than the Indian variety, exactly resembling an ordinary lion in colour; hence the local name, as it might at a distance be very easily mistaken for a small lioness. The specimen I had got turned out to be an unusually fine one, and in perfect health.

We were now encamped on the north fork of Beaver Creek, and were to remain here until rejoined by Evans with the necessary stores. The camp was not altogether well-selected; there was plenty of wood and a beautiful little stream of water close by, but we were not sheltered from the fearful cold wind, which came tearing down from the mountain range to the westward.

The long-threatened storm broke on us here, and we had a time of it, with a vengeance, for the whole week of our stay. The first day, although the storm had begun, was not so bad as to prevent my going out in the afternoon for a hunt with Herridge. We were lucky enough to get a stalk on two large bull elk in the timber, the finest of which I got, and wounded the second; but this one went away straight over the range, and notwithstanding all "Ned's" efforts to turn him and bring him to bay, we failed to get him. We nearly had an accident with the other bull, from trying to finish him without firing another shot, and so further disturbing the ground. After the first shot the poor beast had gone on a little way and laid down, and was so sick that he could not rise again; he had, however, the full use of his head, and it was a matter of danger to get too near him. Herridge said, that by getting the horns round a small tree he could keep him

R

down whilst I finished him with the knife. Knowing the strength even of a red deer under these circumstances, I rather doubted Edd's powers, but as he was an old and experienced hunter, I waived my own opinion, and consented to take my part in the operation. At the first touch of the knife the powerful beast violently released himself from Herridge, and, fortunately for me, I either fell or was thrown out of reach of his horns. One attempt was enough for both of us, and a cartridge with a half-charge of powder was quickly called into requisition.

On another occasion whilst hunting from this camp, I took out Curly as my assistant, but it was the last time I troubled him. The "boy" used to carry about an old soldier's rifle, which, judging from its shooting, must have been of the ram's-horn pattern of grooving. Certain it was that scarcely a beast had been slain by it during the many months Curly had been on the hunt, in spite of frequent and easy chances. If, however, it did not kill, it "scared" as much as the most accurate "express." Curly was moreover very ambitious, and I had had more than once to declare most positively that only with my leave was he ever to use his rifle. Up to this time he had behaved remarkably well, but to-day the spirit of keenness overcame his obedience, and taking advantage of my stopping to try some very heavy timber with "Ned," he went off on the hunt on his own account. I missed him, but not thinking much of it went on alone. Presently I spied with my glass two fine bull elk in an open place amongst the timber, and having thought over quietly how they were to be got at, proceeded to carry out my plans.   Imagine my disgust on hearing, when within some 500 yards of the deer, the sharp crack of a rifle, followed by another and another, and yet another!   On scuttling up a little rise as fast as I could, I saw my two bull elk tearing up the range at full speed quite uninjured, while the worthy Curly was standing below, evidently disgusted with his misses, and gazing after the fast retiring forms !

But his hunt was not over yet; he had capital walking powers, so following on through the timber, he had actually three more chances at other wapiti, with equally futile results.   After this he came back, found my tracks, and followed me, having come to the conclusion, probably, that it was no use any longer trusting to his own shooting.   I had gone on in a fever of indignation, and when he joined me I naturally gave him a bit of my mind; so too, I fancy, did some of my men on his return to camp.

Such trials of temper one must be prepared for in these regions, where it is often necessary to re-member and put into practice, if the trip is to be enjoyed, the advice of old Horace, to preserve equanimity under trying circumstances.

The storm continued with increasing intensity for several days, the cold being truly severe.   All our meat had to be cut with an axe, and my beard and eyelids were constantly frozen during the night. One day I tried to make a watercolour sketch, but the colour became ice before it had time to be ab-sorbed into the paper.   The ink inside my bag froze, everything, in fact, froze that could freeze.   We seemed to be approaching almost the miner's description of the cold on one of his expeditions, when he says,—

> "Cold up North ! I've known a name
>   To congeal in my mouth ;
> And that is how the saying came
>   About the 'frozen truth.'
>
> "Yes ; and I have seen still stranger feats—
>   You know, Jim, I'm no liar—
> The flames freeze into solid sheets
>   As they rose up from the fire."

A fiercely strong wind generally prevailed, and this made camp life just now anything but pleasant. Sometimes it was no easy matter to keep the fire from being blown clean away, which added considerably to the difficulties of cooking. Still I was wonderfully well, and fit and able to enjoy and take advantage of any break in the storm.

A very enjoyable day after wapiti I call to mind especially—a red-letter day both in weather and sport. One of Edd's friends, Lee, had volunteered to come with me that day; and a very good assistant he proved.

Mounting our bronchos, we started for the range lying to the north of our camp. Many herds of antelope were passed on the way, but they had no attraction for us to-day; we were bent on a wapiti, and no inferior game would suffice.

Having hobbled our horses at the mouth of one of the small cañons which come down to the plain, we started up into the range. We had not gone far on foot when we spied two magnificent bull elk lying in the open, in a sort of little corrie or punch-bowl. They were well placed for a stalk, so having marked our ground, we got the wind all right, went round, and crawled in to the edge of the little hollow.

On looking through the long grass, a sight met my eyes quite sufficient to make even a more tutored heart beat fast. There they lay within easy distance, two gigantic bulls, with horns " like young trees," as Lee whispered, in perfect and blissful ignorance of any of the human race being within a thousand miles. It was a beautiful sight and well worth enjoying more leisurely, but one knows from experience that, in stalking, a favourable opportunity is not to be dallied with. Selecting, therefore, the best head, I took every care to direct the contents of the first barrel to a vital spot and fired. Up they jumped and stood for a moment, trying to make out whence came the disturbance; this gave me a good chance for my second barrel at the other bull, and down the hill he staggered, bleeding profusely and evidently mortally wounded. In the meantime, the first bull stood stock still, but as he did not drop, I thought it advisable to put in another cartridge, and make sure. This brought him down; so telling Lee to go after the other and gralloch him, I gave my attention to the first.

He was a magnificent beast, a real prize; and well satisfied did I feel on seeing him stretched on the ground before me. The length of his horns from coronet to tip was fifty-eight inches and the beam round the coronet twelve and a half inches. The other head was also very good, the horns being almost palmated, and on this account very peculiar. This made me regret the more the misfortune which befell it in " packing " it to camp, when the horse which carried it fell down the hill, and smashed it to pieces.

After this great piece of sport we continued our

hunt, and ran some risk of finishing the day with a real tragedy. Lee was leading the way through thick timber in which we expected to come across elk or deer, when all of sudden he dropped down and whispered to me, that he saw an elk feeding close in front of us. With my rifle to the fore I took Lee's place, and certainly did see some beast pushing forward through the thick underwood, but I could not make out his head or his form, and waited anxiously until he should get to an open place a little farther on. I was of course at full tension, my rifle at the shoulder and at full cock, forefinger round the trigger, and eye along the sights, but mercifully did not fire, as Lee urged me to, until I could get a more certain view of my game. Well it was that I took my own line! For when the beast did assume a more definite form, it was that of one of our own horses, mounted by Herridge! He was followed closely by another of our ponies led by Hank, on which was secured the head of the elk I had killed two days previously. I must say my blood chilled; but no harm was done, and it all ended in a hearty laugh, in which Lee joined the loudest.

The weather continuing fearfully bad, we became very uneasy about Evans, who should have rejoined us some days ago. Herridge proposed to go in search of him on horseback; and this being settled on, he left us early the following morning with the intention of making our old cabin on Mount Independence before nightfall. The storms had driven the game further down—a long and fruitless trudge through a lovely game country convinced me that the sooner we shifted our ground the better.

The cold continued intense, and the gale very severe; it was therefore in every way desirable to get down from this elevated region; but until Evans had been heard of no move could be made.

Those who have not experienced the winter gales of these high districts cannot conceive their severity and fierceness and the danger of being out in them. It was at times a difficult matter to cook our food, the wind blowing the camp fire away. Then after dark it was hardly possible to keep a light in the tents, and had it not been for a small coal-oil lamp I purchased before leaving civilization, I should have often been in darkness even at my meals. We had great trouble to keep the tents up; in addition to the ordinary ropes we had to press into the service all the lariats from the horses, and even then I some- times thought, during the fearful gusts of wind at night, that I should be buried underneath canvas and snow before morning. No real damage, however, occurred during the whole gale, but it was monotonous and trying work when for many days we could hardly get outside our tent from morn to night. My men scarcely ever remembered such fearful weather, and certainly not before Christmas.

Poor old " Ned " was the only one who had any sport during the worst of these weary days of storm, and this was of doubtful enjoyment even to himself. Near to our camp, in the banks of the stream, was a burrow of skunks. Curly had trapped one, but the stench was too strong for him even, and he had thrown it away, trap and all. Master " Ned," being bored, I suppose, at his confinement to camp all one day, thought he would stroll out in the evening and have a hunt. Very foolishly he selected a skunk as the object of his *chasse*, and he must have been ignominiously defeated, for he came back very dejected and crestfallen. Worse still for him, he was so odoriferous that I simply could not bear him inside my tent; and although very sorry for the poor brute, for the cold was fearful, I barricaded the tent-door with every possible obstacle before turning in for the night. Three times "Ned" charged, and on each occasion would have carried the work had I not used my voice as a second line of defence. Eventually he gave it up, and then with extraordinary sagacity waited until the camp fire was out, and dug himself a hole where it had been. The next morning he was not only alive but quite warm and "tickled" (Angl., jolly), and, moreover, had so singed his coat that all skunk smell had been burnt away, and he was once more endurable.

During these days of inaction the men seemed to pass the time pretty agreeably to themselves. They used to sit huddled together in their tent, with a frying-pan full of glowing embers in their midst, round which they played cards and told stories. The smoke of the smouldering wood made it impossible for any ordinary mortal to exist in the upper strata of this atmosphere; even to squatters on the ground it was so pungent as to cause the eyes to water and smart in a most unpleasant manner. The stories were chiefly of their own experiences in their many wanderings, and episodes in the early life of the frontier towns, all of which were told in the purest western vernacular and phraseology.

It was, as may be imagined, very difficult to

keep oneself warm in such weather. In the day time my own outer clothing was of Scotch tweed, which I found very ill adapted to meet the severity of the weather. The wind seemed to treat two flannel shirts and two waistcoats as if the whole was net-work, so fearfully did it penetrate to one's skin. Buckskin is capital for keeping out the wind, and is well adapted to this very cold dry climate; but I had not been "posted up" in such matters before starting and was ill-prepared for intense cold. I had tried to get a suit of buckskin sent up to me when Loyd left; but it had been forwarded to Laramie Station, "C.O.D." (i. e. cash on delivery), and my messenger had not the wherewithal to pay, and so it had returned to Denver whence it came. As soon as I could I got a suit of "Californian goods," such as are worn by most of the ranchmen, made of a close brown canvas, lined with Californian blanketing, which I found excellent, being as impervious to the keen wind as buckskin, and at the same time warm and light. Under this I wore two flannel shirts, and what is called here a "Cardigan," or knitted waistcoat with sleeves. I found my English woollen under-garments and stockings far superior to what can be got out here, which my men designated as "shoddy." The material best suited for outer clothing should be light and close in texture, so as to prevent the penetration of wind, and at the same time allow free action to the limbs when walking. Some old hunters prefer the Californian goods even to buckskin, which they think has a rheumatic tendency, and which, no doubt, if wet, becomes disagreeable to wear. In all this cold I did entirely without stimulants, nor did I feel the want of them in this fine dry atmosphere. I had one bottle of cognac with me, but only for medicinal purposes, in case of accidents or illness, and my only drinks were tea and coffee. The men would have indulged freely in spirits, I have no doubt, but all they had was purchased by themselves, and therefore limited in quantity and soon exhausted. As long as it lasted they used to take a nip before breakfast of a drink composed of half rye-whiskey, half hot water, mixed with a little salt butter and sugar and nutmeg, and its flavour was by no means bad, odd as it may sound.

The second afternoon after Edd left, a joyful shout was heard in camp. The snow had been falling so heavily, and the weather was altogether so miserable, that I had scarcely been outside my tent the whole day; I could not conceive therefore the cause of this ebullition of spirits, and I rushed out, not knowing exactly what to expect. I was just in time to see Edd's and Griff's arrival, the former on horseback, the latter driving the light waggon. A curious sight they were, for scarcely anything but shapeless forms of pure white snow were to be seen in their respective places.

Griff's story was soon told. He had waited at Pinkham's Ranche for the arrival of the stores from Laramie city; the storm had come on, and the stores had been delayed on their transit. He had only left Pinkham's the previous morning, and had made the cabin on Mount Independence before dark, where he had found Edd Herridge. They had left the cabin very early that morning, and had had a fearful drive. Griff said it was so bad that he did not know how Edd had been able to find his way at all in the blinding frozen snow, driven with the whole force of the north-westerly gale. There was a general feeling of relief in camp at the whole party being reassembled, and many were the vows not to get separated again under any circumstances. Griff brought much news, but all was strictly of a local character, such as the freezing to death of a man near Tyseiden; the severity of the storm even in the comparatively low Cache la Poudre district, where two feet of snow had fallen; old man Pinkham too had had a successful hunt after the bison, of which he and his partner had killed five. But no intelligence of any sort or kind reached me from the civilized world, and I could not expect to get any now for many a week to come.

CHAPTER XII.

"Spreading between these streams are the wondrous, beautiful
    prairies,
Billowy bays of grass ever rolling in shadow and sunshine.
Over them wander the scatter'd tribes of Ishmael's children,
Staining the desert with blood ; and above their terrible war
    trails
Circles and sails aloft on pinions majestic the vulture,
Here and there rise smoke from the camps of these savage
    marauders."

Longfellow's " Evangelina."

ALTHOUGH the next morning was almost as bad as any
of its predecessors, we were so sick of our present
camping-ground, the quantity of snow, and the extreme cold, that we determined to make an attempt
at pulling out and getting further northwards to less
frozen regions. It sounds odd to talk of going north
to seek warmth, but so it is here. The lie of the
elevated country slopes towards the north ; the

river, itself the North Platte, flows northwards,
running in a cañon cut through a land of open
wastes and granite rocks. Our course lay over a
plain nearly parallel with the river, with a range of
high mountains on our left, and a region of rocks
and foothills on the right. The slope to the north
is pretty rapid, so that we hoped before many days
to get out of the snow-covered country. We had
now had so much of it that we were quite wearied
of the white world, and I could well enter into the
feelings of one of my men who informed me that when
he saw bare ground again "he would lie on the
ground and roll, like a broncho."

The day of our move from Beaver Creek was a
trying one, and it was with great difficulty we
reached another stream called "Grand Encampment," although it was only some ten miles off.
Here we found a small cabin, inhabited by the most
curious weather-beaten old buckskin conceivable. If
that old fellow's adventures and experiences were
chronicled, I am much mistaken if they would not
be a trifle startling. He seemed to have known
western life in every phase; but he was not communicative, except in his sleep, when I used to hear
him talking away like a lunatic. I should like to
have "interviewed" the old fellow, although I
doubt whether I should have got much out of him; for
even when all the rest were busily employed gossip-
ing round the camp fire, very little came from his
dry parchment-like lips. His present employment
was minding a few head of cattle for their owner,
named Bang, who had removed to a more genial
climate. My men had no hesitation in taking possession of the cabin, in which proceeding, I must

say, the old fellow most fully concurred, and too glad
were we to exchange flimsy canvas for solid logs of
wood, as a shelter against the inclement elements.
We had, however, even in the ten miles improved our
climate; there was far less snow, and we had caught
up the antelope, which, like ourselves, were retiring
before the driving storms.

Had I wished to kill a large number of antelope,
now was my chance; herds of them were to be seen
feeding within a very short distance of the ranche, and
I shot two fine bucks one morning within 300 yards
of the cabin door. But I had already obtained some
very good heads, and my great object was to get as
far as I could a representative of all the *mammalia*
worth killing. What I hoped for in this locality
were mountain sheep. Vain hope! Griff and I
hunted hard, but not a trace could we find; nor did
our old buckskin lead us to believe that any existed
in this neighbourhood, and I fancy the old fellow
was above the average run of hunters. We determined therefore to make without delay for the range
of mountains lying further north and to the right of
the Platte, to which belong the well-known Elk and
Sheep Mountains. On them I hoped to find my *oves;*
but on our way thither we came across a hunter
friend of Herridge, who gave so deplorable an account of the game prospects there that we changed
our course and struck straight away for the Medicine
Bow Range and the other mountains still further
northwards.

What a pity it is that civilization must destroy all
wild life! From this aforesaid Elk Mountain only a
few years ago, at the time of the making of the
Union Pacific Railroad, one celebrated hunter, named

Jack Watkins, was able to send sufficient venison to feed the whole army of "constructors" on the line between Laramie city and Fort Fred Steele.   Now-a-days an elk is rarely met with on the whole range; and as for sheep. inviting as the rocks of Sheep Mountain looked, it was considered too poor a " show " for even a flying visit.

Jack Watkins was, by-the-bye, a well-known and rather a respected character in these parts.   He had the reputation of being one of the best shots and hunters ever heard of ; but when the railroad was completed, and the large demand for meat ceased, he seems to have given over his Nimrodian pro-pensities, and to have taken to the less healthy and very lawless vocation of "running a drinking saloon " without a licence.   This was considered so serious a breach of the law, and such an injurious precedent, that even in these out-of-the-way parts it was decided that it must be put a stop to. Accordingly, his apprehension was resolved upon; but, knowing their man, and that he was not likely to be taken without some trouble, the authorities deemed it advisable to send a whole company of soldiers to effect his arrest.   The soldiers were halted at a short distance from the ranche, and the officer in command advanced towards the door.   Here he was met by Jack Watkins, armed with his Winchester repeating rifle, who quietly remarked that he would probably have heard that he, Jack Watkins, was a remarkably good shot, and not likely to miss his man, and that, if the soldiers advanced any further, or did not at once " make back tracks for their camp," he would shoot every one of them, commencing with himself, the officer. The latter seemed to have thought it probable Jack would keep his word, and that it was better therefore to retire while still intact, which he accordingly did. " What do you think of that, Sirree ?" said my informant, Lee, glowing with admiration at Jack's successful defiance of the authorities. " Well, I should have gone the next day with a battery of artillery, which would soon have knocked the ranche about Jack's ears," was my reply, at which, and my enthusiasm for law and order, Lee seemed " quite put about."

Our camps now were generally in close proximity to the frozen Platte. The strong winds and fall of

CAMPING-GROUND NEAR THE FROZEN PLATTE.
From a Sketch by A. P. V.

snow had ceased, but the cold continued intense. My thermometer, as I have already stated, was made to register only a few degrees below zero, and had struck work long ago, so I could not take the temperature myself; but we were here at a far greater elevation and higher up in the valley of the Platte than Fort Fred Steele, where, during these severe nights—at the end of November—the Government observations had registered 25° below zero. From our position, I think it would be within the mark to assume that we were at least 10° colder, in which case we should have undergone 67° of frost! Pretty cold for under canvas!

All our surroundings continued covered with a thick coating of snow, and when the sun was out the dazzle and glare became most painful and trying to the eyes. Some of my men wore coloured goggles, and blackened underneath their eyes with charred wood. By adopting this latter expedient and using dark glasses I got on pretty well, though often in the forenoon I was unable to look about much. Snow blindness is not uncommon in these parts. The boy "Curly" had had an attack, and dreaded much a repetition.

My men now left off pitching their tent at all. They preferred to lie on it, with a couple of large fires built on either side of them. Fortunate it was for our comfort that stillness prevailed, and that we were able to enjoy in peace the great luxury of the roaring camp fires. We had luckily plenty of dead cotton wood for fuel, and for food the primest venison (antelope and elk). We despised mountain hares—called here "jack rabbits"—as also the "sage hens" or "cock of the plains" (*centrocercus urophasianus*). These are magnificent birds, as large as capercailzies; the cock measuring as much as two and a half feet in length, and weighing up to six pounds. They live entirely in the open, and take long high flights

s

like black game. The plumage is of a brownish
grey, sprinkled with white, the cock and hen being
alike in colouring, but the former is larger, and has
a somewhat long and pointed tail, which the female
does not possess. They usually keep in packs, and
are not difficult to approach. From feeding on the
sage-bush their flesh tastes very strongly of that
dwarf shrub, and this flavour was insurmountably
unpleasant to me, and apparently to the men
also, for none of those I killed were ever cooked.
Coues says, in his "Birds of the North-West," that
this disagreeable flavour can be got rid of by taking
out the intestines immediately on being killed. He
states also that this bird has the peculiarity, in a
scientific point of view, of possessing no gizzard, the
stomach, instead of "being hard and very muscular,
as in other gallinacea, is soft and membraneous, like
that of the birds of prey." As they were no good to
us for food, as soon as I had obtained as many as I
wanted for specimens, I gave up shooting them, but
before this they were nearly the cause of a disagreeable adventure. It happened that one day I was
riding near the waggons, when some of these birds
got up and flew away behind us. I marked them
down, and leaving the teams to continue their jog,
started back alone for a stalk. When near the spot
I got off my broncho, taking care to throw the bridle
over her head, a proceeding which hitherto had had
the desired effect of stopping her from rambling.
But some demon possessed the animal on this
occasion; for having had my shot and secured three
of the heavy birds, I retraced my steps, meaning
to remount and gallop on after the waggons, which
were by this time out of sight. The broncho had

other views, for no sooner had I got within twenty
yards of her, than away she galloped, and, worse
still, in an opposite direction to that in which the
waggons had disappeared. She stopped to graze
some half mile off, when I approached her again,
and with the same result. After this second flight,
I sent "Ned" round her, which had the effect of
stopping her for a few minutes, but very soon she
broke the bay and bolted off again. I must say I
felt anything but comfortable. It was getting
towards night, the waggons were so far away that I
had no chance of catching them on foot, even if I had
been able to keep the track ; I had no food, and there
was no fuel but sage brush for fire, and to be without a fire all night in this cold meant freezing
before morning. My only chance then was to come
to terms with my pony. Dropping the sage hens,
I now set about a regular quiet stalk, and was lucky
enough this time to get within distance of the dragging reins before she made her rush, on finding
which she soon succumbed. Glad enough was I to
feel myself on horseback once more, and "making
time at a good round lope" after the waggons,
which I overtook just before they made camp.

We had now left the close proximity of high mountains, and were passing over a large prairie, through
which the North Platte drags its sluggish course
towards the Medicine Bow and Sweet-water country.
On this plain were plenty of antelope; one day I
killed three, but beyond taking an occasional stalk
when they came on our line of march, I did not pay
much attention to them. After leaving the higher
mountains we lost all signs of elk, but I hoped
to fall in with them again when we struck the

ranges further northwards, a hope destined to be
disappointed.

The Platte, here about thirty yards across, was so
hard frozen that the waggons could cross it almost
anywhere. It seemed a curious phenomenon of
nature that at one spot on the banks of this ice-bound
river a hot spring should be bubbling up on its
very margin. I did not ascertain the temperature
of the water, but it must have been very considerable, for steam was coming off freely. A sort of
little establishment had grown up around this
spring, consisting of small log huts, in which were
located the owner and a few invalids undergoing a
course of the waters. Amongst these latter was,
curiously enough, a true cockney, born within the
sound of Bow Bells. He had been in America
thirty years, and had suffered greatly from rheumatic
pains in his limbs, which had become lately so
severe that the doctors had wished to amputate the
affected parts! Fortunately he had heard of these
springs, and was obtaining very great relief from the
use of the waters. My native townsman was very
keen to hear all he could about the little city, and I
gratified him to the best of my ability.

Cattle ranches were now pretty frequent, and we
found at all of them great readiness to afford us
shelter, and to furnish us with any necessaries we
required. Some of these ranches kept a lot of milch
cows, and made a large quantity of butter; others
were able to secure stocks of hay, which realized
$22 (4*l*. 8*s*. 0*d*.) per ton, delivered at the Govern-
ment post of Fort Steele.

The great object of my ambition now was to get
a good specimen of the mountain sheep or big horn

THE "MOUNTAIN SHEEP" (OVIS MONTANA).

(From a Sketch by A. BIERSTADT.)

(*ovis montana*). These much-coveted animals, corresponding to the *ovis ammon* of India, and the *mouflon* of Sardinia, inhabit elevated regions, in which rocks and ledges abound. They are scarcely ever seen in the plain, even in the immediate neighbourhood of rocks; but should they be found there, woe betide them, for any ordinary dog can then "tree them," that is, drive them on to the nearest isolated cliff or rock, and then the poor beasts can be shot at pleasure. Their habit is to fly when disturbed to the nearest precipices, from the ledges and points of which they can survey with composure their old enemies, the wolves and the pumas. The latter are said to have a marked partiality for them as a prey, and no wonder, for their meat is second to none, savouring more of venison than mutton. They seem to be the connecting link between deer and sheep. In size they run up to a red-deer, a full-grown ram weighing as much as from fourteen to eighteen stone " dressed " (Angl., " clean "). The skin is covered with a very fine deer's hair, and the feet and legs are also like a deer's. But notwithstanding that it has so many points like the deer kind, yet the head, shape, and movements are so entirely sheep-like that the animal conveys much more the impression of a sheep than a deer. In capacity for scrambling it equals, if not surpasses, the chamois, rushing and jumping down such steep faces of rock as it would appear impossible for any creature even to crawl down. The heads of both rams (or "bucks," as they are here called) and ewes are furnished with horns, those of the male attaining a magnificent size. I have been told of horns seventeen inches round at the base, and of enormous length; of a head that weighed sixty pounds; but I never saw one more than ten or twelve inches round the coronet, or weighing over twenty-five or thirty pounds. It was an old idea that these animals were able to save themselves by falling upon their horns when jumping from great heights, but I need scarcely say that this, like many other hunters' tales, is without the smallest foundation. In consequence of the quality of the meat, and the estimation in which it and the heads and skins are held at the stores and trading posts, I am sorry to say that this quaint and attractive creature is becoming very scarce. It is very shy of civilization, perhaps more so than any of the deer kind, but it is met with at times and places when little expected, and on this account there is more of luck in hunting it than most other animals. It is excessively quick-sighted, trusting more to its eyes than to its nose to give notice of the approach of danger.

I feel sure, after what I have said, that my brother sportsmen will enter into my feelings of keenness to secure a good specimen of this half-sheep half-deer. But the fates were against me, and I utterly failed. I believe, however, another week's stay at one locality would have put me in possession of more than one good head, but at that time I was obliged to move off elsewhere. And so it happened that I had eventually to turn homewards without a moun-tain sheep's head.

But to return to our progress down the Platte. Not a single likely place for sheep was passed which I did not try. Griff Evans was both an experienced and successful sheep hunter, and I had the benefit of his knowledge and advice. But experience and hard work were all of no avail, for we came across nothing but tracks, more or less old.

If, however, the actual success was wanting, the hunt took me amongst the most magnificent scenery, where no human being but a sheep hunter ever thought of going. High ridges of bare red granite, split into peaks and precipices, on which, wherever the slope would allow, flourished cedars and splendid red pines. Through these rocky wilds wound the frozen Platte, hemmed in by perpendicular walls of rock hundreds of feet high, producing grand cañons which would be difficult to equal in wildness, grandeur, and desolation.

One of the finest and wildest of these mountain ridges was in the neighbourhood of a ranche beyond the Medicine Bow Creek, occupied by a man of the name of Austin. A rough, but very hearty stock-man, he was one of those hardy characters to be met with only in the advanced positions of civilization. In past life he appeared to have been always ready to fill any position that came across his path. At one time engaged as a soldier in the Northern army, fighting against his brethren of the South; then taking his turn with his comrades in one of those wretched Indian wars; and he was now settled down here with a partner of a kindred spirit, possessing about 800 head of cattle and a score of horses, in a country but very lately held by the warlike and cruel Sioux, and probably still to be subjected to their raids. Here he retained much of his soldier's training. Everything in this ranche was done systematically and by clockwork. Early hours were strictly observed. We breakfasted by lamplight ;

and directly supper was over, about nine o'clock, turned in, when the solitary coal-oil lamp was turned out. This did not altogether suit the lazy habits of some of my men; but, as it offered greater chances of sport, it agreed well with my own keen spirit.

The only piece of luck I had during my stay here was getting a coyoté (prairie-wolf), which, being pressed with hunger, actually penetrated to the cattle-sheds by the ranche. We were sitting at breakfast one morning, when in rushed a cattle-boy with the information. Seizing my rifle, I ran out; it was so dark I could scarcely see the form of the animal, much less the fore-sight of my rifle, but I could hear the beast snapping his jaws at one of the dogs. He allowed me to approach so close that I could almost have struck him with the end of the barrel, when by a lucky shot I put a ball through his heart.

On leaving Austin's we had to cross a low divide of the Seminole range, and when on a high, bare *plateau* came in for another of those fearful snow-storms. It was with difficulty we made way against it, and glad were we when we sighted once more our old friend the Platte, on the banks of which we had decided to camp.

On crossing the river on the ice, the first and only accident happened which befell any of our party in its wanderings. Griff Evans, who was, as usual, driving one of the teams, was jolted off the high driving-seat, and falling on the side on which he carried a six-shooter, drove that weapon violently into his ribs. Luckily the result was nothing more than a severe bruising, but Griff did not for many a day

afterwards, take at all a hopeful view of his injuries.
He was at first apparently but little hurt, and was
able to take the leading part in a most disagreeable altercation between himself and Edd Herridge
as to where camp should be made. Griff wanted to
go some miles back to an old cabin on the side of
the mountains; Edd said it was too late in the day
to go so far, and that he and the others would
camp on the river, whatever Griff did. High words
ensued, and at last I saw Griff's waggon, with my
blankets, clothes, and other necessaries going in
one direction, whilst the other waggon, driven by
Hank, and containing all the food and cooking
utensils, was bound in another. Then I thought it
was high time to assert my authority. To be without the contents of either one of the waggons,
even for a single night in such a climate, was too
serious a matter, so I ordered Griff back, and both
disputants to camp in a spot selected by me. This
succeeded, and things went on much as usual. But
when Griff's temper began to cool down, the pain of
the bruise began to come up, and he bemoaned
his sufferings loudly and persistently. Unfortunately, none of my outfit were adepts in the surgical
art, and his groanings were such that I really
began to be afraid he was seriously injured. I
thought perhaps some ribs were broken, and had
pierced the lungs or done some other internal
injury. The affected part was so tender that he
could not bear any one to touch it. I could feel his
pulse, which was so quiet that I was reassured and
endeavoured to comfort him, but without much
success. By this want of "grit," as my men called
it, Griff did not rise in their estimation; they

declared that there was "too much of the grand-
mother about him."

It was pretty evident that we should be detained
here some days, before Griff would be so far recovered as to be able to move. Fortunately we were
in the neighbourhood of a cañon of the Platte, said
to be very good for mountain sheep; and that there
moreover resided at a ranche close by, a first-class
old hunter, whom I hoped to induce to accompany
me on the hunt, and to show me the likely country.
I found him most willing, and it was soon arranged
that we should have a hunt the next day. Starting
from his abode, which was close to our camp, we
walked some little distance up the cañon on the
frozen river; and then turned up a very stony gully,
between steep granite rocks, a sort of place which
would be called a "screten" in the Highlands.
The scenery was magnificently grand; through
the narrow and precipitous cañon flowed the usually
roaring river, now silenced in most places by a
coating, not of inches, but of feet of ice; only here
and there, where the torrent was so rapid and
weighty as to preclude freezing, was anything to be
seen or heard of its waters. In these spots the
stream appeared of a bright green colour, boiling up
through the dull white of the surrounding snow and
ice. Magnificent walls of red columnar granite rose
abruptly from the very edge of the river to a height
sometimes of 1,500 feet, often in strange and castel-
lated forms, like ruined strongholds. Occasionally
isolated rocks stood out like solitary giants; at other
times they ran up in one sheer face almost to the
level of the mountain plateau above. It was curious
to observe how in every little nook and hollow capable

of holding a handful of soil, luxuriated the cedar,
the pine, or some of the many varieties of dwarf
red shrubs which grow in these parts.

A CAÑON OF THE PLATTE.

From a Sketch by A. P. V.

Up one of the most practicable of these slants we
toiled, until we had reached the level of the mountain
country. From the first it required but half an eye
to see that my companion, Bennett, was a hunter of
no ordinary merit. It did one good to see the care
with which he scanned every rock as it came fresh
into view, and took note of every track we came
across. We had got the wind all right, blowing
straight down from the country we were going to
hunt, and I felt full of hope.

As we approached the ridge Bennett evidently
thought we were near game; he advanced to the
sky-line with as great care and caution as the most
experienced Highland stalker. I watch him closely,

and feel he has seen something. With an expressive gesture he motions me to keep low, and a gleam lights up his weather-beaten face. Crawling forward a little I am enabled to take in the ground he sees. Yes, by Jove! there they are at last! The beasts I have toiled so hard after for so many weeks, and almost within a long rifle-shot. What a heart-beating sight! a herd (or " band " as they are here called) of about a dozen ewes and lambs and two bucks, one, a grand old fellow, the other a three-year-old. What game, quaint-looking creatures they are, with their rich brown and white coats and queer horns. They are lying and feeding on the other side of a gulch, or little glen, about 400 yards from where we are. Some of them are evidently suspicious, for their heads are up, and the old ram is already thinking of moving. Bennett is, however, as cool as a cucumber, and surveys quietly the intervening ground with the eye an old stalker. Quickly he pronounces the attack hopeless from this quarter, and whispers that we must get back as quietly as we can, return down the slope and get in on them further up the cañon. This we at once commence to carry out, and I hope, as we move away, that the beauties will settle down again, and that we shall be able to get a good chance at them from above. But, alas! here I am again doomed to disappointment, for when we come next in sight of their whereabouts, not a beast is to be seen—all have " skinned out." What a disappointment, and after such days of toil and hardship! But it is no use bemoaning our luck, so we are soon on their tracks, following them up the cañon as fast as we can. They had, however, made good their escape, and we saw them no more that day.

As a sort of consolation, on our way back in the evening we came on a fine cow elk, which I killed for camp meat, and very fine steaks she furnished.

Besides being a good hunter, Bennett was unusually good company; most of his life had been spent as a trapper, and he was full of anecdotes of his experiences. One story I cannot help repeating, as, from the reputation of the man who told it me, and his whole manner, unlike many bear stories, I believe it to be true. It was as follows :—Bennett and two partners were "after furs," that is, on a trapping expedition. Having got "quite a number," one of them had gone down to dispose of some at the nearest post and to bring back necessary stores. A night or so after his departure a bear came and took away three tame beavers, besides a quantity of meat. This so enraged the hunters that they determined to set a trap for the marauder. Accordingly half an antelope's carcase was pinned to the ground, around it a line was stretched and fastened to the trigger of a rifle, loaded and pointed at the savoury bait. The trap was skilfully conceived and carefully set. Very soon after the hunters had retired to their "bunks" they were aroused by the discharge of the rifle, and on going out found a grizzly bear's cub lying dead. Pulling the body inside the small tent, they reset the trap and turned in again. In a very short time they were made aware of a most unwelcome visitor, in the shape of the old she-bear herself. She had come to look for her cub, and having scented it, had followed it into the tent. The poor beast fondled the dead offspring and licked it and whined over it, sometimes in her movements actually treading on the hunters' feet and legs. The

wretched men scarcely dared to breathe, knowing
perfectly well that that moment she discovered them
would most likely be their last. At last she left,
when, fearing that she would return they lost no
time in leaving the tent and getting up the nearest
tree. She did return and remained "quite a while,"
but, although now safe, our friends were by no
means to be envied, for the night was bitterly cold,
and they were "up a tree" in the lightest of costumes. Eventually she again retired, when Jack at
once declared "that he could stand it no longer, no,
not for all the bears in Wyoming," so down he came
and lighted a fire, and fortunately the bear did not
again appear.

As might be supposed, after having once sighted
sheep, I was not likely to leave the locality without
another try for them, but again without success. Once
indeed we found them high up the cañon, but they
had seen us and were scuttling up through the rocks
like rabbits. I fired and my men fired too, but the
enfilade resulted in neither killed nor wounded. This
second time the three-year-old ram was with them,
but the old fellow had taken himself off, no doubt
thinking himself like many an old red deer stag,
safer in perfect solitude than with the rest of the
herd.

In this cañon we came across the den of a mountain lion, a large hole between great boulders of
granite. The smell from it was most offensive, and
quantities of bones of animals and birds scattered
around the entrance testified to the destructive power
of the formidable owner. The men who were with me
pronounced him "at home," but as we had no means
of bolting him, nothing could be done. Unfortu-

nately, we never thought of smoking him out, which I believe would have been practicable, and which operation—so Griff told me—was on one occasion successfully carried out in Estes Park. The " boys," however, were so scared at the sudden appearance of the lion amongst them, that they all fired wildly and the brute escaped unscathed. Bolting mountain lions, after the manner of ferreting rabbits, would at any rate have been a novelty in the sporting line, and I wished much that we had thought of the smoking expedient.

Evans was now so far recovered that we were able to make a move, and glad enough we were to do so. Our camp here had been anything but a good one; the locality abounded in sand, which in the windy weather which prevailed, was a source of real discomfort. Nothing could keep it out; it penetrated food, clothes, and bedding. When mixed with one's victuals it was especially disagreeable and distasteful. A slight misfortune, too, had happened to our store of sugar; the can of "coal-oil" (paraffine) for the lamp had leaked, and some of its contents had found their way into the bag. This oil certainly possesses a wonderful power of penetration, for although only a few drops apparently had escaped, yet the whole contents of the bag were tainted and uneatable as sugar. Hank contrived, however, to make a very passable syrup of it by simmering it in a frying-pan for a long time over a dull fire.

Our line of march from here lay at first north-east, along the right bank of the Platte, which we then crossed and headed due north across a sandy, alkaline prairie. Although very little grass appeared on the surface, great quantities of cattle were thriving on it. It is said, however, that owing to the alkaline deposit on these plains they lose their teeth prematurely. Here and there were enormous bushes of sage (*artemisia tridentata*), usually only a few inches high, but in this locality luxuriating by the side of the streams in the most wonderful way, and attaining the size of large shrubs. In one spot they were over my head on pony-back, and I had some difficulty in forcing my way through them. A decoction of this shrub, which goes by the name of " sage tea," is in much repute amongst the hunters and others for the treatment of all sorts of illnesses, especially what is locally called " mountain fever," which seems to be of the typhoid type and occasionally ends fatally. My men had a story of two men suffering from it at one of the frontier towns; one of the cases was scientifically treated by the army doctor, the other with sage tea by the local tailor. The sage-tea patient got well, but the other succumbed to the disease. The most common growth on these true alkaline plains is what is locally called " grease wood," a spare, small, and at this time of year (December) leafless shrub, from which, when burning, a sort of oil or grease exudes, hence the local name. It is too quick burning for a good camp fire when used alone, but when mixed with sage-bush does very well.

The margins of the little lakes, of which there are many in this locality, are covered with a thick coat of an alkaline salt. I did not keep any for analysis, but judging from the taste the chlorides of sodium and calcium appeared to be the chief ingredients of its composition.

We were still in the land of antelope, though less

numerous than further south, and on one occasion I
nearly spent a night out through hunting them. As
was my custom when on the march, I was riding
within sight of the waggons, but so far ahead as to
get a sight of game before it was disturbed. A herd
of antelope had attracted my attention, and I had
ridden off alone for a stalk. The men had seen
me, and I had got my shot so soon that I was
afraid almost of firing, so direct were the waggons
in the line of fire. Having killed, I waited by the
dead antelope, expecting one of the men would come
back to "dress" it, and "pack" it to the waggons.
When, however, after waiting some time no one
appeared, I gralloched it myself, and cutting off the two
haunches—called here "hams"—and the head, and
packing them as well as I could on my saddle, set
off in pursuit of the waggons. But nowhere could
I strike the trail; the soil was light and sandy, and
a strong breeze was blowing, so that it was, to
my comparatively obtuse sense of sight, quite oblite-
rated. What was to be done now? If I rode
after the teams, it would be at a great risk of
never seeing them again, at any rate for that day,
for Edd Herridge himself, our chief pilot, had been
in doubt when starting of the exact course to be
steered, and he meant to make it out as he went
along. I must confess to feeling very uncomfortable;
but I was mounted, and had meat, and could make
a fire, so, had I only had my blankets with me, I should
have had nothing to fear, unless one of those awful
winter storms had broken upon me.

After carefully considering my position, I came to
the conclusion that the first thing I had better do
was to mount a hill which I saw not very far off,

and take a survey with my glass ; perhaps from that elevated spot I might see something of the teams. This I did at once but not a vestige was to be seen of my outfit. I spied all the country most carefully, and hoped for some time that the teams might be in some hollow, and would come suddenly into sight ; but no ! they had evidently " made good time " after I had left them, and got clear away over some distant sky-line.

It was now late in the afternoon, so I had to make up my mind quickly what to do. The weather was fearfully cold, and even with plenty of food and a good fire, a night without blankets was a thing to be avoided.

On speering around I was able to make out with the glass, in the far distance, a sort of habitation which had the appearance of an Indian lodge, or "tepee." We had passed within sight of it in the morning and I had heard some of the men discussing what it was. I had gathered that they believed it to be some sort of white man's ranche. I now could see it plainly with the aid of my stalking-glass, and could moreover make out figures moving about, and smoke rising up near it, so that at any rate it was inhabited. On consideration I thought that I had better ride back to this place, where most likely, I should get shelter and perhaps assistance in refinding my outfit, the loss of which in itself was an awkward matter in this boundless country. Taking the exact bearings with my compass, I descended the hill and rode straight away for the edifice. I was rather uneasy about the reception I should get on my arrival at these strange quarters, but I had uniformly experienced nothing but hearty

welcomes from the " cow-punchers " of the west.
If then they were whites I was not apprehensive ;
but what if my men were wrong and they were
Redskins ! We had heard there were two camps
of the Arrapahoes out on the war-path a little further
on ; they were nominally after their old enemies the
Utes, but the " young bucks "—as the young
warriors are called—are said to be not over particular
" whose hair they lift " when they are out on the
war-path. But, I argued to myself, these frontier
men are not often mistaken, especially in the matter
of Indians; besides, I will take the precaution not to
go straight into camp until I have reconnoitred. At
any rate shelter at night at this time of year, in case
of a storm, is most needful, so I determined to
push on.

I made such good speed, that I had bright daylight for approaching the curious-looking erection,
but when I was hundreds of yards off I was able
easily to determine the nationality of the occupants,
by that peculiar western vernacular which issued
from many lusty throats at once. It was evident
that there was here a large gathering of ranchemen, and it seemed that they were employed on
some cattle matter, but what that was I could not
for some time make out. On getting nearer I at
last discovered that the process called " branding " was being carried out on a considerable
scale. No one noticed my approach, so intent were
they all on their work. At length I got one of
them to attend to my queries, and from him I
ascertained that there were amongst the company
two old acquaintances whom I had met further
up the country. They were delighted to see me,

and gave me a hurried but very hearty welcome. I was at once asked to partake of the shelter of their small tent, but as there were already three in it, and no spare blankets, I must "bunk with Jack Rogers," i. e., sleep under the same blankets with that worthy individual. Well, shelter was everything, and Jack was a very good fellow, so this was soon settled. They were fortunately short of meat, so my haunches of antelope came in very acceptably, and were much approved of.

Perhaps I should not weary my readers were I to say a few words on that process in stock-raising on which the whole party was here engaged, namely, branding cattle.

Besides the original branding of the calves, when stock changes hands in these parts it is necessary that the old brand should be crossed through, and that of the new owner placed alongside. When a herd is sold, the plains are scoured far and near for the cattle with the required mark. These are all gathered and confined in a "corrall" or pen or fank, formed of timber, which is called "corralling." At one corner of the corrall is a passage formed of strong and high posts and rails, so narrow that only one beast can get through it at a time. At the end of this passage, opening on to the prairie, are some strong slip rails. The stockmen force the cattle in the corrall into this narrow passage. Outside the corrall is a blazing wood fire, in which the branding-irons are heated almost to a white heat. These are pressed on to the flanks or quarters or shoulders of the cattle as they get jammed singly into the narrow passage. A couple of men stand at the slip rails, and let them out as they are operated upon. They can thus be branded and taken stock of at the same time. The burning portion of the process sounds cruel, but it was quickly over, and I saw no sign of after-suffering on the part of the liberated animals.

Several occupants of neighbouring ranches had come together here, besides those directly interested in the transaction, their object being to see that none of their own cattle got transferred in error, and to lend a helping hand. The bellowing of the half-wild cattle and the shouting of the eager stockmen can be better imagined than described. The latter became greatly excited when one of the cattle broke out of the corrall before it was branded, which occasionally happened. As there were ten or twelve ranchemen, and over 800 cattle taking part in the branding, it is not to be wondered at if the proceedings were a trifle noisy, but I saw no loss of temper.

During supper a lively conversation took place on various matters, connected with cattle and agriculture. One question causing great discussion was as to when a calf became a head of cattle? The decision arrived at was that every beast born after the preceding month of March was still a calf, and therefore not paid for as a unit of cattle.

Then arose a mighty debate as to the agriculture future of the territory of Wyoming. The Colorado men did not believe in it as a grain-bearing district, but the Wyoming boys stuck up gallantly for their native territory. One of them brought forward a very telling argument in support of the fertility and capabilities of its soil. "It could grow strawberries," he said, "for he had been in the summer time prospecting for a tie camp

(i. e. looking out for a locality where railway sleepers could be cut), when he struck some elegant strawberries." Having ate until he was "crowded," he wished to take some back to camp, but had nothing to carry them in. At last he bethought himself of his socks, filling both of which, he returned satisfied to camp! "Were they good, Frank?" I asked. "You bet, sirree, a way up," was the heartfelt reply.

Amongst the ranchemen assembled here was one of those marked examples of what steadiness and application will do in this new world in the person of an Irish Canadian, Tim Foley by name. He had come into this country ten years ago; since which he had led the varied life of a rancheman, settled on the extreme frontier of civilization. Many a skirmish had he had with the Indians of Arizona; on three occasions he had been wounded. He was said to be a very good "Indian fighter," and a capital shot. Although reported not to have had a dollar in his pocket when he first came into the States, he is now valued at $100,000 (80,000*l.*). A remarkable trait about him was that he never swore, a proof that swearing is not a necessity, even for a "cow-puncher." Besides these rougher qualities he bore such a reputation for straight dealing as any one might have envied, and was universally respected by all who knew him. What a pity it is for this young country that there are not more such characters, but I fear Tim Foley was in many respects a great exception to the common rule.

The following morning I tried in vain to get some one who knew the country to help me in finding my outfit, but every hand was engaged with the all-important branding.   All they could do was to give me the fullest directions in their power how to reach the " Sweet-water," on which they thought my party would certainly have camped.

Having ascertained my route as well as I could I started away alone, and within fifteen miles struck that small river, along the banks of which passes the old emigrant road to Utah and the other western countries.   After following this road a mile or so, I was delighted to see in the distance a figure riding towards me, which I soon recognized to be little Griff Evans.   Although in truth enchanted to be with him again, I could not help giving him a bit of my mind for his neglect in not waiting for me the day before.   His excuse was that they thought I had not killed, and would be sure to get their tracks and follow on directly.   When I did not make my appearance they began to be uneasy, thinking that I should be out all night and have a hard time of it, and that morning early a general search had been organized.   Hank had gone out in one direction, Edd and Lee in another—with the hope, too, of getting some camp meat—and little Griff had taken the back tracks of yesterday.

They had made camp near the celebrated Independence Rock, close to which was a large cattle ranche.   We soon reached it, passing on the side of the deeply-worn emigrant road the graves of three soldiers formerly of the 11th Ohio Cavalry, who, as stated on the little grave-boards, were killed near here by Indians in 1863.   This route being one of the best known to California, has been the scene of many a skirmish, especially about the time of the first discovery of gold in that state. The Indians most hostile to the whites were the Sioux and the Arrapahoes. The former have now betaken themselves further to the north, but the main body of the Arrapahoes are at present located on the Platte River, near Fort Casper, about twenty-five miles from this. They are, I am told, an off-shoot of the Sioux, and generally act in concert with them in all their wars. Just now they are supposed to be friendly to the whites, and are in the winter quarters assigned to them by the United States Government; but the settlers do not seem to have much faith in their professions, and are of opinion that when the spring comes, and they can afford to be independent of Government for their supplies, their good behaviour will be abruptly terminated.

In the range of ruddy peaks to the eastward is encamped a large party of Ute Indians on a hunting expedition; the smoke of their fires being at times visible from our own encampment. This tribe has been of late years friendly to the whites, but a deadly feud exists between it and the Arrapahoes and Sioux. The two latter are tribes of the plain, and the Utes belong to the mountains. The Redskins fight to advantage on the kind of ground they are accustomed to, and in their skirmishes victory follows accordingly; if the fighting occurs in the plain, the Sioux win, if in the mountains, they are " whipped." The report that there are now two small bands of Arrapahoe bucks on the war-path encamped near here, is confirmed by one of the " boys " from the ranche, who had seen their camps. Their alleged object is to pick up some of the Utes from the mountains above, but this news is not agreeable either for ourselves or the ranchemen. For us it is unpleasant, for these Indians cannot be trusted, and if they were to come across one or two of us away from the rest, the temptation might be too great, and beside this, there is the risk of having our horses run off. This latter danger is shared by the ranchemen, and in consequence they are obliged to go round their stock once or twice every day.

The so-called Independence Rock itself is a curious round-topped granite rock, nearly a mile in circumference at the base, and a couple of hundred feet high. Being so directly on the main emigrant road, it has always been a well-known halting-place, and the base of the rock is literally covered with names and dates.

A few miles further up the river is the " Devil's Gateway," where the Sweet-water makes its way through a range of granite mountains. Fine walls of rock rise on each side of the river to the height of between 300 and 400 feet, affording some bluff and desolate scenery.

CHAPTER XIII.

"Mightiest of all the beasts of chase,
  That roam in woody Caledon,
Crashing the forest in his race,
  The Mountain Bull comes thundering on.

"Fierce on the hunter's quiver'd band,
  He rolls his eyes of swarthy glow,
Spurns with black hoof and horn the sand,
  And tosses high his mane of snow."

Sir W. Scott.

I was very anxious, before finally giving up the hunt, to obtain a few good specimens of the far-famed American buffalo, or, more correctly-speaking, "bison." I was told that I had a better chance of finding them within a few days' journey of this than in any other locality I was likely to visit. Accordingly sheep-hunting was put aside for the time, and a start was made for the buffalo country.

We had to get over a good bit of ground before we could hope for anything but antelope, and heavy work it was with our "played-out"

teams. We were not made the more comfortable
by coming across the tracks of Indians on the war-
path, moving in the same direction as ourselves,
and not more than a fortnight old. There was
the trail plain enough; the single line of ponies
with round-cut hoofs, and, as Edd Herridge pointed
out, no sign of lodge-poles, clearly showing that
they had no squaws with them and were "after
hair." Edd was so well up in Indian lore that he
was able to say from the trail that they were
Arrapahoes: it is probable too that he was unusually learned in such matters, from having himself
married an Arrapahoe beauty. After this unpleasant discovery it was necessary to be somewhat
cautious in our movements.

As it happened, that very afternoon we had a
"scare." Griff Evans was walking some little
distance ahead of the teams, stretching his little
legs after a spell of driving, when all of a sudden
he was seen running for us as fast as he could
toddle, gesticulating frantically. We halted at
once, and were naturally all anxiety to know what
he had seen, "Either buffalo, or Indians' ponies,"
he did not know which, and only about a quarter
of a mile further on, in a little gulch to our left
front!

Here was excitement indeed, whether it turned
out to be Indians or buffalo. The waggons were
drawn up close together, Hank and Griff left behind
with them, whilst Edd, Lee, and myself cantered
on to solve the burning question. Edd, who thought
very little of Griff, said we should find a lot of old
tree stumps; Lee believed that it would turn out
to be Indians, whilst I went in for buffalo. When

we had got to within 100 yards of the edge of the hill overlooking the little basin, we dismounted, made our horses fast, and advanced cautiously to the ridge, with our rifles at the ready. Then lying down, we crawled on and peeped through the undergrowth into the little corrie below. A very pretty sight awaited us, and the scare was over, for within 300 yards of where we lay a very nice little family party was quietly enjoying itself, consisting of an old and young bull and three cow buffalo of different ages. I am not ashamed to confess that my heart jumped at this my first sight of a beast of which I had heard so much all my life, but had never dreamed of seeing. But there was no time for sentiment. It was already very late and dark, and not a minute was to be lost.

On carefully surveying the ground we found there was no cover of any sort to hide us after we got within 200 yards of the still unsuspicious beasts. Thereupon Griff Evans was called up and a council was held. Griff and I were for taking the long shot that evening, late and dark as it was, but Edd Herridge, the only one of us four who had ever seen buffalo before, was so energetic against it that we were overruled. Edd argued, that it was so dark now that there would be no " show " at all that evening, but that the buffalo were sure to be in the neighbourhood in the morning, when we should be able to stalk them at leisure. Eventually we gave in, but most reluctantly, to Edd's judgment. We knew the chances of hunting, and experience had taught us that a "bird in the hand was worth two in the bush;" but Edd was a very old hunter too, and knew buffalo, so taking his advice we turned back with heavy hearts to the waggons.

Camp was formed about a quarter of a mile off, behind a few little ridges, to lessen as far as possible the chances of the buffalo being disturbed by our proximity during the night. All however, to no purpose; for when the next day came the closest hunt for miles around gave no trace of buffalo.

This little lot must have been a solitary party, which had strayed away across the range from the main herds. Our fire, and the unavoidable noises of camp, or, perhaps, some of our stock wandering, had scared them during the night, and they had probably made away across the range for their accustomed haunts. Often afterwards did I think of that little family, and wish I had stuck to my own opinion. I should most likely have wounded the old bull and got him with the aid of the dogs, dark as it was. Regrets in the morning were of no use, so after a fruitless search we " pulled out " and moved camp further towards the range, beyond which we had every reason to hope we should find more buffalo.

The following evening we made camp on the banks of a little rushing open stream, called " Horse Creek." Why it was not frozen I do not know, unless it was a warm spring, as my men said they believed it to be. Here was some grazing for the stock, which were beginning to get very poor, notwithstanding that they had had oats all the time. The question of food for them was now of so much importance that we determined not to attempt to take the waggons over the range of mountains which we were approaching, but

to "pack over" on some of the most suitable
of our bronchos, and leave the remainder with a
couple of men to recruit until our return. Before
doing so, however, Edd and I made a reconnoitring
expedition. We got over the divide late one
evening, and on looking down on to the plain
below saw right under us, only about a mile away,
three splendid bull buffalo. Edd was again for
delay ; would pack over here to-morrow and be sure
to find them again ; the buffalo were so placed that
no one could possibly "creep" them ; it was too
late for us to make camp afterwards, &c. &c. But
all these excuses were of no avail with me this time.
One lost chance was sufficient—I had learnt my
lesson ; so I stuck to immediate action, and down
we rode towards them.

The buffalo is a wonderfully keen-scented beast,
but he does not see or hear as well as the deer tribe.
Being able on this occasion to keep both out of sight
and to windward, we had no difficulty in riding to
within a quarter of a mile of them. Here we dismounted, and doubly secured our horses with the
lariats and hobbles, taking care to remove the
saddles, and bridles. In the vicinity of buffalo
horses cannot be too carefully seen to, for it is a
well-known fact that nothing scares a horse so much
as the sight or smell of a buffalo. A regular stampede will set in which nothing can stop, and should
they once get away, "it may be for ever" in this
wild country.

After leaving the horses we got into a sort of
frozen "creek," which, by occasional long bits of
very flat crawling, kept us well out of sight.
With some little difficulty we at last reached a

turn in the burn where the banks were tolerably high; and from here we were able to get on our feet, but had still to keep low, until we got under the very bank upon which the bulls were feeding. Edd had marked his ground well, for when I looked very cannily through the growth on the top of the bank, there were the three huge beasts within thirty yards of me. Cautiously pushing the muzzle of the rifle through the grass, I aimed carefully behind the shoulder of the nearest bull and very low, in accordance with previous instructions. It seemed as if it would be impossible to miss the huge lump— it was like shooting at a small haystack; but, like a haystack, there was no bull's-eye on it, no particular spot at which to take aim. Just as I fired they seemed to see or hear something, and were off; but I knew the great beast must have got the ball somewhere, so I turned my attention with the second barrel to one of the others, which were running straight away from me. I fired and saw him get the ball in the back just behind the shoulder, and he fell away at once from his companion.

Telling Herridge that I would follow this one if he would attend to the first, which was crawling on badly wounded, off I ran with my old dog "Ned." On crossing a small ridge, I sighted my friend about 300 yards off, making very bad time over the broken ground. I at once put "Ned" round him, and away the colley went as cheerily as if he was going to herd a domestic cow. Directly the buffalo saw him he turned about and made a magnificent charge, with a momentum sufficient to knock a house down. "Ned" saw him coming, waited very quietly until he was quite close, then jumped a few feet on one side, and directly the buffalo had passed commenced yelping again at his heels. The bull did not turn again, but continued his retreat at a jog trot. On observing this, I called in "Ned" and followed on. When the bull caught sight of me he pulled up, but being very young at the work, I foolishly went on towards him, just as I should have done in the case of a deer. I wished to make sure work, so did not fire until I had got within thirty yards, when I dropped on my knee and let go both barrels. Most fortunately the second ball broke one of his forelegs bringing him partly down, and he then gradually rolled over on to his side. I cannot make out why he did not charge me before I fired. It was a most dangerous proceeding on my part, the result of absolute inexperience, and Herridge was quite scared when he came and saw from what a short distance I had fired the *coup de grâce.* Edd had had no difficulty in coming up with the first bull, but had been obliged to fire several shots before he finished him. They were both magnificent old bulls, and most perfect specimens of their kind. I measured one of them with the following results :—height at shoulder, six feet exactly ; girth of neck, eight feet ; girth behind shoulder, ten feet. The weight was estimated as twenty hundredweight when "dressed," and a business it was to dress him, Edd almost disappearing into the cavity in the process.

When we had got them nearly ready, I volunteered to go down and bring up the bronchos. I found them all right, and got them saddled and bridled, and was leading them up quietly, one by the bridle, the other by the lariat, when, without the

smallest apparent reason, a scare seized them and
the one I held on the lariat tore past me like a
locomotive. The sudden and violent tightening of
the lariat threw me instantly on to my hands and
face; upon which the second brute, of course, followed suit, and there I lay flat on my face, being
dragged along the hard frozen ground as fast as
they could gallop. Fortunately I was not entangled
in the rope, and was soon able to shake myself
loose. My feelings when I picked myself up re-
sembled what I remember in my boyhood, after
a fall when running on a hard gravel path; the
palms of my hands stung and tingled fiercely, and
all the wind was knocked clean out of my body, leaving a most uncomfortable vacuum. On getting on
to my feet again, I felt inclined to let go at the fast-
disappearing forms of our ill-conditioned bronchos,
but was able luckily to hold my hand. Well, here
was a pretty mess! Nearly dark, many miles away
from camp, with the horses gone, perhaps to be seen
no more! There was no use, however, in lamenting
or raving, so on I walked for the ridge, over which
the brutes had disappeared, and had the satisfaction of seeing them picking at some tufts of buffalo-
grass about half a mile further on. A cautious
stalk brought me within reach of the dragging
lariat of the one, and after a short struggle he was
secured. Then with the assistance of the first, I
was able to get hold of the second; so, fortunately,
there was no harm done, beyond the loss of
Herridge's heavy Californian stirrups, which had
gone adrift in the stampede, and the shaking I had
come in for myself.

The following day we took some of the ponies to

fetch back as much meat as we wanted for camp use, but to our disappointment all was tainted and uneatable. The fact is that the hides of the bulls are so thick that, unless taken off at once, the meat immediately heats and spoils. All we could do, therefore, was to skin both beasts, cut off the heads, and return with these to camp. We poisoned the carcases for coyotés, and got a couple by the proceeding. The heads and hides were very heavy, and as much as two bronchos could carry.

In consequence of this beef spoiling, we were now, for the first time, short of camp meat, and reduced to a sort of hash, enjoying a very rough epithet amongst the western hunters, and composed of odds and ends of past meats, with bacon, and flour, and pepper, &c., which was by no means palatable, and very greasy. But this unsatisfactory state of the commissariat did not last long, for the next day we were after buffalo again, and I killed a fat three-year-old bull, which afforded excellent food for the remainder of our hunt. At the same stalk I killed a second bull, from which we had only time to secure the hump and tongue.

We had a good deal of difficulty in finding the buffalo on this last occasion, but when found they were in vast numbers. From one spot I was able to count, with the aid of my glass, no less than eleven separate herds! The size of the herds varied from hundreds to units. As far as I could make out they were all bulls, for this district, being nine or ten thousand feet above the sea, is too cold for the cows, which keep further down in the plains.

Although at first rather dispiriting and very fatiguing, this last day's buffalo hunt was not with-

out its excitements. In the first stalk I had
just shot the fattest young bull we could see, when
all of a sudden there was a scream of "Look out,"
from Lee, who was behind, and a terrible rushing
noise broke on us. There was no time to move
before a herd of buffalo, with their heads down,
tore past within ten yards of us, in blind terror!
Nothing could have saved us had we been in their
way; but, fortunately, we were just out of it. We
supposed that they must have heard the shots, and
not knowing where the danger was, had become
mad with excitement and fear, and had rushed
into the very teeth of it. Hank, who was an
old and experienced buffalo hunter, gave me
to-day a practical illustration of the ferocity of a
wounded buffalo. One of those I shot was, by the
first ball, only incapacitated from getting out of a
small hollow into which he had run. On seeing us
close by him, he became perfectly frantic, and persistently endeavoured to get up the bank at us. Hank
threw him his hat, which he knelt on, and gored,
and rammed into the earth with his massive head
in a perfect frenzy. I never saw such a determined exhibition of ferocious intentions, and felt
thoroughly convinced of the small chance any one
on foot would have of escaping, when charged in
open ground. I do not, however, for a moment
believe that a wounded buffalo will "go for" a man
when he thinks he can get away. He always looks to
flight as his best mode of preservation from his
great enemy, and it is only when he feels he cannot
escape by aid of his legs that he will charge. I
should have had no difficulty in killing almost any
quantity in this locality, and glad enough would my

men have been to take part in the proceeding; but all the excellent meat would have been lost, as we should have been unable to pack it, and I could not be a party to such a shameful waste.

Poor Bison Americanus! I fear you are destined soon to be reckoned amongst the good things of the past. But before saying a few words on this interesting question, I will touch very briefly on the beast itself, and the modes of hunting it.

A BULL BUFFALO (*Bison Americanus*).
From a Sketch by A. Beverly.

As is now generally known, the American buffalo is, properly speaking, no buffalo at all, but a bison, one of the great distinctions being that the latter is invariably covered with a woolly hair. The American variety seems to correspond with the European auroch (*bison*, or *bonassus Europæus*), but is somewhat smaller. This question is fully entered upon in an exhaustive article on the bison in the United States Government Report, by Mr. Allen, who was attached to Dr. Hayden's surveying party of 1875.

There are two ways of hunting buffalo, viz. "creeping," *i.e.* stalking, on foot, and riding them down on horseback. Of the first only have I had any personal experience.

Hunting buffalo on foot very much resembles any other kind of stalking. Attention must be paid to the seeing, hearing, and smelling powers of the animal, especially to the last, which I believe to be as acute as those of a deer. When they are numerous, and the ground broken, I can quite understand that one would soon get tired of this sport. I doubt very much, however, whether I should not get sooner sick of the second mode, which is riding into the herds, and shooting them down with a rifle or heavy six-shooter. There may be an art in singling out the most desirable beasts, and Colonel Dodge, in his interesting book, "Hunt-ing Grounds of the Great West," says that there is, but from what I have been told by men who have tried it, one "run" has generally been sufficient for them. The riding down must, at any rate, lead to a greater waste of life. It is said that for one bagged masses are wounded, which afterwards die, and are never found by the hunter.

As to the comparative danger of the two modes, there is, with ordinary care, but little in either. In riding buffalo no harm is likely to happen, unless the ground is very bad, and your horse comes down. If the horse is an old stager he will take very good care of himself, both against the roughness of the ground and the charges of the buffalo. In stalking them it is only needful to keep out of sight of the wounded buffalo, or at such a distance as to make a charge improbable. Want of care in this respect has often led to deplorable accidents. At the time one of my men was hunting on the Republican River, a young hunter was killed in the following way. With a friend he had fired at an old bull, and wounded him. Finding the range too great to finish him "right away," he had attempted to get nearer without being seen, but the bull "picked him up" and "came for him." On perceiving this his nerve seems to have failed him, for, dropping his rifle, he tried to escape by running. Of course he was speedily overtaken and gored to death before his companion's eyes, who could not get to him in time to help him.

So much for the two ordinary modes of killing buffalo; but such has been the miserable and wanton destruction of this fine beast during the last fifteen years, and the apparent apathy of the Government in checking it, that but a short time must elapse before it will be difficult to obtain a buffalo by any method. It is only a marvel, when one reads of the thousands, aye, millions, which have been slaughtered, how any even now survive. But it is very evident that they are getting terribly reduced in numbers, and are now found only in a comparatively small portion of the country. The Government Report says:—"Instead of roaming over nearly half of the continent, as formerly, they are restricted to two small, widely-separated areas."

It is easy to discover the reason of the great

diminution of numbers. In old times the buffalo's two enemies were the Red Indians and the grey wolf; and it would appear as if the natural increase had been sufficient to meet these two causes of waste. When, however, the white man came on the scene, armed with repeating rifles and six-shooters, and possessed with a wanton spirit of destruction, this was no longer the case, and the almost countless herds soon became both smaller and less numerous.

To show to what an extent the wasteful and sinful slaughter was carried on by the whites, we read in the Government Report before referred to (p. 554), that "the number of hides shipped from Dodge City alone in three months, from September 23rd, 1872, was 43,029, and 1,436,290 pounds weight of meat, and *that only the saddles were saved*"—the remainder of the animals being left to rot on the prairie. That "at least 50,000 buffalo were killed here in these three months; but the return for January exceeded those of the preceding months by over *one hundred and fifty per cent;*" thus making the number of buffaloes killed, "merely around Fort Dodge and the neighbourhood, for this period of four months, exceed *one hundred thousand!* This does not take into account those killed in wanton cruelty—miscalled sport—and for food for the frontier residents." A little further on another report of about the same date is quoted from, which states that "thousands upon thousands of buffalo hides are being brought here (Wichita, Kansas). . . . . It is estimated that there are south of the Arkansas, and west of Wichita, from one thousand to two thousand men shooting buffalo *for their hides alone!*"

Another account states that "during the season

1872-73 not less than *two hundred thousand* buffaloes were killed in Kansas, *merely for their hides!*" All this means that an untold quantity of the finest beef was lost for purposes of food, and was actually allowed to putrefy where the poor beasts fell.

Again "it is stated" that, "in 1874, on the south fork of the Republican, upon one spot were to be counted *six thousand five hundred carcases of buffaloes, from which the hides only had been stripped, the meat was not touched, but left to rot on the plains!* At a short distance hundreds more of carcases were discovered, and, in fact, the whole plains were dotted with the putrefying remains of buffaloes. . . . It was estimated that there were at least two thousand hunters encamped along the plains hunting the buffalo. One party of sixteen stated that they had killed twenty-eight hundred during the past summer, *the hides only being utilized!*"

I will not go on with such sickening data; suffice it to say, that any amount of such evidence can be found, not only in the Government reports, but in other public as well as private documents. Is it possible to conceive a more wicked waste of the bountiful gifts of a Good Providence? Be it remembered, too, that in all probability the great mass of these poor slaughtered beasts were old or young cows, which are easier killed than the bulls.

At any rate—it may be thought—a good price for the hides could alone have promoted and permitted such a state of things. But pursuing the Government pages a little farther we find that the hide market "became glutted to such a degree that, whereas a few years before they were worth three dollars (12s.) apiece at the railroad station, *skins of bulls now*

bring only a dollar (4s.), and those of cows and
calves sixty and forty cents (about 2s. 6d. and 1s. 8d.)
respectively!"

When you add to this wanton and unremune-
rative slaughter the masses which are killed for
food by the whites, and by the Indians in other
parts of the States, and, further, the very large
quantity killed for no purpose whatsoever, but
solely for the sake of the amusement of killing, is it
any wonder that the poor buffalo is rapidly becoming
so scarce that there should be a general opinion he
will soon be altogether a beast of the past? Is it
not rather a wonder that he has survived to this
day?

One of my own "outfit" had been an old buffalo
hunter on the Republican, and quite confirmed the
foregoing accounts of the deplorable waste. He
told me he had seen *acres of putrefying carcases!*
His story was that the waste arose in consequence
of the inhabitants of the cities refusing to give the
hunters a fair price for the meat; that as long as
they got five cents (2½d.) per lb. it was all "hauled,"
but that when they could not get more than three
cents (1½d.) it was not worth the hunters' while to
haul it to the towns and stations, and *all was left to
rot!* In the winter of 1872-73, he himself and a
partner, with two or three "skinners" to assist,
killed over 2,500 buffalo, for the hides of which they
got an average price of $2½ (10s.) for the bulls, and
$1½ (6s.) for the cows. At first they got 10c. (say
5d.) each for the tongues, but such was the glut on
the market that afterwards they were literally
worthless.

I will conclude these few remarks on the buffalo

question by quoting a paragraph from the Government Report (page 556), bearing, as it does, on future legislation. It runs thus :—" These facts " (*i. e.* evidences of the extraordinary decrease in numbers of the buffalo, and of the very diminished area of their wanderings) " are sufficient to show that the present decrease of the buffalo is extremely rapid, and indicate most clearly that the period of his extinction will soon be reached, unless some strong arm is interposed in his behalf. As yet no adequate game laws for the protection of the buffalo, either by the different States and territories included within the range, or by the general Government, have been enacted. In a country so sparsely populated as is that ranged over by the buffalo, it might be difficult to enforce a proper law ; yet the parties who prosecute the business of buffalo-hunting professionally are so well known that it would not be difficult to intercept them, and bring them to justice if found unlawfully destroying the buffalo. It is evident that restrictions should be made not only in respect to season, but the young and the bearing females should be protected at all seasons. The Government might even set apart certain districts within which the buffalo should be constantly exempt from persecution." So writes Mr. Allen, a gentleman who has given the question great attention and is well able to form an opinion as to the character of the law to be framed and the possibility of carrying it out in these far-off regions. The difficulty appears to be not only the execution of a law, but the possibility of framing a measure which could so efficiently protect the comparatively small remnants as to give hopes of preventing their total extinction. It is now very late in the day, and the region to be supervised is very large, but the general obedience to the law is remarkable in these wild districts, and I was often astonished at the quiet way in which these western men accept the decisions of Congress, and submit to the authority of the executive. It seemed as if they generally thought active opposition quite hopeless in the long-run, and so content themselves with outspoken grumblings. I have little doubt, therefore, that the local authorities could enforce a new law. Perhaps the necessary protection might be provided by the issue of licences to professional killers at the outfitting towns, on the granting of which a heavy deposit might be required as a security for the observance of the law. The suggestion, too, of setting apart certain districts as "sanctuaries," within which the buffalo should never be molested, is one well worthy of consideration; but it is to be hoped that these would be better respected than the Indian reservations have often been. But, as I said before, the great difficulty seems the details of the Act. How are the cows to be dealt with? are none to be killed, or only a certain proportion? How is the slaughter for the hides alone, and the consequent waste of such masses of good meat, to be detected? How is the Indian hunting to be regulated? or the wanton shooting into the brown, so constantly indulged in by the whites, to be put a stop to?

Many indeed must be the difficulties of legislation, but all, I trust, are to be overcome when taken in hand by men acquainted with the evil and its practical bearings. And be the difficulties ever so great, the question is one well worthy of the consideration of even that busy assembly, the Congress of the American nation, involving as it does the destruction of thousands, aye, millions, of tons of food for the people.

Sincerely do I trust too that the opinions of many well able to judge may prove incorrect, namely, that it is now too late for legislation; for even so good an authority as Colonel Dodge says (p. 139), " The buffalo are virtually exterminated. No legislation, however stringent or active, could now do anything either for or against the trade in the buffalo product." At any rate it is the duty of the Government to make a determined effort to prevent the total cessation of what has hitherto been an important addition to the meat supply of both the red and white citizens of the west.

OUR CAMP IN THE SWEET-WATER COUNTRY.
From a Sketch by A. P. V.

CHAPTER XIV.

"Lost! lost! lost!"
Sir W. Scott.

AFTER we had had our buffalo hunt, and I had
secured two splendid specimen heads, we commenced
a retrograde movement on the "Sweet-water"
country, in which I hoped for some black-tail deer

and perhaps even sheep. The first camp we made was misplaced in one very important respect, and that was that the water of the beautiful-looking lake which had attracted us thither, was so impregnated with alum, I believe, as to be more like a dose of Epsom salts than anything else. Of course it was useless to man or beast, and we had to melt snow for all our wants. The water thus obtained possessed a most unpleasant taste of sage, and this important want settled us to move camp forthwith to the banks of the frozen river, which was within sight and only a few miles to the southward. Our intentions, however, were doomed to be frustrated; for the following morning (December 18th) all our horses disappeared in the most sudden and unaccountable manner. Herridge and I had seen them about nine o'clock before starting for hunting, and at ten o'clock when Hank went to fetch them in for moving camp, they were nowhere to be seen. At first we thought they had strayed, although they had hitherto been remarkably wellbehaved in this respect, but we thought that perhaps the want of good water had sent them off in search of that necessary commodity. When some days, however, had elapsed and nothing had been seen or heard of them, although most of the "outfit" had been engaged in tracking and scouring the country, we began to suspect the Arrapahoe bucks, who were still encamped in the neighbourhood. From the circumstances which afterwards came to light it is extremely probable that this was the right solution, and that these worthies had "run them off."

We had possessed altogether eleven of the horse

kind, nine of them " bronchos," six of which were
the property of the Estes Park Company, for which
I was personally responsible ; two belonged to Lee
and Hank, and one to Herridge. All these had had
very hard work, and were comparatively of little
value. The other two quadrupeds were the property
of Edd Herridge, and were large American horses,
great prizes in the eyes of an Indian. The nine
played-out bronchos were ultimately recovered,
having probably been released when found to be of
little worth, but poor Edd's horses were never seen
by us again ; most likely they had been taken to Fort
Casper, where the main body of the Arrapahoe tribe
were encamped, at the same time that the bronchos
were set free.

Here we were then, literally " planted," for we
had no means of dragging the two waggons containing our little all. It certainly was a lovely spot
to be " planted in," but anything like involuntary
detention is uncongenial, in fact it is disturbing to
the minds of most men, especially of those keen on
a move. I had intended to be in California ere this
—the middle of December—for my time was getting
short. But there was no help for it, so stand by I
must, at any rate for the present.

Fortunately our camp was at no great distance
from Independence Rock, near which there was a
stock ranche occupied by a man called Macdonald,
who, as might be supposed, was of Scotch extraction. This man good-naturedly hired out to us a
couple of his own bronchos, the best of which I kept
for my own hunting, whilst the other was employed
in looking for the stock. The first few days after
our loss I did pretty well, hunting chiefly alone,

but sometimes with one of the men when not required in the search. On one of these occasions, I had the misfortune to get my broncho hanged, the poor beast having got "scared" by something, after I had dismounted and left her fastened to a tree by the lariat. She had fallen down on the rope, and choked herself, although the knot had been made so as to be incapable of slipping. I was very sorry for the poor animal, and for myself, too, for that matter, in having to pay up $85 (£17), and to trudge back after hunting to camp, about eight miles in the dark.

Another day, when out with Lee, we discovered a well-made *cache* within a couple of miles of our camp. For the information of the uninitiated in hunters' parlance, a *cache* is a hole or cavity where something has been hidden. The superincumbent ground, in this case, had all the appearance of not having been disturbed since it was made, and what added to the interest of its further investigation was the discovery in close proximity of a white man's skull and other human remains, as well as a horse's skeleton. Various were the surmises as to the probable history of these thought-stirring relics. The most likely seemed to be that in the old days, when the overland road was well traversed by emigrants, a robber had lived in this sheltered hollow, that he used the *cache* for secreting his ill-gotten gains, had come back wounded from one of his raids, had died where we now found his remains, and that his poor horse had been left to starve where picketed. Supposing this to be the true solution, we thought it well worth while to take some trouble in opening up the *cache*, which, from its

A MOUNTAIN RANGE, WITH BLACK-TAILED DEER.   (From a Sketch by A. Bierstadt.)

Chapter XIII., page 368.

careful and solid construction of slabs of stone, and
great depth, took us some time to accomplish. Indeed, so hard and tiresome was the work that we
gave it up before the cavity was fully opened out.
Our labours were entirely thrown away, we found
nothing, and I had to console myself for trouble
and loss of time by thinking that it was something
to have seen a well-made *cache*.

It was now getting on towards the latter end of
December. The weather was bitterly cold, and
there were threatenings and prognostications of a
coming storm. I had killed in the vicinity a couple
of good black-tailed bucks, one of which was judged
at 200 lbs. (over 14 st.) "clean." There were signs
of sheep about, for which I still had a very keen
longing, and this keenness nearly cost me my life in
the following way.

One day when out with Griff Evans, we had come
across sheep tracks so very fresh that we thought
we must "jump" or sight them every moment.
All day long we hunted and spied, but without
getting a glimpse of our game. It so happened that
I had made an arrangement for the next day with
the rancheman Macdonald to convey me and some of
my goods in a light waggon to a place called Sand
Creek, whence I could get on to Rawlings, on the
Union Pacific Railroad. As it was not more than
twenty miles to Sand Creek, and the track over the
plain pretty fair, it was thought that the journey
could be made in daylight by starting as late as one
o'clock in the afternoon. The sight of the fresh
sheep tracks had fired my hopes, and, as the range
on which they were, lay somewhat in the direction
of Sand Creek, I settled with Macdonald to wait for

X

me at three o'clock at a certain spot a little distance
on the way; my object being by this plan to hunt
the range again the next forenoon and have another
chance of my longed-for sheep.

At a very early hour next morning Griff Evans
and I left camp, anxious to make our last day's
hunt as long as possible. We worked the rocky
ground of yesterday, but again unsuccessfully; the
sheep, we thought, must have moved, and having
got across the ridge by about three o'clock, we
gave up hunting and turned towards the place
where it had been arranged that Macdonald should
meet me. On coming in sight of the spot, there was
the waggon with Macdonald and Edd Herridge
moving slowly onwards, being then about a couple
of miles away. In order to make it clear that I
was on my way to join them, Griff suggested that I
should fire a shot, which apparently had the desired
effect, for the waggon instantly stopped. As Griff
Evans was not going with me, but was to stay
behind with Lee and Hank to search for the missing
stock, and as my direction now was straight away
from our old camp, neither he nor I thought it of
any use for him to come out of his way any further,
so I sent him and my old dog " Ned " back to camp,
and I then started off alone as direct as I could for
the waggon.

In descending the steep hill-side after parting with
Griff the formation of the ground soon hid the waggon, but as I had got my marks, I felt no uneasiness
on this score. The two miles or so were quickly
covered, but when I got to the spot where the waggon
had been, nothing was to be seen of it or the men.
I soon, however, got the track; and as the ground

was undulating, I thought they must be waiting for me in one of the hollows near. At any rate, I argued, let the worst come to the worst, it is not more than fifteen miles or so to Sand Creek ; I am still fresh—although I had been walking all day and had only had a "biscuit" (Angl., a roll) since a very early breakfast—and I think I shall be able to "make" the distance in the three and a half hours still remaining of daylight.

Now that I think all over it again, I know I was wrong ; I ought not to have attempted to follow on. On not finding the waggon, I ought to have made back at once for the old camp, and not have ventured on tracking a waggon fifteen miles over a country quite new to me, and with only a limited amount of daylight still left. Moreover it was mid-winter in a most severe climate, and there was impending one of those fearful storms which, if it had broken on me that night, must have proved fatal. But I was very anxious to get on ; all my arrangements had been made for leaving, and I hoped to be in more civilized parts on my way to California by Christmas-day, which was now very near.

On I pushed therefore, making, I thought, five miles an hour. The ground was hard and elastic, the air fine and bracing, and the track of the waggon easy enough to follow. I felt pretty comfortable as long as the light lasted, but when it began to wane—at about half-past six o'clock—my troubles commenced in earnest. About then, too, the character of the surface of the country seemed to undergo a change, the herbage became more and more sparse, and there were large patches of light loose sand, which under the influence of a smart breeze had partially filled up the wheel tracks, making them very difficult to follow. Then came the quickly-fleeting twilight of those regions, and with what regrets I saw the dear old sun go down that evening perhaps few have experienced. The difficulty of keeping the track increased every minute, until at last I spent most of the time on my hands and knees, groping for the very shallow ruts. A quarter of an hour or so more, and this failed me, and I found myself off the track and *lost !*

It soon got pitch dark, so dark that I could not recover a white handkerchief which I had laid down close to me as a mark, around which I might grope on hands and knees for the lost wheel-ruts.

What was now to be done? On cool consideration I thought I had come so fast for the first few hours that I must have " made " the fifteen miles, so ought to be very near Sand Creek, and acting on this I fired three shots in rapid succession, which ought, if heard, to lead to investigation. As it turned out afterwards I was actually only a quarter of a mile from some of the cabins, in fact so close that Herridge and Macdonald, when they heard the shots, thought they were from some of the " boys " in the cabins.

When I had fired the shots, I sat down, waiting anxiously for a response, but none came. What my feelings were then no one who has not been lost can imagine. Fearful stories of freezing to death and of the accompanying agonies came across me; amongst others, of a poor young trapper, who, meeting with an accident whilst hunting last year in this vicinity, was no longer able to endure his suf-

ferings from freezing and took the strychnine, which
he had in his pocket for the wolves.   Then I thought
that possibly, and even probably, starvation awaited
me.   Truly, at first, I had as much as I could do
to keep my head; I felt inclined to give it up and
lie down; if I did this I knew my fate was sealed,
and that probably I should never awake again.   I
realized fully that my life depended on keeping my
head, and I prayed for help to do so, and it was
granted to me throughout that fearful night.

It was now a little past seven o'clock; I knew the
moon would rise about half-past nine, and that possibly I might be able to recover the track in the
bright moonlight, if I could only stay here till then.
But a cutting wind was driving down from the
snow-covered mountains and *I soon began to freeze!*
I had no extra clothes, only those which I had
walked in all day, and there was no possibility of
building a fire, for there was no fuel, not even a sage
bush as big as a cabbage, anywhere within reach.
I attempted walking about, but I soon felt that in
the darkness I was getting further away from where
the track lay.   If I remained here, freezing stared
me in the face.   What then could I do?   The only
other course open to me was to try and make my
old camp on the "Sweet-water," which I thought
would be about twenty miles from here.   I had come,
I imagined, a south-westerly course since leaving
Evans, I therefore argued that north-east should
bring me back again.   At any rate I ought by this
course to strike the somewhat isolated range of hills
on which we had hunted, or perhaps I might strike
the Sweet-water river and if I did, it would be easy
enough then to find camp.   The stars were scarcely

visible through the cold haze which hung over the earth, but I was able at last to make out the North Star, to shape my course by.

It was evident very soon after starting again that I was not on the line of country I had just come over, the nature of the surface was so entirely different. Sometimes I was amongst boulders and rocks, sometimes almost on the edge of a precipice, whilst at other times I was ploughing through deep sand. It was a difficult matter to keep my course, as I had so often to make detours to avoid sudden and deep drops, but I kept on pretty straight, and what between fast walking and at times almost running I travelled at a good pace.

A little before ten the moon rose, and I saw to my right a faint outline of mountains. I hoped, and thought at first, that they were the range I sought for. Away to the left I saw some abrupt cliffs which looked like the Devil's Gateway on the Sweet-water; if so, I ought soon to strike the stream, and I walked on with redoubled vigour. But no, I was wrong; the river was not to be found where it should have been had my conjecture been right, and I wandered on down-hearted and dispirited.

At last I was all but "played out," and for other reasons too felt that I must have rest and a fire. Fuel was now a necessity, and I therefore made for the mountains, on the side of which there would most likely be some trees or shrubs. Mercifully, I soon came across a dead pitch-pine tree, and having matches in my pocket, and having luckily learnt the art of building a fire, I soon had a blazing one. I sat down before it and rested, my first real rest since early morning.

It was now past midnight; all was strange and weird around me; the very trees and rocks took uncanny forms; the only noises which broke the silence of the night were the wild howlings of the prairie wolves and the sighing of the wind through the pine trees. I could not rest long here, I began to be uneasy about the Arrapahoe Indians, who, I knew, were encamped not far below our old camp on the Sweet-water, and I did not know how near I might be getting to them. If they saw my fire, it might lead to an investigation on their part, and an easily-obtained white man's scalp, with rifle and ammunition, would probably be too great a temptation for the "young bucks," out, perhaps, on their first war-path; so at one o'clock I was off again, heading the same course as before.

The tops of the mountains were now enveloped in mist; not a single landmark could I recognize. Once, when coming over a low ridge, I fancied I saw a herd of antelope close to me; rather thoughtlessly I fired into them, hoping for meat; but, alas, it was only a few shrubs waving in the wind.

By three o'clock my strength was again failing me; I had had nothing to eat, except the one biscuit, since the early breakfast of the previous day, and I had been walking hard almost ever since. I was forced again to rest, and Indians or no Indians, I *must* have a fire. To add to my uneasiness, I felt too I might be going further and further away from all my known haunts and landmarks.

This time I got into a cleft in a rock, and built a fire in front of me, which had the double effect of preventing the fire from being seen except from the direct front, and of protection from the wind and from a rear or flank attack should the Indians by chance come on me.   Here I sat with my rifle across my knees—not daring to let myself fall asleep—until the first streak of early dawn appeared in the east, a little before seven o'clock.   How rejoiced I was to see it, an end at last to that miserable night, if not to my difficulties.   With the daylight I hoped to be able to make out some known landmark, and with this object I toiled up the steep hill-side immediately behind the spot where I had been rest-ing.   Broad sunlight soon reigned; *but not an out-line, not a feature, in the whole landscape, could I recognize!*   Broken-down, disheartened, exhausted physically and mentally, I again almost gave up; but I had mercifully got through the awful night, and I felt I must hold on.   I had still a few matches left, and my rifle and nine cartridges, so I might get on for some days longer unless assailed by a storm or Indians; besides, I would have another look from a mountain about a mile off, which I saw was much higher than the last, and would therefore command a better view.   For this I made, and again forced my weary limbs to the top.   This time, after a long survey, I thought I recognized the jagged ridge of a range of granite mountains which was visible from our camp on the Sweet-water, and amongst which the Utes were encamped.   If this was so, I must be down on the divide between the Platte and the Sweet-water, and close to the junction of these two rivers.   Near this spot I had understood the Arrapahoe camps to be, but I was relieved at not seeing anything of them.   How glad I was to believe I knew an outline can scarcely be ima-

gined. I was only afraid lest I should be again
wrong; but no, I felt the more certain the longer I
looked at the distant range. But in this case what
a distance I must have walked in the night; for I
had started a long way to the south and west of
Independence Rock, and would be now many miles
to the eastward of it.

Pulling myself together, I started at once in the
supposed direction of the rock, and at last reached
it about eleven o'clock. I need not be ashamed to
confess that I was completely exhausted. I had
eaten hardly anything since early the previous
morning, and had walked since parting with Evans
over sixty miles—at least so said one of Macdonald's
ranchemen, who the next day happened to pass over
a portion of my track—and this, too, after a long
day's hunting. The distance from the hill, from
which I had taken my last survey, to the rock was
fourteen miles in an "air line."

This night will be ever remembered by me. The
feeling of *being lost* was a strain on my nerves such
as I had never before experienced, and trust I may
never again be subjected to, and I can quite understand that a man might lose his senses under such
circumstances. Colonel Dodge narrates the following incident :—" When serving in Texas, a soldier of
my company became lost while returning to the post
from a small village two miles off. A party was
sent out in search for him, and on the second or
third day came upon him almost naked in a little
thicket. As soon as he discovered the party, he
bounded off like a deer, and was pursued. After an
exciting chase he climbed a tree, from which he was
taken by force, and with the greatest difficulty—

struggling, striking, and biting like a wild animal. He was brought back to the post perfectly wild and crazy, confined, and watched, and attended with the greatest care for over a month, before he recovered his mind. He was an excellent man, more than usually intelligent; but I doubt if he ever fully recovered the shock. He recollected nothing but going a little distance off the road for something, and getting 'turned round,' and realizing that he was lost." So sudden a loss of reason may seem improbable to those upon whom the fearful sensation of being lost in a trackless and inclement wilderness has never been forced; I have no difficulty in believing it.

It turned out in my case that I should not have been looked for for some days, inasmuch as each party thought I was with the other. It appeared that Edd Herridge and Macdonald, on coming to the rendezvous, had found the fresh track of a pony, and had taken it into their not over-wise heads that I had ridden on, and that they had not heard the shots I fired before Griff Evans left me. Not finding me at Sand Creek, they thought I had gone back with Griff to the old camp after hunting. They would not, therefore, have looked for me without further information. Griff and the rest of the outfit naturally thought I had joined Macdonald, and was at Sand Creek, so they would not have thought of my being lost until informed of that fact by the others.

Not a little astonished were they when I walked into the ranche that morning, and still more so when I told them of my adventures. "All's well that ends well," but I mean to take every human precaution

on any future occasion not to run the risk of a
repetition of that awful night.[2]

[2] I lay the following episode in this night's wanderings before my
readers, simply as a curious natural phenomenon, to be accounted
for, I daresay, by the learned, but perfectly inexplicable to myself.

I was passing over the prairie land between the mountains in a
moderately clear moonlight about ten or eleven o'clock p.m., when
I suddenly saw a bright light flash up on my right hand, at first
apparently some distance off, in the direction of a line of mountains. I thought it was some of my men who had come out in
search of me, and had, as is often done, lighted a fire to let me
know their whereabouts. I stopped, therefore, and faced the light,
so that I might watch it more closely. To my great astonishment,
it appeared to me now to be approaching rapidly. What it could
be I could not imagine. Face it I must, whether Indians or
anything else; so, cocking my rifle, I awaited its arrival. When
apparently about forty or fifty yards off it stopped. It seemed to
be about the height of a torch carried in a man's hand, and partook
of that character of light, but I could connect it with no figure of
any sort or kind. I felt that I must, if possible, find out what it
was, so I walked towards it with my rifle ready. It then retired,
keeping the same distance from me. I then put my rifle up to my
shoulder, but without producing any effect on the movement of the
light.

Thinking that it must be some delusion, and that, at any rate, I
could do nothing, I resumed my former course. The light came
on too, moving parallel with me, keeping all the time the same
distance from my right side. Mile after mile I travelled on, over
all sorts of ground and elevations, sometimes faster, sometimes
slower; but whatever my movements, whenever I turned my head
to the right there was the mysterious light, always in precisely
the same relative position. At last I resolved to make a fire, and
I altered my course accordingly towards the mountain side; still
the light accompanied me, and it was not until a bright fire blazed
forth that I lost my uncanny companion, which did not reappear
in my after wanderings.

I give the foregoing incident just as it occurred and for what it
is worth. I may mention that when the light first appeared to me
I had been walking for about sixteen hours, during five of which I
had been under the mental strain which inevitably accompanies
a situation such as I have described, and during that period I had

only eaten one small roll. At the same time, watching myself narrowly, I was unconscious of any unusual excitement, or of being in a frame of mind inconsistent with forming a sound judgment on any natural phenomenon which might present itself. On the contrary, I had been able to keep my head quite clear in the many matters, such as the course to be steered, obtaining fuel, and lighting the fires, &c., which, although small in themselves, required consideration and execution.

CHAPTER XV.

WITH the last chapter finishes the actual hunting
portion of my trip ; but suffering still from sheep on
the brain, I could not resist wasting a couple more
days later on, in fruitless pursuit of the coveted
animals.

The last of these, although unproductive, was
so full of enjoyable excitement that I cannot

help fighting it over again. It so happened that none of my old " outfit " were with me. All except Herridge—who had returned to his Indian wife at La Porte, on the Cache la Poudre—were still searching for the lost stock in the Sweet-water country. My own companions were two in number—one a hunter of much reputation in military circles; the other a well-to-do rancheman, by name George Ferries, who had formerly been a successful trapper, and who still loved dearly the wild mountain life. He now owned a ranche and a herd of cattle, the former far above the average both in size and comfort, and in it we had slept the night previous to the last day's *chasse.* Besides being one of the best hunters I had met on this side of the Atlantic, George was a first-class stockman, and, moreover, bore a high reputation for straightforwardness and honest dealing.

The scene of our hunt was a cañon, through which flowed our old friend the North Platte. I had great hopes of success from this hunt—not only on account of the reputation of my companions, but from the promising reports I had had of sheep in this neighbourhood. The prospects of fine weather on the previous evening had been rather doubtful, for although it was bright and still, there were signs of one of those fearful winter storms. Fortunately it held off a few days longer, and the morning of our hunt was all that could be desired. George Ferries looked all over like business—the brown suit of " Californian goods " and small felt hat he wore, by no means assimilating badly with the colour of the rocks and ground among which we had to seek our game. But I cannot say so much for the get-up of our other comrade, who, in his present costume, would have done well for a stage brigand, and would have spent the rest of his days in the best deer forest in Scotland without the remotest chance of a kill. On his head he wore a gigantic thin felt *sombrero*, or wide-awake, which flapped with every breath of wind, like the wings of some colossal bird; his jacket and pants were of dark brown corduroy or fustian, and round his ample waist he wore a broad crimson sash; long "rubber" boots completed his attire. How he was ever to get near the quick-eyed sheep was a puzzle to me; but I was told that he was a most successful hunter, and that I was very fortunate to secure his services. I could only, therefore, imagine that he either did not always clothe himself like this, or that he must be a remarkable good hand at never showing himself to game. But he was a good-natured, cheery fellow, and I had great confidence that his workmanlike companion would so manage matters after we had got into the game region that our friend should do no harm to our hunt.

The early morning found us all three galloping away on very fair steeds for the high ground leading up to the cañon. In about an hour we had reached the likely ground, and our eyes were "kept skinned," searching the snow for the heart-shaped tracks. Presently George had "struck" them leading down a sharp slope into a gulch below. Leaving our horses, we followed them a few hundred yards, when we came suddenly on some black-tailed deer. They stood for a few moments gazing wonderingly at us, affording a most tempting chance, but no shot was fired, sheep alone being the object of the day. When the deer had thoroughly made us out, they jumped away with that peculiar bounding action in an opposite direction from the tracks we were following, so without injuring our prospects of sport. On peering over a ridge a little further on, our eyes were gladdened by the sight of a band of some twenty sheep—of which two were good " bucks "— about 500 yards off in the gulch below. Although they were not actually moving when we first saw them, yet they were " suspicious " and uneasy. Maybe they had had a glimpse of our friend's flapping *sombrero*, or got a touch of our wind; at any rate, in a very short time they had made up their minds, and were on the " lope." George evidently knew their haunts well, and the rocks they were likely to make for; for, hurrying us back to the horses as quick as he could, we commenced a quick movement along the high ground parallel to the course of the galloping sheep below. It was now a regular race for several miles between ourselves and the sheep, our object being to cut them off from the highest part of the range. Gallop we did most certainly, and over some roughish ground; but eventually they beat us, and we were just in time to see the last of them tearing up on to the precipices about half-a-mile ahead of us.

Even then our chance was not gone. George knew the locality well, and commenced at once stalking on foot the likely rocky ledges. One of these he thought offered a very good chance, and we approached the ridge above it with rifles all ready for a shot. Nothing could be seen at first, and we had almost turned away, when G—— saw a ewe or two under a flat rock; drawing back, we were getting round quite close to them, when bang went a rifle behind me. Our friend of the sombrero had set his rifle on the hair trigger, and it had gone off by accident in his excitement! *Eheu fugaces!* to rush to the edge and snap at the bounding animals as they almost fell down the face of the sheer rocks was the work of a moment, but with no results, as might have been expected.

George's indignation was great, and my feelings certainly none of the gentlest. G—— suggested that if it was his, "he would fling the said rifle down the precipice after the sheep," and our *sombrero* friend looked downcast and sheepish enough, only remarking that "it had never happened to him before, but that his hands were so cold"—a good time for a hair trigger, forsooth! However, it was no use lamenting over our luck; besides which, the bucks were not with the ewes, and might still be behind; so we searched for them as carefully and long as circumstances would allow, but it was now getting late in the day, and commencing to storm, and we were compelled at last to give it up disheartened and thoroughly beaten. Thus ended my last day after sheep, as unlucky as all other days after these much-coveted animals. Sorely was I tempted to remain on, and hunt until I got one; but my days in America were numbered, and I was forced to be off for more civilized parts.

But all this is digression, and I must now return to the ranche at Independence Rock the day after I was lost. I was able most fortunately to get a lift over to Sand Creek on a very rough waggon, driven by a loquacious Irishman, which happened to be going that way for some chance stock purposes. On

Y

arrival there I found that Macdonald and Herridge were still here, and had taken up their abode at a stamp-mill, erected some years since for dealing with the auriferous quartz from the mines situated in the Ferries Range, north west of this. These ores have not proved of sufficient richness to compensate for the difficulties attendant on the situation; amongst which are the distance to the railroad, and the cost and scarcity of labour.

We slept in the log hut attached to the mill, rough enough in every way, but too glad was I to feel a roof over my head again, and to be in the company of my fellow-creatures.

The following day we travelled on towards Rawlings, or Rawlings Springs as it is sometimes called, on the Union Pacific Railroad. Our conveyance was a light cart, drawn by two small horses, the property of Macdonald, who did driver. Besides Herridge, we had as a passenger, a rather amusing character in the person of an old "stage driver," who had followed his vocation for many years in Utah and other Western parts, but had now abandoned it for the less-stirring work of cattle herding. He was possessed of a very fair voice, and whiled away the weary time with songs, which though not of the most select description, were decidedly quaint and strange to civilized ears. Macdonald had also a musical turn, but, alas! possessed not the smallest idea of tune. He droned away hour after hour at the same wretched ditty, the refrain of which was—

" We roll'd away quite merrily, but I often look'd behind ;
  For the rocks and woods of Dixie were passing through my mind."

I concluded this was meant to have some reference

to a melody called "Dixie's Land," but thought it wiser not to inquire, for fear of further infliction. On he droned—oh, how sick I was of it!—and on we jolted over the most execrable road, or rather track, in a bare, alkaline country, until a cañon was reached, called Brown's Cañon, perhaps named after the same Mr. Brown as the famous "Brown's Hole," on Bear River, which bears the reputation of being the home of many a desperado and outlaw. A good-sized stream flowed through this in summer time; but now it was hard frozen and silent. The rocks of this locality appear to be a sort of quartz schist, the geological section exhibiting a series of ledges or terraces of soft and hard rock. From this point the road improved, and we were soon able to make our entry into the quiet railway town of Rawlings, where I was speedily housed in the decent railroad hotel, very fairly clean and comfortable.

Everything in this little settlement has to do, directly or indirectly, with the Union Pacific Railroad. It is the centre of one of their systems, and consequently the residence of a number of officials and labourers, with the requisite stores or shops. Usually it is by no means a lively abode, and was well described to me beforehand as a "one-horse town;" but being now Christmas time, the place is quite lively. The second night I was there a ball took place at my little inn, at which the neighbouring ranchemen and trappers attended. Although much was strange to my eastern eyes, there was no uproarious drunkenness or brawling, and the next morning all appeared as cold and quiet as usual. But I had no time to lose, if I wanted to see anything of California and Nevada before my return to England; so, after "expressing" my heavy luggage and frozen buffalo heads, &c., eastwards, I got "on board" the through express train for California.

How comfortable, and even luxurious, the Pullman sleeper seemed to me after my camp life. How cold and queer the sheets felt, but neither so warm or comfortable as the blankets. The feeding seemed unnecessarily refined, and the quantity of new faces and voices perplexing and strange.

And now, having returned to the so often and well described route of the Union Pacific Railroad, my observations on the many interesting scenes passed through will be of the very briefest description. Before starting away for the long run to the Pacific coast, I would merely remark that west of the Mississippi the general character of the topography of the country is given by three great and main lines of elevation, which traverse from north to south. These are the Rocky Mountains, the Sierra Nevada, and the so-called Coast Ranges. Between the two former is a large plateau, over 500 miles wide, and extending in length far into Mexico, of an elevation varying from 4,000 to 8,000 feet. For the information of geologists, the Sierra Nevada is composed of granite, and metamorphic slates of the Triassic and Jurassic periods. The Coast Range is made up mostly of far more recent rocks belonging to the miocene. On going westwards, after reaching the Rocky Mountains, there is a vast improvement in the scenery; for, although on this western slope there are hundreds of miles of dreary, sandy, alkaline plains to be passed over, covered only with a small growth of sage bush, and grease wood, yet there is much more mountain scenery, abounding in rugged and wild cañons, pine-covered slopes, and precipitous cliffs.

The distance from Rawlings to San Francisco is a little over 1,200 miles, and the time occupied by the express from sixty-four to sixty-six hours. The rate therefore is not what we should call "express speed," being only something over eighteen miles an hour, inclusive of stoppages for meals. Half an hour is allowed three times each day for these repasts; breakfast about seven or eight a.m., dinner about one or two p.m., and supper about five or six p.m. After supper the occupants of the Pullman's sleepers gradually turn into their by no means uncomfortable berths, and by nine p.m. or so, all is quiet for the night. I was fortunate throughout to secure a lower berth, which has the twofold advantages of fresher air and the command of the two windows, which I appreciated immensely. There was something very enjoyable in being able to look out from one's bed in the bright still moonlight on the wild scenery through which we were running, and especially so when crossing the mountain ranges, or following the rivers through curious weird-looking cañons.

Although the highest point of the line has been passed at Sherman, 160 miles east of Rawlings, where the elevation is 8,242 feet above the sea level, yet the track is still at the latter station over 6,700 feet, and continues over 6,000 feet for 300 miles, till the Weber Cañon, on the other side of the Wahsatch Range, is reached. The actual watershed of the continent is crossed about three miles to the west of a small station called Creston, nearly 200 miles west of the highest point on the line, and more than 1,200 feet less in elevation. There is at Creston no rocky pass, no well marked ridge, to call the attention of the traveller to the fact that he is crossing any divide, much less the "Great Divide,"—the backbone of the great American continent—but that fact once realized, many curious thoughts crop up. It seems so strange to think that here one drop of water may find its way into the great Atlantic, whilst its companion, which fell only a few inches off, may be destined to add to the even larger wastes of the immense Pacific. The locality of the watershed is a bare, dreary plateau, devoid of almost all vegetation, and swept by fearful storms of snow and wind during the long winter season. Both going and coming the express train passes over it in the middle of the night, so I cannot give any opinion on the distant views, which are said to be very fine.

My first meal after joining the train was breakfast at Green River, and a very good one it was, served in a long room, liberally ornamented with heads of deer and buffalo. Near this the quaint forms of the isolated rocks of shale are striking and picturesque. Thin beds of lignite (brown coal) are found in the neighbourhood, and the shale is often full of bitumen, but I believe neither of these products is found in such quantities as to be, as yet, of commercial value. Fossils of fish abound in this locality, and very fair specimens are to be bought at the railroad refreshment bar at a somewhat excessive price. This river is said to take its name from the unusual colour of its water, but whether it is really as green as it is said to be, I am unable to certify from my own observation, as on both occasions when I crossed it was covered with a coating of ice, strong enough to bear a waggon and team of horses.

The next station of importance is Evanston, on the Bear River, a stream of great repute amongst hunters. This is the last town in Wyoming Territory, and is the dining-place for the western express. Here the traveller going west will first come across the Chinese. He will see them employed at the buffet as waiters, and at all the various kinds of work connected with the maintenance of the permanent way.

Evanston seems to be quite a centre of fitting-shops, foundries, &c. Lignite of a very fine quality is worked in large quantities in the neighbourhood. So dense and bright is it, that, at a distance, the lumps might easily be mistaken for its very superior relative of the old carboniferous formation. I am told that the largest quantity is raised in the so-called Ahna district, and that a short branch enables it to be brought with ease into the markets in connexion with the main line.

As regards the geological position of this lignitic formation, Mr. Lesquereux, of the United States Geological Survey, considers that he is authorized in deducing the following conclusions from the Government geological investigation : "that, independent from the Cretaceous under it, and from the Miocene above it, our Lignitic formations represent the American Eocene" (Dr. Hayden's Survey, 1872, p. 350); and I believe that most of the American geologists consider that the Eocene of their country is identical with the Eocene of Europe. This report contains very interesting articles on the lignitic formations of the Rocky Mountains. I do not gather that it seems quite certain that the beds will supply for very long the great requirements of the railroads, and of the other local manufactures, and the waste incurred in the mining, but as the formation extends over a very great area, new beds of the mineral may be discovered and opened out. It may be, too, that hereafter discoveries may be made which will enable the bituminous shale of the formation to be used with advantage for various purposes for which lignite alone is now employed.

To give some idea of the value of the lignite producing heat, I see that the average of thirteen analyses of different varieties by Mr. J. T. Hodge gives the following results; volatile matter 35.27%; fixed carbon 49.66%; ash 4.25%. The rest was water, varying from 3.28% up to 15.00%. The specific gravity ranged from 1.00% to 1.34%.

Soon after leaving Evanston we passed out of Wyoming and entered the territory of Utah, and very shortly we found ourselves amidst the wonderful scenery of the Echo Cañon. The red sandstone rocks on each side of the track assume the wildest and quaintest shapes, and, as is usual in a country frequented by tourists, are named after the objects which they are supposed most to resemble, such as the "Castle," the "Kettle," "Jack-in-the-pulpit," the "Steamboat," "Sentinel," &c. &c. The rocks put me much in mind of those isolated cliffs on the South Devon line between Dawlish and Teignmouth, though more numerous and larger. Echo Cañon leads into Weber Cañon, through which flows the river of that name. Here the rocks are greyer, but more striking even in shape and quaintness than those in the Echo Cañon. It was a lovely bright afternoon when we ran through these mountain gorges, and the strange abrupt outlines were shown off to the best advantage in the horizontal rays of the gorgeous winter sun.

We reached Ogden soon after emerging from the Weber Cañon. Here are situated the termini of the Union Pacific and the Central Pacific Railroads. Here, too, is the branch to Salt Lake City, of which more on my return journey. A stoppage of about an hour and a half, spent in changing Pullmans and at supper, and then away again westwards in what is called a "Silver Palace Car," which, to an ordinary individual, appears to be nothing more than a modification of a Pullman, and possessing the same comfortable berths, which we soon turned into.

The morning found us at Elko, where we breakfasted, having accomplished during the night about 275 miles out of the 882 from Ogden to San Francisco. The "outlook" is now enlivened by a good many Shoshone Indians, a miserable-looking lot, small and ungainly by nature, and many of them rendered even less pleasing of aspect by being clothed in dirty, loud-coloured blankets and tawdry finery. Their lodges are to be seen all along the line, truly wretched-looking hovels for human beings to inhabit, but their occupants appeared to be quite happy in their squalor and idleness.

From Palisade station a three-feet gauge line runs to Eureka, a large mining district ninety miles distant, of which more hereafter.

We were now travelling through Humboldt county, in the State of Nevada, renowned for its mineral wealth, especially of copper and argentiferous lead ores. There seems to be too an agricultural future for this country, with the aid of irrigation from the Humboldt river.

Battle Mountain is reached by dinner-time. It gets its name from an action fought here in 1857 between the Indians and a Government Surveying Expedition. Pretty specimens of the red oxide of copper are to be seen at the station, which may be purchased for a handsome consideration. About a quarter of a mile from Golconda station there are some hot mineral springs, the steam from which is visible from the railway. Winnemucca station, 468 miles from San Francisco, and 414 from Ogden, apparently "taps" the Idaho country and the eastern part of Oregon. Humboldt, with its good buffet, is reached by supper-time, such a wonderful little "oasis" of green trees and water in the midst of a barren, desolate desert. The river Humboldt, by which we have been running all day, loses itself near this place in a lake without an outlet, the water going off in evaporation and by absorption into the sand, as fast as it runs in.

During the night we had passed out of Nevada, the richest mining State of the Union, and had entered California. About midnight Reno was reached, from which the line to Virginia city branches off, and at four a.m. the highest point in crossing the Sierra Nevada, at a station called "Summit," 7,042 feet above the sea. It is a matter greatly to be regretted that this part of the journey is not performed, going or coming, in daylight, but both the eastern and western expresses cross this divide in the night. We were fortunate so far, that the night was fine and clear, and that a good moon did its utmost to light up the grand scenery. It is annoying too that some of the most beautiful views are lost owing to the provoking, but necessary, "snow sheds," which are very numerous hereabouts. In this part of the transcontinental crossing a wonderful change occurs very suddenly in the scenery. In a few hours we rush from the miserable barren-looking plains of the Humboldt country to the luxuriant timber-covered slopes of the beautiful Sierra Nevada Mountains. This portion is certainly very enjoyable; such magnificent forest and mountain scenery and such a deliciously light and invigorating atmosphere. All around seemed so bright, green, and luxuriant as in early morn we "snaked" round the elevated ridge of Cape Horn, the north fork of the American River rushing along many hundreds of feet below.

We saw plenty of signs of gold-mining in the descent towards Sacramento, at first chiefly of the so-called "hydraulic mining," but afterwards of the older "placer working," or "gulching." Most of these "placer workings" are now abandoned by the whites, and afford only a bare living for the hard-working and abstemious Chinaman. These latter live on one-tenth of that required by a native white, and are amply satisfied when they can make a dollar per day, or even less, whereas the regular miner is not content with less than from three to four dollars for his day's work.

As we run down towards the plains the vegetation changes rapidly; oaks and other hard woods take the place of the varied and beautiful pines, and agricultural clearings become frequent. From being spread over so long a distance—nearly 100 miles—the incline or "grade" from the summit to the Sacramento valley is by no means steep. Newcastle Station, where the elevation is first under 1,000 feet, is seventy-four miles from the summit, so that the 6,000 feet difference is spread over that lengthened distance.

We breakfasted at Colfax, and reached Sacramento in a couple of hours afterwards, passing over a monotonous dry-looking country about Stockton, which, however, on occasional seasons grows marvellous crops of wheat. A large irrigation canal is being constructed for this district, when no doubt it will become a more regular corn-producing locality. The town of Sacramento is prettily situated on the river of that name, and is about 125 miles from San Francisco. The rest of the journey may be performed by steamboat, but as they run generally by night, nothing is to be gained in the way of scenery. If however the town itself, or the Chinese, who muster strong here, are objects of curiosity to the traveller, he may in this way obtain a few hours wherewith to satisfy his craving. Sacramento used to be the chief starting-point for emigrants bound for the interior, who came here from San Francisco by water, and commenced their land journeys from this point. But the railroad has interfered with this outfitting business, and the town is now rather a central camp or *depôt*, from which a large agricultural district and some mining communities draw their supplies.

Six hours' more rail over a flat corn-growing country, thickly covered with ranches and villages, and we are finally deposited at Oakland, a suburb of San Francisco, but on the opposite side of the harbour. Although I must guard against any attempt at a guide-book description of this well-known metropolis of the west, yet I cannot help saying a few words *en passant* to bear my testimony to the beautiful *coup-d'œil* on approaching it from this quarter. The quantity and variety of shipping, riding securely in the great land-locked haven; the imposing position of the town itself, the beautiful chain of mountains known as the Coast Range; the lovely colour of the sky and sea; the queer-looking gulls and other sea birds, disporting themselves in apparent security close around us; all these when first seen in the glories of a winter's setting sun, made it one of those pictures which memory loves to dwell upon.

But we had not much time to enjoy the beauty of the scene. The fine ferry steamer had soon transported us across, when we were forthwith taken possession of by the representative of our respective hotels. My selection was the "Palace," one of those monuments of American enterprise and conceptions which so astonish us less speculative and less ambitious inhabitants of the Old World. It is said to have cost $5,000,000 (1,000,000*l.*), and to have been the outlay of a single individual. It can make up over 1,000 beds, and everything else is on the same surprising scale. In the basement there are shops or "stores," but, after my first evening's acquaintance with them, when at the hair-cutter's I was charged $1 (= 4*s.*) for cutting and washing my hair, and $1 more for washing my brushes, I did not see any advantage in patronizing them any further. The hotel itself was comfortable, and not more expensive than others of far less pretensions.

I was not particularly struck with the architecture

of "Frisco." Some of the buildings are fine, but these are the exception, and the general effect fell far short of what I had anticipated. From being the abode of so many millionaires, very good private residences might be looked for, but of such I saw scarcely any. But that rich men do abound in Frisco there seems no doubt, for I saw two dozen names given in one of the leading newspapers of men possessing over $4,000,000 (800,000*l.*) each, and it was further stated that the four principal owners of the Central Pacific Railroad are credited with an aggregate fortune of $50,000,000, or $12,500,000 (2,500,000*l.*) each! I believe many of these gentlemen live out of town, and that some of their country seats are most sumptuous and magnificent.

Some of the environs are charming, especially the entrance to the harbour, called the "Golden Gate," and the "Seal Rocks," and both of these

THE SEAL ROCKS, SAN FRANCISCO.

From a Sketch by J. P. V.

are within an easy afternoon's drive. The view from the Cliff House on to the vast Pacific Ocean,

with the Seal Rocks in the foreground is very fine,
and it is made the more interesting to an Englishman by the feeling, that in gazing westwards here
he is looking towards Australia and not America,
as from his own native land.

These Seal Rocks are extremely striking and interesting. They are literally covered with sea lions and
seals. There they are to be seen any day, bellowing and
disporting themselves in full enjoyment of nature's
freedom, and that, too, within a few miles of this large
and populous city, and within a few hundred yards of
a suburban resort, like Greenwich or Richmond. So
curious a sight of wild nature is simply unique, and I
can well understand that the authorities have hitherto
jealously guarded the sea monsters from molestation.
It seems difficult to believe, but apparently a well-
grounded rumour is now abroad, that it has been decided to destroy this, the greatest curiosity of San
Francisco, on account of the number of salmon and
other fish which the poor beasts kill! Surely such a
step will not be taken without the most undoubted
and incontrovertible evidence that the mischief done
is really excessive and seriously injuring the fishing
interests, and moreover that it is directly trace-
able to the seals. A scarcity of fish may arise
from so many causes—such as natural bad seasons,
destruction of the spawn or fry—that the poor
phocæ might easily get blamed and destroyed for
an evil by no means of their creation. When
they are destroyed the true cause of failure in the
fisheries might be found out, but too late to resus-
citate the departed wonders, and this most curious
sight would have become a thing of the past.

But a few more words on the town itself before

leaving it again for other scenes. The streets are
crowded with a motley energetic mass, hampered
occasionally in their busy movements by groups of
business men standing in knots outside the banks
and Stock Exchange, or by squads of idlers and
loafers on the look-out for anything and everything
which may occur. These latter worthies have obtained the local name of "hoodlums," and are said
to be the great instigators in the movement now
raging against the hard-working Chinaman. I
believe this would-be persecution has arisen simply
because the Celestial is ready to work for less
wages than the native, and that in this way
he is producing a downward tendency in the
labour market. Unfortunately the "hoodlum's"
views have been taken up by some popularity-
seeking stump orators as a political platform, and
men of influence have pledged themselves to pro-
pose to Congress a bill for expelling Chinese subjects or at any rate for their exclusion in future.
That Congress should seriously entertain such a
proposition is more than an outsider can imagine.
I have always understood that one of the funda-
mental laws of the United States is that every one
is on a perfectly equal footing and cannot be interfered with so long as he conducts himself in con-
formity with the laws of the country, and I
never heard it asserted, even by his bitterest
enemies, that John Chinaman was not a well-con-
ducted individual. He is acknowledged, I believe, by
all to be a law-abiding, industrious inhabitant, and
so long as he continues such, how, in the name of
justice, can he be expelled? Moreover, how is it
possible to taboo a country, by passing a law that its

inhabitants shall not become the citizens of a free country, such as this? As far as I saw in my very brief stay, the Chinese element seemed to have become almost a necessity in this part of the world. In all phases of the working portion of society, from the domestic washerwoman (or rather washerman) to the railway labourer and the miner in "placer" workings, the curious-looking celestial was conspicuous. I happened to visit a large tailoring establishment in this town. Here at work in long rooms or lofts were scores of Chinese, laughing and jabbering away in their own lingo. I do not doubt that San Francisco and other communities would be able eventually to get on without them, but I question whether many establishments and interests, and amongst these especially domestic households, would not feel it very difficult to supply the vacuum caused by the expulsion of the 90,000 Asiatics; and whether such a measure would not produce a very large increase of expenditure to all concerned. To an outsider it would rather appear that the right and proper course for the government of this free people to pursue would be, not to give way to this popular but unjustifiable cry by imposing a capitation tax—as some of our own colonies have tried—or any such doubtful and protective measure, but rather to endeavour to improve the social position of this useful citizen by well-considered measures for the moral training of his children and for bettering the social and sanitary condition of his dwelling-places.

And now a few words about the climate and productions of San Francisco and California generally. Judging from my own short personal ex-

z

perience of the former it appeared to be very mild and relaxing, but treacherous and subject to cold blasts of wind off the ocean. This must make it trying for invalids, notwithstanding that the mean temperature is so high and equable. The average temperature in the month of January is no lower than 49°, and of July not above 57°. Southern California seems however to possess a more desirable climate for a winter residence. The mean temperatures of the month of January at Santa Barbara is 54°; at Los Angeles, 52°, and Santa Monica, 52°, and they are not, I believe, subjected to the same sudden changes as further north. Great quantities of all sorts of fruit are grown in these districts, which are sent preserved or canned by rail to the Eastern States. A pumpkin outside one of the stores here, from Los Angeles county, weighed 155lbs., and I heard extraordinary accounts of the height to which the maize grew in those parts.

The drainage question seems likely to be a source of trouble to San Francisco. Great cause for uneasiness would seem to exist, for the head of the sanitary department has stated in his report that " death from zymotic causes was 34.8% of the total mortality during the past year, against 19.1% for the previous year." The whole of this document is most interesting, and shows that that gentleman (Dr. Meares) is well up in all the improvements of the modern system of house and town drainage. He makes mention of, and advocates strongly, ventilation not trusting solely to traps, which in times now happily past have doubtless often been the cause of fearful outbreaks of typhoid and other fevers. More than ordinary care will have to be taken to ensure a full supply of flushing water, on account of the long periods of drought which occur here.

The annual rainfall of California seems to be extraordinarily variable. It is most curious to observe how the prosperity of all branches of the community seems, directly or indirectly, to depend upon its abundance. To the agriculturist, it is not only a question of good corn crops but even of the actual preservation of their flocks and herds. To the miners, so many processes of gold-winning depend on a full supply of water, that to them an abundant rainfall is of paramount importance. In these Western States the prosperity of the whole community depends upon these two great industries, on the results of which in the year 1877 I will just cast a glance.

Although California is no longer the leading mining State, its production falling far short of that of its sister State, Nevada, and although it is fast becoming primarily an agricultural State, for according to the miner's ditty—

> " But I tell you what it is,
>   The times they ain't no more
> In Californy as they was
>   'Way back in Fifty-four.
>
> " Hit's swarming with them Chinese rats
>   Wot's tuk the country sure—
> A race that lives on dogs and cats
>   Will make all mean or poor."

Yet in deference to its past mineral celebrity, we will first compare this part of its productions with those of the other Western States and Territories. On referring to the " Annual Review " for 1877, published at the *Commercial Herald* office, San

Francisco, I find that the money value of the precious metals produced in California were as follows: gold, $15,237,729 (= 3,047,546*l*.); silver, $2,936,987 (= 587,398*l*.) making together a total of $18,174,716 (= 3,634,944*l*.); whereas the value of the bullion produced in Nevada is stated as $51,580,290 (10,316,060*l*.). The total worth of the precious metals produced in all the States and Territories (inclusive of California and Nevada) west of the Missouri River and including British Columbia, and some received in San Francisco from the west coast of Mexico, is put down as: gold, $26,525,331 (= 5,305,066*l*.), and silver, $71,891,423 (= 14,378,285*l*.), giving together a value of $98,421,754 (= 19,683,351*l*.). This is stated to be an increase of some $7,000,000 (= 1,400,000*l*.) on the production of 1876, notwithstanding "a greatly restricted water supply." Nevada, Utah, Arizona, Oregon, Washington, Idaho, Colorado, and Dakotah show an increased bullion production, while in California, New Mexico, Montana, British Columbia, and Mexico there has been a falling off. This review goes on to state that "since the discovery of gold in California, which event occurred thirty years ago this present month (January, 1878), there have been created in the countries lying west of the Missouri River, and mostly on American territory, bullion values to the amount of $1,948,000,000 (or 389,600,000*l*.); of this sum, about $1,586,000,000 (or 317,200,000*l*.) has been composed of gold, very little silver having been produced here prior to 1861, when the Comstock deposits, discovered three years before, began first to turn out this metal in notable quantity." The value of the gold in the bullion produced from the Pacific States and Territories goes on decreasing every year, whilst the value of the silver greatly increases. Since 1861, inclusive, "the production of gold for the entire coast has been $876,000,000 (= 175,200,000*l*.); silver, $372,000,000 (= 74,000,000*l*.), while last year, 1877, the value of gold and silver in the bullion was not far from being equal; the gold being $51,000,000 (= 10,200,000*l*.), and the silver $49,000,000 (= 9,800,000*l*.)." It appears now, however, to be an established fact in the case of many of the most important silver-mines that the lodes become more and more gold-bearing as they increase their depth from the surface. This takes place with the celebrated Comstock lode in Nevada, the bullion from which during the past year has been very nearly of equal value in gold and silver, the latter being still slightly in excess, but on this more anon.

It is the practice in the assay offices of San Francisco, as in other parts of the States, to give the results of an assay in monied valued, not in contents, as with us.

One of the chief conclusions to be deduced from a perusal of the mineral statistics of these regions is, that their prosperity is subject to frequent variations. Some districts seem on the whole to be doing well and producing largely, others again are "playing out," and amongst the latter must be placed, if taken as a whole, the State of California.

Now as to agriculture, the agricultural prosperity of California and of the other States and Territories on the Pacific slope during the past year was greatly affected by the before-mentioned small rainfall. The grain crop is said to have been not more than one third of that of an ordinary year, and heavy losses have been suffered on sheep and cattle.

The State of California is as large as many countries of Europe. I believe the area is 188,981 square miles or 120,947,840 acres. Of this quantity it is said that 40,000,000 acres are fit for the plough, and that as much more presents excellent facilities for stock raising, fruit growing, &c; while little more than one eighth of the whole area is at present cultivated. Besides this, there are mountain grazings capable of producing excellent meat in years of moderate rainfall.

From the above figures it will be seen that " the agricultural area exceeds that of Great Britain and Ireland together, or the entire peninsula of Italy." The population, however, is at present far too small to occupy effectually so large a quantity of land. It is said to be one million; while it is calculated that ten times that number would be required to do justice to such a territory.

The southern and south-eastern provinces seem to be developing very fast in growing grain and fruit as well as meat. Systems of irrigation are being planned and carried out which will compensate for the scarcity of water with which they have hitherto had to contend. In addition to these prospective benefits, they are already deriving great advantage from being tapped by the Southern Pacific Railway system.

To give some idea of the rapidity and the scale on which things are done in this country I read of a single ranche of 7,000 acres now irrigated and under

the plough and producing grain, vegetables, and fruit,
where three years ago there was a complete waste.
The size to which things grow is astonishing.   It is
said that many of the potatoes from this same ranche
weigh from one to five pounds each, while some
reach ten pounds and even more.   Its farm stock at
the end of last year (1877) was as follows, 4,000 cattle,
7,000 sheep, and 2,000 hogs, and a large number of
horses, mules, poultry, &c., besides 6,000 tons of hay,
5,000 sacks of barley, 2,600 sacks of wheat, and very
large quantities of corn (maize) and roots for the
sheep and cattle !

It would seem from the foregoing statement that
California, as an agricultural producer, is still in her
infancy, and that when capital is brought to bear
and irrigating canals constructed to meet the destructive droughts, we may anticipate a very considerable increase of importations from her.   Perhaps
one of the best criterions of the productiveness of
the land is to be found in the exports of grain, and
I extract therefore the following table, showing the
exportations from San Francisco for the last five
years :—

	Flour.	Wheat.	Barley.	Oats.
	barrels.	centals.	centals	centals.
1873	479,117	9,175,960	269,896	5,725
1874	535,695	8,054,670	222,596	78,354
1875	497,163	7,505,320	126,188	5,377
1876	508,143	9,967,941	351,897	3,721
1877	434,684	4,931,437	90,330	4,544

China was the best customer for flour, having
taken in 1877 over 164,000 barrels against 157,000

taken by Great Britain; but for wheat and barley the British market—independent of her colonies—stands out as pre-eminently the greatest outlet. Of wheat Great Britain took 4,870,069 centals, and of barley 72,744 centals.

As an additional proof of the effect of a small rainfall on agriculture, the decrease in value of exports of grain in 1877 over 1876 is estimated at $8,810,672, or 1,762,186*l.*

So much for the grain productions, but there are other exports of great importance besides bullion and corn. Perhaps the article next in the list would be wool. Last year the clip was over fifty-three million pounds. In 1876 it was fifty-six millions; in 1875 forty-three millions; in 1874 thirty-nine millions; and in 1872 twenty-four millions. The total production since 1854 inclusive is stated to be 381,579,780 lbs., of which probably 333,000,000 lbs. may be credited to the last ten years, the production having in that period been stimulated by a large home demand.

In some parts the cultivation of the vine is attracting much attention, and wine already takes a leading position among the many and varied productions of the State. In 1876 seven million gallons were made, but last year the yield fell to four millions, in consequence of a hot sirocco wind, which prevailed for some time and shrivelled up the fruit. There were besides 20,000 cases of champagne produced in 1877 and a considerable quantity of brandy. The names of European wines, such as port, sherry, champagne, &c., have been generally adopted, which is now looked upon as a mistake, and it is thought that it would have been

better to have adhered to the original local nomen-
clatures.

It is indeed wonderful how bountiful nature has
been to these regions. It is sufficient to visit the
market of San Francisco to be convinced alike of
the fertility of the soil, and of the resources
of the rivers, lakes, and forests. Not only are
out-door vegetables and fruit obtainable at almost
any season of the year, but in early summer they
are in astounding quantities. Last year 2600 tons
of green fruit were sent eastwards; and the re-
ceipts of strawberries during the latter part of
April averaged 650 chests per day, weighing eighty
pounds each. In one day thirty-four and a half tons
were received in the market! Oranges and lemons
are being now largely grown, but both comparatively
recently.

Then as to fish, I saw magnificent salmon from
the Sacramento River, and less inviting-looking lake
trout, from that very elevated inland sea Lake Tahoe,
of good size, but long and lanky, and unsatisfactory-
looking in a fisherman's eyes. It is stated that
170,800 packages of salmon, of the value $960,000
(=192,000*l.*), were sent away by sea in 1876, and
160,982 packages, of the value of $1,023,446
(=204,689*l.*), in 1877.

Game is said to be still plentiful at a little distance
from the towns, but far less so than formerly, and
legislation has been invoked to prevent its further
destruction. The beautiful pastures of the slopes
of the timber-covered ranges are true paradises for
the deer tribe, and if only a proper close time and
fair play are secured, there would be no danger of
extermination or even of scarcity. It appears, how-

ever, that of late the glove trade has required so much buck and doe skin that both sexes of deer have been slaughtered at all seasons and at all ages to meet the demand of the factories. Laws have now been passed by the local Legislature to meet this evil, and it is to be hoped that they will be successfully enforced.

Small game is plentiful. Quail and ducks are to be found in great numbers at the proper season. I heard of one gentleman killing 114 canvas-back ducks in a single day. Unfortunately I had not time to take advantage of some tempting invitations to try my hand at this enjoyable but difficult shooting; my holiday was nearly over, and I had most reluctantly to say nay.

I have said enough on the natural capabilities of California. Any number of dry statistics could be collected in proof of its mineral and agricultural wealth. But with all these advantages it does not strike one as altogether a desirable country to settle in. Man does not seem as yet to have arrived at a just appreciation of the gifts of a bounteous Providence, or to understand that only a due observance of those social duties which enable people to exist together, and to contribute to one another's welfare and happiness, will permit him to reap advantage from a fertile soil and a fine climate. For the proof that nature's gifts, however bountiful, will not alone make a country happy or great, the inhabitants have only to look to the adjoining Mexican Republic. It is quite true that in California a more sober-minded people predominate, but the alloy is considerable. Originally, at the time of the gold discovery, a very rough sample from all parts of the world was collected here. Whether this roving element has died out, or moved on, or still remains to give future trouble to the more order-loving portion of its citizens, is a question which disturbs the peace of many a worthy member of the thinking portion of society. It would seem to an outsider as if the capital and labour question was destined to give more trouble here than perhaps in any other part of the world. The rowdy meetings against the Chinese portend no good, and if the lowest and laziest elements of society succeed, as seems not unlikely, in their unjust demands, what will they next assail? Will communism be the next plunge? and if it should succeed, what miserable internal fightings must follow; and then of what avail are nature's bounties? However favoured a country, we may rest assured that man's duty towards his fellow-man must be observed; social order must be preserved; capital and labour must play their respective parts, or even California, with all its surprising natural advantages, will fail to become the happy and envied home of a contented and prosperous people.

CHAPTER XVI.

"Gold! gold! gold! gold!
Bright and yellow, hard and cold,
Spurn'd by the young, but hugg'd by the old
To the very verge of the churchyard mould!"

Hood, "Miss Kilmansegg."

"Murther most foul, as in the best it is."

Shakespeare, " Hamlet."

As it was now, perhaps, the worst part of the year,
namely the beginning of January, there were some
doubts expressed at San Francisco as to the prac-
ticability of an excursion to the far-famed Yosemité
Valley. It was feared that the depth of snow on the
"divides" would be too great, certainly for wheels,
and possibly for pack-horses. But I thought that,
to return home without having visited the Yosemité
and the Big Trees would be not only a great
disappointment, but a blot on my wanderings.
Accordingly I determined to make the attempt, and

arranged with an obliging ticket-agent at Frisco to put himself in communication with the local agents, in order that no unnecessary delay might occur to my movements. I was accompanied by a Welsh gentleman, who was as anxious as myself for the excursion.

During the proper season the trip is made from San Francisco with the most perfect ease and comfort, a return ticket costing $80 (16*l.*), and the time occupied being about four or five days.

The Yosemité Valley is a cañon of the Merced River, and is situated about 140 miles slightly south of east from San Francisco. It is nearly in the centre of the State of California, north and south, and exactly midway between the east and west bases of the Sierra Nevada range, which is here about seventy miles across. The ordinary route from San Francisco is by rail to Merced, distant about 139 miles, on the Central Pacific Railroad, which takes nearly seven hours to accomplish. Then sixty miles in a "stage," by Mariposa, to Clark's Ranche; then by stage again into the valley about twenty-five miles more. The return journey is often made by way of Coulterville to Merced, where the rail is again joined, after a somewhat long drive of ninety-four miles.

In our case we had no choice of routes, only one being deemed practicable, on account of the snow on the divides.

The first night we slept at the Railway Inn at Merced, and started early the next morning for Mariposa in a wretched old vehicle, which out of the season did the duty of the "stage." Our road at first lay over a most uninteresting plain, the greater part of which seemed to afford only a doubtful existence to scattered flocks of Merino sheep. Where irrigation had been brought to bear, enormous tracts of stubble testified to the great extent to which this district had contributed to the grain crop of the past year. Our driver was a queer specimen of a western Jehu, very quaint in his ideas, and quite noted even out here for the way in which he expressed them. He was rather of a morose turn of mind, and the " nipping and eager air" of the early morning did not improve this natural tendency. Moreover, his amiability was not increased by a breakage which occurred to the springs of the old rattle-trap very soon after starting, which delayed us some little time. As we were the only passengers, with the exception of an occasional " pick up," we saw and heard plenty of our friend before the day was out, and he rather improved on acquaintance, perhaps from the external influence of the sun's rays, or the internal glow imparted by sundry drinks of whiskey. The first and only change of horses was at Hornitos, twenty-three miles from Merced, before arriving at which we had begun ascending out of the plain, and had reached an elevation of about 700 feet.

We were now in what had been once a rich and celebrated gold-mining district. Signs of old workings were to be seen on all sides, and perhaps, a few words here on the systems of gold-mining in general use will be of interest to my readers.

The most common and general modes of mining gold seem to be three in number, and go by the name of "placer," "hydraulic," and "quartz" mining. The so-called "placer mining" is the most ancient system, being the only one practised when gold was first discovered. It consists in "washing" and "dressing" the alluvial gravel deposited in the river-courses, gulches, &c, by means of "pans," "rockers" (which are not unlike a baby's cradle), "long Toms," and "sluices," &c. The alluvial deposits in early times were very rich in gold; but most of them have now been washed over several times, and are no longer capable of returning to the operator as much as a dollar per day. Such earnings do not suffice for white men, consequently, as I have said before, nearly all the placer-operations are now carried on by Chinese.

The "hydraulic" system can be worked only at such places where a head of water is obtainable. The water is led through pipes, to the end of which hoses and nozzles are attached; and such is often the head of water and consequent force, that to be struck by the jet is instantaneous death. Banks and deposits of auriferous quartz gravel left in the beds of the old or "dead" rivers, (whose courses are supposed to have been interrupted by volcanic disturbances,) can be operated upon on this system with great success. Some of the large mining companies work only in this way, a scanty rainfall therefore is felt as much by them as by any other class of the community, and often puts an entire stop to their operations.

The third system is the "quartz mining." This is perhaps the most extensive and successful of all. It seems to have been first introduced about 1851, when the shallow diggings began to show signs of exhaustion. Owing, however, to its having been often at first tried on lodes not sufficiently rich, and also to very great and unnecessary expenditures being incurred in erecting machinery and stamp-mills, this system at first proved a failure, and was to a certain extent abandoned until 1853, when it was resuscitated, and seems to be now steadily on the increase. It consists in simply winning and working the auriferous quartz veins, in the same way as if they were ordinary metalliferous lodes, by means of sinking or driving shafts or levels to suit the lay of the strata, and other local circumstances.

I am told that the expense of treatment in hydraulic mining is very small indeed. It is said to pay to treat stuff worth originally only 20c. (say 1s.) per ton; whereas in " quartz mining " it should not be worth less than $7 or $8 (28s. or 32s.) per ton to return a profit, even if the mill in which it is afterwards crushed and treated is close at hand, and the property of the same adventurers.

Here in the neighbourhood of Hornitos a great deal of placer-mining has existed, and some is still being carried on, in a small way by, the Chinese.

There are also some quartz mines close by; one of them about five miles off, called the Washington, is of considerable importance. The shaft is driven on the slant or dip of the quartz vein in a slate and granite " country rock," as it is here termed. At this mine a mill of twenty stamps has been erected, and over a hundred men are employed by the company.

A great difficulty is often met with in the treatment of much of the ores from auriferous quartz mines, on account of their containing a blackish substance, called by the Mexicans " plumosa," which makes the ores " rebellious " or " refractory," and entails a loss of produce in the after-treatment by amalgamation with quicksilver. I saw specimens of ore from this neighbourhood, showing a considerable quantity of this " plumosa," which in appearance resembles thin layers of zinc blende (" black jack "), but I could only examine it in a very cursory manner, and cannot speak with any certainty.

A small mine I visited near here was sunk on a quartz vein, lying at an angle, I should say, of 50°. The lode itself consisted of a dense milk-white quartz, containing a very little finely-disseminated native gold, but great quantities of auriferous iron pyrites. It varied from five to twelve feet in thickness, and I was told that ore had been taken from it, worth from $50 to $200 (10*l.* to 40*l.*) per ton, but that it was very " rebellious."

I was told that at the Washington mines they treated the " rebellious " ores by " chlorodising," but that even then there was a considerable loss of produce, and that nearly all their gold output was from "free" (or native) gold contained in the quartz. Here we have, then, a metallurgical problem which will well repay any one skilful enough to discover a practical solution, for there appears to be no doubt that great quantities of gold are now thrown " over the heap" in the ores too "rebellious" to treat profitably by the existing known modes of extraction.

The auriferous quartz veins occur principally in a slate formation, which the great American geologist, Mr. Clarence King, has satisfactorily determined by fossils—such as belemnites, ancellæ, and others—to belong to the Jurassic period. In much the largest number of cases the veins coincide in dip and strike with the rock in which they are enclosed, although in a few instances they appear to cut the slate at a slight angle. Mr. King states that, "Nearly all the veins which occur in the granite, and they are quite numerous, have the same dip and strike, as those in the slates; a few, however, run at right angles to these" (Geological Survey of California, vol. i. p. 226). There appears also to be cross courses of more recent volcanic rocks very similar to what occurs in other metalliferous slate formations. The granite is of a light grey colour, crystalline and compact. In some places beds of carboniferous limestone may be seen interstratified with the auriferous slates.

After leaving Hornitos, the scenery became much more interesting and enjoyable. We now passed through the foothills of the Sierra Nevada, with no great growth of forest trees, but covered in places with a dense undergrowth of "chaparal," composed principally of the crooked, but picturesque red-barked manzanita, a sort of maple, and what is called here "buck's-eye," resembling in growth a dwarf fig-tree. Amongst the forest trees were oak, spruce, and cedar; but I saw no very fine specimens of any of these until after we had passed Mariposa. The hill-sides appear to have been recently denuded of timber for the use of the mines, which would account for the scarcity of fine forest trees. In the summer time the beauty of these braes must be very wonderful, for, besides the many flowering shrubs and undergrowth, the sward is covered with masses of gorgeous wild flowers, wherever they have any mould to grow in. To give an idea of the beauty of nature's carpet, Prof. Brewer, in the

Government Report of California in 1864, says—
that "there are 1600 flowering plants, and 100
species of mosses growing naturally within the
limits of the State!" In the spring the whole
country must indeed be one beautiful garden.

Our road now lay through Bear River Valley, one
of the most productive mining portions of the famous
"Mariposa Estate." This so-called "estate" is a
nice little property of seventy square miles, or 44,380
acres, containing within its circuit the richest mineral
districts of the State. On it were located the once
famous mines, "Josephine," "Pine Tree," "Mariposa," "Mount Ophir," and "Princeton." The
past history of the property is so interesting and
peculiar that I cannot help giving a very short outline of it.

This most valuable tract was granted originally
by the Mexican Government to one of its own
subjects, from whom it was purchased in 1847 by
J. C. Fremont, the great explorer. This gentleman
had his rights confirmed by the United States in
1856, not long after the country came into possession
of the American people.

Very soon afterwards a nice legal question arose
as to whether Fremont had a right to the minerals.
It appeared that the original Mexican grant did not
convey it; but a law-suit resulted in the decision
that an American patent for land carries the minerals
with it. The occupiers of the mines would not,
however, concur in this decision, and defied the
officers of the law. "The mines were converted
into fortifications; the mouths of the tunnels were
barricaded; there were besiegers and besieged, and
several men were killed. But at last, in 1859,

Fremont triumphed, and, under his Mexican grant, obtained land which the Mexican Government did not intend to grant, and minerals which it systematically reserved." (Government Report, " Resources of United States," 1868, p. 22.)

A short time after this the monthly yield of gold from the quartz mines of the estate became very large. In 1860 it averaged $39,500 (7,900*l.*) ; in 1861, $53,500 (10,700*l.*) ; in 1862 (although great damage was done this year to mills and mines by floods), $43,500 (8700*l.*) ; in the first five months of 1863, $77,000 (15,400*l.*) ; in May of that year it produced $101,000 (20,200*l.*) worth of bullion. " It seemed then to have reached the figure of $100,000 (20,000*l.*) per month, with a fair prospect of still further increase. It was at this time that the estate was sold to an incorporated company in New York, and the stock put upon the market in the midst of the San Francisco mining-stock fever, which extended its influence across the continent. The prospectus of the company presented a very attractive picture to speculators. The average monthly yield for three years had been $50,000 (10,000*l.*), and for half a year the net profits had equalled that sum." Then followed in the said prospectus, most hopeful reports and flourishing accounts of future prospects from various mining engineers, and consequently " Large quantities of the stock were purchased, and there were large quantities to be purchased ; for the paper capital of the company was $10,000,000 (2,000,000*l.*). The company was organized by Fremont's creditors, who had become owners of the property ; but instead of cancelling the debt and taking stock for it, they took a mortgage for $15,000,000 (3,000,000*l.*),

payable in gold, and issued the stock subject to that
debt, which was supposed to be the only encum-
brance on the property; at least, that was the
supposition of many who bought the stock. It
soon appeared, however, that there were $480,000
(96,000*l.*) in gold due, besides $300,000 (60,000*l.*)
on the Garrison lien, $50,000 (10,000*l.*) on the Clark
mortgage, and $130,000 (26,000*l.*) to workmen and
others in California. Moreover, with the new pos-
sessors, the yield at once fell off; it seemed as if
every nerve had been strained to make the yield of
May as large as possible, and that as soon as the
sale was made the production decreased more than
fifty per cent. The yield for the first five months
in 1863, before the sale, was $385,000 (77,000*l.*), and
during the last six, after the sale, $186,993 (37,399*l.*).
In the former period there was a net profit of
$50,000 (10,000*l.*) per month, in the latter a net
loss of $80,000 (16,000*l.*)." Matters appear to
have gone from bad to worse, until, in 1867, a
receiver was appointed. I quote the foregoing
history of this curiosity even in western mining
transactions from the Government Report of the
Mineral Resources of the United States for 1868.
No comment is required from me to call attention
to the more than ordinary uncertainty of human
affairs as exhibited in this western mining property.

But to return to our Yosemité trip. In consequence of the delay at the commencement of the
stage portion, we had been behind all through the
day. Our driver had, however, "made good time"
through Bear Valley, and we had hoped to reach
Mariposa before it was dark. We had travelled, if
not very rapidly at any rate very jauntingly, for the

roads were infamous. On our way we had passed many signs of the extensive mining operations of the aforesaid Mariposa Company at Princeton, Mount Ophir, and elsewhere. We had reached to within a mile of our destination, the town of Mariposa, and were going at a gallop at the bottom of one of the many little dips or " gulches " which we had hitherto so successfully "sprung," when, all of a sudden, without the slighest warning, snap went the kingbolt, and thud on to the hard ground dropped the after-portion of our miserable vehicle. The horses and the fore-wheels continued their course as if nothing had happened, with the wretched driver hanging on to the reins, vociferating in the most endearing western vernacular to his beloved quadrupeds. Vain were his blandishments; along the hard road they continued to drag his prostrate form, until at last he was forced to let go, and return bedraggled to see what had become of us. Fortunately no real damage was done to any one, and comparatively little to that portion of the vehicle which remained *in sitû* ; so, after a certain amount of bad language towards the old rattle-trap and all concerned, it was arranged that we should proceed on foot to Mariposa, and send out assistance, whilst the driver stayed to guard the baggage. Amongst this was the " treasure-box " of Wells, Fargo, and Co., the well-known express agents, containing $25,000 (5,000*l.*) in gold, rather a tempting piece of plunder for any passing " road agent." It was not very dark, so we had no difficulty in keeping the road and in finding our way to the small inn, which rejoiced in being the best " house " in this uninviting little town. Our horses had arrived some time before us, and had successfully steered the front portion of our late vehicle into the yard in which the "stage" was in the habit of bringing up. It was at once guessed that an accident had happened, and a relief party of three men and a waggon and our own horses had already been organized to go to the rescue. We did not care to go back ourselves, so directed the party to the scene of the accident.

But the old vehicle had not yet finished its career of mischief. A second disaster followed, and this time not quite of such a harmless character. It appeared that the men took with them the fore-wheels, and made them fast to the after-part of the carriage. They then tried to bring the patched-up wreck into town on its own wheels. Allick, our driver, went inside with two others, whilst George, —a noted Jehu and our future guide,—handled the "lines." This time the hind-wheels took to running sideways, and in a very few minutes the trap was capsized. Away bolted the horses, dragging the stage on its top; the unfortunate occupants— enclosed as in a box—were only set free when the edifice was completely smashed up. Allick had his head broken and face cut, and gave a most amusing description of his sensations when being dragged, which he said was like "thunder inside that there stage." George and the others presented very swollen and sanguinary appearances, and were for the rest of the evening objects of unusual interest to the bar-loungers of the wretched little hotel.

We had found this "house" crowded to excess, and were scarcely able to get one room for the two of us. Special assizes were being held for the trial

of some " shooting cases," which had lately occurred
in this, the Mariposa county. These so-called
" shooting cases " are really murders, and often of
the very worst description. In these parts they
appear to be of terrible frequency, and a disgrace to
the country. What could be more cold-blooded and
barbarous than the case which was now being tried?
And as the evidence was so circumstantial and
peculiarly conclusive, I will venture to give an outline of it, illustrative, as it is, of the state of society
here. Two farmers, or ranchemen, lived within a
few miles of each other. The one, an old Scotchman,
by name Patterson, a settler of many years' standing, had reared a family out here, and bore an
excellent character. The other, a young man from
Kansas, called Clow, had come to the neighbouring
ranche two years ago, and was evidently of that
rough type which is reported to be pretty numerous
in Kansas. It appeared that the latter envied Patterson's ranche, and "jumped the liens" of some
little piece of ground which Patterson had lately
taken in. Clow seemed to have already tried to
pick a quarrel with Patterson, and had on one occasion savagely assaulted him with "knuckle-dusters,"
for which he had been fined. A few months ago
the old Scotchman's wife died, and left him alone
with a lot of young children. Very shortly after
this sad event his body was found with a rifle-ball
through it. The shot had come from behind, and
struck him down whilst riding on his own farm.
Clow's horse was tracked to where the shot was
fired from. The ball was extracted from the body,
and found to be from a Remington rifle. An
empty cartridge-case (called here a " shell ") found

close by, was also of the Remington pattern, and
on it was a peculiar mark, as if there had been
something wrong with the extractor. Only two
men in the county had Remington rifles, Clow and
another man. This other individual was proved
to have been many miles away that day from
the scene of the murder. There could, therefore,
be but little doubt that it was Clow's rifle that had
fired the fatal shot. But, as if to make doubly
clear and beyond the smallest doubt that this was
so, the extractor of Clow's rifle on being examined
was found to be out of repair, and to mark the
cartridge-cases precisely like that picked up. I
went to hear a part of the trial, and when I was
there the prisoner, a most unprepossessing young
man, happened to be undergoing cross-examination
by the prosecuting lawyer on this particular part of
the evidence. He was sitting down, picking his
teeth, by the side of his lawyer, apparently quite at
his ease, and answering the questions at his leisure.
But even a Californian jury could not ignore such
evidence. They were obliged to find Clow guilty of
murder of the first degree; but having, in this
county, the power of determining the sentence as
well as of finding the verdict, they did not sentence
him to be hanged, but to penitentiary for life, which,
I am told, is very often commuted after a few
years have expired. If one may judge by the
frequency of crimes of violence, this tendency to
indiscriminate leniency has a disastrous effect on
the state of society. I was told that in this little
county, with a population by last census of 4,572
inhabitants, there have been no less than ten murders by shooting in the last three months. The

sentences have been invariably light, not a single
individual having been hanged (or "tightened hemp,"
as Allick familiarly termed it); and it is doubtful
whether the sentence on this occasion would have
been as heavy as it was, had not the continual fees
of $750 (150*l.*) to the prosecuting lawyer for each
case, besides other expenses, appealed to the pockets
of the ratepayers. From what I heard I believe
that life must be safer and certainly far more agreeable amongst the rough but hearty western cow-
punchers than in this old-settled part of the
country. Violent deaths seem indeed to be fearfully common here; on passing a graveyard, Allick
casually remarked " that very few boys lay there but
had turned up their toes in their boots," i. e. had
been killed.

The general appearance of the court in which the
assize was being held was anything but dignified
or impressive to English eyes. I certainly believe
that the absence of all distinctive costumes, and
of the outward signs of the majesty of the law,
detracts from the calm dignity which a court of
justice should possess. Judge, jury, counsels,
prisoner, witnesses, sheriffs, and sheriffs' officers
were here all arrayed alike, in ordinary dark
clothing. The only thing that distinguished the
judge was his somewhat isolated position. No
constables, or peace officers of any sort, were
distinguishable. All police work is done by the
sheriff, who can swear in whom he likes to assist
him in the execution of his duties. No staves or
weapons of any sort were visible, but probably
there was in that court many a loaded six-shooter
reposing quietly in that purposely-made pocket at

the back of the trousers, and ready for use on the slightest provocation.

On our return from the Yosemité the trial had just been concluded and the jury had found their verdict. The place was in a great state of excitement, for a report had gone abroad that the prisoner was to be rescued from the gaol that very night by a secret society called the " Rangers' Association," of which he was a member. So serious was the position considered that the sheriff swore in a quantity of citizens, who had during the night to patrol around the prison walls, armed with six-shooters.

Our little inn had afforded accommodation to many of those closely concerned in the trial, for besides some of the jury, and counsel, the prisoner's wife and children lodged here, and were present at the public meals. When the sentence was made known, the hat was sent round for their benefit, in which proceeding the jury themselves seemed to take a great interest, and apparently subscribed liberally.

There seemed to exist here a general inclination of antagonism to the law and of sympathy with the prisoner, but the sheriff is armed with such unlimited powers that such feelings seldom assume any outward form of opposition.

But, it would seem that the general system of appointments to the American courts of justice is very ill calculated to result in the employment of the most learned and upright men, if it is true, as I was told, that the judges, except of the very highest courts, are elected for a certain term, and that they need not even have had the training of lawyers. In consequence of this the appointments are frequently both unsuitable and corrupt. Rumour says that political tailors have been appointed "right away" from their boards, for services rendered to government "bosses." Some of their worships' after-proceedings have been worthy of their training, and have not contributed to the "punishment of wickedness and vice," or to the dignity of the bench.

The stories of judges are almost as numerous and incredible as the bear stories, but I cannot help giving one, which I believe to be worthy of credence, of a judge who had a very lofty idea of his own legal capacity, and was at the same time anxious to sustain the dignity of his court. A "shooting case" came before him; there was no direct evidence as to the perpetrator of the murder, but the individual was well known, and indeed confessed it. When brought into court his worship cautioned the prisoner not to commit himself; that he must remember his rights as a free citizen, &c., &c., and that above all things he must not interrupt the proceedings of the court. After this friendly warning, the judge proceeded to state that he, the prisoner, was accused of having on such a date shot the deceased. Whereupon the prisoner broke in, "Well, and so I did." The judge was indignant at the interruption. "Hold your tongue, sir; haven't I told you not to commit yourself nor to interrupt me? I shall commit you for contempt of court if you do so again." He then repeated the accusation, upon which the prisoner again broke in, "I have told you before that I did kill —." Upon this second interruption, the judge's indignation was very intense. "Mr. Sheriff, what is your evidence?" "I have nothing but circumstantial evidence, your honour, and the prisoner's own confession." "Then," said the judge, "I discharge the prisoner on this charge, but commit him for contempt of court!" I was told this by a most respectable gentleman, absurd and improbable as it may seem to us; and many such stories are rife in the Western States, and are generally credited.

CHAPTER XVII.

" Per invias rupes, fera per juga,
    Clivosque praeruptos, sonantes
    Inter aquas, nemorumque noctem."
        Gray's Poems, " Alcaic Ode on Neighbourland
            of the Grande Chartreuse."

I was not sorry to leave Mariposa and its abnormal
excitement and to be once more on the move for
the Yosemité. From here we had to travel on
horseback, as it was not considered advisable to go
any further on wheels, and in consequence of our
half-bred guide, George Munro, having been hurt
in last night's accident, it was late in the morning
before the horses were ready and we were fairly
under way.

Our road at first lay down a valley, the alluvial
gravel of which seemed to have undergone many
washings for gold. Then we turned easterly towards the range, of which we crossed three or four

spurs or ridges in the day's ride, and passed the small trail which leads by Hite's mine into the valley. Hite's mine is a large and prosperous quartz undertaking owned and worked by a single individual. There is a curious and romantic story attached to it. It is said that many years ago, when the present owner was a lad, he met with an accident whilst hunting which incapacitated him from moving. He was found by an Indian woman, who took him to her lodge, and nursed him until he was well. Then she showed him the very rich quartz vein, on which the present mine is sunk. Out of gratitude he married her, and they lived together very happily until she died. This event only happened a short time ago, and the man's experience of the family was such that he has since taken her sister to wife.

As the day wore on we gradually attained a much higher elevation and found a marked difference in the forest trees. Oak and small conifers had given way to grand cedars (many over 100 feet high), Douglas Spruce, and that magnificent and most striking perhaps of all the pines, the sugar pine (*pinus Lambertiana*) which I now saw for the first time. Its stately stem sometimes reaches to eighty feet without a branch, and enormous yellow cones hang down from the horizontal limbs like golden bunches of fruit, striking with admiration and wonder even a casual observer like myself. As the reader will probably have found out long ago, I am sadly ignorant about trees. I admire them none the less, and as it may be of interest to some to have a good authoritative account of this, one of nature's most

celebrated arboreta, I will quote a description given
in the Government Survey of California, 1860—1864
(vol. i. p. 335), the botanical department of which
was under the charge of Dr. Brewer. Speaking of
this western slope of the Sierra Nevada Range, he
says,—

" The great forest belt of the mountain, however
lies higher " (i. e. than the foothills), " at an elevation of from 4,000 to 7,000 feet above the sea. Of
this belt all the most conspicuous trees belong to
the family of the coniferæ, and the forests of this
region, as well as their continuation along the coast
further north, are unsurpassed, and probably un-
equalled in grandeur by those of any other part of
the world. Ten or twelve species occur, but the
principal effect is produced by eight of them, all of
which attain at times a diameter of over six feet
and a height of over 200, while several are often
over 250 and some as much as 300 feet high.
These species are sugar pine (*pinus Lambertiana*),
pitch pine (*pinus ponderosa*), and pitch pine (*pinus
Jeffreyi*), bastard cedar (*librocedrus decurrens*),
Douglas spruce (*abies Douglasii*), three different
sorts of firs (*picea grandis, p. amabilis,* and *p.
nobilis*), *pinus contorta, p. Balfouriana* and *p.
tuberculata.* Two or three species of fir and
spruce, besides those named before, also occur,
but are not among the common and conspicuous
trees. Of these species the sugar pine is the
grandest tree. It occurs at all altitudes between
3,000 and 6,000 feet, but attains its greatest dimensions between 4,000 and 5,000 feet, when it is frequently 300 feet high. Its trunk is perfectly
straight, its head symmetrical, and from the slightly

drooping ends of the horizontal branches the enormous cones hang down in bunches of two or three, like tassels. One tree measured by us was found to be 300 feet high, without a flaw or curve in its trunk, and only seven feet in diameter at the base. These forests are rather open, the trees being seldom densely aggregated; and owing to the dryness of the air, their trunks are very free from mosses and lichens. As we go higher on the sides of the mountain, among the forests we find the pines decreasing in number, while firs are constantly becoming more abundant. *Picea nobilis* is the predominating species at 7,000 to 7,500 feet. All the species of firs which are found here are very beautiful. They all attain a large size, are very symmetrical in their growth, and have a very dark green and brilliant foliage, which is very fragrant. The branches are often very regularly and primately divided, producing a most brilliant effect. The colour of the sky is perceptibly darker, as seen through this peculiar foliage raised in a canopy so high above the observer."

Although the foregoing technical and scientific description refers properly to another part of the western slope of the Sierra Nevada Range, namely Mount Shasta, yet it so clearly describes the forest growth passed through on the way into the Yosemité, and recalls so vividly that charming ride, that it could not have been more applicable had it been written of this special locality. The beauty of the views from the ridges, embracing miles of dark foliage stretching to the plains beyond, and terminating only with the distant mountain ranges, must be seen to be understood. The colouring of the landscape on that lovely evening was enchanting, and such as I had never seen before; it ranged from the almost black green of the timber-covered foreground to a light cobalt on the far-distant mountains, each tint so striking in itself, yet so toned down by nature's delicate hand as to be deliciously soft and harmonious as a whole. Gladly would I have lingered over the more beautiful points of view, but the shades of evening were already beginning to creep on us, and George kept on croaking of the distance we had still to " make " before the " Big Tree Station " was reached.

And George had some reason, for it was dark before we arrived at Clark's Ranche, notwithstanding that we had taken advantage of the " down grade " of the last few miles, and made it at a good " lope."

Although still called "a ranche," this establishment has long ceased to be mainly concerned with agriculture. Clark himself exists no longer, at any rate in this locality; that individual sold his interests many years ago to Messrs. Washbourne, who " run the stage," and are now the " bosses of the route " between this and Merced. The ranche is now a small but comfortable and roomy inn, and during the tourists' season is often filled to overflowing.

Besides having constructed the twenty-five miles of capital road hence into the Yosemité Valley, Messrs. Washbourne are again showing their enterprise by making a road direct to Merced, the object of which is to save thirty miles over the present Mariposa route.

The weather was so threatening, and a fall of snow seemed so imminent, that we meant to have pushed on into the valley the next day, but, unfortunately, my companion was so fatigued with yesterday's ride that we had to rest a whole day here. This we employed in a very satisfactory manner by making a longer visit to the far-famed Mariposa Big Tree Grove than we had intended.

I will not say that I was disappointed with these monsters; it is difficult to be so with such colossal productions of nature, but I do think that from the position in which they are placed one fails to take in at first their extraordinary proportions. This arises, no doubt, from the trees around, to which the eye is at once attracted, being themselves so gigantic. The neighbouring sugar pines and cedars are truly magnificent, and of such extraordinary height that they would be considered wonders anywhere else, and this marvellous growth applies to all the other forest trees of this peculiar locality.

As is generally known, the scientific name of these giants is "Sequoia Gigantea;" the substantive in honour, it is said, of a chief of the Cherokee tribe of Indians who first endeavoured to educate his people; the adjective is apparently varied from "Gigantea" to "Wellingtonia," and "Washingtonia," it may be to suit the different nationalities of tourists. The number of Big Trees in this, the Mariposa Grove, is said to be 600. In the King's River Grove, further to the south in this same State, and situated about 6,000 or 7,000 feet above the sea, the trees are not so thick, but extend over a far greater area. The Mariposa Grove must be at about a like elevation, for the ascent from Clark's Ranche is considerable, and the ranche itself is 5,500 feet above sea level.

On the size of the trees I cannot speak from my

own measurements. I can only say that I rode easily through the stem of one of them, an archway having been burnt through it, and that I was told, on undoubted authority, that one which had fallen down in the King's River Grove measured 450 feet in length, and that my informant was able to ride upright along through a portion of the stem which had been hollowed out by fire, until he came to a knot which had fallen out, and through the hole thus formed he had passed out again into the open air! In the Government Survey of California it is stated that a big tree in King's River Grove measured 106 feet in circumference at the base, but that it was partially burnt, so that the original circumference must have been 115 or 120 feet! This tree was not more than 276 feet high, which is less than might have been expected from such an enormous girth. But so many have borne testimony to the colossal size of these giants, that no doubt can exist thereon, and I will give no more dry details.

The stem of the sequoia grows straight and thick, and is covered with a reddish velvety fibrous-like bark. It is sometimes 100 feet or more before the branches begin to show, and these have the appearance of being puny and stunted, and quite out of proportion with the sturdy solidity of the stem. Many of the trees have been greatly damaged by fire, originated probably by carelessness. The finest specimen of this grove is a tree called the "Grizzly Giant," a picturesque old fellow with grotesque withered branches, sprawling about like ungainly arms. It is stated to be 100 feet in circumference at the base!

A wretched cockney-like habit prevails of labelling with fancy names these splendid growths, just as if they were show potatoes or turnips produced by some would-be famous manure. Nailed on to the grand old giants are flat white boards, on which are painted such names as "Caroline," "Andrew Johnson," "The Fallen Monarch" (the two last have fallen), "The Faithful Couple" (a tree which is split into two a short way up), &c. &c. Visiting cards are also often affixed, and names cut into the bark, still further disfiguring the grand old stems. Now that the grove is the property of the State and possesses regular custodians, it seems strange that this bad taste should be allowed to exercise itself. It certainly mars the enjoyment of nature's works to have miserable placards staring you in the face at every turn, a practice which prevails to a still greater extent at Niagara, where advertisements of wonderful oils and successful pills are painted on the face of the splendid cliffs and rocks.

All the giant trees I saw here appear to be past their prime, and becoming rapidly withered and rotten. There seemed moreover to be a great want of a young stock to take their places. Whether this is really so I was unable to ascertain, but the Government Report of California (vol. i. p. 444) speaking of another part of the State, says that there (near Visalia) "specimens of it (the 'Big Tree') may be found in every stage of growth, and the smaller ones are sawn up for lumber at Thomas's Mill, above Visalia." As to the age of the present giants, one was cut down in the Calaveras Grove, which, at six feet from the ground—where it measured twenty-three feet in diameter inside the bark—had 1255 annual rings, with a decayed centre of about one foot through, so that it is safe to assume this tree was at least 1300 years old!

The next day, my companion being recovered

sufficiently from his fatigue, we made an early start in the first rain I have encountered since I left Canada, and a thorough downpour it was. However, if we did not reach the valley before there was a fall of snow we might not be able to get there at all, so we determined on pushing on. As we got higher on the mountain-side, the rain gradually became snow, until I was once more in a white world. But a little luck was awaiting us to cheer our drooping spirits. We sighted a herd of deer, and by a lucky shot with a ball out of a smooth bore from the road I killed a perfect little buck. It was fortunate that I had brought a gun with me, for on my way up to Clark's I got some specimens of that beautiful little bird the Californian mountain quail. Whether the buck I now killed was a black-tail or white-tail I have been unable to find out. George, our guide and no mean hunter for these parts, said he was a white-tail, and undoubtedly he was much smaller than any black-tail I had seen before. His head, however, appeared to me to be more of the black-tail type, though very diminutive, and I am inclined to think he was a veritable black-tail. I soon "gralloched" the little animal, and with George's assistance hung him up in a tree to abide our return.

As this completes the bag of my tour, I may as well, although perhaps somewhat out of place, jot the total down.

Moose.	Cariboo.	Buffalo.	Wapiti.			Deer.	Antelope.	Puma.	Bear.
			Bulls.	Stags.	Hinds.				
1	1	4	7	2		3	10	1	1

Besides a certain quantity of small game.

Had I been able to add to the above a good mountain ram I should have been more satisfied, but I suppose a gunner is like a farmer, who is always said to be happier with a grumble, and I must confess, from all I have since heard, and considering the quality of my specimens, that in my case regrets are ungrateful.

To resume our ride; the snow became deeper and deeper as we approached the summit of the divide above the Yosemité, which is 6,000 feet above the sea level, but our hearts were soon lightened by the breaking of the clouds, and a cessation of the steady downfall. By the time we got to "Inspiration Point," from which the first view of the Yosemité is obtained, the weather had taken up, and it was tolerably fine and clear.

I could not describe this magnificent view if I would; let that be for others capable of putting into language one of the finest " *coups-d'œil* " known to man, one of those which remain impressed on the mind ever afterwards. I was really half lost in wonder and admiration of the scene before me, it was so far beyond what I had anticipated, so extraordinarily grand, and stupendous. Some words expressive of my wonder at the deep gorge below me must have escaped my lips, for my reverie was interrupted by, " Yes, sirree, quite a dig out, I guess," coming from the laconic George. What a view it was ! Hundreds of feet below us was spread out the park-like bed of the valley, here not more than half-a-mile across, in which luxuriated masses of magnificent specimens of rare conifers, rhododendrons, flowering shrubs, &c., &c., amongst which wound the sparkling little Merced stream. Beyond rose the gigantic mass of grey granite called " El Capitan," presenting a perpendicular face of 3,300 feet, and over a mile in length ("quite a stone" according to the irrepressible George). On the same side, further up the cañon, were the cliffs called the "Three Brothers," over 3,800 feet out of the valley. Then to the right, on the same side as ourselves, rose up in succession the "Three Graces," 3,750 feet, the serrated points called the "Cathedral Spires," 2,660 feet; the isolated perpendicular crag called "The Sentinel," over 3,000 feet, and further off the grand rounded mass of the "South" or "Half Dome," the latter considerably over 4,000 feet. But the highest mountain of all lies beyond, and is said to be 5,700 feet above the valley, and possesses the appropriate and euphonic name of the " Cloud's Rest."

> " Mountains, on whose barren breast
> The labouring clouds do often rest."

After enjoying this charming view as long as we could, we trotted at a good pace down the well-engineered road into the valley, where we were soon surrounded with an almost southern vegetation, although we were still over 4,000 feet above the sea. The surface of the bottom of the glen appeared like a well-kept pleasure-ground. It was clothed with a soft velvety turf, studded all over with rhododendrons, white and evergreen oaks (*quercus lobata* and *crassipouta*), magnificent pitch pines (*pinus ponderosa* and *Jeffreyi*), cedars, cottonwood (a sort of poplar like the Balm of Gilead), and many other trees and shrubs of which I had no knowledge.

We had just time to admire the frozen Fall of the " Bridal Veil," with its unbroken descent of over 600

THE CATHEDRAL ROCKS IN THE YOSEMITE VALLEY.

(From a Sketch by A. Bierstadt.)

Chapter XVI., page 376.

feet, when the light began to wane, and we were obliged to push on to save the brief twilight for our ride to Liedig's Hotel, under the "Sentinel Rock."

Our host was glad enough to see us, for tourists are very scarce commodities at this time of the year, and he determined to celebrate our arrival by exploding a dynamite cartridge, that we might at the same time enjoy the grand echoes. These were doubtless extraordinary, but I am free to confess I would rather have gone away without hearing them than have experienced the anxiety of mind, and real risk to body, which preceded the pleasure. It appeared that the large dynamite (or "hercules powder") cartridge had frozen, and had to be "thawed," which operation was performed under the stove of our sitting-room! In vain I expostulated, pointing out the imminent danger of its exploding and blowing ourselves and the house into little pieces. Not a bit of use; our host was as obstinate as a mule, and would have it. There he sat, surrounded with his children, watching the thawing process, and occasionally feeling the cartridge with his fingers to see if it was mastic enough to allow of the percussion-fuse being inserted. Glad was I when he pronounced it sufficiently soft, and departed with it to the scene of action. A few minutes later we heard a loud explosion, followed by reverberation after reverberation from the surrounding crags and precipices, a joyful announcement to us that all further risk was over.

The next morning broke damp and hazy, but the clouds gradually lifted, and we were able before starting on our ride back to Clark's to see a little of the valley beyond the "Sentinel," in which is the famous Yosemité Fall. This waterfall is 2,550 feet high, 1,500 feet of which is a perpendicular *chute* before a ledge of rock is struck by the water. Then comes over 600 feet of cascades, and then a final plunge of 400 feet into the river below. This year all the water in the valley, except the main stream, is frozen over, and snow lies thick on the tops, with a fair sprinkling in the valley below. We saw these wonders therefore under peculiar and exceptional circumstances, and whether for the better or the worse it is difficult to say.

We had thought of leaving the valley by the Hite's Mine route, but it was deemed wiser, on account of the threatening aspect of the weather, to abandon this plan, and to take the same route back, leaving everything we could do without at Clark's, to be picked up on our return. We had venison steaks to-night for supper off the little buck killed on our way into the valley, and which we had packed home on one of the bronchos.

An uneventful but somewhat tedious journey by the same route brought us back to our old quarters at San Francisco, which, however, I had so very soon again to leave on my homeward journey.

CHAPTER XVIII.

" Of monies, and gold and silver."
" *Merry Wives of Windsor*," *Shakspere.*

My great object now, before turning homewards, was
to see something of the mining "adventures" on the
world-famed Comstock Lode of Nevada, and as this
chapter must contain much of interest only to those
who may care about such technical matters, I must
forewarn the general reader and suggest liberal
skipping.

Through the courtesy of Dr. Price, the well-known
assayer and mining engineer at San Francisco, I
was soon provided with letters to Mr. Mackay and
other gentlemen at Virginia city, where are located

the headquarters of the main workings on this lode.

The journey of 346 miles from San Francisco was made in sixteen hours, by steamer up the bay to Vallejo, and then by rail for the rest of the distance, the main line being left at Reno.

The approach to Virginia city is up the barren, dreary-looking valley of the Carson. Steep and bare mountain-sides rise up from the margin of the little stream, along the side of which the railway winds its snake-like course. Groups of flimsy, uncomfortable-looking houses denoted where mineral wealth had been discovered, and mining camps had been formed. Virginia city, which came into existence about 1859, and now contains over 20,000 inhabitants, is strikingly situated on the eastern slope of a huge mass of syenite called Mount Davidson, the summit of which is 2,000 feet above the city, and nearly 8,000 feet above the sea. The surrounding country bears unmistakable signs of volcanic origin, and is wild, bleak, and destitute of vegetation.

On arrival I lost no time in presenting my letter to Mr. Mackay, locally called the "boss of the big bonanza," who is the resident partner and manager of the Consolidated Virginia and California Mines. He most kindly asked me to visit these undertakings under his own personal guidance, and I quickly came to the conclusion that I could not have seen things under more favourable conditions; for Mr. Mackay was not only the "boss," but had the intimate knowledge of details of a manager of each separate department.

This celebrated Comstock Lode or "Ledge," called after one of its earliest "prospectors," or discoverers, seems to be a "fissure vein," that is, a fissure or rent in the older formation, which has been filled by a more recent and ore-bearing rock. In this case the filling matter is a sort of porphyry called "propylite," which in appearance resembles much our Cornish "elvan." To adopt the local term, the "ledge" varies considerably in thickness, sometimes being as much as 700 feet wide (not half of it, however, being metalliferous), sometimes it narrows to less than seventy feet. I have seen it stated that as a general rule it narrows with depth, that is, that the two sides of the fissure approach each other as the depth increases. The gangue or vein-matter is quartz. The length of the ledge is stated as about three and a half miles, and on it are located about twenty-one mining sets, varying in extent from 3,325 feet, which belongs to the Sierra Nevada Mining Company, to ninety-three feet, which is the property of the Kentuck Company. The richest sets are those of the Consolidated Virginia and California, which measure together between 1,300 and 1,400 feet. The productive portion of the ledge is comparatively small, as barren portions of great extent intervene between the "bonanzas," or ore bodies, or bunches. It is said that the "bunches" as a general rule become smaller as they get deeper, and their composition more "rebellious" to treat, but of this I heard personally no confirmation. The strike of the ledge is nearly due north and south, it dips to the eastward at an angle of from 38° to 45°. But the "foot" and "hanging walls" have a few inches of a sort of clay slate between them and what is termed the "country rock."

Of frequent occurrence in the ledge are what are locally called "horses;" these are wedge-shaped masses

of soft, practically-barren, porphyritic rock, supposed
to have been detached from the hanging wall, between
which there often occur belts of metalliferous quartz.
A piece of the "horse rock" I brought up gave by
analysis 4·3 ozs. of silver per ton. A piece of the
soapy clay rock yielded 1·1 oz. of silver, and both
had traces of gold, thus testifying to the extraordinary way in which even the adjoining rocks are
impregnated with the precious metals.

The ledge is won at the Consolidated Virginia by
a vertical shaft sunk to the eastward in the
"country" rock, from which drifts or cross-cuts are
driven at different levels to cut the ledge. At this
present time the lowest of these is 1,750 feet from
surface. The shaft down which I descended would
strike the ledge, it is said, at about 2,400 feet from
surface, but it would only be continued down in the
event of the ore bodies continuing to prove profitable to the deep. At present it stands at about the
1,750 feet level.

We got out of the cage, in which we had been
expeditiously and smoothly lowered, at the 1,650
feet level, and here Mr. Mackay handed me over
to one of the "captains" to show me all I wanted
to see. Proceeding to some of the working ends I
found the heat intense, far greater than was to be
accounted for merely by the depth from surface. I
have little doubt the excess of heat is occasioned by
the chemical decomposition of the iron pyrites by
water. I had no thermometer with me, so could not
take the temperature, but I have seen it stated to be
100° to 120°. My own impression was that it was at
least 120° (Fahrenheit). The men seemed to feel
it considerably, judging from their general appear-

ance, and by the scarcity of their clothing. In their endeavours to cool their hands and throats as much as ten tons of ice are consumed per day.

The mine water is too impure to be used for any purposes. The boilers and condensing engines have in consequence to be supplied with the water of the town, which is brought thirty-five miles in iron pipes. In order to economize it as far as practicable, that employed for condensing is cooled, after use, in large reservoirs, from which it is pumped back to serve again and again.

The mass of solid ore which is being operated upon is quite astounding. There appeared to be regular " faces " or " breasts " of it, much as if it was a vein of coal instead of bunches of ore. And this is the chief secret of the Comstock wealth ; it is the enormous quantity of ore which is worked, more even than its richness. Over 1,200 tons of ore of an average value of about $45 to $50 (9*l.* to 10*l.*) per ton are said to be the daily output of these two mines, the Consolidated Virginia and California. We thus have 12,000*l.* as the value sent daily to surface to go to the credit of these fortunate adventurers ! The ore varies much in value, some of it is as low as $15 or $20 (3*l.* or 4*l.*) per ton, but some again reaches $85 to $90 (17*l.* to 18*l.*), and I was given the foregoing as a fair average value as it comes from the mine without any " dressing " or preparation of any kind.

To produce this large quantity, about 900 miners are employed, who work in shifts of eight hours each, and continuously from week's end to week's end without cessation. The accidents of all sorts are said to average one a day, of which one-fifth are fatal. The

working miner earns on an average about $4¼ (17s.)
a day, but tempting as these wages may sound to
the ears of our own poor fellows in these bad times,
there are many expenses, drawbacks, and incon-
veniences from which they are exempt. Amongst
these may be mentioned houses, which I believe are
scarce, dear, and bad, and the excessive cost of many
of the ordinary commodities of life. Tea is sometimes 6s. per lb., sugar 1s. per lb., salt 4d. or 5d.
per lb., and all articles of clothing and bedding are
enormously dear. Fortunately amongst the expensive goods are spirits, common rye whiskey, of very
inferior strength, costing as much as 5s. per quart.
Besides these physical there are many social drawbacks to be encountered by a respectable miner in
his every-day life, more especially should he have a
family to care for.

The majority of the miners are Cornish, and I
am happy to say that they seem to be more appreciated here than in Colorado, where a certain
jealousy and ill-feeling exist towards them for
having, as it is asserted, brought down the rate of
wages. The Irish element seems to be both large
and prosperous. The captain who took me into
the "ends" was of this nationality, and with so
strong a Fenian tendency that he could not help
holding forth immediately on the wrongs of his
down-trodden native land. His chief instance of
oppression was that at the time of the famine so
many fowls had been sent to England. I suggested
to him that the money paid for them came back into
the country to buy bread for the peasants who had
voluntarily sold them. But of no avail; he insisted
the fowls ought to have been kept and consumed at

home, and not sent to feed the hated Saxon. In his own calling he was a well-informed, shrewd, practical fellow, and I was much amused at his opinion of a common acquaintance, who was in the habit of holding forth learnedly on mining matters. "Mr. ——— knows a good deal about mines, doesn't he?" I inquired. "Ah, faith, he just knows enough to lose his money," was the brief but telling response.

But to return to the mine. Ingersoll's and Burleigh's rock-boring machines are extensively used; both are highly spoken of, though the former, I am told, is the favourite. The "shooting" (blasting) is done with what is here called "No. 3, giant powder," a sort of slow dynamite which is quicker and less violent in its action than black powder. On this account there is less chance of loss through the scattering of small bits of ore amongst the heavy timbering, &c.

The ore being of such great value, all the ore-bearing portion of the ledge has to be taken out clean. Large cavities are thus formed, which have to be "timbered," and the following solid and costly system has to be adopted: Heavy logs, twelve and fourteen inches square, laid horizontally, are morticed together in a rectangular form with very strong vertical posts, about seven feet, sometimes only five feet, apart, and the space thus enclosed is filled up and made as solid as practicable with waste material from the mine. Notwithstanding this exceptionally strong timbering, a "crush" will sometimes take place within a very few months, and great difficulty is often experienced in keeping the places open even for the short time required to fetch the ore out. I am told that eighty thousand

feet of timber are supplied daily to these two mines.
As may be imagined, the mountain-sides, far and
wide, have been denuded of every stick to meet the
requirements. Even the roots and stumps have
disappeared, having been grubbed up for fuel. The
present supply is brought from great distances, even
as far as from the neighbourhood of the famous Lake
Tahoe, and the eastern range of the Sierras. It is
brought down in mill races as it were, the water
being confined between wooden planks, called here
"flumes," in which flows a sufficient stream to float
the largest baulks. This wonderful demand has led
to large companies being formed to supply the
mines, by "tapping" new and well-timbered districts with flumes and railroads. I am told that
nearly all is now being cut off Government lands, the
State receiving a royalty of $1\frac{1}{4}$ (5s.) per acre.
Considering that most of the land is useless after
it has been denuded of its natural covering, this
royalty would appear very low, yet, notwithstanding,
the wood for fuel costs about $10 (= 2l.) per cord;
and as it takes $1\frac{1}{2}$ cords to do the work of a ton of
good coal, it would appear that it costs here 3l. to
get as much steam raised as would be produced
in many mines in England for about 10s. or 12s.
This very important item in economical working is
becoming more and more scarce and costly as the
distance increases from which it has to be brought.

And now a few more words about the ore itself,
and its subsequent treatment. In appearance it
is a dull grey mass, presenting here and there
metallic spots. Two pieces I brought up with me
from the 1,650 feet level in the California mine gave
by analysis 858·3 ozs. of silver and 37·8 ozs. of

gold, and the other 1,122·0 ozs. of silver and
37·6 ozs. of gold per ton of ore respectively, with
about 2°/₀ of copper. Probably the whole of the
gold is present as "native," but the silver, besides
being "native," is in combination with sulphur,
as silver glance; with sulphur and antimony, as
"stephanite" and "ruby silver;" and with chlorine,
as "horn silver" and "polybasite." The presence of
this latter mineral may account for the small amount
of copper shown in the analysis.

I am told that the ore costs $18 (= 3*l.* 12*s.*) per
ton, delivered into the amalgamation works from the
Virginia Consolidated and 23 cents (say 1*s.*) more
from the California mine; this slight difference
arising out of certain law expenses.

The first process after being delivered from the
mine into the mill, or works, is pulverising under
stamps with water until the ore becomes a very
fine slime or "pulp." The mill I visited was
driven by steam and contained eighty such stamps,
each weighing 940 lbs., about 1½ horse-power being
required for each stamp.

After passing through vertical sieves of fine wire,
the slime is run into large pans, in which revolve
iron arms or fans, requiring eight-horse power to
drive each set. With the slime is mixed quicksilver,
copper vitriol (sulphate of copper), common salt,
and a little soda, and the whole mass is heated by
steam. Chemical decomposition of the silver combinations takes place, and the well-known affinity
of metallic gold and silver for quicksilver leads
them at once to combine and form an amalgam.

After being strained through blanketing to recover mechanically as much of the quicksilver as is

possible, the amalgam is heated in retorts, when the quicksilver is driven off in fumes, which are condensed and collected in the metallic form.

The residue in the retorts is an impure gold and silver mass, which is taken up into the melting-house, and run down in graphite pots, capable of containing about 3,000 ozs., which is laded into three bars of bullion. The value is then stamped on them and they are "expressed" by rail to San Francisco, where the gold is separated from the silver and coined, and the silver is sold as ingots.

The great advantage of the amalgamation process is its extreme simplicity. Its drawbacks are loss of quicksilver by volatisation, and loss of that part of the produce which cannot be recovered from the so-called "tailings." These latter are caught in a series of slime-pits, until the assay shows a value of not more than $7 or $8 (28s. to 32s.) per ton, below which they do not consider it profitable to throw back and treat over again. It is possible that better produce might be obtained by alterations and modifications on the existing process, or by the substitution of some of the many other well-known metallurgical methods for the extraction of silver, but whether this would be remunerative is another matter, and everything seemed to me to be so well managed and considered here, that I have very little doubt any improvement of real practical value, having regard to local conditions and circumstances, would be very speedily adopted.

The discovery of quicksilver in California has been of the utmost importance to these works. It costs here now 50 cents (2s.) per lb., and is obtained from the sulphuret ("cinnabar"), which has been of late years found in such quantities that not only is the home consumption fully met, but last year over 46,000 flasks, of a value of $1,625,310 (= 325,062*l.*) were exported, chiefly to China.

A run through the assay and melting-house, which is the property of the Consolidated Virginia, but which does the work of the two companies, completed a most interesting visit, and I came away from Virginia city impressed both with the wealth of the Comstock Ledge and with the gigantic scale of the undertakings I visited.

As a practical exemplification of the wealth, it is computed that $350,000,000 (70,000,000*l.*) worth of bullion has been produced from this lode up to the present time, and the following is the produce of the Consolidated Virginia alone, since 1873 inclusive, as stated in the annual report of the President, Mr. C. H. Fish:—

	Gold.	Silver.	Total.
1873.—	$314,289 = £62,858	$331,293 = £66,258	$645,582 = £129,116
1874.—	2,063,138 = 412,688	2,918,016 = 583,609	4,981,184 = 996,297
1875.—	7,635,207 = 1,407,042	9,082,188 = 1,936,137	16,717,395 = 3,343,479
1876.—	7,378,146 = 1,475,629	9,279,501 = 1,855,901	16,657,650 = 3,331,530
1877.—	6,270,519 = 1,254,104	7,163,500 = 1,492,700	13,734,019 = 2,746,804

$52,736,130   £10,547,226

Of this vast amount it appears that $35,640,000 (7,128,000*l.*) has been paid in dividends! I am not aware what the actual capital now employed amounts to; it would seem, however, that $438,490 (87,698*l.*) was expended before a dollar was returned.

The California mine accounts are also both interesting and instructive, and testify equally to the riches of the Comstock. In 1876, the average value of the 127,540 tons raised was about $105 (21*l.*) per ton, and the total value of the bullion was $13,400,841 (2,680,168*l.*), of which $6,488,640 (1,297,728*l.*) was gold, and $6,912,203 (1,382,440*l.*) silver; the dividends paid to shareholders in this year was $8,640,000 (1,728,000*l.*)! Last year (1877) the ore raised from the California was 213,683 tons, of an average value of $88½ (17*l.* 2*s.* 9*d.*) per ton. The dividends paid to shareholders amounted to $12,960,000 (2,592,000*l.*)! The cost of working and after treatment of the ore was $25.70c. (5*l.* 3*s.*) per ton; of this amount the labour for getting the ore was $3.57c. (say 14*s.*); hoisting (or winding out of the mine), 86c. (3*s.* 7*d.*); after-treatment, $10.39c. (2*l.* 3*s.* 3½*d.*). The silver extracted weighed 464¾ tons, of a value of $9,538,104 (1,907,621*l.*)! and about eighty-three tons of gold, of a value of $9,386,745 (1,877,349*l.*)! So that the total value of the bullion was $18,924,849 (3,784,270*l.*)! The wages paid were $776,362 (155,272*l.* 10*s.*), of which $712,536 (142,507*l.*) was to miners at $4 per day; the average wages throughout the concern was $4.33c. (18*s.*) per man per day.

I do not know that anything gives a better idea of the scale on which an undertaking is carried on than the actual balance-sheet, so will now give what purports to be that of the Virginia Consolidated for 1877, as stated in one of the San Francisco daily papers. There appears to be a mistake in the addition, which I am at a loss to account for, the credits being correct, but the debit side should be $15,529,996.82, a difference of $1,630,339.27, or about 326,068*l.* However, the figures will suffice to show the very large amounts expended on the various items, which are so amply met by the great value of the bullion produced.

CONSOLIDATED VIRGINIA, 1877.

Receipts.	$	£
Yield of the mine for the year	13,734,019.07 =	2,746,804
Sundry ores sold during the year	68,201.38 „	13,640
Received from sundry parties for assaying	62,424.31 „	12,485
Balances outstanding	35,012.79 „	7,002
Last annual meeting since settled	$13,899,657.55 =	£2,779,931

Disbursements.	$	£
Cash and bullion samples in hand, Superintendent at Virginia	10,743.06 =	2,149
Cash on hand, San Francisco Office	1,353.25 „	270
Balance of cash in Nevada Bank	1,088,349.01 „	217,670
Virginia office expenses	3,284.45 „	657
Team account	1,271.20 „	254
On purchase	93,933.53 „	18,787
Surveying	700.00 „	140
Assay Office expenses (Virginia)	38,269.90 „	7,654
Books and Stationery	1,614.45 „	323
Legal expenses	299.07 „	60
Advertising	199.50 „	40
Water	6,000.00 „	1,200
Real Estate	1,652,000.00 „	330,400
Hoisting—balance paid above receipts	3,142.14 „	628
Taxes	282,579.23 „	56,216
Reduction (crushing)	1,449,188.60 „	289,838
Interest and Exchange	89,934.39 „	17,987
Bullion Freight	48,402.19 „	9,680
Dividends (Nos. 33 to 40 inclusive)	8,640,000.00 „	1,728,000
C and C Shaft	131,000.00 „	26,200
Bullion Discount	975,416.05 „	195,083
Supplies	391,505.87 „	78,301
Salaries and Wages	615,545.50 „	123,109
San Francisco office	5,265.43 „	1,053
	$15,529,996.82 =	£3,105,999

The board of management is, I believe, a committee of five, elected yearly at a general meeting of the

shareholders, who have the power of calling a
general meeting between-times, and altering the
composition of the committee. Most mining companies in these parts are incorporated under an Act
of Congress similar to our own Limited Liabilities
Act. If a company is not under this Act, the
liability of the shareholders is unlimited.

I must not quit this locality without saying a few
words on that great work for which an Act of
Congress has been obtained, and which will be of
such importance to the mining adventures situated
on this lode. I mean the Sutro Tunnel. This
tunnel (or adit, as we should call it) has for its
main object the unwatering of the mines, at a depth
of 2,244 feet from the surface, by branches or cross-
cuts; but, besides this, it is expected to prove of
great value as an intake of fresh air for the deep
workings, and as a base, as it were, for exploring
operations.

The mouth of the adit is between Corral and
Weber Cañons, a little over four miles from the
Comstock outcrop, but as the ledge dips to the east,
it is expected to cut it in 20,178 feet, or three miles
and 1,446 yards. To expedite the work and procure fresh air for the men, four shafts are to be
sunk in this distance, about 4,500 feet apart, the
depth of which will vary from 443 to 1,942 feet.
The rock through which it has to be driven is said
to be on the whole easy to deal with, and to con-
sist of trachyte, trachytic breccia, and trachytic
greenstone, the latter partially decomposed, and probably requiring timbering for its whole length of 300
yards or more. The vertical section through the
self-supporting rock is described as "a circle of

twelve feet diameter, with offsets three and a half feet from the bottom, about one foot wide, which support the superstructure of the railroad track, to be used for removing ore and débris from the mine. The space under the superstructure is for drawing the water from the lode. Where timber supports are required to sustain the adjacent rock the top is level, and ten feet wide, clear of the framing; height, eight feet to the bottom of the timbers supporting the railroad, where it is twelve feet wide in the clear. Below this there is a triangular space, three feet seven inches in depth, forming the water way." (Government Report, 1868, p. 398.) It is estimated that 10,535 feet will be through solid rock, and 9,643 feet through decomposed rock requiring timbering. It was originally computed that the time actually required to carry out this great work would be a little more than two and a half years; but allowing for delays and contingencies, it was thought that it would probably take from three and a half to four years. But as it was begun in 1871, and is not yet connected with any of the workings on the Comstock, we may assume that unexpected difficulties have been met with. Burleigh's drills have been extensively used; and in the month of December, 1874, 417 feet were driven (13 feet per day). Up to the end of 1877 the total quantity completed was 18,607 feet, the year's work being 3130 feet (261 feet per month). There would then be about 1,500 feet still to drive to reach workings on the Comstock lode.

The importance which such an adit would be to mining undertakings continually troubled with water, only miners themselves can fully appreciate.

In some cases it may make the difference of actual existence, whilst it will place at the disposal of all in connexion with it a large intake for the purposes of ventilation, which may prove of very great value in the future, in dealing with the heat question. It is anticipated, too, that a great hydraulic power will be developed for the benefit of all mines connected with it.

Before leaving the Comstock I may be expected to say a few words on the probable future of this " mine of wealth," although I feel it somewhat presumptuous in a mere visitor like myself to make even a surmise. The surface extent of the fissure is now pretty well known, but the problem yet unsolved is whether it will continue its peculiar wealth to the deep? whether the same precious metals will continue to predominate, or whether the lode will not alter its character as the depth increases? Such an occurrence as the latter is by no means uncommon in metalliferous lodes, as an example of which, many of the copper-mines of Cornwall may be mentioned which have turned into tin as they have increased their depth from surface. The scientific investigators who have had the best opportunity of forming an opinion of this ledge seem to think that it will continue of much the same character as at present. Baron Richthofen, in his Report to the Mechanics' Institute in 1865, on the Sutro Tunnel, writes: " The value of a deep tunnel will, of course, chiefly depend upon the question whether these mines will ever be worked to considerable depth; that is, whether the Comstock vein will extend far down, and whether it will retain its metalliferous character in depth. Both questions will have to be decided from the

study of the structure and nature of the Comstock
vein, and from comparing the results with the
observations at such mines in other countries which
have already been worked to great depth. My
experience on the Comstock vein is based on close
and repeated examinations of nearly all the mines
on its course. I believe I concur with almost everybody who has had equal experience about them, in
the opinion that it is a true fissure vein, of extraordinary length, and extending downwards much
further than any mining works will ever be able to
be carried on. It would be too lengthy to enumerate
the various reasons which lead most positively to this
conclusion. It is now assumed almost universally
as a fact, and the number of those who consider it
as a gash vein, or a system of gash veins, is fast
diminishing. As to the downward continuance of
the ore-bearing character, every instance goes to
show that the average yield in precious metals
remains about the same at every depth. Some mines
had accumulations of ore near the surface; in others
they commenced very near under the surface; at
others, again, considerable work had to be done
before bodies of ore of any amount were struck;
and some which had no ore heretofore appear to
have good prospects to find it soon. . . . . There
is no reason to doubt that the equality of average
produce and yield throughout the entire length of
the vein will continue downwards to any depth;
besides the very obvious theoretical conclusion that
vast amounts of silver could not be carried into
the fissure from the overlying or enclosing rocks,
but naturally had to rise from unknown depths,
through the channel of the fissure itself, to be

deposited in it where the conditions for sublimation or precipitation were given in its open space. Experience in other countries by no means shows of a regular decrease or increase in yield as of common occurrence, though either of them may happen. More commonly, the produce of true fissure veins in precious metals has been found to be about constant."

So wrote Baron Richthofen in 1865, and his views were thought of such weight, that they were published in the Government Report of 1868 on the " Mineral Resources of the United States " (p. 391), with an observation that explorations made since " strongly confirm the views expressed by him."

Should these views prove correct, and the lode continue wealth-producing to the deep, a serious question will present itself, namely, how to meet the rapidly-increasing high temperature. Even at the present depth of about 1,700 feet in the California and Consolidated Virginia the heat is causing inconvenience, and requires artificial means to counteract it. But this inconvenience, at the present rate of increase, will become a positive trouble by the time the depth of 2,000 feet is reached. In this matter the Sutro Tunnel will doubtless prove of very great value as an " intake," and the natural draw of the deep shaft and the heated atmosphere of the workings may easily be assisted by artificial means, such as fans, in the same way as if an inflammable colliery was being dealt with. At any rate we may rest assured that should the valuable nature of the lode continue downwards, science will come to the rescue, and enormously deep workings will be carried on before heat alone is allowed to drive the determined miner from his vocation.

CHAPTER XIX.

" A land of space and dreams ; a land
Of sea, salt lakes, and dried up seas !"
Joaquin Miller, " The Great Plains and Desert."

" Restore to God His due in tithe and time :
A tithe purloin'd, cankers the whole estate."
Herbert, " The Temple."

IT had been my intention before leaving the western
slope of the Rocky Mountains to visit the well-
known Eureka mining district, but Parliament was
now summoned, so this and other pleasant and
interesting expeditions had to be abandoned, and I
had only time for a flying visit to Salt Lake City on
my way back across the continent.

Eureka is reached, by a branch three-foot gauge
line 90 miles in length, from Palisade station on the
Union Pacific Railroad 595 miles from San Fran-

cisco. There is only one quick train daily on this
branch each way, and they are so timed that two
days must be consumed on the trip. I should have
much liked to have seen this locality, which must
be most interesting in its mineralogical and geological aspect, but it was not feasible with the
time I had left. I was told, on good authority,
that the ore is nearly entirely a carbonate of
lead, and that it occurs in connected vertical
pockets in the limestone. These pockets are enclosed within walls of quartz and a sort of shale,
impervious to water. It would appear that the
ore was originally galena (sulphuret of lead),
and that the passing of water down through the
vein has decomposed it, and that it has become a
carbonate, a natural chemical process by no means
uncommon in other localities. Occasionally lumps
of galena are found coated and surrounded with the
new-formed carbonate. The practical result here of
this process is an ore admirably adapted for metallurgical treatment—the approximate contents of
which are about 35°/₀ of lead, and 45°/₀ of oxide of
iron, with about 135 ozs. of silver, and 4½ ozs. to
5 ozs. of gold per ton of ore. The gold probably
occurs as " native " in the quartz and the silver as
a sulphide. Such is the ore as it is raised from
the mines without any "dressing" or expenditure
upon it whatsoever; and in this condition it is
delivered to the works. It is then treated in high
furnaces, each of which smelts about 75 to 80 tons
of ore per day, with a consumption of 25 bushels
of charcoal.

There are two large companies at work here, both
of whom mine and smelt their own ores. One of

the companies is composed chiefly of San Francis-
cans, and is called the Eureka Company; the
other, the Richmond Consolidated Company, is an
English adventure. A lawsuit has lately been going
on between them, in which the chief point in dispute
was whether the occurrence was a "fissure" or a
"pipe," and on this the verdict depended. It was
eventually ruled, I am told, that it was a "fissure."

The base bullion made in this district in 1877
(which contained over $16°/_0$ of gold) was of the value
of $12,000,000 (= 2,400,000*l.*), and the Richmond
Consolidated Company alone produced 5,200 tons
of pig lead, from which the precious metals had
been extracted.

At Ogden—883 miles from San Francisco—I
branched off by the Utah Central Railroad to Salt
Lake City, distant 36 miles. The line runs in close
proximity to the beautiful Wahsatch Mountains,
the peaks of which are more than 12,000 feet above
the sea. This range forms, as it were, the eastern
side or slope of a great interior basin, of which the
Sierra Nevada is the western. Geologists say, that,
in comparatively modern times, this basin was one
great inland sea, and state as one of the proofs of this,
that the calcareous and arenaceous beds, which are
deposited over the intermediate space sometimes
to a thickness of 800 and 1,200 feet, often abound
with fresh-water shells. At that time the higher
peaks of the smaller mountain ridges lying between
these two main ranges must have appeared as
islands above the surface of this vast extent of
water. A large portion of this inland region does
not find any direct drainage to the ocean. To this
special portion, the early explorer, Fremont, gave

the name of the "Great Basin," which has now passed into general use.

It is worthy of note that on the line of the Union Pacific Railroad the mountain ranges tend generally nearly north and south, and are locally parallel. In their geological structure they would, I believe, exhibit, as a rule, a section of a sedimentary rock, more or less metamorphised, overlying volcanic or igneous rocks, the latter generally forming the high peaks and rugged outlines of the ridges. Well worthy of a trip would the Wahsatch Range prove to any enterprising members of the Alpine Club who may be no longer satisfied with the mountains of old Europe. Amongst these wild peaks and precipices they would find ascents difficult enough to please the most indefatigable, and be rewarded with distant views in this clear transparent atmosphere which would be impossible in our moister hemisphere.

Salt Lake City is a bright, quiet little town of about 20,000 inhabitants, clean, regularly built, and picturesquely situated. The long, broad streets and roads, laid out at right angles to each other, are formal and stiff. There is here nothing attractive to the eye of a stranger, at any rate on his first acquaintance, nothing differing much from what he might expect to see in any other western town. The only object which would strike him as peculiar would probably be the hideous exterior of the "Tabernacle," a long elliptic brick building, 250 feet in length by 150 in breadth, with a wooden-shingle dome-shaped roof. The interior of this edifice is capable of seating 12,000 people, and possesses extraordinary acoustic powers. In order to give me an opportunity of

judging of these, my guide, who possessed a very
good tenor voice, sung a few bars "*pianissimo*" on
the platform, whilst I stood at the other end of the
building, and I could hear every note distinctly.
The organ is very large, and of native manufacture,
some of the pipes are fifty feet high and two feet
square. The way in which the seats were arranged
struck me as peculiar yet practical, the floor being
on a gentle slope from the platform to the opposite end of the building, so that all the audience is
able to see the preacher over the heads of those in
front of them. This building is not used in winter,
on account of its not possessing any heating apparatus; the congregation has then to attend the
meeting-houses with which each of the city wards is
provided.

I understand that about three-fourths of the
population are Mormons in the city, but that in
the territory of Utah the proportion is greater,
for out of the 100,000 inhabitants, about 85,000
are Mormons and 15,000 Gentiles, as the non-
Mormons are here commonly called. The Mormon
element is said to be on the decrease, in consequence of the unwillingness on the part of
some to pay the tithes on all produce as required
by the elders. In such cases instant dismissal
from the community follows. I suspect that the
proximity of Camp Douglas, where the United
States Government keeps a small military force,
encourages and renders possible resistance to the
edicts and commands which would not have been
ventured upon formerly. Yet the sect must be
still prosperous and financially strong if one may
judge by their public buildings and domestic

D d

dwelling-houses. A very fine new tabernacle of dressed granite is being erected for their ceremonies, and substantial stone edifices form the abodes of their "bosses." One of these latter, a very nice-looking house, had five small doors opening on to the street. I was told that these five openings demonstrated that the proprietor was the possessor of five wives, each of whom had her own door. Another had three doors for the same reason; and another, said to be that of Bishop (!) Sharp, formerly a Scotch collier, had two doors. Another, with a like number, belonged to an old brute of an elder, who had very recently lost a wife, and had just replaced her with a young Scandinavian girl.

Brigham Young's establishment is enclosed within walls, with the exception of the Amelia House, a part of which his favourite wife still occupies. He himself used to reside in the Bee-Hive House in which he died, and he was buried in the grounds attached to it. A watchman's hut has been erected in the garden for the purpose, it is said, of guarding the grave.

It is sincerely to be hoped that not many years will elapse before polygamy will cease; and the following circumstance would seem to point that way. The United States Governor, Emery, opened the Territorial Parliament a few days ago, January 10, 1878, and is reported in the Salt Lake *Daily Herald*, a Mormon organ, to have used the following words in his " message :"—

" The majority of the people of this territory, belong to a religious sect known as the ' Latter-day Saints.' I do not intend to discuss the merits or demerits of this new religion, but to refer to one of its distinctive features, polygamy. This system of marriage has continued here for thirty years, and for fifteen years in violation of law. In all the States and Territories except Utah it is considered a grave offence, and is severely punished. Polygamy is no less a crime here than in other portions of our country; and yet the law remains a dead letter upon the statutes. I regard this system of marriage an evil, undermining the peace of society brought within its influence, and carrying with it dark shadows, which rest like a blight upon the offspring of these illegal relations, and the women who are maintained in them. The number of polygamous wives in Utah is large—how large I have not the means of knowing—yet it is safe to say they number thousands. Such a condition of things is an anomaly nowhere else to be found in a Christian country. This, gentlemen, is a serious question, and should be met openly and with candour. It is for you to decide whether from all the surroundings you will take action in the premises and provide against the continuance of these criminal relations, or ignore the consequences of this state of affairs. Congress has reserved to itself the right to approve or disapprove of any territorial legislation, and also to enact such laws as may appear necessary to the welfare of the people. Yet, notwithstanding these reserved powers, it is more than probable that Congress would acquiesce in any measures inaugurated by yourselves looking to a permanent and equitable settlement of this question. The territories are the wards of the national Government created by Congress, and whatever privileges are enjoyed within them are extended

by that body, all of which Congress has the power
to modify or revoke. The policy of the Government has been to allow citizens of the territories to
legislate for themselves, and no doubt it will continue in that policy, provided they enact judicious
laws, such as are in accordance with the general
government, and in harmony with those of the States,
and not otherwise. Polygamous marriages are so
frequent and so numerous throughout this territory,
and the sentiment of the majority of the people so
much in their favour, that the officers of the law,
though charged with the duty of enforcing the law,
find themselves unable to do so without further and
more stringent legislation on the subject. This
legislative body has sufficient jurisdiction over the
matter to provide such enactments as the circumstances require; but if it fails to act in the premises, then it is the duty of Congress to take
cognizance of the fact and to provide such legislation as will meet this case, or abolish the law which
makes polygamy a crime."

Some further remarks follow, but I think I have
quoted enough to show the feeling of the Government towards this practice, and the apparent probability that it will soon be suppressed by special
Act of Congress, should the Territorial Parliament
refuse to deal with it themselves. Considering that
a very large majority of this local legislature are
Mormons, who should support polygamy as one of
the tenets of their religion, its suppression would be
a bitter pill for them to swallow; but abolish it they
must, or pressure will be brought to bear from the
east. The Salt Lake *Daily Herald* of January 16th,
1878,—the Mormon organ—in an article comment-

ing on the message, alludes to this passage in the following off-hand way:—"No message by a 'Gentile' governor of Utah would be complete without a reference to polygamy; hence his excellency, who doubtless desired that his communication to the assembly should be lacking in nothing, devotes a portion of the document to that practice. He talks as if he was expected to say so much on the subject; but we doubt if the governor dreams that his words will have any effect upon the members of the dignified body, a majority of whom are presumed to practise what he asks them to abolish, and all of whom belong to a religious faith and organization, one of the tenets of which is this doctrine of plural marriage. His language on this subject ought to pacify the radical anti-Mormon class."

This is certainly a somewhat cool way of treating a message from the Central Government as if it were mere bounce to be put aside. They make, however, some little *amende* by pronouncing that "on the whole the production is very fair," and to be rated, in market parlance, as "above fair to middling." The foregoing passage from the message gives too an interesting and official view of the relation existing between the Territorial Legislatures and Congress. The elected Territorial Parliaments are allowed to legislate on local matters and their recommendations, if not in contravention of the acts and views of Congress, are sanctioned by the latter body and become law.

One of the most charming views of the city and its lovely surroundings is to be had from the United States Government post of Camp Douglas, situated

about three miles off, under the Wahsatch Range.
This is an entrenched camp, capable of accommo-
dating seven companies of infantry, and possessing
about a dozen brass field-pieces in a commanding
position.   At this time there were only three companies here, the remainder of the garrison being, as
usual, in pursuit of phantom Indians, a work of
fatigue and hardship, and attendant with but little
glory.

I found the officer in command most civil and
communicative.   Like most officers in this small
service, he had had a very large and varied experience of military life.   Indeed, it cannot well be
otherwise after a few years' service with the United
States army of scarcely 25,000 men, who have to
occupy more than 200 posts, scattered over such
an enormous extent of country.   Like our own,
these troops are subjected to great changes of
climate, from the parching heats of southern Arizona
and New Mexico to the intense colds of northern
Wyoming and Montana.   The service is not a
popular one, and less so with the privates than the
officers.   To be one of the "boys in blue" is looked
upon by the indigenous western men as a career
not to be tolerated even under the most pinching
necessity.   Probably the life is too fettered for
their ideas of liberty, and consequently, although
the pay is good, $17 (3*l.* 8*s.*) for privates, and $32
(6*l.* 8*s.*) for non-commissioned officers per month, and
all found, yet a native American in the ranks is
the exception.   I am told that nearly all the rank
and file are Germans or Irish.   Enlistment is volun-
tary, and for a period of five years.   Great induce-
ments are offered to the men to save.   They need

not draw their full rations, when they receive value
for the same; and when their uniforms and kit are
not worn out at the stated times, a very full allow-
ance is made them in money, which is placed to
their credit in the regimental accounts.

I am told that a captain's pay is at first $2000
(400*l.*) per annum, with an increase of ten per cent.
for every subsequent five years' service, besides
many extras and facilities for obtaining articles of
food, clothing, &c., from the Government stores at
cost price. This latter system does not, I believe,
exist in our service, but it is much appreciated here
by the married officers, and enables them to live at
a far less cost than if they had to buy at the ordinary trading stores.

The acting commandant of Camp Douglas had
served in the North and South war, and in many small
campaigns against the Indians. Last year he had
been engaged under General Cook against the Sioux,
in the country north of the Black-hills of Dakotah,
and had undergone great privations and hardships.
His belief was that this tribe had been so thoroughly
" whipped" that they would not break out again at
present, but that the flame would smoulder, and
should the Government make any false step, such as
the further reduction of the already too small army,
the Indians would at once seize on the opportunity,
and again take the war-path.

I have heard but one opinion as to the incom-
petency and corruption of the Indian Bureau, or
Ring, in its past dealings with the Redskins. Many
believe that the United States army officers could
undertake the management of the whole matter in
the same way as in Algeria, where a selection of

French army officers constitute the so-called "Bureau Arabe." At any rate, it would seem that no change can be for the worse.

From its commanding position, Camp Douglas, as I said before, possesses a most extensive and beautiful view, and not only of the city and the near Wahsatch Mountains with Emigrant Peak, and the lofty Twin Peaks 12,200 feet above sea level, but also of the Great Salt Lake, the Oquirrh Range, and the country beyond. Salt Lake City and its environs are full of interest, both social and physical; but they have been so often and so fully described by those who have had both leisure and opportunity to investigate them thoroughly, that my remarks will be very few, and these confined chiefly to natural objects.

In the first place, a few words about that curious inland sea, nine or ten miles to the north of the city, the Great Salt Lake. It is said to be from 75 to 120 miles in length, and from 15 to 40 miles in width, and to be situated 420 feet above the sea level. As it were, it entombs the Jordan River, on which the city is built, for after it disappears into this vast expanse of water, like Bear River, it is seen no more, for curiously enough there is no visible outflow from this or any of the other lakes situated in the Great Basin, the surplus water being disposed of by evaporation and absorption. The water of the lake contains from seventeen to twenty per cent. of common salt, besides about two per cent. of other alkaline salts. My hunters used to tell me that no bird could rise off the surface after having once settled on it, but this I cannot vouch for. The bathing is said to be delicious, which is also the case in the warm salt springs about a mile to the north of the city. The water of the lake scarcely ever freezes, even in the coldest seasons of this very severe climate. Beautiful specimens of crystallized salt are found on the sage-bushes growing on the margin, when they happen to grow so close as to be occasionally immersed in the water.

It would appear, from the geological investigation which I have alluded to before, that this and other lakes of the Great Basin are the remains of gigantic inland seas spreading over vast areas of country, and that in those times the water was scarcely, if at all, salt, fresh water shells being found in certain localities in great abundance. Professor Hayden, in the United States Government Report, 1870, p. 170, says that "The smaller ranges of mountains were scattered over it" (this sea) "as isolated islands, their summits projecting above the surface; that the waters have gradually and slowly passed away by evaporation, and the terraces" (or 'beach lines') "are left to reveal certain oscillations of level, and the steps of progress towards the present order of things; and that the briny waters have concentrated in those lake basins which have no outlet. The entire country seems to be full of salt springs, which have, in all probability, contributed a great share to the saline character of the waters."

One of these ancient beach lines has been found on the mountain-side as much as 300 feet above the present water level. There are now no fish in the lake, although various articulate insects have been discovered and reported upon.

In the distance beyond the Great Salt Lake rises up the Oquirrh Range, not so beautiful in outline or so high as the Wahsatch, but possessing equal attractions to the miner and geologist. As in the Wahsatch, the sedimentary rocks found in this range belong to the silurian and carboniferous formations. I believe the section would be quartzite (a gritty sandstone), overlaid with limestone of the carboniferous period, and below the whole an old volcanic rock, like granite or syenite, perhaps in some localities metamorphosed into gneiss. In the limestone occur the lodes of rich lead and silver ores, which have made the mines of Utah so celebrated.

The far-famed Emma Mine, of unenviable notoriety, is situated about 8,400 feet above the sea, at the head of a gorge called Little Cotton Wood Cañon, in the Wahsatch Range. The particular locality is so well described by Professor Hayden, in the Government Report of 1872, that I will give the account of his visit almost in full, feeling sure that many of my readers will be interested to hear the description of so distinguished a geologist of a mining district which has since caused such a sensation on both sides of the Atlantic. It is as follows :—" Leaving Salt Lake City we take the State road, and after a ride of ten miles in a south-easterly direction, passing between thriving farms dotted with comfortable-looking houses, we turn to the left and strike across the country to the mountains. Directly before us is the highest point in the Wahsatch Range, the Twin Peaks, over 12,000 feet above sea level. As we ride along we see distinctly marked on the sides of the mountains in front of us the water-lines of the former shores of the Great Salt Lake. These old shore-lines are distinctly marked on the mountains, on all sides of the lake, and on all the islands of the lake. We pass over numerous terraces, and at length reach the mouth of the cañon. Here there are no less than seven distinct terraces, some of them, however, due to the action of the Cotton Wood Creek. Near the mouth of the cañon there are smelting works, to which ore is brought from the mines at the head of the creek. Inside the cañon we find ourselves between high granite walls, rising precipitously on either side of the creek. The first thing to attract our attention is the conspicuous bedding of these granites. The dip is east, at an angle of fifty to seventy degrees. The granite is of a light-grey colour composed of white feldspar (orthoclase), quartz, and black mica. The bottom of the cañon is strewn with boulders of granite, which lie scattered over it in inextricable confusion. In many of them I noticed veins of feldspar, of about two inches in width, crossing each other at right angles. Another noticeable feature in these granites is the occurrence of rounded pebble-like masses, of a dark colour, enclosed in the grey matrix. Professor Silliman (Silliman's Journal, vol. iii., p. 196) referring to these, says, ' These granites are probably metamorphics of conglomerates, an opinion first suggested to me by Professor W. P. Blake,' and he further states, ' there is a pebble-like roundness in the particles of quartz in this granite, which points to a mechanical origin. The rock is quite uniform in its structure.'

" A mile or two in the cañon we came to a small village called Graniteville. It is near here that the granite of which the Mormon temple is being built is quarried. Instead of working into the rock on the sides of the cañon, the quarrying is confined to the huge blocks of granite which are scattered over the bottom on both sides of the creek. Some of these blocks are immense, measuring thirty feet square. They are split into the required size.

"Our road for about five miles leads us between the granite walls that tower far above us, surmounted by dome-like masses, whose summits are covered with snow, giving origin to the numerous falls and cascades which abound on the side of the cañon. The Little Cotton Wood Creek flowing past us falls about 500 feet to the mile. It rushes along furiously over its rocky bed, seeming to be at war with the immense boulders that dispute its right of way. As we proceed we leave the granites behind us, and above us project the sharp jagged edges of quartzite beds. These quartzites have a reddish colour, and are followed by slates, upon which rest thick beds of white limestone, the lower beds are crystalline and probably silurian, although I was unable to find any fossils in them. The upper layers are dolomitic, and are carboniferous in age. It is in these limestones that the ores occur. The principal mine is the 'Emma.' Unfortunately, owing to a disturbance at the time of our visit, I was unable to see the Emma Mine, but visited the 'Flagstaff' and the 'Silver Star.'"

Then follows an analysis of an average sample of eighty-two tons of first-class ore from the Emma Mine, made at Swansea, South Wales, in April, 1871, showing over 34% of metallic lead, 0.48% of silver, nearly 41% of silica, 3.54% of iron, the remainder made up of small quantities of sulphur, antimony, copper, zinc, manganese, alumina, magnesia, lime, carbonic acid, with 9.58% of oxygen and water by difference. "The quantity of silver obtained from this lot was 156 troy ounces to the gross ton of 2240 pounds."

I am told on good authority that the lode or fissure operated upon by the Emma dips north-east; that it is sometimes as much as fifty feet wide, and is filled with a gangue consisting chiefly of quartz and carbonate of lime; that the lead is present as pure galena (sulphuret), and the same decomposed into the carbonate; that the ore contains as much as 40% or 50% of galena, and is besides worth $100 (20*l.*) per ton for silver. There are still a few miners at work in this once-famous mine, being employed by the mortgagee, a Mr. Pearce, I think.

The general opinion of those I met in this locality seemed to be that the "Emma" had originally every prospect of becoming a good mine. The ore was there, and plenty of it; but that the undertaking was swamped in the stock market by being made to carry three times the amount of stock it required. This seems, in the opinion of most local men, to have been the chief cause of its ruin. I am told that much of the mine is now so flooded with water as to be as good as lost; but that some good ore is still got out from the other portions.

The Flagstaff Mine, situated in this same cañon, and on a parallel lode, is now turning out large quantities of fine ore.

The Prince of Wales's Mine is situated about one and a quarter miles from the Emma, in the Big Cottonwood Cañon, and is the property of the Messrs. Walker, Brothers, of Salt Lake City, from whom I received very great courtesy. It is supposed that this mine is working the same lode as the Flagstaff. The ore is of a precisely similar character, namely, galena, often decomposed into the carbonate, and rich in silver.

The Bingham and Telegraph Mines seem to be the two principal undertakings " located " in the Oquirrh Range. Their ores are argentiferous and auriferous sulphurets and carbonates of lead, but I am told that they are somewhat less rich than those from the Wahsatch Range.

It would appear as if a kind nature had meant the ores of these two ranges to be treated in the same smelting works. One contains much silica, the other is rich in oxide of iron, so that together a most happy mixture is formed for metallurgical treatment.

The fuel used at the works is charcoal and coke, which is brought all the way from Pittsburg, and costs, it is said, $30 (6*l.*) per ton.

Most of the miners in these parts are from old Cornwall, and they seem to be much appreciated for their untiring energy and working capabilities.

Here, as in nearly all other mining districts of the Western States, there is no observance of the Sabbath. That day is like any other as far as actual labour is concerned. The only bright exception I heard of was at the Hans Peak Mines, on the borders of Colorado and Wyoming, where a church has been built, and the officials encourage the men to go to it. At the Prince of Wales's Mine, before-mentioned, they tried to stop work on Sundays, but such fearful scenes of gambling, brawling, and shootings ensued, that the day of rest had to be abandoned. I was told that the Protestant Bishop of Salt Làke City had said that it was " far better to have it a working-day than to incur such dreadful scenes of vice." True enough, no doubt, but is it right to let the matter drop here? Would there be those scenes if the men, as in the old country, had places of worship to go to with their families, and were encouraged in so doing by their ministers and their superiors? Surely there is no reason for assuming that their natures are changed by the voyage across the ocean, and that the Sunday would be less well kept here than it is in their recently left homes, in the mining districts of Cornwall and elsewhere, were the same opportunity for keeping it properly provided for them? Is there not, moreover, an undeniable duty, a moral obligation, incumbent on those who are now benefitting by the miners' labour, and amassing by it such enormous fortunes? should they not, in mere gratitude, do what they can to provide for the spiritual welfare of their hardy labourers?

There is really something miserable in the feeling that the weary, dreary round of work goes on continuously from week's end to week's end, from year's end to year's end, without a day of rest of any kind. "Work, work, work," the only cry; the "almighty dollar" the only object. Here is surely a field for the missionary, where he can labour amongst, as it were, his own kith and kin? many of whom have been brought up actually in our midst. In former days in the old country they have been accustomed to keep the sabbath in such an orderly way as to be an object of remark to the passing stranger. Hard times have come upon them, and they have been obliged to emigrate. Now they find themselves in regions where, apparently, scarcely any attention is paid to religion. They are surrounded with fellow-workmen, many of whom are hardened in profanity. Soon the religious tendency of early life dies away, having nothing to nourish it, and eventually they become as careless of religion as the mass of those amongst whom they live.

Now this may be thought to be mere pedantic talk on my part, but I have heard it from more than one of themselves, and I feel it right to state the facts.

But it may be asked, how is this unfortunate state of things to be remedied? what is to be done? Well, let the owners of mines and others in authority provide places of worship, however humble, and let them countenance and encourage ministers of religion to come and dwell amongst them. I feel little doubt that, at any rate, those newly-arrived would appreciate such efforts; and moreover that many who have left their wives and little ones behind in old England, would, if they found schools and places of worship in their new homes, quickly get them out to them where they are much needed, instead of leaving them in the old country, often to become mere dependents on charity, or be supported by the rates.

I believe that, even in a selfish and pecuniary point of view, it would eventually prove to the advantage of the adventurers were a properly kept day of rest established. I cannot conceive that there can be anything more exhausting, more demoralizing to body and soul, than this continuous, grinding wear and tear of the human frame. Irreligion is, to my mind, *the* great blot on this otherwise bright and joyous portion of God's earth, and all sincere and earnest well-wishers would do well to consider so lamentable a blemish.

CHAPTER XX

" Breathes there the man with soul so dead,
  Who never to himself hath said,
  This is my own, my native land ?
  Whose heart has ne'er within him burn'd,
  As home his footsteps he hath turn'd,
  From wandering on a foreign strand ?"

Scott, " Lay of the Last Minstrel."

HAVING seen all I could of Salt Lake City and its surroundings, in the very limited time at my disposal, I reluctantly resumed my journey eastwards. I would gladly have lingered on and seen far more of that remarkable district, which, to quote a paragraph of the Governor of Utah's message, is " rich in agricul-ture, gold, silver, lead, copper, zinc, sulphur, salt, iron, and coal, with climate unsurpassed by any other in America;" but Parliament was on the eve

F C

of meeting, and there remained but a few days before I was due to sail from New York. The morning I left the "harem of the West," was truly lovely; a bright winter's sun was rising from behind the Wahsatch Mountains, the rough face of which was in the deepest shade; the most exquisitely delicate rose-tints tinged the snow-covered peaks of the Oquirrh Range, below which in peaceful repose lay the bright green waters of the Great Salt Lake. What a scene for Bierstadt's brush! but even he would have run the risk of being charged with exaggerating effects while only adhering truly to nature as she appeared on that beauteous morn.

But the "All on board" was shouted, and we were hurried along to Ogden, and soon deposited amongst the busy throng of the overland train from San Francisco. Once more the regular daily routine of train life is entered upon, and with no special incidents to enliven it.

By dinner-time we had arrived at Evanston, where I spent the half-hour allotted for that meal in looking over the collection of snow-ploughs kept ready at this season of the year for immediate use. The locomotive superintendent acted as my guide, and was most ready to give me information on the various machines. They have three different sizes of ploughs, which are used to suit the work to be done. The largest and most powerful is a machine in itself, and a most imposing-looking structure it is. It stands no less than seventeen feet off the ground, and weighs twenty-one tons. The share of the plough is a **V** shaped arrangement of steel plates, bolted securely together, in form something like the share of an ordinary land plough, the plates

being at an angle of about 30°. This share is the
first to encounter the opposing masses of snow. It
is supported from behind by a massive framing of
horizontal flat steel plates, carried down to within
one-eighth of an inch of the rail itself, and carried
by what are called "shoes," i. e., rounded pieces of
steel, which run on the rail from about a foot behind
the plough. Behind this arrangement, and mounted
on a separate carriage, is what is called a "flanger,"
which is constructed of flat pieces of steel, reaching
almost to the top surface of the rail, and just clearing
the sides. This scrapes off the snow and ice from
the top surface and sides of the rail. About three
feet further back on the same carriage are fitted
steel brushes, which sweep the rails clean of the
broken-up ice and snow. This ponderous machine
is so arranged as to be forced ahead into a bank of
snow, by six locomotives acting together, and is said
to be capable of clearing the way of seventeen feet
of fresh drift.

No. 2 plough weighs about five and half tons, and
stands about twelve feet high. It is very similar
in shape and arrangements to No. 1, but is much
smaller and more handy. It is adapted to be
worked by a single locomotive, and is capable of
dealing with eight to ten feet of snow. This No. 2
machine, I should say, was well worthy of the attention of those northern lines of the old country,
which have so frequently had their traffic interrupted
by the severe snow-storms of the past winter. In
it we have an arrangement the results of a very
large and constant experience of perhaps the most
ingenious mechanics in the world.

No. 3 plough is simply an ordinary "cow-catcher,"

tipped or shod with steel plates, and capable of removing two or three feet of snow.

From what I was told the process of snow clearing is at times somewhat exciting. On one occasion, on the Kansas Pacific Railroad, when my informant was riding on the engine, the snow-plough ran into a herd of buffalo, and broke the leg of one, which was afterwards finished with a shot. On another, a wretched deaf man was "quite scared and white-like" on being lifted up and landed "right away" on to the plough, which was, fortunately for him, travelling very slowly. He was quickly laid hold of by some of the men on the locomotive, and suffered no injury beyond the scare.

It often happens that both amusing and instructive companions are to be met with on board the American trains; and, as far as my experience goes, they are always ready to meet a stranger a liberal half-way. On the present occasion, amongst the many passengers was one of the "bosses" of the Black-hill stage route from Cheyenne, bound for Ohio to take possession of a farm which a "road agent" (highwayman) had bought with the proceeds of one of the robberies of the said stage. The robber had got away with the plunder, had bought a farm, and had intended to settle down with his family to peaceful agricultural pursuits in this far-off land, when the poor wretch was tracked and apprehended just as he had completed the purchase.

Another of my fellow-passengers was a gentleman from the Black-hills, who was able to give me much information about that recently-discovered mining district. I heard from him that the two most common rocks in this locality are a soft granite and a greenish slate. The richest "ledges," he said, were found at the junction of the slate and the granite, and that "horses," of a sort of porphyry, occurred in the "ledges." The ledges themselves are composed of a sort of soft, quartzy granite, and vary from five to thirty feet in thickness, lying usually at an angle of about fifteen degrees. He stated that the alluvial deposits at the beds of the creeks form into a sort of conglomerate, in which specks of free gold are often visible to the naked eye; and that ore as low in value of gold as $4 to $5 (16s. to 20s.) per ton can be treated with advantage in this district. A large company from California are now erecting stamp-mills and works, at which they hope to be able to deal with ores for $2½ (10s.) per ton.

Then agriculture came in for its share in relieving the *ennui*, and afforded an extensive subject for observation and conversation as we glided through the fertile fields of Illinois. One of the most important crops in this State is Indian corn or maize, besides which large quantities of wheat and oats are raised. The latter, they tell me, is of such a quality as often to weigh 48 lbs. per bushel. At this date, January 22nd, the spring wheat was quite green and well above the ground. Very little snow had fallen here as yet, but at this time it often covers the ground three feet deep. The wheat harvest begins here about the 1st of July.

The following day I discoursed much on oysters with a large oyster-merchant, who happened to occupy a neighbouring berth in the Pullman. With him I had much in common, partly from a very strong partiality for that excellent mollusc, partly from having sat on a House of Commons

Committee, having for its object the better preservation and future increase of that now costly
luxury. On this side of the Atlantic, oysters are as
much in favour, or perhaps even more, than they
are with us. There are several varieties of American
oysters, differing much both in size and quality.
Some are quite excellent, and would compare very
favourably with our "natives;" others, again, are
large and coarse; in fact, individual taste can be
accommodated from flesh the size of a saucer to
that of a half-crown. In New York the large sorts
are called "Counts," and sell for about $1 ($=$4s.)
per 100, whilst the smaller sorts, called "Culls,"
do not realize more than 55 cents ($=$2s. 3d.). The
railway charge for conveying them from New York
to Chicago is now $1 per 100 lbs., or exactly 1 cent
($\frac{1}{2}$d.) per lb.; but before an amicable arrangement had been arrived at between the competing
companies, the carriage was as low as 25 cents
per 100 lbs. In the cold weather, when the thermometer is below zero, the transport is made in the
so-called "refrigerator cars," which keep the cold
out and prevent them from freezing. Hay is often
wrapped round them with the same object; but the
best preservative of all against freezing is said to be
paper. My informant told me that on the American
beds oysters are rather on the increase than otherwise, notwithstanding the very great demand made
on them. A universal close time exists from 1st of
May to the middle of September, not secured by
law, but enforced by nature, as during the summer
heat any oysters dredged would infallibly be spoiled
unless consumed on the spot.

I took the same route homeward as that by

which I came out, partly from my wish to see
Niagara in its winter garb, and partly from wishing
to pay a flying visit to Professor Ward's museum
at Rochester.

On the 23rd of January I enjoyed a long visit to
the Falls. The little town had a forlorn and deserted appearance; nearly all the stores were closed
and emptied. Even my friend the naturalist was
gone; he who had warned me on my former visit
of the fearful dangers of cariboo hunting; how a
hunter had told him he had nearly had his brains
kicked out by an enraged specimen, and had saved
himself only by getting behind a tree! All was now
cold and deserted. The weather was clear and
bright, but bitter; the thermometer was only just
above zero at midday, and a piercing wind drove
over Goat Island, laden with particles of frozen
spray, which cut like bits of glass. I walked over
the islands, and visited the most striking points of
view. The river was flowing full and dark, contrasting with the virgin whiteness of the surrounding snow and ice. Every cliff and rock was completely encased in ice, which appeared in piled-up
masses at the foot of both Falls. All the foliage
was covered with frost, and sparkled like a Twelfth-
night cake in the sunlight. Anything more fearfully
cold and desolate than some of the views, could not
well be imagined, and yet there was something
which made one doubt whether Niagara was not
more striking and interesting in this truly Arctic
desolation than when I saw it before in all its
autumn beauties, the object of admiration to scores
of one's fellow-creatures.

Having seen as much as the time would allow

of this peculiarly-attractive wonder, I resumed my
journey to Rochester, where I spent some time with
Professor Ward, visiting the fine Natural History
Museum of the College, and going over his own
stores of mineralogical and zoological treasures.
These are chiefly the productions of America, but
they are by no means exclusively so ; for Mr. Ward
is a man of extraordinary energy, and has collectors
in many parts of Europe and Asia, and is thus enabled to furnish very complete collections to colleges
and other institutions. One of the latest additions
to his natural history collection is a true " white
elephant" in the shape of a complete skeleton of a
mammoth, which he has obtained from the icy regions of Northern Siberia. This little addition was
beyond the capabilities of Professor Ward's previous buildings, and required an edifice of its own,
around the inside walls of which now hung my own
spoils of the chase, which I had from time to time,
as occasion offered, sent to him for preservation.
They had been most ably handled, and appeared to
me naturally remarkably fine; but in this opinion
I was delighted to find myself supported by the
Professor, who pronounced some of the wapiti heads
and my cariboo to be unusually good, and one of the
buffaloes as the largest he had ever set up. In fact
he only regretted I had not sent him the whole
beast for preservation ! but I consoled myself by
thinking that had I done so I should not have quite
known how to lodge him, and, like the Professor
himself, should have had to build a special addition
for my newest arrival.

New York reached, a whirl of sight-seeing, but
alas, only for a day and an evening, and then away

for Old England in the magnificent White Star liner "Germanic," Captain Kennedy, of 5,400 tons. The voyage home was in every way fortunate—a splendid ship—excellent company—unusually fine weather—and last, but not least, a good commissariat and most comfortable quarters. As to the ship, bad sailor as I am, I did not dislike, nay I actually enjoyed the voyage. When about six days from New York, we encountered what was logged as a "strong gale;" but it had little effect on our gallant ship or her internal economy, beyond breaking a few dozen tumblers; for such is the power of these fine specimens of naval architecture, that, although the wind was almost dead ahead, we accomplished on that day 323 knots. As it may interest some of my readers to know the rate at which the Atlantic is now traversed, I annex the log, as it appeared daily on the companion :—

Date.	Lat.		Long.		Distance Run.	Remarks.
	deg.	min.	deg.	min.	knots.	
January 27	40	40	66	24	346	From Sandy Hook
,, 28	41	16	58	32	359	Light breezes
,, 29	42	00	50	44	355	Strong breezes
,, 30	44	39	43	27	350	Fresh gale
,, 31	47	04	35	56	346	Fresh breezes
February 1	49	10	27	44	352	Strong breezes
,, 2	50	45	19	44	323	Strong gale, 380 miles west of Fastness Light
,, 3	51	23	10	18	360	Fresh breezes
					87	To Queenstown
					2878	

On Saturday morning, the 26th of January, about ten o'clock, we left New York; the Sunday afternoon week, about five o'clock, we were in Queenstown. Here we parted with a few of our fellow-passengers, and the whole of our mail-bags. Home news came on board, and then away again for Liverpool. The Channel sea was so calm that I paid a lengthened visit to the engineer's domain, and admired the smooth working of the fine engines, which were driving our floating palace at a sixteen-knot velocity through the dancing waters. This great speed is only attained by the expenditure of more than ninety tons of coal per day, and the attendance of fifty-five hands to the engineer's department.

The Mersey is speedily reached, but a heavy fog put an end to our gallop, and we had to grope our way slowly to the moorings.

And now my tale is told; my wanderings are ended; and in a few hours more I am amongst familiar sounds and faces in the lobbies, waiting for the first division of the Session. I confess to a very comforting sensation at being once more in old haunts. Greatly as I have enjoyed my run amidst so much that was new and strange, I have returned, if possible, more English than I went out, and more thankful to a kind Providence for casting my lot in the " Ould Countrie."

FINIS.

GILBERT AND RIVINGTON, PRINTERS, ST. JOHN'S SQUARE, LONDON.